SECRETS OF THORNS

FLEUR DEVILLAINY

Secrets of Thorns

Fleur DeVillainy

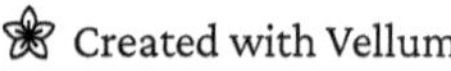 Created with Vellum

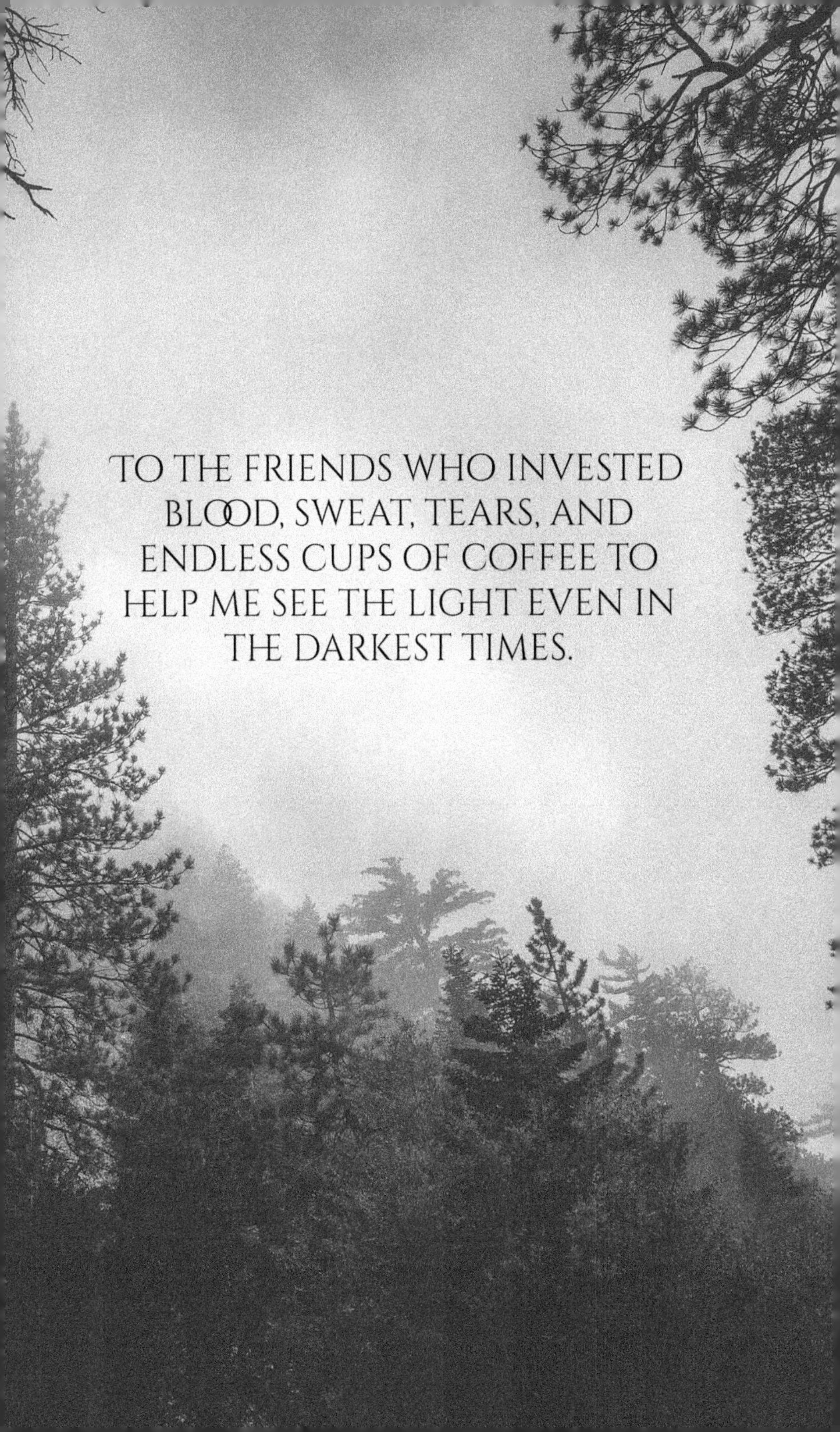

TO THE FRIENDS WHO INVESTED
BLOOD, SWEAT, TEARS, AND
ENDLESS CUPS OF COFFEE TO
HELP ME SEE THE LIGHT EVEN IN
THE DARKEST TIMES.

Acknowledgments

Creating a world may often be a solitary endeavor, but when it comes to creating a book, it is anything but. Throughout my journey as an author, I have come to realize that although the characters reside solely within my mind, it has truly taken a village to bring them to life on the pages.

I am immensely grateful to the many individuals who have played a significant role in this process - from my dedicated editing team to my invaluable betas, supportive friends, and devoted readers. Your contributions have undeniably made this book so much better. Even during the moments when I found myself emotionally torn over the difficult task of "cutting my darlings," you all stood by me, offering words of encouragement and support. It is thanks to your unwavering belief in me that I was able to meet my deadline and breathe life into the second book of this series.

I would like to extend my heartfelt gratitude to Charlotte and Johnna, my fellow authors, for their unwavering support and encouragement throughout this journey. Additionally, I am immensely grateful to Victoria for her constant belief in me and for being a loyal friend. I cannot thank her enough for our late-night talks, where we delved into the depths of plot intricacies, and for her dedication in keeping the team engaged and excited. To Alyssa, Reema, and all my beta readers, I am incredibly thankful for your invaluable help in transforming my manuscript into the beautiful book it has become.

To my husband, daughter, and parents who always support me in all my wild hobbies and adventures and who never let me stop dreaming.

Well, here it is! Part two in the Vandeleur Trilogy. Thank you, dear readers, for taking a chance on it. I hope you love this continuation of Sybil's story.

- Fleur

About This Book

This book contains explicit content and dark elements that may be triggering for some. For a full list of warnings, please turn to the trigger warning section at the end of the book.

SHADOWVALLE
KALLISTAR

PROLOGUE

Deep in the mountains, a great beast slumbers.

Smoke, dark as ash, curls from its nostril and spirals into the air, twisting like rings around the long stalactites hanging from the stone ceiling. The rumbling of its snoring is the only thing breaking the silence, the sound so deep it makes the ground vibrate, almost as if the mountain itself is breathing. There are sconces anchored to the rough-hewn walls of the cave; they are worn and tarnished, and in their flickering light, the beast's golden scales glimmer. They are sharp and defined, reflecting an ethereal glow, as if they bore secrets untold from a time long before shifters and elementals were at war on the continent of Craeweth. In truth, no one knows for how long the beast has been lost to its dreams or why it fell asleep at all, yet the Goddess knows it will soon have to wake, for it has a role to play.

When a cold draft from the mountain peak seeps through the forgotten tunnels, the scent of ancient earth and dampness permeates the cave, mingling with the metallic tang of tarnished bronze. The beast moves and stretches, its wings tucked tightly on its sides, casting large shadows that engulf the chamber. A heap of coins and riches tumbles over as the creature's barbed tail lashes out with tremendous force in a tinkling chorus of metallic clinks and clatter reverberating through the cavernous stone walls. The crack of thunder peels outside, and the creature peeks open its eyes.

It is time.

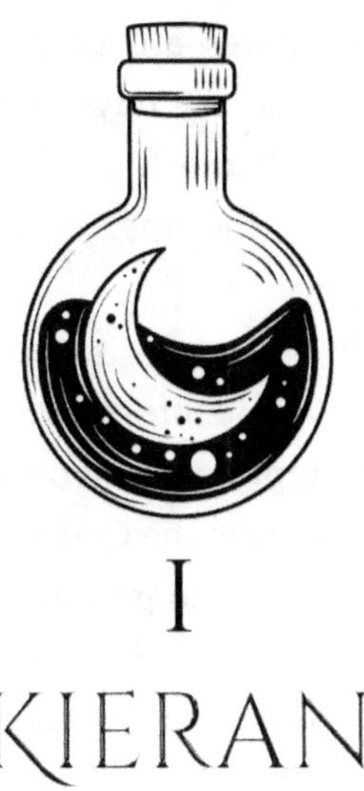

I

KIERAN

She is going to kill me.

I rake a hand through my disheveled hair and stare into the silver mirror before me. I struggle to recognize the man looking back at me. Even in the gloominess of my chamber, I can see his bloodshot eyes with dark circles, a shadow of stubble on his cheeks, and his normally immaculate mage robes are wrinkled and hang loosely on his body.

I am a complete wreck.

A sigh leaves my lips and I grimace, rubbing a hand across my aching brow. I pushed my magic reserve to its limit last night and now my head feels like a pot left too long on the boil. Not that this is the first time this has happened.

I turn toward the desk littered with dark green glass vials and jars containing potions and herbs meant to help my mind expand. Another sigh. Leaning against the table, I feel the splintering wood under my fingertips, and I try to ignore the rest of the mess surrounding me. There are heaps of clothes littering the stone floor, the bed with its pristine white sheets is unmade, candle nubs are resting on every surface, and parchment filled with notes are scattered everywhere. The chamber is a testament to the days and nights I have spent tirelessly seeping through the future. Searching for a damn unicorn and an imbecile princeling. Searching for the one thing that will make *her* happy.

What am I doing?

I have spent my whole life seeking her attention, her approval. Hoping her sapphire eyes would see more in me than a means to an end. How cruel the Goddess is, to make one love so fiercely, only for that love to go unnoticed. Unappreciated. Sure, it would be easier if I could just carve this love out of me, and leave Tricella behind as if she never existed. Yet, I'd rather keep this painful love locked within me than live a life not having loved at all. Even if now, after all these years, it has begun to wear on me mentally and physically.

No matter. My discomfort means little if I can succeed. If I can have Tricella back.

My temples throb, starlight flashing at the edge of my vision as I frantically sort through the assortment on my desk. I reach for the pot of brewing tea at the edge of the table and pour myself a steaming cup of what I hope will be the solution to my aching mind.

"Where are you hiding?" I whisper as I roam over the map before me and take a sip of the brew. My eyes focus on a piece of parchment pinned on a small village north of the castle. There's a number scribbled in dark ink.

112

It's the number of shifters we've caught on our last attack. One hundred and twelve shifters we can siphon magic from. And yet, none of them are what we truly need.

I take another sip, and my eyes water from the pungent aroma.

I would be lying if I said I'm remorseful for the events that have led me here. For turning the key in the locks of all those cells in the dungeons where shifters now lay and wonder what fate has in store for them. For helping Tricella research the darkness and grasp the power she craves. Because once upon a time, when Tricella was not a queen but a girl, her ambition and brilliant mind superseded her desire for cruelty. Her dream was to be happy and loved.

So, when she whispered to me one day by the fire, "I *need* the power the stories talk about, Kieran. I long to be powerful so I can make them all pay. I will never be weak again," I helped her find the book of dark magic and climb the social hierarchy until they crowned her queen. And when she wanted immortality to stop the hours and the minutes so she could keep that power and not see it taken from her by the thief called time, I found her the last unicorn known on the continent.

Sybil Vandaleur.

The sole creature able to grant such a gift out of the purity of its magic. The same unicorn I must now find again, before she understands her true power and becomes my queen's undoing.

Because what the future had not shown me all those moons ago was that dark power is saccharine. It melts on your tongue and makes you wish for more as it slowly takes pieces of your soul until you're no longer yourself. That is my only regret: to have given her the thing that extinguished the very spark in her eyes that made me follow her blindly, that power that has turned her into this cruel and bloodthirsty version of herself.

I did it all for a dream. *Her* dream.

I set my empty cup on the side and start following the borders of Shadowvale with my index finger. A knot of unease twists in my gut. Tricella is going to call for me soon and I will have to tell her, once again, that I find no glimpse of Sybil Vandeleur in the uncertain haze of the future. Every time I try, visions blur so fast I can't pick them apart. And maybe this time her rage will be enough to end my life.

I grab the edge of the desk, my knuckles blanching white as I'm hit with a wave of nausea from the pain of my throbbing head. The brew has done fuck all.

Opening the bottom drawer on the right-hand side of my desk, I breathe a sigh of relief, shoulders sagging when I find the bottle I'm looking for. I pour myself another cup of brew but this time, I also pour a heaping dose of the poppy syrup into the steaming mug of tea before collapsing onto the stiff wooden chair.

Agony flickers behind my closed eyelids—a sharp, stabbing sensation that nearly derails me. Thunder booms outside, shaking the thin pane of glass before sleet pelts the window, intensifying the pounding in my head. Winter was quickly melting into spring, despite the clusters of snow clinging to the ground. I didn't have time to waste.

"What to do?" I ask myself out loud, my throat scratchy from the hours spent in silence.

I'd do anything for her.

My hands are already stained crimson, and I doubt the Goddess will ever take a soul as rotten as mine into her kingdom. So, if killing the useless king, his son or anyone else hindering this plan would be the solution, they'd already be seven feet underground. But I've been playing this game for far too long to waste a valuable pawn.

I push on, focusing intently as the steaming cup in my hands burns my fingers. I strain to find the prince amidst the swirling visions. Gritting my teeth, a stifled groan escapes as I endure the pain, my resolve unwavering as I strive to capture a single image of their whereabouts.

The first thing I see is snow. Aramis and his second in command are cutting south through the thick snow in the mountains. The unicorn is nowhere in sight.

This can't be.

I pull harder on my magic, pushing past the pain, seeking the truth. The images keep coming, one after the other in a kaleidoscope of colors. But no matter the time or place, they remain together in all my visions. As the vision starts to blur, I mentally grapple with that single image. They could be anywhere in Shadowvale. I need more information.

Mental claws scrape across the inside of my skull as I focus closer, attempting to hone in on anything that could give me their location.

I take a deep breath, my hold onto the cup tightening. I cannot fail her again. Not now. Not when we're so close.

"Come on." Frustration laces every word. Nothing but snow and ice fills my vision.

"Fuck," I curse, throwing the empty cup against the wall and slamming my fist into the desk.

Kieran.

My body tenses, skin prickling as Tricella's voice echoes in my head. Pushing to my feet, I straighten my robes and comb a hand through my hair before opening the door that separates my study from her chambers.

"Yes, my queen?" I bow, my body protesting the movement.

Tricella sits on a plush lounge chair made of red velvet, reminiscent of the throne she sits on in the throne room. Her chambers are grand and fit for a queen. A large fire pit crackles in the corner, covered by an ornate golden brazier and decorated with twisting thorny vines. Heavy vermillion drapes hang over the window, muffling the booming sound of the thundersnow storm outside. My eyes are drawn toward the wooden table at the center of the room, pristine save for the dark tome and an empty crystal goblet, its edge stained with the imprint of her lips. As always, I ignore the right-hand side of the room, where the sound of shackles and a shifter's quiet whimpers break the silence.

"You've been quiet." She taps her nails restlessly on the arm of the chair as she turns to face me. My heart clenches at the sight of her long golden hair. "What news do you have for me?"

"They've gone into the mountains–"

"I asked for an update, not a repeat of what I already know," she says sharply, pushing up and grabbing my chin, her fingernails biting into flesh as she forces my head up. I allow myself a moment to study the new dark purple veins streaking away from her darkened fingertips until I meet her gaze. My stomach clenches, roiling with a sudden onset of nausea at the sight of her sharp gaze. I look for the woman I met on a summer's day. In the marketplace, her cheeks lit up with a warm blush as she greeted customers with a genuine smile. Her basket, filled with plump, freshly-picked apples, was extended to anyone who caught her attention. She paid no mind to the stares that lingered on her bare, soiled feet and torn clothing. Undeterred, she gracefully moved from stall to stall, immersing herself in the vibrant atmosphere of the market, determined to sell her meager basket. It was her unwavering determination to better herself that drew me to her.

She's still there, barely.

"I'm sorry, Tricella," I say, my lips pressing into a tight grimace. "I saw the prince and his dog heading south, but the unicorn was not with them. Something or someone has blocked her from my view. I'm trying–"

"Oh Kieran," she coos, her voice dripping with honey as she releases me. "We do not have time to lose her. You will find her, or you will *finally* find where the rest of the unicorns are hiding. Either way, I will get what I need."

The unspoken words, "or else I'll find someone to replace you," hang in the air between us.

I can't fail her. I *want* her.

With her back turned, she carefully examines the tapestry on the wall, recently relocated from Queen Rose's crypt. It depicts a serene scene of unicorns grazing in the fields of Shadowvale.

"Tricell—"

"Your Majesty," she retorts sharply while advancing toward the table and firmly placing her hands on either side of an expensive black tome. "Just because you have wormed your way to my right-hand side does not give you leave for such *familiarities*." Her words hit me in the gut, and I try to mask the pain they've caused me.

"Your Majesty," I echo with a slight nod, lips pressing firmly together as I move to stand by her side whilst she pours over the damn book that caused this whole mess.

The tome reeks of dark magic. Its presence is suffocating, as if it's absorbing the very air around us. Yet it is also alluring, it sings to me like a siren—songs of knowledge and sweet power written in curled letters and runes penned with dark ink. I attempt, as always, to read the words but fail when I am met with a language that is not of this world or this time. Tricella caresses the yellowed pages with the gentlest touch one would reserve for a lover. The Goddess only knows how long I've been longing for that touch. I clear my voice and mind.

"The unicorns have not been seen or heard of in over two

hundred years, save for Sybil and her family. There are no records of their existence, except this tapestry."

"Rose would not have made this tapestry if they weren't alive... somewhere." She flips the pages and runs her fingers along the unfamiliar runes, then flips her attention to the male chained against the far wall. "Alfred, read it to me again."

I force my gaze to follow.

"Reading it for the hundredth time will not reveal the answers you seek," he says, voice cracking from screaming. The old man's clothes are tattered and bloodied, purple bruises are scattered on his body. He's a shifter, but his use to us went beyond stealing his magic. We apprehended him a while back at Verdigris Falls before he boarded a ship. He originated from Shadowvale but had spent his life traveling the world, studying ancient magic and language.

I try not to roll my eyes at how unnecessary this spectacle is. Personally, I prefer more subtle ways to make people talk, but the queen has developed a penchant for blood.

Tricella's body tenses beside me before she lifts a hand and dark shadows fly from her fingers, hosting the male up and slamming him against the wall, chains rattling. I clench my hands, hiding them in my sleeves and will my expression to remain impassive at this new manifestation of her magic.

"Read it to me. *Again*," she whispers coldly as the shadows writhe across her forearms and up her neck as she moves toward him.

"I've read you the book front to back a dozen times. You know as much as I do. I don't know what that book is, everything in it makes no sense. I can read it but... it's incomplete," he says through clenched teeth, sweat beading on his brow.

Her eyes flash and the veins in her neck pulse.

"Then you must be hiding something, so I'll give you one

last chance," she says, using her magic to lift the book before him.

"Or what, you'll torture me and steal my magic as you have dozens before me? Who will read the book for you then?" The man laughs, showing his bloodied teeth. "I only know of four people on this continent who can read it, and you've already killed one."

The shadows pour out of Tricella, the dark veins slithering under her skin as if alive and a wicked smile, dangerous as it is breathtaking, paints her red lips. I brace myself for what's about to happen.

"I spent my whole life searching for this book. It all started with a fairytale; you probably know it too. My father used to tell it to me before he abandoned us. How was it? Ah, yes. The Goddess Alpheaia created Craeweth and the first gift she bestowed upon the land was magic. But she soon realized magic was wild and needed balance, so she wrote two books to guide those who would cherish the use of magic. Books filled with every spell, every ritual and rune, books with the key to unlimited power."

Her eyes have a dangerous light to them. Hungry and unbound. Like clouds gathering before a storm.

"The book of light and... the book of darkness," Alfred whispers in disbelief, eyeing the tome again. He shakes his head. "But that's impossible."

"Oh, Alfred. I knew you were smart. Now, where were we before you so rudely interrupted me?" Tricella taps her long nail on her chin. I pretend to look through the other books stored in her library, knowing all too well where her story is headed.

"Ah, yes. The books. You see, I never believed it was just a fairytale like so many other small-minded idiots like you, because even fairytales are born from a kernel of truth. So, when I was left to rot by my drunken shifter of a mother, rejected, abused and ridiculed by both communities because my elemental father made me a halfling, I went on a little adventure."

Tricella steps closer to Albert, who is surprisingly intrigued by her story. So much so that he does not notice her shadows slowly coiling around his wrists and ankles like serpents.

"I spent most of my life searching for the books. Researched and studied. I crossed kingdoms bargaining and gathering clue after clue from the ancient creatures that roamed the earth around the same time the Goddess created the books and... I found them." Her voice is filled with pride but also bitter at the part of her life she'd rather wipe from existence.

I turn back in her direction and cross my hands behind my back, nails biting into my palms. Does she remember? I ask myself. Does she remember I was by her side following those seemingly pointless clues? I swallow the knot in my throat.

"Well, I found one," Tricella corrects herself with the flick of her wrist. "And after all I've been through, I will not be denied the answers I seek."

As the shadows caress his neck, Albert is reminded of where he is and starts shaking violently in fear. "I've told you everyth—"

My headache is slowly creeping in again, and I hope this spectacle ends soon. I focus my eyes on her golden hair once again and try to remember the feeling of cursing my fingers through it. This nightmare has to stop.

"Ah, ah, ah!" She lifts a finger, and the shadows cover Albert's mouth for a moment. "If the book didn't contain the boundless power the stories speak of, Alpheaia wouldn't have concealed it so deeply in the mountains."

"You possess more power than any person should rightfully have, except for the Goddess herself. The darkness consumes you, even now," he says with a shake of his head.

"You know nothing of what you speak," she spits out, body shaking with rage. "I will never be taken advantage of again, never feel powerless."

Enough.

"Your Majesty." I step in, and the corners of my lips pull up as I cross my arms and lean against the doorframe. "Perhaps he will become more talkative if he goes without food for another day or two in the dungeons."

"I don't have time to wait," she says, glancing at me over her shoulder, her blue eyes glimmering with rage. "I need answers *now*."

Catching us both by surprise, the prisoner laughs. "It all makes sense now," he says between laughs. "There's a reason why the Goddess put the two books to rest together. You won't find the answers you seek without the other half. Magic is limited. You need balance. Darkness is merely the absence of light," he says.

"I don't care about light magic, healing magic. It is weak. I want strength, I want power. Everything I need is within these pages!" She turns back toward him, dark shadows curling up her arms and licking at her flesh.

Tricella's anger radiates as she fumes, her fingers tightly clenching into a fist. The male figure chained before her unleashes a chilling, unholy scream, his body contorting against the wall before finally collapsing. The room falls into a stillness, broken only by the sound of blood trickling from his nose, staining the icy stone floor.

She turns to face me, her face a mask of cold indifference.

"Find me the unicorn."

2

ARAMIS

The sun is finishing its descent across the sky, painting it the sweetest shades of reds and pinks. I mindlessly clutch the crystal around my neck and hope my mate is safe.

"How much further until we reach the village?" I cast a sharp glance at Nero as he jumps down from the branch above, landing on the forest floor beside me.

"We should be there before nightfall. I can see smoke rising in the distance."

Out of all the discomforts I have experienced whilst en-route in the wilderness, walking in snow-soaked boots is the one I hate the most. It's been days since Nero and I left the tunnels where the avalanche separated us from Sybil. My fingers are a painful, angry shade of red from digging through the wall of snow. It had taken all my strength, and Nero's stern voice, to convince me to leave her and look for the rebel shifters camp. The one Kela was taking us to.

"Sybil has survived on her own for years. She's told ye so

and proven herself, not to mention she has all the equipment and her wits. If there is a way, she will find it," Nero had told me then, and I had to believe him, or I would have found a way to bring that mountain to the ground with my bare hands and the power of my wind magic.

She is safe, I remind myself.

The hand clutching the crystal travels down my thick coat and rests at the center of my chest, where the bond between me and Sybil feels like a gentle caress. I must trust her just as she has trusted me.

"Come on, lad. We need to get there before dark. I don't think we'll get as lucky to find a roof over our heads again." Nero interrupts my thoughts; his eyes have a note of worry in them when he notices my lost gaze and the hand on my chest. I nod and take a deep breath, boots crunching on the icy path.

In an unexpected turn of luck, we had stumbled upon a village the night before, but the excitement of a hot meal and soft bed had soon vanished when we realized it had been abandoned. The faded curtains and doors hanging off their hinges painted a desolate picture. We had sheltered in the only hut with a complete roof, but the deep claw marks on its side were unmistakable. Memories of Kela, the wolf shifter, sacrificing herself with the shadow demons cross my mind, and I nearly trip over the frozen root of a big pine tree.

"Fuck," I mutter, Nero pretends not to hear me.

Seeing the village after everything I had discovered in the past weeks had been a slap in the face. The signs of my kingdom falling apart were everywhere. I had been too oblivious and naive to notice. Too concerned pointing my finger to the shifters, fueled by my own prejudices. Tricella has weaseled her way into my father's bed, and sown the seeds of discourse not only to me but my kingdom.

I have lived for over a century, trained in the art of war,

commanded the royal army, fought giant beasts while standing knee deep in gore on battlefields next to my soldiers and yet... here I am, torn with uncertainty and apprehension for the future that lays before me. For the future of my kingdom.

I must make amends.

"And you're sure there are elementals living amongst the shifters?" I ask with a raised brow, breaking the silence that will otherwise make my mind run wild. The fact that elementals had joined the shifters' cause had sparked feelings of pride for my people, at first. But also shame for having taken so long to see the truth in front of my eyes.

You have to find *her* first, a voice in my head whispers. The bond tugs again.

"Aye, as well as other creatures and witches. It's a refuge of sorts, for anyone displaced by the attacks or anyone wanting to dethrone the queen."

An army.

If there are water and earth elementals, we could find a way to prevent the snow from coming down as we dug her out.

My heart constricts in my chest at the thought of war.

"They couldn't possibly mean to take on Tricella and the royal army." I glance over but his face remains serious.

"Aramis, these people—our people—are willing to risk anything if it means freedom and peace."

My head hangs, chest heavy. My hands are starting to shake, and my heart rate is increasing.

"I have to free them, Nero. I have to save her."

"Aramis-"

"Tricella is hunting us down as we speak. What if she gets to her before we get help?"

"I dinna think Tricella will-"

"We don't know what she's capable of!" I stop in my tracks,

turning to face him, nostrils flaring. "Look at what she's already done. I will not idly sit by any longer and let her destroy Shadowvale."

"Aramis." He sets a hand on my shoulder, but I swat it away. "No one blames ye–"

"I aided her. I brought shifters to her to be questioned and sent off to the mines." Flames of heat surge through my body as I forcefully wrench my gaze away from him, my quivering muscles pulsating with pent-up anger. "I stole Sybil and brought her straight to the queen."

"Sybil forgave ye. She sees the goodness in your heart as I do." The sound of twigs cracking fills the air as he shifts his weight behind me.

I lift the stone chained around my neck before me, flexing my fingers around it as the sunlight filters through the trees, but it does not glow and does not give a hint of where we should go.

Has even the Goddess forsaken me?

"What if the rebels don't want to help us? What then?" Nausea churns in my gut. I shake my head, trying to clear away the thoughts.

"They will help us. They're eager to meet Sybil after Kela's visions of her." This time, he falls silent, shoulders and wings slumping. "I should have been faster and saved her."

"Her death was not your fault."

A muscle ticks in his jaw as silver lines his eyes. He brushes them with the back of his hand and turns away from me. "Aye, but I will carry her death and all the others who came before her and after her. I wish I had told ye earlier about my heritage and Tricella's corruption—"

Guilt churns in my gut. If I had been a better friend—if I hadn't let grief blind me for so many years—he wouldn't have needed to hide half of himself from me.

"Nero, it isn't anyone's fault except Tricella's. We were outnumbered and unprepared." With a comforting hand on his shoulder, I quietly swear under my breath, hoping to provide him some solace. "We will avenge her. We will avenge all our people."

"Thanks, mate," he says, the corners of his lips turning up, but the smile doesn't reach his eyes.

"Well, if it isn't Nero Lockheed." A low, rumbling voice reverberates, resonating with power and depth akin to a wolf's growl. Emerging from behind a towering tree, a man of impressive stature with close-cropped hair and a thick, matching chestnut beard comes into view. I stop, rooted to the spot instinctively, as his piercing, almond-shaped eyes, a shade of light blue, fixate upon me.

"Aries," Nero growls a low warning, his body tensing beside me.

"You know this male?" I raise an eyebrow inquisitively at him as I step to his side, hand poised on my sword handle.

Shifter.

With each step he takes toward us, exuding an unmistakable predatory energy, my instincts scream at me to fall into the defense.

"Unfortunately," he grumbles.

"And you brought the little wind princeling with you." He sniffs the air and his eyes flash in challenge. "But not in chains, I see."

"Aramis comes of his own free will. We come to seek the council's aid and bear news." Nero's body is rigid beside me.

"Oh, the council will not like this." He grins, baring sharp canine teeth.

"We will speak to the council and let them decide," Nero says. "Now, lead us or move aside."

"You'll find much has changed since you last brought us

news, Lockheed." He draws out the last syllables and spits at the ground at our feet.

"Ye don't seem to have changed one bit." Nero stands protectively beside me, heat radiating off his body as his hands curl into fists. I reach out an arm to hold him back.

"Where is the unicorn?" Aries walks closer, flexing his claws. "And Kela?"

"That's why we're here," I utter, stepping toward him when a chilling hand presses against the back of my neck. Suddenly, my strength evaporates, and I crumble, sinking to my knees. Aries' cocks his head to the side and crushes his fist into my nose.

"Fucking hells, Aries." Nero slams into the man's chest, who merely laughs as he staggers backward. "What is the meaning of this?"

Agony surges through my face, a sharp and searing pain. In my blurred vision, flickering stars dance, accompanied by the metallic scent of warm blood trickling down my face.

"Can't be too careful, draken. I don't think you've met my newest prodigy. She has the most peculiar power." I glare up at him, but my body feels as heavy as lead. I'd like to wipe the smirk off his face, but my wind feels eons away and my muscles barely respond. Wherever this prodigy is, I cannot see her.

"Unfortunately, she hasn't mastered the strength to take down more than one person without draining her own reserves and requires a week to recover her magic. Count your-self lucky."

"I did nothing to provoke this," I seethe through clenched teeth as shadows dance along the edge of my vision, threat-ening to overwhelm me.

"Your very presence is provocation enough, *Prince*. You are no friend to the shifters, and you've just willingly walked into the wolves' den."

Nero growls at Aries, his narrowed eyes flicking between me kneeling on the ground and the bastard who busted my nose. "Ye may be a member, but ye do not speak solely for the council, Aries," he grumbles.

A smirk plays on Aries' lips as he crosses his arms over his chest. "No, I suppose I don't. But do you think they'd really fault me for protecting this village from a traitor?"

Traitor. Liar. Disgrace.

I push the words away, refusing to let them distract me. I've let rage and guilt blind me from the truth once before, but never again. Meeting his hate-filled gaze, I defiantly state, "I am no traitor. We have come to see the council. We're here to bring news that will help save the kingdom."

He scoffs at my words. "So you've said, but do you really think I am going to let you, the Prince of Shadowvale, waltz into the heart of camp just because you say you're one of us? Do you not think I have heard about your many escapades?" Aries steps toward me, seizing my arms and forcefully binding them together.

"Glad to see yer still a piece of shit. There's no need–" Nero argues. I know seeing me in this state pains him, but we both knew this was going to happen. It is only fair that the shifters harbor doubts when it comes to the Prince of Shadowvale. So if I have to endure this to ensure peace and win their trust, so be it.

"Nero," I interrupt and gather all my strength to look into his eyes. "It's fine, brother." Silent understanding passes between us and the rough texture of the rope burns into skin as he tightly secures my hands. Aries hoists me upright, his grasp unyielding.

Suddenly, a cool hand grips my elbow. I snap my head to

the right, where a strange girl with pale silver eyes and a snow-white bob is carefully examining me. My knees start shaking ever so slightly when I feel the girl's magic enter my veins, sapping my strength.

"His magic feels different than the others'," she observes with a small voice, strands of white hair falling in front of her milky gaze. I am both terrified and in awe of this young woman.

"Leave him be, Solari. Your job is merely to incapacitate him until the council determines his fate." Aries turns to Nero, a smirk still on his face. "Now you both can come with me."

"Where do you plan on taking us?" I ask, breaking the silence as we both follow Aries to the camp. Each step is more laborious than the last, thanks to Solari's magic, which grips my body like hundreds of pins and needles pricking my skin.

"Somewhere you cannot harm anyone in this village, but where you cannot escape trial either," he says. As we make our way through the edge of the tree line, I notice runes carved into the trunks of trees. Passing through them and into an open field, the landscape before me shimmers like a mirage. In the distance, shapes of buildings and tents fill the ground, smoke spiraling into the sky.

Magic to keep an entire village hidden from those who did not know it existed?

"I told you before, I'm not leaving until I speak with the council. I have no intention of leaving."

"That remains to be seen, *Prince*," he sneers, forcefully pushing me against the rough bark of the tree. The impact sends a burst of stars dancing at the edge of my vision, accompanied by a sharp pain in my head. "Kneel."

"No," I say defiantly, eyes narrowing. I will not kneel to his man.

"I thought you would say that." He grabs my shoulders,

pushing with his enhanced shifter strength. With my wind hindered by Solari's magic and my hands bound, there's little I can do to counteract. He slices through my binding before yanking my arms behind me. A searing agony burning in my sockets as they are tightly bound around the sturdy trunk.

"Aries, that's going too far," Nero says, stepping between us.

"Lockheed, unless you wish to join him, move out of my way. The council will not look favorably if you intervene." I watch as my friend tenses, a muscle ticking in his jaw before he relents. Aries is right. Nero must remain diplomatic, or they'll start doubting him too.

"Ye cannot mean to leave him here, tied up and defenseless until the council convenes?" Nero's eyebrows shoot up in indignation as he dramatically spreads his arms wide.

"That's precisely what I intend to do, and that is a valid point." With purposeful strides, he moves closer, unbuckling my sword belt and removing the two daggers secured to my thighs. "Can't leave you armed. Solari, make sure he doesn't leave before we return."

My eyes never waver from Aries, locked in a tense gaze. "Go," I say icily to Nero, my voice filled with resolve. I do not trust Aries to portray our purpose to the shifter council. Sybil's words about not all shifters being evil ring in my ears; I hope she can prove me wrong again.

"What's taking them so long?" I pull against my restrained arms and growl in frustration. The sun had set, bringing nightfall and the late winter chill with it. The forest behind me comes alive with the sound of owls hooting and wind whistling through the trees. And here I stand tied up.

Powerless.

I glance to the young woman standing beside me, one hand on my elbow, her eyes never leaving the village in the distance. Her magic is a passive net over my strength and magic; however, I can feel its force has begun to ebb and wane, yet not enough to free myself.

"Solari," I say, remembering the name the wolf shifter had called her earlier. She breaks from her reverie, her strange silver eyes peering up into my face. It is hard to judge her age based on her pale, flawless cream skin, but she looks near to Edmund's age.

Edmund. How is he taking all of this? What must he think of me?

She cocks her head to the side, her white brows furrowing as she stares at me. "But of course."

My breath catches in my chest.

Hope.

"How many–"

She turns away, staring toward the village. "Someone comes."

I watch as a figure shrouded in a black cloak moves toward the two of us, carrying a dark object in their arms. They nervously look over their shoulder back toward the village every so often. The moon breaks out from behind a cloud, illuminating her small figure, honey-colored skin, dark hair and rich brown eyes. It's a woman, and the object she is carrying resembles a bucket. She stops a few paces away, and in the dim light, I can see her tremble. A long feline tail twitches behind her as she glances between me and the girl at my side.

"Are you who they whisper about?" I strain to hear her barely-audible questions over the quiet slosh of liquid in the bucket, but it's clear that she is talking to *me*.

"What do they whisper?" I reply, voice hoarse. I dart a

tongue, barely moistening my dry lips as I think about when the last time was that I had anything to drink.

"They say." She takes a few timid steps closer, tiny claws digging into the wood of the bucket. As the silver glow of the moonlight peaks through the clouds once again, I notice the thin pink scars marring the smooth skin of her forearms. There are hundreds of them, each telling a story of pain and endurance. A story I hope I had no part in.

"They say you are Aramis Adrostos, Prince of Shadowvale. They say you've spent your whole life hunting down shifters to bring before the crown for trial."

"Yes," I reluctantly reply and swallow the knot in my throat. My cheeks burn as I drop my chin to my chest. Solari doesn't move or interject in the conversation, so I push on with a whisper, "What happened to your arms?"

"Shadowvale soldiers. Whipped for not bowing low enough during the first few years of Tricella's reign." She sighs. "That was just the beginning. I fear what would have happened had I not fled to the country."

I hear a shuffle of feet and sigh, pressing my eyes closed as the weight of reality settles on my shoulders. I will never escape the ghosts of my past. These people will never accept me. They despise me and I can't blame them for it. Am I any better than Tricella?

The wooden bucket lands at my feet with a thump, water sloshing over the side, and I look up, meeting her warm brown gaze.

"They also say you come to repent, that you want to join our cause and rebuild Shadowvale with a united people." She kneels, staring at my bound arms, sleeves pushed to my elbows in my struggle, revealing the scrapes, bruises, and mud from our grueling journey.

"I have failed my people, and I have done unjust harm to your people for which I vow I will do everything I can to undo. But it's true. I come to ask for forgiveness and help." My throat constricts as I admit my weakness.

The silence stretches as she sits, watching me before pulling a small wooden cup from her pocket and filling it from the bucket.

"Why?" She holds the cup between her hands, studying me.

"Because..." The words die on my lips. Sybil's beautiful star mark comes to my mind, her strength and relentless strive to be better and to do the right thing. Nero's nervous smile when he first revealed his draken form to me, terrified his secret would be the end of our friendship. My mother's kindness. Edmund's unprejudiced affection for Sybil. Kela's courage. Those are the foundations on which I want to rebuild Shadowvale. That's why I must earn forgiveness from the shifters.

"Because when my time comes to leave this life behind, I want to know I have done everything I could to ensure every creature has the right to freedom and peace," I whisper hoarsely.

I hold my breath as she leans forward, lifting the cup to my lips. Solari's hand tenses on my other side and I feel a slight surge in her magic. Otherwise she maintains her vacant observation. I drink greedily as the water touches my tongue, relishing as the cold liquid parches my throat. She could have poisoned the water, and it would not have surprised me, but denying her offering would mar the fragile first acceptance I have created.

"Your journey will not be an easy one, Prince Aramis. Trust is not so easily earned, but everyone deserves a second chance. Don't waste it." She glances over her shoulder before picking up the bucket and disappearing on nimble feet into the dark forest. I realize I didn't ask for her name. Will the other shifters show me just as much kindness?

3
ARAMIS

The sound of a dagger slicing through rope is a symphony to my ears.

"Glad to see yer still alive," Nero says, sheathing his dagger back into his boot. I wince, rubbing my chafed wrists as sensation and blood flow return to my hands. The sight of him and two other men approaching as the first light of dawn graced the sky had filled me with relief.

"Thanks," I say to Nero as I glance up at the burly, tall man standing next to him with chestnut brown hair and piercing blue eyes who had been silent. I can't put my finger on it, but I could have sworn I've met this male before. "I am Aramis."

"I know," he says, nodding to my best friend as he examines me. "Nero told me as much. You both look worse for wear."

Glancing down, I grimace at the disheveled state we're both in from traveling. From our mud-coated boots to the green stains on our once-tan pants, it becomes evident that we are in desperate need of a proper bath. Running my hand over my jaw, I feel a week's worth of growth, emphasizing the need for both a bath and a shave. The lingering scent of sweat that surrounds us reinforces the urgency. I look more like a peasant than a prince.

"We traveled hard and fast to make it here." I square my shoulders, standing to my full height and raising my chin. "I must speak with the council."

"We are eager to hear what you have to say." He holds out a hand and we shake firmly. "My name is Roger. Roger Macgregor."

Macgregor.

I school the shock from my face. He couldn't possibly be related to Kela. But as I look at him, I can't deny the unmistakable tilt to his head, the way he holds his body, and his eyes. She had *his* eyes.

"Let's go," Aries barks out. "Unless you want to look worse in front of the council by being tardy." He snickers and turns, walking away. Nero's improved mood gives me hope that I might not be walking straight to the guillotine, so I step forward, nearly stumbling at the weakness of my body.

"Woah there, Aramis. Need a hand?" I cut a sharp glance in Nero's direction, willing my body to listen to me, but I sway on my feet.

"Solari is still learning to control her magic. You'll feel weak and shaky like you're recovering from the plague for a few hours at least. Her touch has put even the strongest of us to our knees." Roger's lips purse together as he stares toward her and Aries in the distance.

"What is she?" I ask, reluctantly accepting Nero's help. I lean heavily on him, my legs wobbling like gelatin as we make our way toward the village.

"She's a halfling. Her mother was a python shifter, but she never spoke of the father. Her mother passed away sixteen years ago. She caught the vermillion fever at the end of her pregnancy and passed hours after giving birth to the babe. She was born with pure white hair, porcelain skin and silver blue eyes. We didn't think she'd make it, especially after everything her mother went through, but she held on."

"She is just a wee bairn," Nero says. "I've never seen her when I've come before."

"She is a strange child, as if she only has one foot in this world. She used to keep to herself and we mostly let her. But then her *peculiar* powers started manifesting a few years ago and Aries decided to take her under his wing." The tone lacing those last words betrays a note of discontent in regard to this choice.

"And her other heritage?" I ask, my curiosity getting the better of me.

"We haven't been able to figure that out and her mother didn't leave any hints. She hasn't shown any sign of shifting or other powers, but we've never seen or heard of anyone else like her."

Children with abnormal powers, elementals fated to shifters; this can't be a coincidence. Something is coming and even the Goddess is intervening.

The gentle sounds of a village waking from slumber start getting louder as we approach the camp. My battle instincts kick in, observing and categorizing everything I see.

Following a dirt road, we pass hundreds of tents in multitudes of colors, their walls illuminated by flickering flames. Clotheslines hang from tent to tent, where garments sway gently in the breeze. Shoes seemingly belonging to both adults and children are orderly placed by the entrance. The inviting aroma of porridge sways my way from the big pots balanced above fire pits scattered between tents, making my empty stomach cramp up. The few shifters already active at this time of day sit on the makeshift benches around the fire and send curious looks in my direction.

As we make our way toward the heart of the camp, the tents are soon replaced with cottages in various stages of repair, some with sagging roofs, others with make-shift doors, but nonetheless, people seem to make do with what they have. I cower slightly at the thought of the riches I grew up with at the castle. Before us, in the center of town, stands a tall building with bland walls, small, cracked windows, and a heavy canvas sheet for a door. Aries and Solari are nowhere in sight. More and more people bustling through the dark streets stop and stare and I feel small, as if every sin I have ever committed is clearly visible on my face.

"Wait here," Roger says, holding back the sheet as we duck into the dark room beyond.

Nero supports me as I lower myself to the ground, legs still uncooperative, and leaves again. The room is large, the wood consisting of plain planks of wood without ornament. Worn, moth-eaten curtains cover the cracked windows. Tiny orbs of mage light float above a marred wooden rectangular table surrounded by eight chairs. From my angle, I can barely discern a map of Shadowvale, covered in various hand carved wooden figures. It's a war table.

"Fucking Aries." The fabric covering the door ripples as Nero's wings flair behind him, and I tear my gaze from the table. His body radiates tension as he paces in the cold stone floor beneath us. "That bastard has nay right to let her touch ye, use her magic on ye. It was unprovoked."

How many times did I extend less of a courtesy when we brought shifters to be questioned at the castle?

"If it gets us one step closer to saving the kingdom and winning their trust, I'd do anything," I vow as I gently stroke the golden thread deep in my core. It's what Sybil would want. The way she finally looked at me like a man and not the beast who tore her from her home and everything she loved.

"Be careful ye don't eat yer own words," Nero chuckles.

Murmuring voices outside draw our attention before the door is flung open. Roger, Aries and a group of other people enter the room. By their appearance, they vary in ages from no older than Edmund to as old as my father. Some have prominent shifter features in their demi-form, and others radiate elemental powers, although the majority seem to be shifters. Most wear tattered clothes, in little better shape than my own as though they escaped with only the outfit on their back. Their eyes burn into my skin as they pass, some pointing and whispering, some scowling, and others staring with curiosity etched into their faces. Eight sit in the chairs and turn to face me whilst Nero remains stoically by my side. I push to my feet, willing my legs not to give out on me, but the still lingering effects of Solari's magic mixed with the musty odor of packed, sweaty bodies nearly makes my stomach turn. I scan the gathered crowd, my instincts screaming to fight or flee. I've never been surrounded by so many shifters in one room and here I stand, weak, weaponless and nearly defenseless.

A tall, willowy man with cropped salt and pepper hair and cold, sharp green eyes like cut emeralds stands at the center of the table and lifts his aged hands. There's an air of authority to him enhanced by the deep lines etching his face. A quiet strength that commands attention. I don't need Nero to confirm this man holds most of the power within this camp.

"You should always respect wisdom when you see it in others, Aramis. Leaders respect other leaders." One of my father's few lessons before Tricella turned him into an empty shell, comes back to me. Before the memory can startle me, I am distracted by the mage lights brightening, illuminating the room further.

"Aramis Adrostos. Crown Prince of Shadowvale, you come before the council of Thorns, seeking to speak with us." The man's voice is deep, each word imbued with authority.

I nod, then open my mouth to speak but he turns, facing Nero, and continues, "Nero Lockheed, your absence has been a point of discussion. For weeks you have not reported back to us, yet you return not with the unicorn we were expecting, but with the Shadowvale prince?"

Heat burns along my neck at his dismissal, but I bite my tongue and bide my time. Some battles are better won with words than sword blades.

"Victor." Nero bows his head respectfully. "I apologize for my absence, but much has occurred since our last meeting. Tricella's forces–"

"We are aware Tricella's forces are on the move searching for the unicorn. We've heard the rumors from the scouts. What happened to the unicorn shifter?" Roger says, sitting back in his chair with his arms crossed over his chest.

"That is one reason we are here. Sybil is trapped in the mountain passes. We were on our way down to find you to see if you knew the old entrances to the library of Harpalyke. We were camping in the caves overnight when an avalanche trapped Sybil inside."

"No one has been to the library in years. Not since the beasts took to the tunnels in the war. You're more likely to be eaten than make it there alive," Victor says.

"You cannot mean just to leave her there to die," I say, meeting his gaze, tension radiating through my body. The barest flicker of magic hums in my veins, a wind whipping through the room, causing the mage lamps to bob in the air.

"I told you he can't be trusted! His magic is wild and untamed as his temper. He's as likely to tear this village down in a royal tantrum as he is to report to Tricella," Aries says from his end of the table.

"That was hardly a wild show of power," a female with wild, wavy blonde hair and bright blue eyes chuckles from the opposite end of the table. "If you want a true demonstration of untamed elemental power." She lifts her hand in the air, conjuring an orb of water. Her lips pull back into a grin as she leans over the table, the orb grows spiked projectiles as it spins faster.

"Enough, Evolet. This is not the time to provoke Aries."

"Fine." She leans back in her chair, casually letting the orb spin in her open palm, once again a smooth, opaque ball.

Victor turns back to me, frowning. "That is not what I said," he replies. "We value every life, shifter, elemental and any other who comes to our refuge. We have been looking for Sybil for years after hearing rumors of Tricella's hunt for her parents. For their *kind*. We will have our cartographers look for information concerning entrances to the library, and they'll consider sending scouts to search for her."

"Thank you," I say, clenching my fists and pulling back my magic until it simmers under my skin. My strength is slowly returning, and I stand taller but my heart races. They've agreed to help her, but how long will it take to find the tunnels and search for her?

"Have you heard any word from the castle since you left?" Victor raises an eyebrow, steepling his fingers before him as he stares at the two of us.

"No," I say, letting my head drop, feeling the weight of loss for everything I have left behind: my crown, my friends, and Edmund. Now the possibility of losing my mate too. "We have not had contact with anyone in the castle since we left, but

Tricella knew where we were. I don't know how she found us, unless..."

"Hmm?" He raises an eyebrow, and the crowd falls quiet, leaning in expectantly.

How much can I tell them? Can I trust the shifters with intimate knowledge of who is close to me? What secrets can I reveal without endangering my family further?

"Tricella knows Nero freed Sybil and that I helped her escape when she sent her abominations to attack us in the woods. She has a seer, Kieran."

"That is not news to us. Nero has warned us of Kieran's powers for some time. Our village is warded by the best elementals and witches to protect our people from his sight. It's why we've evaded her attacks for this long. Feeding us old knowledge will not win our favor, Prince. We need help. We need answers to defeat her and stop her reign of terror." His last words are enhanced as he stands, punctuating the air, his voice hitting me in the chest like a physical blow.

"I did not–"

"Tricella has gone on a rampage since you two absconded with the unicorn right from under her nose. Her attacks have become more violent, her shadow demons kill with no regard to who is enemy and who is friend. Did you really think she would not inflict her rage upon others? Innocents? We had to pull all our spies from the castle for fear they'd be found out. Not even elementals are spared from her bloodlust now. And her demon pets are growing stronger by the day. At this rate, neither shifter nor elemental will be able to oppose her madness."

Evolet, the water elemental, bows her head to hide the scorn on her face. Did she flee from the citadel near the castle? What had happened to her?

"Tricella was stealing Sybil's magic, her very life force." I narrow my eyes. "If Nero hadn't saved her—"

The canvas door whips to the side, and we all turn as a female shifter storms into the room, baring her fangs. Anger pours off her in waves as she narrows her hate-filled gaze on the two of us.

"Where is my daughter? Where is my Kela?" The last notes of her voice end in a canine whine, her hands fisted, claws extended at her sides.

My daughter.

Suddenly, my chest feels too tight to breathe.

"Kaitlin," Nero begins solemnly. He holds the woman's gaze, and when the silence stretches on, she furrows her brows.

"Nero. Where. Is. Kela? You were supposed to be with her and the unicorn. She saw it. Where is my baby girl?" Roger pushes back from the table and comes to her side. He tentatively puts his hand on Katlin's shoulder, but the woman pushes him off. Nero, at a loss for words, shakes then bows his head.

"No." Tears line the woman's green eyes as she lifts a trembling hand to her mouth. The pain lacing her sobs is excruciating and my ever-present guilt echoes in my own heart that breaks at the sight of this woman mourning her daughter.

"Kaitlin," Nero says quietly, face falling with grief and anger. "We were ambushed by Tricella's shadow demons on our way here. We were outnumbered and under prepared."

She turns, burying her face against Rogers' chest as she wails. He holds her close, running a gentle hand across her back but his eyes are too hazy with tears.

"We did everything we could to save her. She fought like a true warrior," I say, even though nothing I say will be able to take away from the pain.

She turns to me, glaring with puffy red rimmed eyes. "I don't care what you did or what you think of her. If it wasn't for your family and that bitch ruling these lands, she would still be here." I flinch as she spits at my feet.

"We knew about the attack," Roger says over her head as he rubs comforting circles on his wife's back. "Kela told us as much before she left. She had seen it all. She didn't give us the details but the way she acted... we suspected something unsettling. We tried to convince her to stay, but commanding her was like commanding the ocean to stop crashing along the shore or the wind to stop blowing."

"Roger, if she knew, she should have said something." Nero's hands clench at his side. "If we knew, we could have been more prepared, taken a different route, anything."

"You know her visions didn't work like that, Nero," Roger replies calmly, taking a seat at the table and urging her to sit next to him.

"Where was the unicorn? Why didn't she heal her?" Kaitlin asks venomously, glaring at me. "How is she supposed to save our people if she can't even save one? Kela was only a pup, barely out of her youth!"

"Perhaps the prince is still in league with the queen," Aries starts. "She may even be tracking him here as we argue, a distraction!" He shoves his hand in the air, staring at the crowd around him

A murmur rises from the crowd as everyone begins to talk over one another. Hate filled gazes and pointed fingers move in our direction. I instinctually step back toward the door.

"He is a threat to all shifters," a deep male voice calls out.

"Everyone deserves a chance to change."

"What about Kela? What if it wasn't an accident?" My teeth grind at the obvious insinuation.

"We've already been over this—"

"What if he has already shared the location of the camp with his spies?" They begin to cast accusatory glances at one another.

"He let Kela die. He let hundreds of shifters be tortured by the queen. A life for a life!" Someone shouts from the back of the room.

Nero tenses behind me, hand reaching for the hilt of his sword. My palms begin to sweat, and I reach for my magic to throw a shield around us if needed. They may be out for blood, but I can't hurt them and prove not to be the monster they claim me to be.

"Enough," Victor's voice rings out, the magic lights flaring. The council has all risen from their seats, magic radiating off hands and claws outstretched and I see that it is equally comprised of half elementals and half shifters.

"Violence in response to violence will never break the cycle. We would be no better than the queen herself." Victor's stern voice commands the council to lower their arms and return to their seats, as the crowd quiets and steps back.

"Prince Aramis will undergo a trial for his war crimes against his people and a decision will be made with Alpheias's blessing."

A snarky laugh challenges Victor's sentence, and everyone turns their heads toward the only shifter reckless enough to oppose the old man: Aries.

"He is a threat to our village. You can't mean to leave him to roam free until a decision is made. From the rumors, he could tear down this village with his magic before the night's over. I hope you won't see the day you regret this decision, or we'll all be food for demons." Aries' venomous gaze lands on me and I can tell he'd be happy to rescind my head from my neck if they only give him the chance, just as I'd happily prove to him how good I am with a sword.

But Victor ignores the shifter's words, his sentence now law. The old man nods at the council members before leveling his stare on me. The stone hiding under my coat begins to pulse, matching my heartbeat, and I hold my breath,

"His trial will commence tomorrow at sunset. In the meantime, he will remain locked in the cells, his magic bound with the durgrim embedded in the walls."

4
SYBIL

I used to be afraid of the dark.

The thought mixes with the sound of gravel crunching under my every step and bouncing off the stone passageway.

"Hello?" I call out, pulling the edge of my cloak tighter across my chest. The only answer is my echo. There was a corner in my little cottage in Kallistar that always terrified me come nightfall. It was shrouded in darkness so thick, I often wondered if it was a portal to the depths of hell. The darkness of these tunnels does not scare me. It hugs me gently and guides me further toward the heart of the mountain, eager to show me its secrets. It reminds me that I am no longer that same girl.

"What I wouldn't give for Nero's fire affinity right now," I grumble, the humidity of the tunnels making my hair curl and body shiver. I count our lucky stars that, at least, Lemon and I managed to avoid injury in the avalanche.

As if summoned by my thoughts, he pokes his head out of my pocket and chitters at me.

"I don't know where this path will take us, darling. We'll just have to wait and see." My stomach gives an audible rumble. In the faint glow cast by the lichen sparsely growing on the stone walls, I reach into the pack and pull out some of the carefully packed food. My heart clenches at the memory of Kela packing our bags with her freshly baked treats.

She had known.

The whole time, she had known she was walking to her death. Yet she had never cowered. Tears line my eyes and I quickly brush them away. I can't succumb to grief, not now.

"We're not in Shadowvale anymore, boy, that's for sure." I rub his soft head, then take the last swig of water from the flask. I frown, looking from the empty container in my hand to the dark tunnel ahead."Balderdash, we're out of water. I should have melted the snow before heading down."

I turn forlorn back toward where we have come. I don't know exactly how long I've been walking, but the pain in my feet is indicator enough that it is too late to turn back.

Rocks skitter, their sharp edges scraping against the rough walls and creating an eerie echo that reverberates through the darkness enveloping us. My chest constricts as images of the shadow beasts flash through my mind. I gulp, wiping my sweaty palms, and push down my racing thoughts.

"Hello? Is anyone down here? I'm looking for the library," I call out, shifting the pack onto my back. Silence once again meets my ears. I might no longer fear the dark but being alone still puts me on edge. My arms cross over my chest, fingers fidgeting with the edges of my sleeves. Every heartbeat echoes in my head like a drumroll, increasing in volume and speed with each intrusive thought taking shape. The library could be a myth. The exit to these tunnels could be closed. Hunger and thirst could easily be the end of me... and Lemon.

I can't lose hope, not now.

I pull the reins on my imagination and take a deep breath of cold air. I force my hunched shoulders to relax and roll my neck to diffuse the tension in my muscles. Allowing fear to take over my body and mind is going to be my end, that's certain. Queen Rose and the Goddess have led me here, I need to trust them. I need to trust that Kela's sacrifice was not in vain.

A hero is not the extent of their training. A hero is a hero because, even when hope is lost, even when everything you do amounts to nothing and shows no promise, you keep trying. You fight.

Her words rush back to me and spur me on. I need to trust that Aramis—

The ghost of a caress tickles my cheek. Aramis's calloused hand is taking me back to a memory I've been holding close to my heart, tucked in a special pocket for moments when I need to remind myself I am no longer alone. For moments such as this one.

I should focus on the path ahead of me, but for a moment, I close my eyes and let myself fall back to that memory. The way his touch in the warm water of the spring made my skin tingle. His full lips on mine. Our legs tangling. Breaths hitching.

The ache his absence spurs in my soul surprises me still. My feelings for him are a summer storm raging within me, relentless but sweet after the summer draught. Slowly, my right hand settles on my chest, where my love for Aramis feels like sunshine in spring. I spare a quick prayer to the Goddess to watch over Aramis and Nero. If they followed the plan, they should be looking for the rebel camp now, looking for help.

Tears prick the corner of my eyes as I take a deep, shuddering breath. I am not alone and I can do this. Lemon climbs onto my shoulder, a sandpaper tongue licking away the moisture. With each inhale, I remind myself that these tears, this pain, are temporary. They are a testament to the depth of my emotions, but they do not define me.

Standing a little bit taller, I remind myself of the vow I've made to help my people. I re-open my eyes and keep walking. This is my mission. The library must be here.

As I turn another dark corner, a refreshing breeze gently caresses my cheek, carrying with it an invigorating scent I instantly recognize.

Water.

"Do you smell that, Lemon?" I hasten my steps, careful not to trip on the irregular stone ground, plunging into the depths of the shadows. I hear the faint sound of dripping water ahead.

Where there is water, there is life.

This is the sign I've been praying for. My muscles relax and a small smile plays on the corners of my lips.

With my hand raised, I reach out with my powers, honing in on the subtle vibrations of energy. The lichen pulse around me, illuminating the tunnel, but I feel no other signs of life.

Strange, even this deep in the cave, I should sense *something*.

With caution, I follow step after step, fingertips brushing along the rocky walls as they slowly expand. The tunnel no longer feels claustrophobic as it opens into a large, cavernous room with three other tunnels before me. More luminescent lichen dotted with clusters of tiny long-stemmed mushrooms cover the walls, donning the cave with a greenish glow. I smear lichen on the floor to mark the passage I came through and I thank the Goddess for this little bit of light. The other two tunnels are nearly identical to the original passage, save for the echo of dripping water coming from one of them.

"Well, that narrows our choices," I whisper, disheartened. As I take a step to follow the first sign of direction I have met in hours, a *crack* echoes from under my boot. Shards of something edgy poke my sole and I know it's not the gravel. Eyes fixed on the lichen, I take another step. *Crack.* I swallow the lump in my throat and slowly glance down. When my eyes adjust to the dark ground beneath my feet, my stomach turns, nausea taking over my senses. The lifeless body of a giant cave rat, now nothing more than a barren carcass, lies abandoned in a corner. Some of his bones litter the ground I'm walking on.

The water did not lead me to life, but *death.*

I freeze, hairs rising on my arms. Panic rises within me. Is this the end waiting for me? *Click.* Was this all for nothing? *Click.* How could I believe I'd make it on my—

Click.

There's another sound breaking the silence other than the dripping of water. Clicking noises draw my attention above, to the tall arched ceiling made of dark marble with a white intricate veining pattern. At a closer look, those are not arches at all, nor is it marble. Hundreds of pearlescent ropes weave webs across the dark ceiling, some of them are thin as thread, others as thick as my forearm. Despite the luminescent lichen, the darkness still lingers that far up on the ceiling. I can feel *something* viciously studying me, observing my next move, something other than the darkness who has been my friend so far. I blink once, twice and... notice something else. Legs.

In the center of the ceiling, where the ropes converge in symmetrical patterns, a spider the size of two large stallions lies still as stone.

"Please be dead, please be dead," I chant under my breath as I back slowly toward the closest tunnel, never taking my eyes off the creature. Suddenly, I am aware of the sound of my breathing, Lemon's incessant rustling, the edge of my coat swishing along the shards of bone—

The edge of the tunnel hits the pack, and an apple falls out, rolling to the center of the room, gleaming dully in the lichen's hue. My body stiffens, feeling rooted to the spot as my heart beats painfully in my chest. Above me, the spider opens its beady eyes and stares down at me.

"Well, issn't this an unexpected ssurprisse," the creature says in an ancient tone. Slowly stretching out its eight legs that span the length of the room, the creature blinks languidly and clicks its enormous claws. "It'ss been a long time since Arkin has feassted on ssuch a delectable morsel."

Why did it have to be a giant spider?

My pulse pounds in my ears, drowning out my thoughts. My arms and legs shake as I weigh my options. I could run, trust my legs to follow the tunnel's path and hope it leads toward an exit or, even better, the library. However, the chances this creature knows these passageways better than I do are high, and I don't particularly want to meet the rat's same end. Not to mention that I am done running.

I reach into my well of magic, feeling my horn materialize on my forehead, and strength move into my limbs. I am no longer the defenseless, half-trained healer from Kallistar. Grabbing the dagger from its sheath, I drop my pack to the ground and crouch into a defensive position Kela taught me.

"Until I am meassured, I am not known. Yet how you misss me, when I have flown," he says, his feet tapping against the stone ceiling. Eight beady black eyes blink at me. "You ssmell devine."

"I am Sybil Vandeleur, last living unicorn, and I do not feel like being eaten today," I yell, watching as the spider lowers itself to the ground across the room.

"Ssybil Vandeleur," the spider tastes the air. "Arkin has

heard that name. It is an old name. The walls sspeak of ssecretss, they whissper your name. Do you know why the wind ssings your name?"

"I don't know what you're talking about, creature. Just let me go and I'll leave you in peace," I say, holding the dagger before me and tossing my braid over my shoulder.

"The more there iss, the lesss you sseee," it taunts as it watches me. "You're far from home, horned one."

"Where there is darkness, light can shine brighter," I reply, inhaling steadily through my nose.

"When you don't have me, you want me, but when you do have me, you want to give me away. What am I, Ssybil Vandeleur?" It purrs, rubbing its pinchers together.

"Stop talking in riddles and let me go." My voice quivers. I grip the handle until my knuckles blanch white.

"Arkin hass not eaten unicorn flesh before. I sshall feasst on you sslowly." Saliva drips from its open mouth as it clambers toward where the apple lay on the ground.

Fear coils inside me, icy and unyielding like cold steel.

"I only seek the library of Harpalyke. Let me go and I'll leave you in peace," I say.

"Harpalyke," Arkin shrieks, body tensing before it slams a leg into the wall. I shield my face as dust and webs rain from the ceiling. "What does a tassty little treat like you have to do with those blassted witchess?"

I edge along the room, moving as silently as I can whilst avoiding the rat's bones.

"That is none of your business, I'm afraid." Magic swirls within me, but the lack of rest and food makes it feeble. I do not have enough magic to completely transform, but I could fight in my demi-form.

"You sseek ssomething others have ssought before,

unicorn," the creature mumbles but I try to ignore him. "The quessstion is, *why?*"

I roll my eyes at the cryptic nonsense, but the creature seems to be in a chatty mood so I let him continue—anything to avoid becoming his next meal.

"Arkin has lived in this mountain for eonss, ssince the beginning of time," he continues in a lull. "He has sseen the Goddesss, seen the warss between your kind and the other one. Foolissssh you are. Sseeking power as old as time for your own endss. Magic is balance, tassty one, sshe sseems to have forgotten about it, will you?"

"I have no idea who you're talking about," I say and try to keep my tone calm. The only way I can leave this room alive is if I can incapacitate the creature to stop it from following me through the tunnel. My dagger is no match for its size but maybe I can slice through a couple of its legs in order to gain some time to run.

"Where have you gone, little unicorn?" The spider's legs search along the ground like bony fingers looking for coins in a pouch. Its eyes dart directionless in a murderous frenzy, yet when they land on me, they fail to focus, and Arkin moves the other way.

It's blind?!

I take the opportunity and make haste toward the tunnel door, focusing more on being quiet than unseen. Dodging bones and pieces of dried-up spider web, I turn my back to Arkin, who crawls up the wall to scout its perimeter. The rhythmic clatter of its fangs and the scraping sounds of legs against the stony walls send shivers down my spine, so much so that I don't see the little protruding stone on the ground.

"Goddes—" My hands and knees slam into the rough rock floor. Searing pain followed by thick hot liquid running down my arm as the spider's claw catches the edge of my sleeve, tearing into the skin of my shoulder as I roll away.

"There you are."

The rancid smell of rat droppings permeates my senses as my blood drips on the ground below me. I duck as it swings a long leg toward me, and swipe out with my dagger, the blade whistling as it slices through the air before hitting the hard armored shell of its back.

"Oh, thiss will be fun," it says as its whole body shudders in anticipation. I realize with nauseating clarity that the reason I am still alive is because the creature is playing with me, tantalizing its food one little attack at a time until fear consumes me.

"Ssoft, ssquishy unicorn. You cannot hide from me. I can hear your heart pounding and tasste your fear in the air. You will tasste divine after years of tunnel rats."

I ignore the pain in my knees and hands and pad my way silently across the floor in the opposite direction, moving when it steps to cover any sound of my footsteps. This is so, so bad.

"You cannot run, you cannot hide."

I freeze, willing my thundering heart to slow, taking in slow deliberate breaths through my nose. Think, Sybil. Think.

"There are no happy endingss, horned one," it coos. "Do you know why?"

No, I want to scream but I shut my mouth, hands now sliding away from me as they get bloodier. I pray to the Goddess Lemon stays put in the backpack and doesn't attempt any of his heroics.

"The living sseek happiness, but it is sshort and dessperate attemptss that are forgotten and fleeting as death. It iss the dead who harbor the lingering hope for the joy of life. Sshall you whissper to me your regretss when you are dead, unicorn? What ssecretss will you tell the wind?"

I cannot keep crawling forever.

"I will not die here!" I yell as I push up from the ground and charge, sliding under the creature and slicing at the soft, unprotected underbelly. It moves skillfully and my dagger hits one of its legs instead, nearly yanking it out of my grasp.

"Foolissh girl!" It howls and shoots webbing, slamming and pinning my left wrist against the stone wall. The dagger falls from my hand.

"No!" My heart flutters in my chest as I rip at the sticky silver thread with my free hand but only manage to trap it as well. My feet scramble against the lichen and stone as I struggle to pull from the wall.

"Oh, little ssnack. How you tried in vane and failed. Will the wind whissper your name after this?" With my hands still bound together, the creature grabs me and effortlessly frees me from the wall. Sweeping me upside down by my feet, Lemon slips from my pocket with a squeak and falls to the ground.

"Let me go!" I scream as I buck and writhe in its grasp, pulling on my magic and my strength without avail. I try to stab it with my horn. The spider spins me rapidly, its threads tightly binding my ankles together, causing a dizzying sensation as darkness creeps into my peripheral vision from the rush of blood to my head.

"Who sshall ssave you now, little unicorn?" It snickers before the darkness consumes me.

5
ARAMIS

This is ridiculous," I grumble. My voice echoes off the cold, damp walls as I pace across the worn stone floor of my cell for what feels like the hundredth time.

Running my fingers through my disheveled hair, I take stock of where they've locked me up. The cell is simple, but devoid of life. It contains only a solitary stained wooden bucket, emanating a faint scent of decay, and a humble straw mattress tucked away in the corner, its worn fabric concealed beneath a patchwork blanket. A faint glimmer of the setting sunlight manages to pierce through the narrow-barred window, casting a soft glow that dances upon the swept surface below.

"How long do they plan on keeping me down here?" I ask as I peer through the iron bars. There is no one there to answer. The cold metal barely registers against the weeks' worth of scruff growing on my face. The magical barrier wraps around me, leaving a void where my wind magic resides trapped—a tangible absence in my body. I collapse onto the ground, curling up with my legs pulled to my chest, supporting myself with my arms and chin.

I need a plan. I haven't spent my whole life training to rule this kingdom only to lose it to the very people I want to protect.

I have to believe that Sybil has found a way out of that mountain or the thought of her trapped and alone will kill me. We will be reunited. I will hold her again; I just need to prove my fucking worth first. Raking my hand through my knotted hair,I wince at the pain. Gently, I reach inside and gently stroke the tiny golden thread, the only magic the barrier hasn't suppressed. If only I could talk to her through the bond, make sure she is safe, it would ease my mind.

What to do, I ask myself. I could try to break out, but then what? I'd relinquish the little trust I was trying to gain with these people, my people, and would be back to square one without help. My hands shake as I clenched my fists tightly. I came seeking their help and forgiveness only to be treated... like the villain.

You may not be the bad guy in your story, but you are the villain in mine.

I cringe as Sybil's words come back to me. At the time, when we were traveling through the forest, I did not know it but I was indeed the villain, and not just in her story. I had been the villain for so many shifters by then. I had ruthlessly taken them from their homes and families thinking it was the right thing, thinking it would avenge my mother's death and grant me my father's admiration. The shame of it all tastes acrid on my tongue; it makes me want to crawl into a deep dark hole and never reappear. How will I ever look at my hands again and not see the crimson blood of innocents? I look at the iron bars in front of me, and a little voice inside of me says, *good, this is where you belong.*

Then, there's another voice, gentle and sweet like honey. She reminds me to be kind to myself. That Tricella has molded me into the villain to these people, my people. I have to believe that all those atrocities were not just my doing or I will never forgive myself, like Sybil somehow has.

I won't stand for it any longer. They deserve freedom from persecution.

I'd give Tricella a taste of her own poison. Determination burns in my gaze as I set my jaw and turn to stare out the small window.

The creaking sound of an opening door sends me to my feet in an instant, but as I peer out of the bars, no one is there. The last of the light is fading, leaving the hallway in dusty, eerie darkness.

"Who goes there? Show yourself," I call out.

Silence stretches as I listen for any sound of movement but I immediately jerk back when a hooded figure steps out of the shadows before my cell, two silver blades in each hand and only the glint of their eyes visible. My body tenses, and my hand reaches for the sword that is not sheathed at its usual place.

"What surprise did I have when you decided to leave the capital and walk straight into the viper's nest?" he hisses. As much as I try, I cannot see its face nor recognize anything from its attire that could give me hints about who this is. I stand my ground, refusing to back up any further.

"Who are you, and what do you want from me?" I instinctively reach for my magic, but that too is gone, making me feel utterly defenseless.

"You have made many enemies, *Prince Aramis*. How do you know who to *trust?*"

"I came here and vowed peace," I retort, searching for an accent in its speech. Who the fuck is he?

He jumps, slamming his fists into the cage, bars rattling from the force. "You do not know the meaning of peace," the intruder screams, spittle flying into my face. "You reek of death and destruction. Everything you love will wither under your touch."

"That is not true," I argue, attempting to keep my tone calm and composed. But my mind races to innocent shifters locked in the dungeon, villages burned to the ground, and Sybil trapped under the mountain in the caves.

My right hand shakes as a sharp pain lances my wrist. When I glance down, I see nothing amiss. The cuff sits there untampered, yet it feels as if it's closing on itself, strangling my extremity. I try not to give the pain away but sweat starts beading my forehead. Something is not right.

"Even now, your precious draken is questioning whose side you're really on. Why else would you still be locked in a cell if he had no doubt of your alliance?" The stranger's sharp tooth grin glints from under their hood.

"You speak nothing but lies. Only a coward hides his face and goes against the commands of their superiors to engage in a personal vendetta. Your people granted me a chance to prove myself and Nero would never doubt my loyalty to him and to this cause," I say, even ast my gut twists and doubts fill my mind. The strange pain burns again along my ankles, and I feel the bond inside me turn cold with fear.

Sybil.

The intruder is still speaking but his words are a faraway echo as pure terror laces every inch of my being. My skin shivers and my vision starts tunneling and I widen my stance to keep my balance. I feel dangerously close to losing consciousness. What the hell is happening to her?

"Sybil!" I cry out, grabbing hold of the golden thread, hoping to get more information—anything. The searing sensation of a cold blade slamming into my shoulder pulls me back to reality and terror transforms into blinding anger. Hot blood soaks my tunic from where a silver hilt, simple in its craftsmanship, sticks out.

"You are the spawn of that traitorous queen. You are nothing but her puppet, doing her bidding. For all we know, you're under her magical influence as much as your father is," he sneers before lunging at me with another dagger. I dodge to the side, wincing as the movement causes the first dagger to dig deeper into my flesh.

"She is not my *mother,* and I am not under some spell," I growl and lunge toward him.

I fist the edge of his tunic through the bars, our faces only inches apart but his hood is still secured in place, and I can't see anything other than his lips and jaw. The man drops the second dagger and grabs my wrist, which is still aching from the phantom wound. I wince, and in that moment of distraction, he lunges toward the dagger still lodged in my shoulder, but before he can take it, I pull him down and we wrestle to the floor. My knees slam against the filthy stone floor, my skin splitting at the impact. He grins, sharp teeth flashing in the torchlight before his body begins to morph into the ugliest rat I've ever seen. He is the size of a dinner plate with a sickly-colored fur that reminds me of putrid mold. He is missing his right ear and has a scratch down his left eye. The rat looks at me one last time, head tilted in a mocking expression before running away through a crack in the wall.

A door slams and I turn as Nero storms down the passage, muttering, followed by two more sets of footsteps. I turn around and the rat is gone with no trace.

"Aramis. What happened to ye? Get this door open before I

rip it off the hinges," Nero says over his shoulder as he rushes over and kneels in front of me, brows furrowed with worry as he assesses every inch of my body, as he's done countless other times to make sure I'm in no imminent danger. As he did when we were kids, the night the assassins came for me and my mother, and he spared me her same fate.

There is a jumble of keys as I yank the dagger from my flesh and toss it to the ground before holding pressure to staunch the flow of blood. Nero's face is stern with determination; he is going to raise hell for what happened. Without saying another word, he hands me a handkerchief to press on the wound and goes to light another torch, shedding even more light on the disgusting cells and hallway.

"What's going on here?" Rogers' voice booms. "We've come to bring you to trial, and we find you in more trouble than we left you."

Before I can respond, the ache in my wrist reminds me of more urgent matters. I ignore Roger and turn to face Nero.

"She's in danger, Nero. I can feel her. Something has happened."

"Aye, and I bet she feels yer pain in ken." His words make me flinch as I realize I know nothing about how a mating bond works. To what extent are our souls bonded? Does she really feel my pain, even though she does not yet know she is my mate? The knowing worry that she will never accept the bond haunts me.

Nero waves his big hands in front of my eyes. "How did ye bloody get stabbed while locked up in a cell mate?"

I shake away my worries and look at Nero's handkerchief, now soaked in blood. If the wound does not stop bleeding soon, I'll need stitches. "Why don't you ask the guards why a shifter was let in to attack me while I was defenseless," I say as I glare at Roger over his shoulder.

"Ach, Aramis I dinna ken who came into this cell and attacked ye, but it was nae Roger. He's been with me the whole time. A shifter, ye say?"

"A shifter wouldn't have been able to get inside your cell without the key. It's spelled to block all magic," Roger says, crossing his arms over his chest, brows furrowed and frowning. "But you also were stripped of all weapons before being put down here..."

"I don't know who it was, I just know they stabbed me *through* the bars, then when I grabbed them, they transformed into a rat and took off down the hall," I say, gesturing to the opposite direction of where they entered.

They both turn their heads to where I indicated and sniff, as if they could smell out the intruder over the scent of unwashed bodies and mildew.

Nero shakes his head and helps me to my feet. "Let's get ye patched up and over to the council so we can get some answers."

"Nero——" I begin, resting my hand on his shoulder.

"We will get her." His dark eyes are sincere, and I see my same worry haunting him. "But we need help," he continues. "Trust the Goddess she is fine, Aramis. We have already sacrificed too much; she can't take her too."

I nod as I try to ignore the intensifying pain in my shoulder. Rushed decisions will take us nowhere. Nero is right, we need help. This is our purpose here. I tug on the bond, and it feels calm. There's no longer fear or pain coming from Sybil. Does this mean she's safe or has the threat she's encountered made her unable to feel anything?

I stand before the council of Thorns, Nero by my side as I wait for their verdict. The fresh bandage on my shoulder is wrapped tight around my chest, squeezing the air out of my lungs.

"Aramis Adrostos, the council has discussed your crimes as well as your request for help," Victor says, tapping a finger impatiently atop the wooden table.

I nod solemnly, keeping my face neutral and my emotions in check. I have to play the diplomatic prince. The role I was born and trained to play if I am going to survive this and broker peace in Shadowvale.

"You claim to want to save Sybil Vandeleur, last known unicorn shifter in Craeweth, and you need our help in freeing her. You also claim to see the wrong of your ways, and seek to align your cause with ours, removing Tricella from the throne and ensuring, as Crown Prince, a peaceful future in Shadow-vale where shifters will always be welcome and treated with the same respect elementals are."

"That is correct."

"But you've spent your life bringing shifters for questioning before your father? Torn families apart looking for those accused of treason? Locked countless numbers of shifters in the castle dungeons, including the aforementioned unicorn shifter."

Heat burns along my cheeks, but I give a curt nod. "I was only doing what I thought was–"

He holds up his hand, and I bite my tongue. Victor's piercing blue eyes set on me, and I feel the weight of his role within this community. He is what I wished my father could have been for our kingdom—someone wise and just. I lower my gaze, suddenly conscious of the prolonged silence, and worry I might have overestimated the benevolence of the shifter rebels. These people owe me nothing, whilst I owe them a debt I will never be able to repay. I hear Victor take in a deep breath before I hear his verdict.

"The council has found you guilty of your crimes."

I tense, ready to defend myself but Nero rests his hand on my forearm. Victor clears his throat, eyebrows raised.

"However, Nero Lockheed has vowed on your behalf. He has been loyal to us, helping provide resources, aid, and informing us of the Queen's plans. While not abstaining you from your crimes against your people, we will allow you to prove your worth on two conditions. Your powers will be magically bound until you prove your worth to your people, and you will be under constant supervision by either Nero or one of the council for as long as you are in this village. We also require more than just your word; we need intel. Information our spies would not be able to obtain. Do you agree to these terms?"

Powerless.

I close my eyes, inhaling deeply. If this is the cost of freedom, the cost to gaining their trust, I will do it. I have a lifetime of regrets and wrongdoings against these people—my people. If I am going to gain their trust, I can hold nothing back.

I can feel the color blanching from my face. Not too long ago, in a forest nestled between Kallistar and Shadowavle, an oily voice spoken by creatures in the shadows whispered to me. *How do you judge a man's worth?* And now, I'm asking myself the same question.

"Yes. I will do what I must to prove my word is true."

The council nods their heads, and I am shocked to see elementals at the table.

"Come forth," Victor says as he stands, holding two teal bands. Sweat coats my palms as I anxiously approach the table, all eyes trained on me.

I will not fail. I will not falter.

But who will I be without my powers?

My stomach twists, my mouth going dry as I lift my hands before him, willing them not to shake. A female with jet-black hair rises beside Victor and slides the bands over my wrist. I fight the urge to pull away and rip the bands away as she closes her hands over my wrist.

Her eyes light up a molten gray, hands shimmering as the metal begins to writhe under her fingertips, pulsing with magic. The stone strewn around my neck under my shirt pulsates, my heart beats racing in my ears until everything is drowned out except the sound of wind. Then, there is silence.

6

SYBIL

Someone is screaming.

The screeching sound rends the air, intensifying the throbbing in my temples. I try to open my eyes, but my face feels swollen. I don't remember falling asleep or having a headache. As I try to regain consciousness, a wave of nausea hits when my body starts to sway. I attempt to blink again, and as my vision finally clears, I see Lemon scamper across the ceiling toward me.

How did he get to the ceiling? I wonder in disbelief. *You little rascal, always getting yourself into trouble.*

I attempt to shift my shoulders and extend my limbs, but I can't. My body feels immobilized by constricting coils, and everything is numb—from my ankles up to my neck. *What kind of condition is this?* I wonder, healer brain taking over. I am soon distracted by Lemon standing on his hind legs trying to get my attention. That's when I realize–with utter terror–that he is not on the ceiling but on the floor. Which means...

No, no, no, this can't be happening!

I peer at the sticky strands of web wrapped tightly around my torso and follow them up to the ceiling of the chamber from which I am hanging, like an animal for slaughter. From this height, I can see the intricate web work Arkin has created. His pearlescent strands are woven from wall to wall, a canopy that is as beautiful as it is dangerous. I look at the rocky ground under me, littered with bones,and my breathing accelerates as I wonder how many of my bones I'll break if I fall from here.

"Okay," I whisper to myself, hoping it'll help me clear my mind despite all the blood flowing to my head.

I haven't been eaten alive by a giant spider... yet. But I will, if I don't get out of here. The pounding of my pulse in my ears makes it hard to think but I fight past it. If only I could reach the knives tucked into my boots. The more I move, the tighter the cocoon seems to get, but then I remember. Someone was screaming.

I gasp as the spider screeches, the sound echoing off the small chamber. My eyes scan the ground again, and there, at the intersection between the chamber and one of the tunnels, I see blurred figures engaging in a fierce battle with the colossal spider.

My heart leaps in my chest as sweat breaks along my skin. Who else would be wandering through these tunnels? Is it foe or friend? Someone sent by Tricella to take me back to the kingdom? Or the help Aramis and Nero were looking for?

I am not staying around to take my chances.

Reaching deep inside, I stroke my well of magic. There's not much there but it'll have to do. I materialize my horn and begin rocking my body whilst engaging my abdominal muscles until I curl up, horn nicking and slicing through a few strands of web. I fall back upside down. My heartbeat pounds in my ears like a parade of drums, loud enough to cover the sounds of the fight happening on the ground. The air feels heavy, constricting my chest and making it hard to inhale and replenish my oxygen supply. Dizziness washes over me; I struggle to keep conscious.

Don't give up. A hero keeps trying, even when all hope is lost.

With renewed determination, I hold Kela's words close to my heart, take a deep breath and attempt again. This time,the strands loosen from my wrists to mid-thigh, but my energy wanes as the thick webs constrict my chest and breathing.

Out of the corner of my eye, Lemon scampers up one of the spider's legs, providing a momentary distraction while the three white and gray cloaked figures circle the creature.

It lets out an unholy scream as one of the figures procures a glowing cerulean ball of flame between their hands and sends it flying causing it to hasten backwards toward me.

"Terrible creaturess!" Arkin screeches as it flails, trying to extinguish its burning forelegs. Lemon runs along his back and takes a leap, landing on my bound body.

"Begone, Arkin. You are no longer welcome to wander these sacred tunnels. Seek your prey elsewhere, or feast on my blade," a strong feminine voice cries out as the tallest of the three pulls out a glowing silver blade.

"Arkin sshall eat you all!" Arkin cries as he lunges for the group. The smallest woman pulls a longbow from her back, takes aim, and shoots. The massive spider writhes on the ground, limbs flailing against the walls, knocking down more dust and webs as the arrow hits the joint between his body and foreleg.

"We offered you sanctuary in these tunnels from the shadow beasts under oath that you would not harm travelers seeking the library. You have not upheld your oath. Begone now." The smallest warrior advances, throwing back her hood where long blonde curls tumble around her shoulders, framing a porcelain face with high cheekbones, sharply pointed ears, and bright blue eyes.

"You will regret thiss," he hisses as he backs toward the nearest tunnel whose ground glows faintly with smeared lichen. He turns and flees, the scraping sound of his scuttling feet diminishing with each passing second.

Lemon, my nimble little creature, swiftly scampers up the intricately woven rope of glistening spider silk. With a graceful leap, he lands on me, his tiny paws gently touching the surface where I am suspended. Amidst his hurried chittering, he frantically tears at the delicate strands of the web that bind me.

A whoosh of feathers and the smallest warrior's body stretches until a winged creature with the head of an owl and the body of a tiger stands below me. At this point, with my vision starting to tunnel after being upside down for so long, I am not entirely sure if what I am seeing is real or a fruit of my imagination. The shifter pushes off the ground. Her wings whip wind into the small space as she uses sharp claws to slice through the bindings at my feet. She catches me and lowers me to the ground.

"Thank you." I wince, rubbing my hands and wiggling my feet as the returning blood flow bites painfully into my freed extremities. The chamber floor feels oddly unstable, and I worry I'll fall at any minute if I don't eat and drink something soon. Something this woman had said before shifting that had sliced through my dizzy haze and kept my eyes and ears wide open.

"Did you say the library? Is it the library of Harpalyke?"

"Yes, we are the white witches, guardians of Harpalyke. I am Cassara, that is Marcelene, and this–" She points up at the winged creature above us and to the other cloaked figure. "Is Thalia."

The witches. I have found the witches.

Forcing myself not to gawk in awe of the women before me, I stand a little taller and attempt to rake a hand through my locks, now knotted and matted with spider web. Before I can tell the witches about my mission and the help we need, I notice that the other witch, Thalia, is throwing a sharp glance in Cassara's direction, willing her to stop talking. She has her lips pressed together in a thin white line and assesses me as if I were a threat.

"Who are you, and why are you trespassing in these tunnels?" Thalia asks, pointing a finger at my chest. She is much taller than Cassara, with golden brown eyes and chocolate skin. Her arms are muscular, and her posture exudes the type of deadly agility that makes people cower at a simple glance. I am both in awe and terrified of this woman; a little part of me wishes I was her.

"What did you do to provoke Arkin to attack you? He's sworn peace to these tunnels for hundreds of years." She sheaths the blade, now faded to a dull glow, and crosses her arms over her chest, causing her dark black tight curls to bounce around her waist.

"I did nothing to provoke him," I reply, brow furrowing at her accusations. "I am Sybil Vandeleur and I seek the coven of the white witches who guard the Library of Harpalyke."

"Why?" Thalia raises an eyebrow, leaning back. I feel her raking gaze as she examines the disheveled state of my clothes, ripped from my fight and struggle with the spider. "Or better yet, how did you know of the library's existence?"

"I come seeking knowledge–"

She snorts, rolling her eyes. "The Library of Harpalyke is more than a place of knowledge. Why are you truly here?"

"I told you, I am–"

Before I can respond, she crouches, whips a dagger out, and

holds it under my chin. The steel of the blade presses into my skin, but not enough to cut flesh.

"Have you come to steal from us, little thief?"

"Thalia," Cassara says, laying a hand on Thalia's forearms. "We do not know if she is friend or foe but it is not up to us to be the judge. We must present her to the high priestess."

"Steal from you? I've come to learn from you." My hands ball into fists at my side. I refuse to cower. I have faced deadlier things than a knife held at my neck. "Shadowvale is in danger. The people are being torn apart; shifters stolen for their magic by the queen–"

"Lies. This all sounds like blasphemy," Thalia says. "Our secrets have been guarded by the coven for hundreds of years since the library was first created. We helped broker the peace between Kallistar and Shadowvale after The Armaghdale War."

"I have been at the mercy of the queen's dark magic. She locked me in the tower for weeks while she stole my magic, my essence."

"Dark magic is forbidden," Cassara says, glancing at Thalia. This time, she complies, lowering her dagger.

"That is why I have come. She must be stopped. I have to find a way to free the people of Shadowvale from her reign—"

"We would have known if there was a war going on out there!" Thalia interjects but I see doubt creeping into her gaze. I wonder then, if in keeping the library so secret, the witches too have kept themselves separate from everything else happening on the continent. Am I truly the first person telling them about the atrocities happening out there?

The cat-like creature lands beside Thalia with a ruffle of feathers. Her limbs elongate, feathers and fur replaced by silken, honey-colored skin until she stands proud and tall before me.

"So fiesty," she says in a melodic voice, flashing me a toothy grin, her green eyes twinkling. She wraps her long, lavender blonde hair into a bun atop her head and secures it with a leather ribbon. "I'm Marcelene. So you've come to take down an evil queen. That sounds like a fairytale to me."

"What are you?" I tilt my head to the side, watching her tail flick back and forth behind her. I turn my eyes back to Thalia. "For that matter, how did you find me? I haven't seen a soul since I entered the tunnel, save for Arkin." My eyebrows raise as I push myself up to standing. She reaches out a steadying arm, grabbing my elbow as I sway on my feet. "I've never heard or seen shifters of your kind before."

Cassara points to Lemon, who pokes his head out of his pocket. "I was going about my nightly guard patrol of the tunnels closest to the library when this scoundrel tried to make off with one of my silver arrowheads." She pulls one from the fletching, the silver tip shining in the light of the flame orb bobbing merrily above our head.

"Lemon," I groan, rolling my eyes. Of course that little rascal would run off for help but get distracted by the first shiny object he sees.

"As for what I and Marcelene are, many of the guardians of Harpalyke are meowls. We are an ancient and rare species of shifter granted flight of the snowy owl and strength of the white tigers. The library is a sanctuary to many species; fae, elementals, shifters and spirits all live here in harmony, learning from each other. We've even had a few humans; however it has been nearly half a century since–"

"Come," Thalia says rudely, interrupting Cassara. "Now is not the time for a history lesson. We must seek the counsel of the high priestess to determine the truth to her words."

Lemon protectively scampers up my shoulder and holds on tight to a strand of hair. Meeting the high priestess is exactly what I need. She'll be able to tell me why Queen Rose sent me here and how we can defeat Tricella.

"Look at her, Thalia, does she really look like a wicked thief to you? She's barely skin and bones. It's a wonder Arkin wanted to eat her at all. What she could use is a hot soak and a good meal. A brush wouldn't hurt either," she says with a grin, cocking her head. "Cassara, you can't save every poor creature you stumble upon. The high priestess will decide—"

"She's right," I say, stepping forward in Thalia's direction. "I should meet the high priestess."

I meet the warrior's eyes with determination, and she's both surprised and suspicious by my eagerness to meet her superior. Without hesitating, she cuts a piece of web free and grabs my arm, pulling it behind my back.

"What are you doing?" My heart races in my chest and I pull away, but she holds fast, restraining my wrists with the sticky rope.

"Precautionary. Until the high priestess decides your fate. There are many who have sought sanctuary in the library, we cannot risk their lives."

"I have not come to hurt anyone; I am a healer." My throat constricts, heat licking into my cheeks. I failed to save Kela because I wasn't strong enough. Could I even call myself a healer anymore?

"What kind of healer comes armed to the teeth?" She asks, pulling the hidden dagger from my boot and holding it in front of my face. "Granted, Arkin had you strung up like second breakfast, so maybe you aren't as much of a threat." She shrugs and tucks the blade into the belt at her waist.

"Are you seriously suggesting I venture into a mysterious forest, where lurking shadow beasts and countless other unknown creatures await, while the relentless queen hunts me down, completely defenseless?" I pull at my restrained arms and try to get a glimpse of the witch now standing behind me. Cassara and Marcelene watch us bicker with their hands crossed over their chests, and I could have sworn Marcelene rolled her eyes at every word uttered by Thalia.

"You seem to have a lot going on, Sybil." Her sarcasm does not go unnoticed, but I bite my tongue and remind myself that there's a reason why she is being so thorough. The library is known to hold immense power, the answers to questions that have not yet been asked. It is the temple of knowledge, the beating heart of every civilization in Craeweth, having avidly conserved and collected memories and secrets from those who came before. However, knowledge unchecked and in greedy hands can lead to terrible consequences. Hence why the library's location and workings have been kept a secret so fiercely guarded, that the entire existence of Harpalyke has started to be questioned. So, Thalia's dedication is truly testament to her vow as sworn protector.

"Cassara, Marcelene," she continues. "Make sure she doesn't escape."

I stumble as she pushes past me, leading the way down the middle dark tunnel, the mage light bobbing above her head.

"What about Arkin? That tunnel he went down–" I nod to the ground where there is evidence of my smeared lichen. "That's the tunnel I've been traveling down. There was an avalanche, he won't be able to escape."

"Brilliant maneuver, with the lichen. How long have you been wandering the tunnels?" Cassara says as she scoops my dusty and worn pack from the ground before holding onto my elbow.

"I can't say for certain; I lost track of time without the sun." I bite at my dry bottom lip. "I ran out of water before I came upon this cavern, but we had packed enough food to take us to the rebel camp."

"We?" Marcelene asks from my other side as we head after Thalia, glancing down at the bruised discarded apple at its entrance.

"Before the avalanche, there was a group of four of us. We were ambushed by the queen's beasts. Kela, she–" My throat constricts, chest tightening painfully with tears lining my eyes as I think of her sweet face, laughing as she turns and offers me a freshly baked pastry. "She didn't make it. She was wounded and I didn't have enough magic left to heal her."

"Life is fragile, but she runs in the lands of the Goddess now, may she be blessed." Marcelene pats my forearm. "Grief is a heavy burden, but those who pass to the other side are not wholly gone from us. They watch and guide us."

"And of your other companions?" Cassara brushes a web from her face.

"I do not know what has become of them." I stroke the golden thread praying for any sense of Aramis or Nero, but I am met by silence. "They were outside the cave, taking watch when we were separated. I only hope they have made it safely to the rebel camp."

"I'm sure they are alright and looking for you now." She smiles at me. "But only those granted passage can enter the tunnels and find the library. Rest assured we can scry for them when we return to the library."

"How did you find your way here?" Marcelene asks as we're walking, cocking her head in my direction, her eyes filled with curiosity.

"There are stories about the library being lost for a reason," she continues. "We don't often have guests and those who come, rarely leave as they either join us, or..." She grins and raises her shoulders, reminding me that even though these women are welcoming to me, they are still the white witches of

Harpalyke, sworn protectors of the library and, as demonstrated, fierce warriors I don't particularly wish to confront.

I trail my hands along the cold stone wall interspersed with spongy lichen. "As I was escaping through the catacombs of Shadowvale, one of their ancient queens, Queen Rosalind, spoke to me. She told me to seek Harpalyke. To seek my training."

Thalia stops ahead of us and turns to face me. "Queen Rosalind spoke to you?"

"Well, her spirit did. Did you know her?" I try to meet her steady gaze, but she turns and continues down the path.

"I often traveled between Kallistar, Shadowvalle, and Harpalyke two centuries ago when I first joined as a scholar seeking knowledge. We had bonded over the years. I was sorry to hear of her passing." Her voice, although distant, has a clear touch of sadness that reminds me so much of Aramis when he too talks about his mother.

We continue along in silence as we descend further, the ground sloping. My legs begin to burn, my throat parched. But when my knees start buckling from exhaustion, the tunnel suddenly opens up.

"Welcome, Sybil, to Harpalyke."

7

SYBIL

When I was a little unicorn, merely five years old, my father used to tell me a story. It was always the same, yet I eagerly awaited every sundown just so he could light a candle, tuck me in with the blue wool blanket my mother knitted, and tell me the story of a library lost through time.

Granted, my father was a healer—a man of science not words—so his stories sometimes lacked depth when it came to the heroes and villains. The protagonist was always a little girl with a Starmark above her brow, just like mine, and the villains were always nameless and faceless monsters wanting to destroy everything in their paths for no apparent reason. But there was always one thing in his stories he'd narrate with such care and detail, it made it all worth it: the library.

I remember often thinking what a dream it would be to see the library from my father's stories with my own two eyes. But alas, it was only fiction—or so I thought.

As we venture past the tunnel and into the vast cavern, the air becomes dry and heavy. A palpable aura of power and knowledge wraps itself around me like a cloak and I feel my own well of magic replenishing. Noticing the enthralled expression on my face, Marcelene and Cassara release their hold on my arms. Tentatively, almost afraid to break a spell, I step into the library from my father's stories. My lips part in awe and tears prick at my eyes.

A wide stone staircase carved into the mountain itself curves to connect the platforms above and below. Rows and rows of shelves line the floor, illuminated by bobbing mage lights that cast everything into a golden glow. I move to the edge of the stone railing and take in the sheer magnitude of the room. Hooded figures gracefully carrying stacks of tomes and scrolls walk through the labyrinthine shelves, and I imagine my father amongst them, learning how to save lives and contributing to the community of shifters he loved so much. Leaning over the railing, I peer below, observing how the stairs spiral further down the heart of the mountain. The area is broken into levels with reading areas stretching as far as the eye can see until the darkness engulfs them. Luminescent lichen adorn the entirety of the cavernous dome of the ceiling, resembling a celestial tapestry of hundreds of tiny stars in a vast expanse of stone.

"This is–" I gasp as a winged meowl dives from above to a lower level, a white feather floating in the air in their wake, along with the scent of old wood and well-handled parchment. I inhale deeply as I reach out and pluck the feather from the air.

I hesitate as my hands grip the smooth edge of the stone, polished from years of hands running along its surface. There is so much knowledge contained here within these walls.

There must be thousands of books and scrolls. My hands ache to feel the smooth parchment, eager to run across the velvety leather bindings, savoring the wisdom it holds within. All the questions I have about my ancestors and unicorn magic —questions I never thought I would find answers to—come rushing back. Why did the unicorn lineage end? What is the secret to my magic? How far does my healing power extend to?

I notice a young acolyte with long brown hair peeking from underneath her hood. She is sitting at a long walnut table, feather quill in hand as she notes something down from a big tome, lost in her studies. My hand rests on my chest as I realize it's almost as if I am looking at another Sybil from a different reality. One where she fulfilled her dream of continuing her training as a healer at Nova Esther. A wave of melancholy washes over me, the weight of lost opportunities heavy in my chest. I could have been her, I wanted to be her.

Not be stuck in a war, losing friends...

My breathing stills, chest tight as a silent sob racks my body.

Kela.

I brush away the stray tear running down my cheek. I can mourn her later. Rose sent me here for a purpose and I can't waste a single moment while more shifters suffer at Tricella's hands.

With renewed determination, I turn toward Thalia.

"Take me to the high priestess."

With a nod, Marcelene and Cassara take their posts at my sides again. We're quiet as we follow Thalia down the winding steps, each level slightly cooler than the last as we descend deeper into the mountains. We pass a few other scholars hunched over tables, engrossed in their work, their fingers delicately tracing the intricate text. The silence is broken only by the soft rustling of pages and the occasional creaking of the wooden ladders that lean against the bookshelves. It's a comforting sound, like the library itself is breathing, its vast knowledge pulsating through its veins. The warmth this place emits is a stark contrast to the pressing urgency to find the answers I seek.

I feel a profound sense of belonging, as if I have discovered a part of myself that was missing. The scent of the library fills my lungs and I feel at peace, yet at the same time, I know this is not where I am meant to be. If this were a different time and place, this could have been my home—the family I longed for. But now, my family has blue eyes, a bit of a temper and a golden heart.

We step onto a landing not of shelves but halls and doors, and Thalia comes to an abrupt stop.

"Wait here. Do not let her wander. I will inform the high priestess," Thalia says before knocking on the first wooden door.

"Enter," a voice calls. Thalia slips inside. There is deep murmuring in the room before the door opens again and Thalia gestures for us to enter.

The room, another cave carved into the body of the mountain, is richly decorated in teal and bronze. In the center of the room boasts a shallow bowl of beaten metal, filled to the brim with iridescent liquid, whose surface glimmers in the mage lights bobbing the perimeter of the room. Behind, a female sits, her body covered in flowing white robes stark against her rich brown skin. Her dark hair peppered with barely visible gray curls around her high cheekbones through her hood. It's her eyes that stand out to me as she stares toward me. Milky white covers her entire pupil and iris.

"Come, child," she says, lifting a hand and gesturing toward me with her long fingers adorned with silver rings. I feel the pull of magic in the command of her words, my feet moving on their own accord. I kneel before her and bow my head respectfully.

"I am Daniela, Clan Leader of the meowls and High Mother to the Coven of the white witches."

Moments pass in silence as she observes me. I can sense the power emanating from her and know that behind her calm and composed exterior hides a force to be reckoned with—a warrior, just like the other witches in the coven.

"Thalia says they've caught a thief–" she begins.

"I am no thief!" I cry in defense, pushing to my feet, but she lifts her hand. The corners of her lips turn up as her eyes lift to my brow. I consciously raise a hand to the faint star.

"We've been waiting for you," she says.

I look into her peculiar eyes and freeze, an odd feeling settling deep in my stomach. Ever since the night Aramis came rushing through my door in the middle of the night in my little cottage, I've felt as if I were a puppet whose strings were maneuvered by something I could not understand, something that scared me. And now, standing in front of the high priestess of the white witches, that feeling has returned, but I am not afraid. If they were waiting for me, it means I am on the right path. That whatever is pulling my strings—whether the Goddess or destiny itself—wants me here to save my people and destroy Tricella.

"What do you mean?" I ask and keep pace as she gestures to us to follow.

"Harpalyke was built by the first scholars of Shadowvale, as far back as our records indicate," coven mother Daniella says as we make our way down another spiraling set of stone steps. "Originally, it was a temple to the Goddess Alpheaia but was expanded to hold the knowledge and bloodlines of elementals and shifters throughout the centuries."

My heart leaps in my chest. Could they have records of my family? Distant unicorn shifter relatives?

"But, how did you know I was coming?"

"Rarely, meowl children are born with the gift of prophecy." She steps out onto the platform and lifts her hood back, revealing white hair plaited into a crown around her head. Smiling, she turns her milky white eyes in my direction.

"When I was an acolyte, training to follow in my mother's footsteps, the Goddess blessed me with a vision." She squares her shoulders and crosses her arms behind her back. "I was only a young witch at the time, but I knew it would change everything. I saw a war born out of greed, shifters and elementals brutally ending each other's lives, and then another threat, black and deadly, made of the darkest shadows on this continent. Mind you, Sybil Vandeleur, I saw this at a time of peace, so you can imagine how heartbreaking that must have been, knowing that peace had counted days."

I notice Thalia shifting uncomfortably on her feet in the corner of my eye. She had been shocked at the news of the looming war outside this mountain, had Daniela kept it a secret from the other witches?

"Nevertheless," Daniela continues, pacing the floor and coming closer to me. "The Goddess did not leave me drowning in despair because among that plague of darkness befalls the land, she showed me a healer." Daniela extends her index finger and lifts my chin in her direction.

"Young and beautiful, with a Starmark upon her brow, she will emerge with the light of Harpalyke and reunite the people."

At a loss of words, I mutter, "You think I'm that healer?"

She nods to my forehead. "A healer guided by Nordfeu."

"The northernmost star," I whisper, and a tingle of apprehension runs along my skin. "But—"

"You do not need to see, to know. I can feel the aura of your magic." She lifts a hand in an arch. "How can the library of

Harpalyke and the white witches help you in your mission, Sybil Vandeleur?"

Why have I come?

I steel myself, my thoughts straying to the shifter families in the dungeons and Tricella's plans.

"I seek knowledge and training with the white witches of Harpalyke to help defeat the Queen of Shadowvale and free the shifters. The queen consort, Tricella, has the kingdom enthralled under her dark magi–"

"Dark magic is forbidden, child. Any records of it have long since been destroyed or locked away under our most powerful spells and constant supervision." She shakes her head, hands clasped before her. "It is unlikely Tricella has found a way to learn how to access the darkness in the magical balance. We all harbor a touch of darkness within us to ensure balance is upheld, as the Goddess herself wished it, but it's not enough to enthrall an entire kingdom"

"Then, how do I defeat her? What did the prophecy say? How do I triumph?" Frustration laces my every word. I throw my arms wide as I grit my teeth together.

"Prophecies are fickle things, child. They show you glimpses of the future with no knowledge of the how and the why of it all."

I slump in my chair defeated, feeling like I am going in circles. The thought of waltzing into these halls and finding all the answers I needed was naïve. The exhaustion of the last couple of days dawns on me, and all I want to do is crawl into a bed and disappear.

"Yet," she continues, "you sought out Harpalyke. The library felt your intentions and let you in. Only those with true intent to learn, or brought by one of the scholars, can gain easy access. The library has its own defenses, but it is not impenetrable."

Her gaze, deep and unfathomable, lingers on me as she softly hums. "If you're here, it's because the Goddess willed it. We will offer you shelter and help you gain access to the knowledge contained in this library. That is all we can do. We are sworn protectors of the library, and as such, we have a duty to remain neutral in this conflict to protect the histories."

Shaking my head, I swallow the hysterical laugh bubbling inside me. "With all due respect, you live by a codex that allows tyrants to kill innocent children whilst you hide between the pages of books. Knowledge is useless if there's no one left to share it with." Desperation claws at my throat, my voice cracking and straining, a desperate plea for help. Daniela's milky gaze holds mine in an iron grasp, but I struggle to read her. Have I compromised everything?

"Sybil," Marcelene says, placing a gentle hand on my shoulder, and I feel my strength waver. "Even if we wished to give you the knowledge you seek, that is not how the library works, this place is... unique."

I stop myself from rolling my eyes, tired that everything is never as simple as it seems.

"Acolytes study for years before beginning their training," Marcelene continues. "Rest assured, we will do everything we can to find the answers you seek."

"I don't have time to read every book in this library. People are relying on me. Every moment I waste, she becomes stronger," I say, massaging my throbbing temples.

"How about we start by getting you cleaned up and fed?" Cassara says gently, looking to the high priestess for confirmation.

Daniela nods and goes to sit again. "I must consult with the coven leaders about what's to be done. Witches, take care of our guest, and Sybil, don't lose hope."

"You'll be sharing this room with Marcelene and me for as long as you're here," Cassara states, pushing open the door. She gestures toward the bed closest to the door before placing my bag on a small wooden chest by the foot of a bed.

"Thank you," I say, gazing about. The room is small but cozy, with stone walls and a soft glow emanating from the mage lamp on the nightstand. The beds are simple yet comfortable, each adorned with a fluffy pillow and a neatly folded blanket. The room feels inviting, a peaceful sanctuary after long days of travel.

"There is a large natural hot spring deeper in the mountain, study rooms, and a common dining area for main meals. Many of the scholars keep odd hours, so most of us just eat when we can," Marcelene says with a shrug.

"How do you get food delivered this deep into the mountain?" I ask, gently stroking Lemon's head in my pocket.

"We have a greenhouse where we grow most of our food and house chickens. We don't have a kitchen, though. The library is enchanted to provide necessities, but it can get peevish if you get too particular," she says as she bounds out the door and down the corridor, leaving Marcelene and me to follow.

"Oh," I whisper in amazement. "So when you said that the library is unique, it's because of the enchantment?" I stop in the middle of the hall and peer around.

"Exactly! I thought you'd caught up with that? How else would we have kept the location of this huge labyrinth a secret? Did that spider hit you upside the head too hard? Come on, I'm starving."

"So, how did you end up here?" I ask the witch tentatively, hundreds of questions on the tip of my tongue.

She laughs, the corners of her eyes crinkling up. "I was born here and have been here my entire life. My mother is one of the elder scholars, as was my grandmother before her. I am training in all arts of magic, language, and history to take my place on the council one day. My strength lies in the magical objects and my shifter abilities, so I often guard the tunnels leading to the library. This way," she says, gesturing to the left.

"How do you not get lost down here?" I ask, trying to keep count of the white washed doors set evenly spaced into the pale stone walls.

"You get used to it," Marcelene says with another shrug as we turn the corner that opens up to a large room filled with rows upon rows of shelves crammed with books. We come to a low set table clustered by plush chairs and couches. "Lunch first, then we will get cleaned up and search the library for more information."

"Thank goodness, I'm famished." Cassara settles into her seat. My eyes widen as a plate of sandwiches, a steaming pot of tea, and small cups materialize on the table.

"How–"

"The library," they reply in unison.

"Now, sit down. You look like you're one bite away from fainting, you're so pale," Cassara says around a mouthful of sandwich.

As I sink into the cushions, I take a bite, feeling the delicate bread dissolve against my tongue, releasing a harmonious mix of flavors. An involuntary groan of pleasure escapes my lips.

"This is delicious," I say, taking a sip of the steaming tea Cassara offers. "How does it work?"

"The library? All you have to do is ask for what you need, but it's often intuitive and picks up before you even know what you want."

"Well, color me impressed. I've never met an enchanted

building before, let alone one who is such a superb cook." I reach toward the plate of sandwiches when a bowl of chocolate-covered strawberries and a plate of scones appear before me.

"Why, don't you look at that!" Cassara squeals, clapping her hands together. "It must like you. I've only ever gotten a treat on holidays and my birthday!"

Her words are lost on me as I stare at the warm scones. The tea goes cold in the pit of my stomach, and tears prick my eyes. I don't deserve to be here, surrounded by such friendly company and filling up on such good food.

"What's wrong?" Marcelene asks, concern etched on her face.

"I—" My throat constricts, and I push the plate away, burying my head in my hands. "I appreciate your hospitality, but I can't sit here, pretending everything will be okay. Tricella wants me. She wants my power, but she won't stop there even if she has me."

A stack of velvety linen napkins materializes on the table, their delicate texture inviting to touch. Overwhelmed by the gentle gesture, tears stream down my face.

"You've had a rough journey, Sybil, but you're safe here."

A hiccup escapes as I dab at the tears streaming down my face.

Safe.

I thought I was safe once.

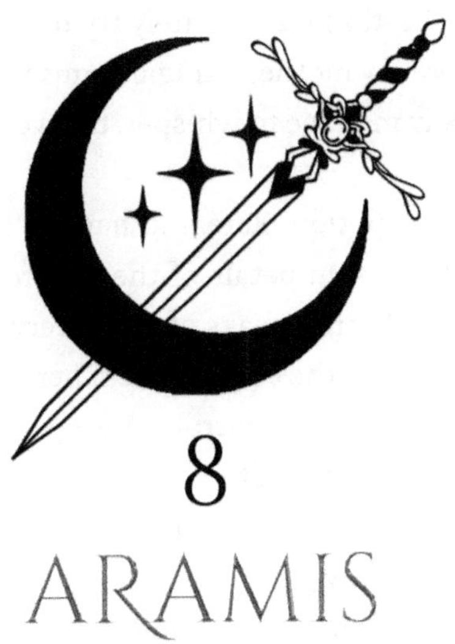

8

ARAMIS

I s this really necessary?" I pull at my doubly bound hands behind my back, metal and rope chafing my skin. The new bands feel strange on my wrists and the lack of magic still echoes within me. Heat flushing up my neck, the guards forcefully push me to the ground. My knees sink into the unforgiving hardness of the council's room floor, sending a jolt of discomfort through my body. Gazing upward, I meet the intense gazes of the council members one by one. Nero was made to leave the room and I'm now a lamb in a wolf's den.

"Aramis Adrostos, son of Lysander Adrastos," Victor says, gaze locking on mine with unnerving intensity. "You have forsaken your magic, ensuring you will not harm any member in this village in exchange for a chance to prove your worth and offer valuable aid and information to help our cause." The weight of his words hangs heavily in the air. I nod in agreement, readying myself for whatever will happen next.

Evolet, one of elementals on the council, holds up a vial of shimmering silver liquid. "Do you know what this is?" Her question hangs in the air, filling me with trepidation. My heart pounds in my chest, as I desperately try to recall the lessons of my youth, before my mother's tragic demise.

"No," I finally manage to whisper, the word barely escaping my lips.

"It's a curious potion. Rare and hard to conjure. It's made from the night blossom petals of the Eashronna plant, which only grows in the barren peaks of the Aldervora mountains in the winter." She spins the corked vial in her fingers.

"What does it do?" I narrow my eyes as the iridescent liquid swirls through the vial.

"It renders the consumer unable to lie," she states blankly, once again meeting my gaze.

My chest constricts, heart pounding erratically.

A truth serum.

I had thought them only a myth.

"Runa, please elaborate," Victor prompts, pointing toward the council member. She has a pixie cut with sleek black hair, deep brown eyes, and a sun-kissed complexion.

"You see," Runa says, rising from the table and stepping forward, her footsteps echoing in the dimly lit room. "You might have convinced Roger and Victor that you tell the truth, but after all our efforts, we'd like to be extra sure."

My heart pounds in my chest as I try to stand, my boots scraping against the cold stone floor. Before I can speak, the guard behind me grabs my shoulders, their grip tight and suffocating. With a forceful slam, they push me back down, the impact reverberating through my body.

"You shouldn't have any problem volunteering to answer some questions under its influence," Runa says, her voice dripping with skepticism. The sound of her words lingers in the air, filled with tension and doubt. "Unfortunately, the serum only lasts twenty minutes or so."

Gritting my teeth, I utter, "Nothing I've said has been a lie." My clenched fists tremble with frustration, and my knuckles turn white. "If I take the serum and answer your questions, will you help me free Sybil?" I ask, voice cracking.

"When we get the answers we seek, we will release you from your cell and allow you freedom to roam the camp," Victor responds, his voice filled with cautious hope. "But only if we believe that you will not pose a threat to this village."

I nod, wanting this done as soon as possible. The air grows heavy with anticipation, and the room falls into silence. The scent of uncertainty lingers in every breath.

I will not fail her and lose her.

I will not fail my kingdom any longer.

I am the Prince of Shadowvale.

Runa grabs me roughly by the jaw, uncorking the vile and pouring the contents down my throat. I gag and cough, writhing against my bound arms as the liquid burns down my throat and fills my veins. I fall to the side, my skin feeling as though it's on fire as the world spins.

I am going to die, and I'll never get to see Sybil again. I'll never get to tell her the truth.

"Mate," I mouth the inaudible word, barely registering the cold floor under my cheek as I hit the ground.I squeeze my eyes closed against the mage light bobbing around the room. Everything feels wrong, my tongue heavy as lead in my mouth.

A few breaths pass before someone hauls me back to my knees. I open my eyes, breathing deeply through my nose as the world settles. I have to think strategically, I have to prove to them that my loyalty has always lain in protecting Shadowvale.

Victor clears his throat. "Let the inquiry begin."

He sits on his designated chair at the head of the table and reads from a yellowed piece of parchment. "You come before the council of Thorns. Tell us who you are."

"Aramis Adrostos, Crown Prince of Shadowvale." The words are ripped from my mouth before I have a moment to think, leaving an acrid taste in their wake.

"What is your elemental power?"

My chest aches at the absence of my power, but the words fall from my lips. "Wind. I'm a wind elemental. I can control and manipulate the air."

"Did you knowingly aid Queen Tricella in the capture of shifters for questioning?"

"Yes, but—"

"How long have you known Nero Lockheed?"

Memories of me and Nero running through the royal wing of the castle whilst his mother tended to mine as her hand-maiden flash through my head. The two of us sneaking into the kitchen for cook's tarts. Our first wooden sword lessons.

"Nearly my entire life, since we were boys," I say confidently, the words coming easily.

"And growing up, did you know he was a draken shifter?"

"No." Cold disappointment curls in my gut. Even my friend did not trust me with his greatest secret.

"And how did you feel when you found out?"

My heart tightens, recalling how frantic I was in the woods, realizing Sybil was my mate. Hating that she was a shifter and then discovering my childhood friend of a century had lied to me.

"How did you feel?" he repeats.

I bite my tongue, but the words stumble out. "Hurt. Betrayed. Angry."

"Why?"

"Because he is a *shifter*. Because he lied to me for a hundred years by omission."

He is a shifter. He lied to me.

The words echo in my heart.

He only held the truth because he was afraid of how you'd respond.

"I think we've heard enough for today. Take him back to his cell."

As I'm pulled to my feet, I sway unsteadily, feeling the tingling sensation as the blood returns to my legs from kneeling.

They mean to paint me as the villain.

My fists tighten as I stare at the intricate metal bands around my wrists. Gone is the coarse rope, but the bands cut deeper than any physical confinement. My knuckles blanch as fiery rage surges through me, fueled by betrayal.

The magic pulsing from the metal feels wrong, causing cold sweat to break along my skin. Rage boils within me, a seething fire that scorches my veins, as the bands suppress the power that normally courses through me.

I lift my head, peering up into the darkness as the door slams at the end of the hall.

"Nero?" I call out, voice cracking with disuse. He had been down a few times to see me over the past week but mostly it was quiet shifters who came to deliver food and water twice a day.

"It wasn't me!" A male's panicked voice calls out. I hear a scuffle and shuffle of feet. "I swear I didn't steal it."

"Sure you didn't," a gruff voice replies as they come into view. Between two burly shifters was a male with pale skin and jet black hair peppered gray at the temples which fell into his face. He wore a rumpled dark tunic, pants, boots and cloak.

The cell across from me swings open and they throw him in. He lands with a grunt in a tangled up mess of gangly limbs and fabric. He quickly scrambles up but not before the door slams shut in his face.

"Let me go. I demand an audience with whoever is in charge for this injustice." He shakes the iron bars, his gray eyes shimmering in the dim light of the torches.

"You'll meet your justice soon enough, thief," one of the guards says before turning and heading down the hall.

"Bloody shifters. Who do they think they are?" he says under his breath as the guards walk away, leaving the man pacing the cell seething with anger. He turns his attention to me, his eyes filled with determination. "Do I look like someone who would steal something?" he asks desperately.

I study him for a moment, taking in his disheveled appearance and the intensity in his eyes. There's something about him that makes me cautious. "I don't know," I reply honestly. "I've learned not to judge based on appearances alone." My lips draw down.

He nods, seemingly satisfied with my response. "The name is Axton," he says before shaking the bars, but they only groan in protest. "And you are?"

"There is no point. The metal is enchanted. I'm Aramis," I reply, turning my head to stare out of the small window giving me a view of the starry sky. "Aramis Adrastos." I should be careful with my name out here but I don't care enough to hide anymore.

"The Crown Prince?" He snorts, giving up his pacing and slumping against the wall. "And I'm the King of Kallistar."

I ignore him, my thoughts straying to her. I lift a hand, my thumb caressing the stone necklace hanging from my neck.

"How did a band of misfit shifters catch the wind elemental prince himself?"

"I came here willingly, asking for help," I say.

"Well, that's a series of rather unfortunate events. How long have you been locked down here?" he asks.

I sigh, my gaze shifting from him to the dimly lit torches on the wall. "It's hard to keep track of time in this place," I admit. "But it feels like an eternity." *Especially knowing every moment I'm stuck in here, she's out there. Alone.* My gut clenches at the thought.

"I was falsely accused of stealing a valuable artifact, and they threw me in here without a fair trial," he complains, grabbing a rock and throwing it through the bars. It bounces and skitters down the hall. "Beasts, they are. What do they have you locked up for?"

I stare at the flames, remembering the way they danced along the cave wall moments before I left her. Shaking my head of the memory, I turn to him. "They believe I am behind the attacks on shifters."

He pauses, examining me. "Ahhh. I think I might have heard a rumor or two about Shadowvale going through a crisis of sorts. I tend to rarely pass through this kingdom, you see. Too much trouble these days. What happened princeling, did you not want to share your toys with shifters?"

I stiffen. "You know nothing about who I am or what I'm capable of."

"Perhaps not, but I do know we need to find a way out of here," Axton says, his voice filled with determination. "There must be a way to prove our innocence and escape this wretched place. Or a way to escape."

I look around the cramped cell, but all I see are cold iron bars and stone walls that seem impenetrable. "Escape is futile. Even with my wind magic, I can't break us out of here. What did they accuse you of stealing, anyway?"

"Oh, you know, the usual," he says as he picks at his nails.

"And did you?" I ask, brows raised.

"Of course not. I was only taking back what was rightfully mine." He puffs out his chest. "I was playing cards down at the Cerulean Dragon Inn, when these two badger shifters cheated over cards and took off with my satchel. I followed them here, intent on taking it back. Low and behold, I stumble on a secret shifter camp. What are they even trying to achieve here?" he scoffs. "Anyway, their guards cornered me. They wouldn't even let me tell my side of the story. They think I'm a spy or something." He rakes his hand through his hair.

"I'm sorry. I'm sure they'll hear you out once everything calms down." Kindness is all I have left at this point.

"Like they did for you?" He snorts.

I turn to lay down on the thin straw bed and close my eyes, wrapping my cloak tighter around my body as he continues to talk to himself.

Waiting in this cell is not a demand of my patience I haven't experienced before. Father used to make me practice for hours, days, on end in the training yard until I had perfected my sword fighting skills. I look at my hands, at a scar I once got from my training. Just when I thought I couldn't physically move from exhaustion, he would make me spend hours pouring over battle strategies and kingdom politics.

My fists clench as I think about the blank look on his face when Sybil and Tricella stood before him. As a boy, he would talk about justice and freedom. I hope with everything I have that when all of this is over, I can become the man he wanted me to be.

I inhale deeply and something changes. The faintest trace of lavender and tea. Surely, I'm imagining it. And yet I can't shake it once it's deep within me, pulling at the mating bond.

The bond.

By the gods, what am I to do?

9
SYBIL

ou don't happen to have a section on how to defeat evil queens by chance, do you?" I ask as I run my fingers along the next row. Marcelene, Cassara and I have been searching this level of the library since breakfast.

Marcelene snorts from two rows over. "The library isn't sorted like that," she says.

"Then, how is it sorted? How do you find anything in a labyrinth of knowledge like this? I thought you said this floor was for ancient texts on magic."

"It is, but the library has a mind of its own. Sometimes it moves things around." Clutching a worn tome titled Magical Creatures of Craeweth, Marcelene walks over. "What about this one?"

I pride myself on being a bit of a mythical creature expert. That, and there isn't a book you could keep away from me.

My heart clenches as Kela's words ring in my ears. Lemon climbs up to my shoulder as I pull the book toward me and look through the index. I shake my head and hand it back.

"I–I don't think this will have the answers I seek, but I'd like to go through it, regardless. There's something I'd like to check. Have you heard of a ramidreju?" I scratch Lemon behind the ears. It took a lot of convincing to have him stop running through the library like a mad man. As cute as Lemon is, having little paws sink into ink pots and leaving prints behind on ancient tomes is not ideal.

She shakes her head, holding the tome to her chest. "I cannot say that I have, but I'm more of a magical object expert than a magical creature one. Why?"

"Someone close to me once said he was not a normal ferret, but a ramidreju. It doesn't matter." I shake my head, turning back to the shelf. "One day, when all of this is behind us, I'll be able to spend hours by the fire with no worries other than if I should read another chapter."

"Now that sounds like a dream." She turns to scan the shelf behind me. My smile falters as I wonder if that day will ever come; I dread what I may have to sacrifice for it.

"An Earth elementals Guide to Curing Winter Ailments, Seven Signs of Sight, Magic on the Defense. Any of these sound good?" Marcelene asks, indicating a red leather bound spine.

"I don't think any of those would help us defeat Tricella, unless she's planning on plunging the world into perpetual winter and unleashing devastating plagues," I say, crestfallen.

The high priestess had not lied when she said that most knowledge about the art of dark magic had been wiped from the archives, and the library did not seem inclined to show us where the few tomes left were hidden. The three witches had tried everything to convince Harpalyke, but all that magically appeared in front of us were tomes that read "How to Save Kingdoms in 10 Easy Steps" and "Spells to Uncover Very Dangerous Books" filled with fairy tales and recipes. Even the library was mocking me. So instead of focusing on the threat,

Tricella, we decided to look for information regarding its potential solution, me.

"We've found nothing of use," I say as I pull Lemon into my lap.

"Well, not exactly nothing," Cassara says. "We found more books on magical creatures that gave you insight on Lemon's ramidreju abilities."

"True. I still can't wrap my head around the fact that he's not an ordinary ferret," I say.

"You are destined for great things, Sybil. You need a strong sidekick." Cassara grins as she pulls her blonde hair into a messy bun.

I shake my head, staring at Lemon laying belly up on the table, snoring quietly.

Why did he choose me?

Marcelene snorts. "I'd like to see him face a beast. They'd eat him up like a snack and use his bones as toothpicks. His greatest use is his ability to steal shiny objects–Ow!" She rubs the side of her head after a small pot of ink flies through the air and lands with a clatter on the table.

"Seems like you're not the only one who befriended the library," Cassara says, keeling over in her chair with laughter. "So this prince of yours," Cassara continues, blue eyes twinkling. "Is he handsome? What about his bodyguard?"

In the last couple of days spent at the library, I told the witches about my life. The coven had eventually deemed my presence at Harpalyke necessary; a sign of Alphaeia, they called it. And even though not a moment had gone by where I did not feel the urgency in my mission, I allowed myself little pleasures, like opening up to these women who had been nothing but kind to me.

A small smile graces my lips as the image of Aramis

standing protectively above me in the hot springs under the open star filled sky fills my mind.

"Nero is a treat, I think you'd love to meet him." I twist my family ring around my finger. "Aramis is... he's different. Sure, he's handsome, but he's complicated and we didn't exactly start off on the right foot."

"I still don't understand how you managed to forgive him after everything he's done to you and your kind," Thalia says as she walks down the row toward us.

"Well, he wasn't aware of what she was doing," I say defensively.

"But don't you think it's odd that he was that blind to what was going on around him? Don't get me wrong, losing a parent at a young age is not easy, but it didn't make me want to eradicate the cause because of it." Her words hit me like a blow to the chest.

"You said his father was under a spell. Could Aramis have been under her magical influence too?" Cassara asks, peeking her head around the corner at us.

"He didn't seem like he was under a spell when I met him, just angry and blinded by prejudice to the point he genuinely believed he was doing the right thing for his people," I say.

"What if that was intentional?" Cassara says as she pushes to her feet. I follow as she counts down the rows of shelves until she turns. Running her fingers down their spines, she stops and pulls a large green leather-bound tome from the shelf and plops on the floor, opening it in her lap.

"What's that?" I ask, sitting next to her. Marcelene sits at my other side.

"Lore of shifters," she says under her breath as she flips through pages, running her finger delicately until she reaches a passage. "Aha! Here it is. Unicorns have the power to cleanse poison from an object, making it pure again."

I snort, pulling the book over to me. "That can't be true. My parents would have told me about that years ago instead of teaching me how to counteract poisons."

"Well, using your magic takes energy. It's not limitless. Having the ability to cure with your knowledge and hands can be useful without draining your magic stores" Thalia says as she pulls a journal from her pocket and scribbles in it.

"What does that have to do with Aramis being under magical influence or not?" I quirk an eyebrow at her.

"Didn't you say you felt connected to him since you met him?" she asks.

"Well, yes. It was as if I had always known him. That's why I never cowered before his stern exterior. I knew what was hidden behind it, so I reached out my hand." I frown and instinctively reach for that golden thread inside me.

What does it mean?

Cassara pulls the book back into her lap and flips the page, pointing to an illustration of a unicorn crying diamond tears, laying their head into the lap of a maiden. "What if through your bond, you're inadvertently purifying the spell placed on him?"

"That seems like a farfetched idea. What do you mean by 'bond?'"

"Don't you know about the bond between fated mates?" She asks, her eyes taking on a dreamy, faraway look.

I had read about fated mates. So many of the books I used to read at my cottage wrote about the rare occurrence of souls born intertwined as the Goddess weaves lives, destined to be together. They were always just that, though, stories written to make reality more bearable and dreams more vivid.

"We are not fated mates, we can't be." I stare at her incredulously, but she only smiles wistfully back at me.

I would know, wouldn't I?

"It would explain your draw to him and how you were able to find each other," Thalia says, putting her journal back into her pocket.

"It would explain how you could fall for the Prince of elementals who has spent his whole life hunting your kind to bring them before his stepmom, and forgive him so easily," Marcelene says, the corners of her lips pulling down.

"Impossible. He hates shifters... well, hated. He was beginning to be more open during the last week we had spent together."

"Imagine a scared, lonely boy who just nearly died by 'rebel shifters,' whose mother was murdered. It wouldn't take much magical influence to turn that fear into hatred and prejudice. Tricella could have put her claws into him, not only with poisonous words but blinding him with her magic. Over the years, she might have thought him so under her thumb that she started pulling back to utilize her magic elsewhere."

"Where would she learn such a thing? Magic to manipulate the mind or control others is a myth. I've only ever heard of it in fairytales and folktales. Stories of knights in white armor fighting great monstrous beasts of darkness and shadow," I scoff.

"All stories are born from a kernel of truth, Sybil." Thalia purses her lips. "There is a story that the Goddess herself built this mountain to create balance between the earth and sky, lightness and darkness, knowledge and secrets. The first coven of white witches built the library here as a temple to worship her."

"What does that have to do with defeating Tricella?" My shoulders slump and a heavy sigh escapes my lips.

"Did you ever notice anything weird between them at the castle?" Cassara asks. "Maybe it would give us a clue where to look to find out how to defeat her."

"I rarely saw Aramis except the night we arrived and the morning I nearly escaped." I bite my lip then shudder as the memories come back. "When Tricella had me chained, draining my power, she said he was blind and would do anything to save his people, not realizing what he was doing. She said kidnapping me hardly took any nudging. Beyond that, the only show of her powers I saw beyond draining mine was telekinesis and the strange mental hold she seemed to have over the king."

"Which would make sense why after finding you, your magic began to influence her hold on him. Purify him of her poison and open his eyes to the reality of what's going on in his kingdom," Cassara says.

"So anything that's been between us has just been because of some predestined bond set upon us by the Goddess herself?" Cold disappointment settles in my gut.

"I mean," she says, closing the book and setting it to the side.

"Sybil, the mating bond has to be chosen by both parties before it can be solidified," Thalia says, meeting my gaze. "You'll feel the connection, sometimes even with each other's emotions. Once the bond settles into place and is accepted fully by both parties, some mates can even communicate through it."

"And does *he* know about this fated bond?" My chest tightens.

If he knew, why didn't he say anything? What if, despite his changing feelings, he still held hatred in his heart against me being a shifter?

"If you can feel the bond, he can feel it too. A mating bond isn't something to take lightly, you're tied for life. It's a sacred blessing."

"Or a curse. How could you love someone who has spent their whole life hating your kind?" Marcelene scoffs.

Could he ever fully accept me, unicorn and all?

"Marcelene!" Thalia chides, clicking her tongue.

I rub at my forehead, feelings warring inside me. "I don't have time to worry about this mating bond. I need to find a way to defeat Tricella." I turn back to the shelf, leaning my head against the smooth wood as I bottle down my conflicting feelings. I need to save my people. But I'm also not going to let the Goddess, fate or anyone else decide my future. Instinctively, my hand goes to rest on my chest, where I feel that familiar tug. For the first time, I revel in it, knowing Aramis feels it too.

The three girls look at each other then back at me.

Thalia tucks her arms together in her sleeves. "I must be off on patrol, but I wanted to check in on your progress. I wish you the best of luck, Sybil Vandeleur."

She turns and heads back in the direction she came, mage robes swirling around her ankles until she disappears. I look at our cart, mostly empty save for a few tomes on elemental magic.

"This floor has gotten me nowhere. Maybe we should try somewhere else."

Out of the corner of my eye, a flitter of movement catches my attention. I turn, but nothing is there. Grabbing the handles of the cart, I push it down the hallway toward a table nestled with chairs by a small grated firepit set away from the books.

Another chortle like the tinkling of bells has me stopping in my tracks.

"What was that?" I turn and find Cassara standing deeply entranced with a book.

"Hmm?" she asks, not lifting her eyes from the pages.

"I swear I heard–" I trail off as the sound comes again, this time from two shelves above me.

"Library sprites," Marcelene says as she dumps another handful of books onto the cart. "Pesky creatures, but they make great messengers. No one knows exactly how, but they can travel from library to library carrying missives. Show yourselves."

Dozens of opal-colored fluffy balls, each the size of a chicken egg, materialize along the top row of books. Each of them has spindly arms and wide, watchful eyes. They swarm together, a tangled nest before jumping into the air and floating down onto Marcelene's awaiting arms. With a burst of energy, Lemon jumps up and down on my shoulder, his chittering filling the air with excitement.

"You can't eat them!" I hiss, pulling him off and tucking him in my pocket with a scratch to his head.

Marcelene brushes them off her arms to float harmlessly to the floor. They scurry away, tickling my ankles as they run past and back into the shelf. As she unrolls the tiny parchment they've left in her palm, concern washes over her face. Her brows knit together as she absorbs the contents of the message.

"What is it?" I ask.

"After your meeting with the high priestess, the coven decided it was our responsibility to know what is happening out there so we've sent out informants."

My heart warms at the thought that my words helped Daniela change her mind.

"There's been another attack," Marcelene continues. "Many have lost their lives, both shifters and elementals alike. Underground escape routes have been put in place by the rebel shifters for those who are trying to escape from the territories around the citadel, but many are refusing to cower and leave their homes. Resources are getting scarcer by the day. Even—"

"What?" I ask, terror already painting hundreds of terrible scenarios.

"There have been strange reports about the soil being cursed. Nothing is growing for at least ten miles from the castle. Even the cattle roaming those plains are dying and the water seems amiss." I cover my mouth with my hand as my mind immediately goes to Edmund still locked in the castle and all the starving shifters in the dungeons. Has Tricella's magic poisoned the land itself? If the witches don't see this as a clear sign of dark magic, I don't know what will.

"There's more," Marcelene whispers, and her eyes meet mine with worry. "The queen is in a frenzy trying to find a unicorn." Her eyes move to me and the star on my brow. I instinctively reach up to brush my hair over my face, as if it could shield me from Tricella until I devise a plan to vanquish her.

You are the healer we have been waiting for. You must seek your training with the white witches in the forgotten library of Harpalyke.

"We're running out of time," I say, sending a little prayer for all those that have lost their lives because of my ineptitude.

Marcelene sighs, tucking the message into one of the pockets in her robes and shakes her head. "I'll need to let the coven mother know this evening."

"This evening? Why wait?"

"The coven elders are meeting and are not to be disturbed. It is the way of things."

My hands cover my face in frustration at these ancient and idiotic rules.

"Can't you see she is growing stronger by the day?" My body trembles as I meet her gaze.

"Why are you not getting involved in the war? You gave shelter to shifters during the last war against Kallistar, did you not?"

"We gave shelter to both elementals and shifters during the Armaghdale War. We did not participate. We recorded the history. Our past helps us understand the present and future."

"What if Tricella destroys it all? There will be nothing left to record! She is a monster, hungry for power and willing to do anything to feed that hunger." My chest aches as I think of all the families hurt by her. What would drive a person to willingly rot her soul with dark magic, driven by a need for power?

Record... Family records.

"Sybil we–" she starts.

"Wait! You said you recorded all the histories of Shadowvale?" I ask.

"Yes, but–"

"Do you keep records of the elemental family trees?" My heart speeds in my chest.

"Yes, another two levels down," Cassara says. "Why would you want to look at records? You're from Kallistar. I doubt we'd have much in your direct family, unless you had cousins in Shadowvale."

"It's not about me, it's about her. I want to learn more about the queen."

IO

ARAMIS

Ye drugged him with a truth serum and questioned his integrity, making him out to be a villain with no one to defend him!" I'm pulled from the depths of sleep as Nero's voice echoes down the stone corridor of the hallway. I rub my hand across the scruff of my beard as I stare up through the bars.

"It wasn't like that," a vaguely familiar feminine voice replies.

"Oh nay? Ye didn't ask specific questions that would paint all the crimes he's committed over the years without a chance to defend himself?" Nero counters.

"He told no lies, Nero. He is guilty of those crimes," she says. Their footsteps echo closer.

The council had dragged me out of this cell on three more occasions, and every time, it was the same routine. They bound my arms behind my back, made me kneel in front of the council, administered the serum, and proceeded to ask question after question. They were mostly curious about the Shadowvale army, a smart move considering there were thrice the number of the shifter rebels adept for battle. In a direct conflict, the shifters would need help to survive an attack from such a mighty force.

They were also curious about the workings of the castle, probably to help spies infiltrate. Questions about my father's rule, Tricella's modus operandi, and even questions about Kieran. From a strategic point of view, my knowledge of their enemy was extremely valuable—the only thing I could offer them—so I never opposed and willingly shared all the information I had. Arguably, the truth serum wasn't even necessary. But every time, after hours of relentless questioning, it ended the same way. They'd ask me if I willingly captured shifters and delivered them to Tricella, to which the honest answer was always a condemning yes.

I blink away the dryness in my eyes, rubbing to clear the blurriness of sleep until my surroundings come into focus. The room is dimly lit, with only a small window high in the wall letting in a sliver of morning sunlight. My body aches as I stretch my arms over my head, the result of falling asleep leaning against the rough stone walls.

"Aye, Evolet, but ye also did not give him time to answer how he's helped his people. Ye haven't spent the last hundred years with him as I have. Aye, he may be a bit naive and stubborn, but at his core, he is honorable," Nero says.

I glance up as their steps slow and they come into focus. Nero stands beside an elemental member from the council, her light brown hair pulled up into a messy bun atop her head.

"Aramis, yer looking worse for wear, mate." Nero's lips pull up, but his smile doesn't meet his eyes. His clothes are wrinkled, hair mussed as though he has been running his hands through it half the night.

"Ye could use a shave." He wrinkles his nose. "And a shower."

"You're one to talk," I say, nodding at his disheveled state. My attention goes back to the female as the key scrapes in the lock of my cell and the door swings open. "No burly guard to tie me up and drag me to the council this time?"

She eyes me appraisingly, raising an eyebrow. "Would you prefer it if I tied you up?"

Nero snorts and I turn, glaring at him. "No, but perhaps Nero over here needs a taste of—"

"I don't sleep with draken. Nothing against shifters, but water and fire really don't mix." She rolls her eyes and gestures for us to follow her.

"They should not have forced ye to answer the questions under a truth serum," Nero growls as he keeps pace at my side. His hands flex, claws extending as we make our way up the stone staircase at Evolet's heels.

"I volunteered, Nero," I say, turning to him and holding up my banded wrists. "I'm willing to do anything, be anyone, to prove my loyalty to my people."

Prove to her I'm changing.

"Yer a good man, Aramis."

Then, why do I feel like the villain?

"You're a good friend, Nero."

"Hurry up, or do I need to find you two a room?" Evolet calls as she opens the door.

Nero pauses with a hand on my shoulder. "I know this is not the situation I'd hoped for, but remember the people are terrified. Show them the prince I've known my whole life, inside." He taps a finger to my chest.

I nod before following Evolet out the door and through the village until we reach the council room. Evolet takes her seat at the table with the other seven members of the council, who are all standing over the large map of Shadowvale. They glance in my direction for only a second and then continue their hushed conversations. No glass vial awaits on the table, nothing to bind by arms. This is *different*. Usually, when I am taken here, they hide all hints about their plans, but this is a war council in session. I stand tall, with Nero at my side.

"Aramis Adrastos, once again, you come before the council of Thorns. Kneel," Aries says, leaning back in his chair.

"I will not kneel before the council," I state quietly, turning to face him.

"Defiant? Would you rather we throw you back in the cells?" he taunts.

"Aries," Roger growls.

I turn my attention back to the council, battle strategies and political treaties whirling in my head. I must play my cards right. They need me just as much as I need them.

"I do not refuse to kneel out of disrespect, but because I come to you as an equal." I lower my chin respectfully. "I come before you to prove my loyalty not to the queen, but to my kingdom and its people."

The council's whispers fill the air, their urgent tone mirroring the desperation that consumes me. Nero's comforting presence offers a sliver of hope.

"Come forth, Aramis," Evolet says, and indicates a chair at the far end of the room, separated from everyone else. I look at Nero suspiciously, who reassures me with a nod.

"The council wants you to audit this meeting. Maybe they're starting to warm up to ya." He winks.

"Hmm, you make a fair point, Gideon." A woman with deep blue hair turns to Victor, continuing a conversation started before I entered the room. "Do we petition for sanctuary in Kallistar?"

"To travel through the forest with this many people,

including the sick, elderly and injured would be ringing the dinner bell for the shadow beasts the Prince and Lockheed talked about. It would also be more difficult to hide from the elementals that still support the crown," the old man explains, crossing his arms over his tunic. The shadows under his eyes have darkened since the last time I saw him. Things must not be going well.

But he's not wrong. If what I saw of the encampment coming in is anything to go off, then they would be impossible to miss if they all moved at once.

"Any updates on the escape routes?" Roger asks, holding his chin pensively.

The woman with the blue hair nods. "We have ten people currently scouring for routes. According to Maeve, there's roughly three groups of five refugees on their way here from the west. They're all that's left from the attack at Stafmore."

Another attack. Tricella has not stopped.

Nero leans my way. "Ye've met Evolet. She's a water elemental. She helps Victor stay up to date with everything. Maeve is an owl shifter. She's able to go airborne without being noticed. My bloody wings would be impossible to miss."

I nod, more and more impressed by the organization the shifters have put in place to counteract Tricella.

"We have mole and weasel shifters trying to dig tunnels from the outskirts of the capital all the way to the citadel," Evolet continues, following lines on the map. "It will be risky and take time to make them secure, but we cannot forget about the people there. They need our help, especially now that resources are scarcer than ever."

"We should attack while we have the element of surprise," Aries growls.

"We are not out to start a war, although we may have no choice if it comes to that. But this is not the time to think about attacks, Aries. We need to help those who are unable to flee," Victor replies.

"The crypts." The words leave my lips without thinking and silence dawns on the room.

Everyone's eyes focus on me, but Victor gestures to continue.

I clear my throat and stand, squaring my shoulders. For a second, I feel like I am back home with my men.

"The crypts lead to the forest on the southwest side of the castle. The moles could use them as entry points to the citadel."

"I used that route to smuggle out Sybil," Nero adds. "I worry it might be compromised now, Aramis."

I scratch the stubble on my cheek and attempt a step closer to the map where the castle, my home, stands at its center.

"But that's not the only way out from the crypts." A faint memory comes back. It's my mother and I walking hand in hand through the crypts to lay flowers to our ancestors.

If you're ever in danger, my love, trust your grandfather's secrets. My mother had whispered, resting her index finger to her rosy lips before pulling a secret lever next to my grandfather's marble sarcophagus. Ancient stairs opened before me, and as she helped me down, we reached a narrow hallway; at the end of which, I could see the golden light of the sun.

The grate at the end of the tunnel has a hook at the side. Open it and run, Aramis. Follow the stream until you're safe. I remember nodding but thinking I'd never need to run anywhere as long as I was with her.

I clear my throat again, gently willing my mother's ghost to disappear. I explain how to access the old water duct to the council.

"This is excellent," Roger says as everyone around the table nods in agreement. "It will give us a way in and out of the castle."

"Would you be able to draw a map? Are you sure Tricella does not know about its existence?" Evolet asks whilst furiously taking notes.

"Of course. And no, the old ducts don't even appear on the castle's plans. As far as I know, my mother stumbled on them by accident," I say. For the first time, I feel like I have finally made a difference in this war, but the feeling is short lived.

"How can you trust him?" Aries crosses his arms behind his head, a smug expression on his face. "Maybe he's in league with her, and he wants us to take that passage to deliver us straight to her. We should just kill him and be done with it. Give the people relief knowing they'll sleep safer with him dead."

"As we've told ye, multiple times now, Aries, Aramis and I come to petition for help and offer aid. We are not working with the queen." Nero is quick to come to my defense and I think, not for the first time, what a good friend he is.

How did he hide this essential part of himself from me our whole life?

I must do more. This is my chance to prove myself.

"I will take your bloody potion and tell you everything again if I must," I say to Victor, head held high.

Everyone turns to the head of the table, curiosity etched on their faces as they wait for Victor's answer. The old man studies me in silence, his determination mirroring mine.

"There will be no need for that. The Prince has proven himself compilable, not giving us any reasons to doubt his loyalty. Knowing about the crypt passages is the type of knowledge we've been after for months. It will help us to save more people, which is ultimately our priority." Murmurs rise from the other council members. Not everyone agrees with Victor and would rather still see me rot in a cell.

"However," Victor continues, raising his hand to reinstate silence. "This is a democratic council, and I understand some of you still harbor doubts about the Crown Prince. Therefore, until we're able to successfully use the passage and can confirm the Prince has not sent us into a trap, he will remain under our control."

Fuck.

The thought of having to return to the cells makes me dizzy. My shoulders slump, eyes landing on the table in front of me. I can't waste any more time. Sybil—

"Yet," the old man mutters and my head snaps up again. "Like everyone at this camp, the Prince too has to pull his weight. We will allow you to roam the grounds as long as you help with tasks. You will be under the supervision of Aries; the Goddess knows Lockheed's relationship to you is too personal, and I have a feeling you two together cause only trouble."

Nero subtly elbows me, and I try not to snicker. This is good. I *want* to help them.

The mating bond tugs in my core. She is safe.

I am coming, my love.

II

SYBIL

"All the family records are kept in here," the scholar before us says. He's as old as an olive tree. Deep lines are etched in his skin, and his long white beard gives him a whimsical look. We follow him through a wide archway and my eyes are immediately drawn to the shelves that line the walls, showcasing an impressive collection of giant leather bound tomes and ancient rolls of papers.

"Is there any particular one you're looking for?" the scholar asks. I am mesmerized by the spacious chamber, with numerous tables adorned with parchment, quills, and pots of ink. I will never grow tired of this place.

"Do you have anything on unicorn shifters in Shadow-vale?" I blurt eventually.

"Oh yes, we have quite the collection of rare shifter families back here," he says, pushing his glasses up the bridge of his nose. He gestures for us to follow him and leads us to a shelf from which he carefully selects a thick tome, its pages covered in a layer of dust. When he places the book on the nearest table with a thump, I cough from the cloud of dust that fills the air around it. Despite my itchy nose, excitement tingles through my hands and I rush to join him.

"Unfortunately," he continues, "there have been no updates in hundreds of years. These records date back to the reign of Queen Elanora and King Mattheo."

My heart sinks like a stone in my chest, a heavy ache weighing me down as I fight to conceal the sorrow etched across my face.

"Oh, that's unfortunate. I'd still like to see it, though." I smile weakly and look over the pages, following the carefully inked lines and looping scrawl over the unfamiliar names until it stops with an expansive blank space on the parchment below. "What of the elemental lines?"

His smile broadens, straight sharp white teeth gleaming in the mage light. "Oh, elementals we have many records of. Any affinity or family in particular?"

Nero.

The mere thought of him and Aramis causes my heart to contract, overwhelmed by a flood of emotions. I can't let that distract me from my goal.

"I'm looking for information on the current queen."

"Ah, earth elementals then." The scholar pulls a brown leather book from the shelf, and after searching through the categorization system, he goes to pick up more books and a few parchment rolls.

This is going to take a while, I think, and I gasp in amazement when a cup of steaming tea appears next to me. Maybe the library was starting to like me after all.

"These are the most recent records, roughly nine hundred years of lineage. You know these elementals, they live for ages," he says with a little chuckle that makes me smile.

An odd question starts flourishing within me and before I can decide on it, I splutter "How are halflings recorded?" I peek into the book closest to me, its yellowed pages as thin as leaves.

"The children of elementals and shifters?" He frowns, tucking his arms into the sleeves of his robes. "Unfortunately, we have been unable to successfully record the offspring of such couplings. In all honesty, miss, they are rare, and most are kept secret. Sometimes, out of pride, one parent or the other recognizes their children without openly admitting who the other parent is. You'll see some inscriptions are partially filled out for this reason." I think about Nero and wonder if his name lives amongst these pages.

"Thank you," I start but fail to remember the man's name.

"Oh, it's Theodore, miss. Don't hesitate to call for me if you need help—or the library for that matter," he says with a nod.

"Thank you, Theodore. I appreciate your time."

With whooshing robes, the man leaves me in a sea of books and parchment. I take the little cart and wheel my treasure and tea to a quiet table at the end of the hall. Only another scholar sits there, his head bowed upon a tome with blacked out pages. Making sure not to disturb him, I take a seat and a sip of my tea.

Green tea, excellent for concentration. I send a little thank you to the library and a cool breeze caresses my cheek. Just like Aramis used to do with his wind magic.

Breathing in, I prepare myself for another day of research. For weeks now, I have been studying book after book, looking in vain for mentions of dark magic or secrets about unicorn magic. Yet, one thing I never took into consideration until now was looking for Tricella herself. Who was she before she became queen? Where was she born? Who were her parents? Did she come from generational wealth? Where did she live?

I settle in the wooden chair and open the first book, hoping that understanding the woman behind the monster will allow me to find a way to slay the monster itself.

Hours pass, and I search page after page, meticulously examining the lineage of every noble family, hoping to find even the slightest mention of the queen. Yet, to my astonishment, the name of the queen is absent from all the royal records. As if erased from history.

How strange.

I would have bet she came from noble origins. How else do you suddenly become Queen of one of the most powerful kingdoms in Craeweth?

I yawn, stretching out my aching back as I glance about the room, mage lights bobbing in the air above us. Lemon stirs awake in my pocket and stretches out his small paw, a silent request for another cheese cube. The library kept sending me little treats throughout the day, something I was very grateful for.

"Something is not adding up," I tell my little companion and sigh, feeling lost again. "I could use a little guidance," I say out loud to no one in particular, and hold my head between my hands.

Almost imperceptibly, one of the tomes sitting on my desk —this one looking much less regal than the previous one— starts moving in my direction as if alive. I narrow my eyes, pull it toward me, and read the title.

"She's a queen," I say to the library and feel a little bit silly talking to the air. "Why would I find her in the records of the small folk of Shadowvale?" The library's only response is to tuck my chair a little bit closer to the table.

"Alright, alright. I'll have a look. It's not like I am stuck in a mountain with no idea what to do whilst there's a looming war outside." I flick through the pages one by one. Each name is followed by a date of birth, name of the father and name of the mother, and when known, their profession. Occasionally, I see incomplete lines as mentioned by Theodore.

It was difficult to pinpoint Tricella's exact year of birth, but I took a wild guess based on Queen Rose and the King's ages. After reading the names of countless farmers, seamstresses and cooks, I stumble on something interesting.

Catricella, known as Tricella. Born in Lyall, Shadowvale: Mother Morgana - UNKNOWN. Father Water elemental, Lord.

The name Catricella is unique enough to have featured only a handful of times in the annuals, and never with the nickname "Tricella" next to it. Could this be her?

Surely not. But I wonder, what if...

"Oh, there you are! I wasn't expecting you to still be down here. The whole day has nearly passed," Marcelene says as she moves through the archway.

"Marcelene!" I almost scream before catching myself and remembering I am still in a library. "Hand me the records of the shifter small folk!"

Startled by my outburst, Marcelene goes to the cart full of books and takes a green cloth bound one. I immediately jump to the same year and start pointing to an incomplete line, ecstatic that I have finally made a discovery during my time here.

Tricella. Born in Lyall, Shadowvale: Mother Morgana, jaguar shifter - Beggar. Father UNKNOWN.

Tricella is a half shifter.

I lean back in my chair and let out an exhausted laugh.

"Should I... worry?" Marcelene asks, standing behind me with a concerned look on her face. She leans over my shoulder and peaks at the annuals, then immediately looks at me, eyebrows furrowed.

"Is that?"

"I think so. Her parents tried to confuse the annuals by switching between her name and nickname," I say, closing my eyes, thinking about all the implications this discovery brings forth; I can't wait to share it all with Aramis and Nero.

"Sybil, I apologize for interrupting this moment, but the coven leaders and mother are ready to meet with you," Marcelene says, putting her hands on my shoulders.

As Marcelene guides me into the large room, the mage lights cast a gentle glow, illuminating the lichen dotted ceiling above. The stone walls are adorned with clusters of crystals in various shades—pearl, violet, and teal—their shimmering reflection dancing along the walls. The air carries a faint scent of ancient magic, mingling with aged parchment and strangely jasmine. In the center, a grand round table commands attention, surrounded by a dozen chairs, occupied by the coven mother and what appears to be the remaining leaders of the coven.

"Sybil Vandeleur," a wizened old male says as he stares at me. "One of the last unicorn shifters. I knew your father well before you were born."

"You knew my father?" I lift my eyes to meet his gaze.

"Mhmm, it was a long time ago, before the war when he was a colt not much older than yourself. My name is Alexander, not that he would have mentioned me. I was teaching a seminar on the art of branching herbology and magic for healing at Nova Esther." He drums his fingers on the table. "I heard of his unfortunate passing from this world."

I nod, unsure what to say and unwilling to show my ever-present grief.

"I hope your time at the library is proving to be fruitful for your mission?" Daniela, the high priestess, asks.

I'm grateful for the change in topic. "Indeed. I am following a lead that is proving interesting. But I am still not sure how to counteract Tricella's dark magic. I don't know how being a unicorn will help me defeat her." I open my arms at a loss. "I need—"

"You need training. As Queen Rose commanded you," Alexander said. "Harpalyke has a tradition to remain neutral in conflicts, a tradition we are currently... reviewing. Yet, there's other ways we can help you, horned one. We have agreed to train you to access your innermost magic." All the witches and scholars present nod in unison and I can't believe my ears.

"But the only magic I know is healing," I whisper, nervous about this sudden pressure put upon me. I start fidgeting with my fingers.

The high priestess chuckles, her face cracking into a broad smile. "There is more power in you than you realize, child. To everything, there is balance. You must be the light to her darkness. Your power comes from the earth, from the Goddess herself. I can sense it radiating off you. You see your magic as the power to heal, but what is healing if not using that light within you to create happiness, peace, and alleviate suffering?"

My healers code, but with a different purpose.

To save the shifters of Shadowvale and all who come after. To save my people.

"You are the embodiment of what it means to be a unicorn. You say Tricella seeks you for your power. She fears your power and wishes to tarnish it, as all darkness wants to swallow the light. Maybe you don't have to understand her magic, just trust in yours."

She will not have me.

I lean forward, bracing my hands on the table as I look at the coven leaders, the three witches standing behind them who rescued me, and finally to the coven mother.

"Teach me."

12
SYBIL

Sybil, you should rest," Cassara says as she sits in front of me, pours a cup of tea, and sets it on the table between us. The faint glow of the mage lights cast dancing shadows on the walls and shelves around us. Her blonde hair is braided and rests on her left shoulder. She is wearing a loose green tunic, which I have come to know is the type of outfit witches wear when they are off duty from protecting the library or aiding with research.

"Harnessing new powers takes time and energy. You've been training with Alexander and the high priestess for hours. No one expects you to learn how to defeat the queen in one day." A reassuring smile paints her lips and I'm grateful for her worry.

The pain in my lower back speaks volumes of the number of hours I have spent on this wooden chair. I roll my shoulders and stretch my neck, but my chest feels tight and the room is heavy with a sense of urgency. Sweat beads my forehead and my shirt is stuck to my skin from trying the exercises Alexander taught me over and over again.

"You'd expect a healer to take better care of herself, wouldn't you?" I say with a low chuckle, the shadow of exhaustion looming over me.

Just as I had asked, we had started with the training immediately. The witch had taken me into an empty room deep within the mountain and challenged me to let my power run loose through me.

"Close your eyes, Sybil. Feel your magic. Don't let that power only be part of you, let it *become you*," Alexander had said. "You are the limits you impose on yourself, child."

For years, I had only ever seen my power as a gift I could access to heal people. I would channel whatever I needed to make people feel better and then tuck it back in the corner between my soul and my heart where magic lived. Almost naively, I had labeled and limited my magic, and instead of regarding it as raw energy cursing through my veins, I had limited its purpose. Now, it was time to unlearn something I had spent years inculcating to myself.

Whilst Cassara pours herself a cup of the steaming tea—black, from its pungent smell—I extend my hands toward the table and they start to tremble. I hold them out, reaching for the dregs of my power and calling forth the light until they take on an ethereal glow, feeling the surge of energy coursing through my veins. The cup wobbles for a moment, teetering on the edge of the table, before finally succumbing to the force of my power. It hovers in the air, suspended by an invisible force, and begins its slow journey toward my waiting hands.

As the cup reaches me, I can't help but feel a mix of excitement and trepidation. Bending the power I possess to my own will, beyond the realm of healing, is something I had never thought possible. Alexander and the high priestess had been delighted by my fast progress, yet this power is both a blessing and a burden. It's a constant reminder of the responsibility I carry and the knowledge that Tricella has had over a century to perfect and hone hers.

I take a deep breath, savoring the moment before taking a sip of the black tea. Its warmth spreads through me, invigorating my senses and sharpening my focus.

"Sybil!" Cassara exclaims, wide-eyed, making Lemon jump from a little nook in the shelf where he was napping.

"It's nothing special," I say, shaking my head. "I can't exactly defeat Tricella throwing cups full of tea in her direction, can I?" Lowering my gaze, I feel stuck between wanting to be proud of what I have learned and knowing it is not enough.

"But every little step will take you closer to it." She tilts her head and sets her cup back on the table. "I believe there's a reason why unicorn shifters have always been rare, ever since the time of the Goddess."

Cassara gently guides her finger along the edge of the porcelain cup, her brows furrowed, trying to put into words something she'd been trying to grasp for some time.

"It's because your existence defies the balance of magic. Most shifters tend to sit in a gray area. Our magic is influenced by the choices we make every day. Not fully light, nor fully dark, but somewhere in the middle." One of the mage light flickers and I wonder if it's the library urging Cassara to finish her thought—just as curious as I am about where this is going.

"We are told that unicorns are pure light. You were born out of the feelings of joy, prosperity and peace the Goddess felt after creating Craeweth. The goodness within you is encompassing, and I think you don't even realize that." Her blue eyes set on mine.

"We all thought unicorns were extinct, Sybil. We grieved that loss in Craeweth, yet here you are. The proof that light will always find a way to shine, even when the night is darkest." Cassara takes my hand in hers. They are calloused and the squeeze she gives me is exuding comfort. "You can do this."

My eyes sting from tears unshed. Being reminded that I am the last unicorn in Craeweth always feels like a punch in the gut, but the witch sitting in front of me is right.

With a gentle breeze smelling of pines and summer rain, a white silk handkerchief appears out of nowhere and lands on the table next to our bound hands. A laugh escapes my lips and with it a tear runs down my cheek. I look up to the cavernous ceiling of the room.

"Thank you," I say to the library and two chocolate truffles appear.

"You really know how to treat a lady, huh," Cassara says to the emptiness. We both laugh.

I set the cup down gently, the delicate sound of porcelain meeting the plate echoes in the room.

"I have to keep practicing," I whisper, the words laced with determination. I bury my face in my hands, threading my fingers through my unbound hair. "Every moment I waste, she gets stronger." Lemon jumps off the shelf and onto the table. He stands on his hind legs in front of me, sensing I am tired and overworking myself once again. He nudges his cold, wet nose against my cheek, his rough tongue scraping against my skin.

"I think it's time for you to go to bed, Sybil. What good will you be if you burn yourself out? Magic isn't limitless," Cassara says.

I fear she is right as exhaustion pounds through me again. The sound of my chair scraping against the floor echoes through the room.

"I will see you in the morrow," I say, picking Lemon up and allowing him to crawl into the pocket of my dress.

"Sweet dreams, unicorn."

I exit the room and take a right toward the main chamber of the library with the grand staircase I saw the first day. There's a handful of scholars still roaming the hallways, but I trust my feet and let them guide me to my bed as a pounding headache starts taking root.

"This is not ideal," I whisper to myself massaging my temples. When I lift my gaze again, I don't know where I am.

Somehow, I have walked myself into a dead end. The corridor in front of me ends with a blank wall made of dark brown bricks, as if placed there to hide something. Gone are the white doors I have come to recognize, and the air here feels damp and ancient. Slowly, I take a step toward the wall, but when I try to touch it, my fingers go through it.

"How stran—" The ground beneath my feet suddenly opens and I fall down a hatch door that was not there moments before.

My body contorts to shield Lemon in my front pocket from the impact. The harsh thud of my hands and knees hitting the ground reverberates through my body, while sharp pain shoots up my limbs. The acrid, metallic scent of blood and scraped skin fills the senses as the rough texture of the stone grates against my flesh. I cough, groaning at the stinging pain that lances up the left side of my ribs.

Pulling on the last of my magic reserves, my hands take on a dim glow so I can inspect my injuries. My eyes are drawn to the wall where the stones vibrate, grating against one another until a tall archway slowly opens. It's made of rough-hewn stone, different from the hand carved doorways I've seen in the rest of the library. There, in its distance, I see a staircase winding downward. Heart racing, I brace a hand against the stone wall, supporting the left side of my ribs as I push to a standing position and drag my bruised body toward it.

How wonderful, yet another dark tunnel.

Old Sybil would have run rather than approach a dark looming entrance. I have no such compulsions anymore. I have a queen to take down.

Lemon climbs out of my pocket, chittering angrily, and I gently stroke his head. As he licks at my palms, a soothing warmth spreads through the abrasions, hastening their healing.

"I'm sorry boy, are you alright?" I cursorily check his body for injuries, but he wiggles out of my grasp and climbs onto my shoulder, sniffing the cold air wafting from the dark tunnel. I glance up at the sound of tiny scurrying and tinkling and spot a small cluster of sprites staring down at me with their googly eyes.

I brush away the tears staining my cheeks with a sniffle before lifting a hand. Three sprites float into my awaiting palm. I bring them closer to my face and can't help but smile as their downy, soft fluff tickles my nose.

"What are you guys doing here? Do you have a message for me?" My heart leaps in my chest but then sinks as disappointment settles. Nero and Aramis wouldn't be anywhere near the library, let alone know about the sprites messengers.

They jump up and down on my palm, making tiny tinkling noises.

"I'm sorry, I don't understand you," I say, glancing around the empty stone corridor before gazing back into the dark archway. "Do you want me to go down there?"

Great, I'm lost and talking to tiny fairies. Maybe I hit my head too hard when I fell.

I frown at the stairwell as the sprites continue to bounce in my palm. There's only one way to see this through. Sighing, I will the sprites to move and I take Lemon from my shoulder.

He stands on my joined palms, paws rubbing on his sleepy eyes.

"Lemon, I need you to get Marcelene, Thalia, and Cassara. Find them and bring them here. I... I have this feeling..." Looking down the tunnel, I know deep in my bones something is waiting there for me. Even so, I must learn from my mistakes and whilst I have to follow this feeling, it does not hurt to get back up too.

"Take them down this tunnel. You can do this, good boy." I lower my forehead to his and his whiskers make my nose tickle. After setting him down onto the rocky ground, Lemon sprints up the brick wall and out of the hatch door. I turn to face the entrance with a newfound familiarity of the darkness.

"251... 252... 253... 254," I count as I descend step after step and wonder if whoever designed the library ever asked themselves how many staircases are too many?

The step at the end of this tunnel feels... different. Its weathered steps are curved, eroded by time and those who have set foot in these ancient chambers before me. Shadows dance along the walls and the air is silent, as if the mountain itself is holding a breath, guarding the secrets that lay at the staircase's end.

I try to focus and ignore Aramis and Nero's voices in my head; they would be enraged if they knew I had embarked on a solo journey down an eerie tunnel that magically appeared in front of me. Nero would scold my recklessness and tell me I have no sense of preservation. Aramis would remind me that this could very well be a trap.

Good thing the boys are not here.

"Three hundred and seventy-five!" I exclaim as I jump off

the last step and enter a compact room at what feels like the bottom of the mountain. The round stone wall holds torches that cast a golden glow on the only thing present in the room. A massive wooden door stands before me, fortified with iron fittings.

Before I go to examine the door, a whooshing sound above me anticipates the arrival of the witches in their mewl form. One of them even has Lemon on their back holding on for dear life. The sprites follow close by. Marcelene, Thalia, and Cassara shift into their humanoid forms and I lose a breath, happy to no longer be alone, but the relief is short lived.

"Goddess, Sybil! What happened?" Cassara exclaims, rushing toward me.

"Look at your dress, are you well?" Marcelene follows examining every inch of my body.

"How on Craeweth do you always get yourself into trouble!" Thalia chides, hands on her hips.

I smile at the three witches and at the irony of having found three more people to worry about me. Cassara places her hand where I clutch my ribs, the warmth of her magic seeping through my chemise easing the sharp pain radiating through my side."What is this place?" Marcellene asks no one in particular, eyes wide.

"I'm not sure. I don't remember there being an archway here before." Cassara looks toward her companions. "Thalia?" The third witch shakes her head and I can see her reflexes sharpening, readying herself for a potential threat.

"I got lost. There was this magical projection of a wall and then this hatch door appeared, and I fell. When I opened my eyes, the stones started moving until this archway appeared," I explain, hoping they have answers.

"I've never heard of the library creating passageways into

the mountain before." Marcellene runs her hands along the hewn surface of the stone arch.

"This is strange," Cassara interjects, "but there's only one way to find out what's going on." She reaches for the door handle.

Before she can turn it, Thalia grabs her arm. "This could compromise the library's security. We should consult the high priestess."

"Thalia." Cassara's tone is firm but kind. "I say this with love: you have to live a little."

Marcelene's eyebrows raise in shock, and she bites her lip to stop her snicker. The tension is thick between the two witches, but Thalia eventually drops her hand and takes a step back.

The metal squeaks, rust sprinkling to the ground as though the door has not been opened in a century. Cassara pushes against it, the door groans and moves a sliver but doesn't open.

"Well it's not locked, but I'm going to need some help."

We line up, shoulders pressed against the wooden frame as Marcelene turns the handle.

"On my count. One–Two–Three!"

Together, we shove against the door. As it creaks and moans under the force of our shoves, anticipation and relief courses through my veins. With a sudden burst of energy, the door flows open, and we tumble out, a chaotic mess of limbs and bodies colliding on the dirty floor. The impact stirs up a cloud of dust motes, shimmering in the air like tiny stars, creating an ethereal atmosphere in the room.

"I thought the library cleans itself," I cough as I wave the air in front of my face. Lemon jumps to the ground, the sprites clinging to his back.

"It does, but I don't think this is part of the library," Thalia says, offering me a hand up and conjuring a mage light.

I stare around in wonder at the circular room with marble flooring and stone walls. There's twelve ornate pillars running along its circumference, one for each kingdom in Craeweth. A dark blue ceiling littered with golden carvings stands out in stark contrast. I stretch my neck attempting to decipher the drawings in the faint mage lights.

There's a woman at its center, standing in front of a towering mountain. She's wearing a long gown; a crown sits on her brow and her arms are stretched out. An open book sits on either side of her. There are carvings of shifters, symbols of elemental magic all around her and creatures hide in the darker corners.

"This is our history," Marcelene whispers.

I follow the Goddess's gaze down to the center of the room where two twin pedestals stand. They grow from the ground as if born from the mountain itself and as I walk closer to them, I feel energy pulsing off in waves, inviting me to have a look.

"Something used to be here," I say, running my hand across the smooth top of the pedestal on my right, which appears to be free of any dust or debris. Magical energy like the first bloom of spring, or crystalline water sings under my palm. It echoes within me and my magical well feels slightly more replenished. Curious, I move to the second pedestal, but as I extend my hand, I immediately draw back. Searing pain, suffocating hurt, and anger flood my senses, making me seethe.

"What is it?" Cassara asks, coming to stand by me.

"Can't you feel that?" I rub my hand, but the dark feelings seem to have seeped through my very skin.

"I don't feel anything," she replies, glancing at Thalia and Marcelene. They shake their heads too.

"I don't know if we should be here," Thalia whispers, her eyes on the door as if it'll close at any minute.

I look back at the pedestal and then up at the ceiling once

again. "I think there used to be books kept in here. Ancient, powerful books. I can feel the remnants of their magic when I touch the wood, like they were down here for so long they left an imprint."

Why did you show me this? I ask hoping anyone, the Goddess, the library, or the mountain itself will answer.

"Think, Sybil," I whisper under my breath.

The Goddess. Two books. elementals. shifters. Balance in magic. The library is told to hold immense power. *Find the library of Harpalyke.*

"Who created Harpalyke?" I ask the witches without glancing back. The clogs in my mind are turning at speed trying to solve this puzzle.

"No one really knows," Marcelene answers, taking a step closer to me. "They say the Goddess gifted it to the white witches at the beginning of time and asked them to protect it."

"What kind of knowledge could have been stored at the beginning of time in this library that needed protection?" I wonder out loud, the air electric. "Unless..."

"Unless there was more to it," Thalia continues, and I turn my gaze in her direction. Her eyes are now lit by the fire of discovery, and I can feel we're close.

"Maybe the library and this whole mountain were created to protect more than the books upstairs." I think back to the fairytales I read as a child about the Goddess. "The first gift the Goddess bestowed upon the people of Craeweth was magic. But raw magic was too unpredictable and chaotic for shifters and elementals to use, so she created balance by dividing it into light magic and dark magic and writing it all down into..."

My eyes raise to the ceiling once again and I feel the witches doing the same, the answer to our question above us.

"Someone must have stolen the books," I whisper, defeated. I was too late, again.

Without realizing, I lean on the pedestals. One hand on each and the rocky base of them starts to crumble.

"Sybil!" Cassara catches me before I fall forward. The tumbling rocks raise a cloud of dust that makes me cough and my eyes sting.

"What's this?" Thalia asks as she scoops down to pick something up from the rubble. I reach for the parchment and I flip the paper over where, drawn with hasty movements, there's a crude dagger stabbing a crimson heart.

"I think this is a clue to find whoever was originally here."

13
SYBIL

We've been searching for days, and we've found nothing." I drag my fingers through my hair as I place the last book on the pile.

The parchment we found in the chamber at the bottom of the mountain was a calling card.

"That's a dumb idea." Cassara had scoffed when I explained to her that sometimes, famous thieves leave them behind as a sign of their work.

We had then returned to the library, where Marcelene had rounded up every book on symbols she could find in the hope we'd discover information about the dagger and heart drawn on the parchment.

The last two days of discoveries have started to take a toll on me, but I can't stop. I finally feel so close to grasping something that will help me make a difference in this war. I take a deep breath and realize I can't remember the last time I saw the sky or felt the sun on my skin.

"I think I have to leave the library," I whisper, breaking the silence. The three witches sitting around the table look at me.

"But you have just started your training with Alexander," Marcelene says, lips upturned.

"I have done what Queen Rose pleaded me to. I sought training, I know the magic we need to defeat Tricella is part of me," I say, placing a hand to my chest. "I simply need to stop being afraid of it."

Scraping one of the empty chairs next to Cassara, I join the witches. They look at me with apprehension except for Thalia, who's determined gaze spurs me on.

"Knowing that Tricella's ancestry lies in both shifter and elemental lines showed us a weakness in her armor we didn't know before. This could be leverage! We know her anger is spurred by her desire for power and immortality but what happened before that? Why would a half shifter turn against her own people?" I shake my head, still trying to grasp how all these puzzle pieces fit together. "And now," I continue, "we also know she is in possession of potentially two of the most powerful books on the entire continent, penned by the Goddess herself. And we might even have a lead on who got these books for her." I slump back in my chair and start fidgeting with the hem of my light blue sleeves. "This might not seem like much, but after losing someone I really cared about, after being tortured and locked away, for the first time, I feel hopeful."

Marcelene claps her hands together, making us all jump. "Right, witches and unicorn, let's get our smart little heads together and come up with a plan."

Thalia rolls her eyes. Cassara stretches her arms as if readying herself for battle. It feels good knowing I won't be alone at the front line. Lemon crawls out of the pocket of my dress and jumps on the table.

"The books," Thalia begins. "We need to find out if Tricella has both. Because if she only has the book of darkness, there might still be a chance the book of light is out there, holding the knowledge of how you can amplify your magic, Sybil."

"If only there's a way we could track the thief using the ca–"

Marcelene's words are interrupted by a thick, emerald leather-bound book plopping on the table between us. Golden swirls depicting a rearing unicorn on the cover glint in the mage light.

"I've never seen that book before," Marcelene says as she traces the intricate design with a finger. The mage light above us flickers.

"That's odd," Cassara says, glancing at its side. "Look on the spine, it has the mark of the prohibited section in the library."

"It's a section only the high priestess has access to," Thalia explains in response to my furrowed brows and confused expression. "They contain spells and secrets passed on from high priestess to high priestess to uphold Harpalyke. We should not have this book." She straightens her back and goes to take the book but it shifts further in my direction.

As my fingers brush the book, a jolt of electricity shoots through me, leaving a buzzing sensation in my fingertips. "Did you guys feel that?"

"Traces of power from their writer are imprinted into the pages of many magical books. The same as the way magical objects are created," Marcelene explains.

"The energy, the magic it feels familiar–" I gently turn the cover and it opens with ease, revealing a loopy scrawling script, *The Power of Wynstar,* without an author.

"Who is Wynstar?" Cassara says.

"Or what is Wynstar?" Marcelene leans over the table. "Is it a place?

That name sounds so familiar...

"I'm not sure, but the library clearly thinks it'll help us," I chime in. "The Power of Wynstar–"

As we stare at the book in contemplation, the pages begin flipping rapidly of their own accord. My eyes stay fixated on the mesmerizing movement, unable to look away.

With my heart racing, I stand from my seat as the pages abruptly stop turning. The book is spread open revealing a page with a neatly scrawled title: 'Seeking a Lost Object,' accompanied by a carefully drawn design and spell.

"Let me see that." Cassara slips the thief's parchment into the chapter and then flips through the pages. "It doesn't look too complicated. Library, could you get us a map of Craeweth?"

Moments tick by before a rolled up old map appears on the table. The aged parchment crackles under my fingertips as I spread the map open across the table. Tears prick the corner of my eyes as my finger is drawn to the small dot where my village was south of the Armaghdale forest.

"Is that where you're from?" Marcelene asks quietly.

"Yes," I say. "It feels like eons ago." My throat tightens and chest aches for the familiar scent of my home, the feel of soil under my hands as I plant the spring harvest.

"Don't worry, Sybil. Everything will turn out as it's meant to be." Marcelene smiles softly at me, then turns to Cassara. "Anything?"

"Thalia, we're going to need your help."

I can sense Thalia's internal conflict between wanting to call the high priestess and helping us. Eventually, she scoffs and leans toward the book.

"I've never seen spell work like this before," she says, looking up to me. She flips it open to our marked page and holds up the scrap of parchment before running her finger along the text. "But it doesn't look too complicated."

She sets the book to the side and peers at the map. Humming under her breath, she pulls a pearl hairpin from her bun and sets it on the parchment and places both at the top of the map. She braces her hands on either side of the map and begins to chant.

> *Thief I seek, come to me*
> *Wherever you hide*
> *I shall see*
> *See the sight*
> *Hear the sound*
> *Be it high in the air*
> *Or low on the ground*
> *Let who I'm looking for*
> *Now be found*

We all stare at the map as the tiny pin vibrates, lifting into the air before falling and rolling off the map.

"What happened?" Cassara asks, catching the hairpin before it falls off the edge of the table.

"I'm not sure," Thalia says, tucking a strand of hair behind her ear. "Either the thief has a protection cast on him, or my magic isn't powerful enough–"

"What if we channeled our powers?" Marcelene asks.

"What do you mean?" I ask, looking at each of them in turn. "I've never heard of channeling powers before."

"It's not done very often, as it consumes a great amount of power. It's how we open the portal. We have to be physically touching and pull deep into the well of your magic."

"The portal?" I ask.

The three witches look at each other uncomfortably, trying to decide whether to let me in on their secret or not.

"The tunnels are not the only way in or out of the library," Marcelene eventually whispers. "This mountain is one of the few places in Craeweth where magic is so concentrated it opens a portal through space, able to take you to different locations."

"Well, we now know it's probably because the Goddess decided to store in this mountain the most powerful magical books ever created," Cassara interjects, raising her shoulders.

"We use the portal rarely as it compromises the library's security," Marcelene continues, ignoring Cassara's logical conclusion. "But in this occasion, it might be useful."

"We can't come this far and not try," I plead but the witches stay silent.

Dread coils in my gut. "We don't have long left."

Cassara lifts her eyes and meets Marcelene's, worry painting her features. "The council would forbid us to use the portal, let alone attempt this spell without further research."

This time, it's Thalia who scoffs and glances at each of us in turn before grabbing the book and placing it directly in front of her, touching the bottom edge of the map. She bites at her lower lip as she silently rereads the spell.

"They won't like this, but I was told we should all learn to live a little."

After a moment of surprise at Thalia's nod, we all burst into laughter, and it breaks the growing tension in the room. If even Thalia is willing to bend the rules of the white witches, then our options have grown thin. Marcelene lifts her hands, placing one on Thalia's shoulder and offering one to me. Cassara stands on my other side and mimics Marcelene.

"For Craeweth," I say, placing my hands in either of theirs.

"For Craeweth," Thalia says, her voice resonating in the

room as she speaks, her hands gently resting on the ancient book.

A surge of electric energy courses through my arms, causing the tiny hairs to stand on end. A sudden gust of wind swirls around us. Delicate scrolls on the table and shelves to cascade to the ground. Above, the mage light flickers and dances, casting an ethereal glow around the room. The air becomes infused with the intoxicating scent of lemongrass and lavender, creating an atmosphere of mystical anticipation.

With each word of her incantation, Thalia's voice grows stronger and more mesmerizing. As she reaches the climax of the spell, the hairpin levitates into the air, spinning wildly in a dizzying display of power. Time itself seems to slow, and we all find ourselves holding our breath in anticipation. The room falls into an eerie silence, broken only by the resounding thud as the hairpin plunges toward the wooden table, embedding itself with a solid impact.

We all collapse back into our chairs, panting as we stare at the small pin lodged into a section of the forest at the base of the mountains near a small town.

"Looks like we've got our destination. Let's catch us a thief."

"May the Goddess bless your journey," Thalia whispers as she stands in front of Marcelene and myself. She hastily pulls our hoods over our heads as her hands tremble with unease. Before she steps away, I take her hand in mine.

"Thank you." The words are filled with unspoken gratitude and the love I have developed for these women in the short time I have spent with them.

Thalia nods and squeezes my hand two more times.

After finding the location of the thief, we all agreed to spitting up our party. The library needs witches like Thalia and Cassara to protect it, now more than ever. Yet nothing could have convinced Marcelene to stay behind. So, while we follow the clues to find the thief, Cassara and Thalia will continue researching about light magic and anything they can find regarding Tricella's past.

I hoist my healing satchel—heavily overstocked with supplies—further on my shoulder as I stand before an apparently ordinary stone archway located almost at the peak of the mountain. However, when the witches had told me about an ancient magical portal, I had imagined something a little bit more... ornate. Marcelene stands next to me as Thalia and Cassara take position behind us holding hands.

"The high priestess will not like this," Marcelene says, shaking her head with a smile on her lips. "Good thing she won't be here to see it." She winks at me and shuffles her feet, ready to sprint at any moment. She's wearing leathers; a large bow and quiver hang on her back.

"I don't know how long we'll be able to hold the portal open," Thalia says, trying to mask her concern. After some discussion, we had all agreed to continue our solo mission without involving the elders. After all, it's easier to ask for forgiveness than permission.

I nod, giving Lemon—hiding in my pocket—a little tap on the head. Cassara and Thalia clear their throats and I see from the corner of my eye a growing light emanating from the two of them. The center of the portal begins to glow iridescent like a large bubble. Marcelene reaches for my hand and squeezes it reassuringly.

"We, witches of knowledge and protectors of the past seek passage to our destination." Cassara holds the map up and it's ripped from her hand in a current of wind before landing on the stones before the portal. The center of the archway begins to lose its transparency and I see visions of forests, lakes, snowy peaks, deserts and plains, rushing one after the other before it settles on a quiet small town where smoke can be seen trickling into the sky barely lightened by the rising sun.

"Now!" Cassara screams and as we step through the portal, I thank the library for showing me the way.

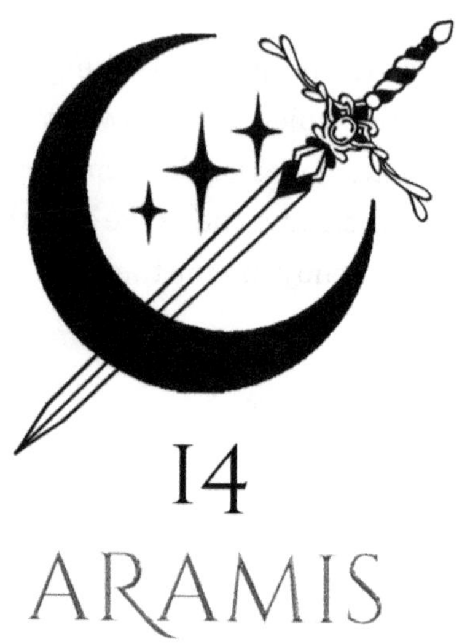

14

ARAMIS

I bet you never had to wash your own linen before, Prince?" Aries snickers as he leans against a tall pine at the edge of the stream. The afternoon sun filters through the trees, and I take a moment to appreciate the scenery.

"I don't know what idea you have of the life I lived at the castle, but I can assure you I have slept more nights on rocky grounds by the fire with my men than on silky sheets."

My fingertips ache from the freezing water but I ignore it and dunk the sheet in again. This newfound freedom at the rebel camp had come with responsibilities in exchange for better comfort. The first night I spent in one of the little huts away from the stench of the cells and Axton's incessant chatter had been glorious. But when the morning came, with it also came Aries, my "guard," and a list of tasks I had to do to pull my weight at the camp.

I have done everything from cooking to chopping wood and even aiding with the injured, although my healing skills were embarrassing compared to Sybil's. Occasionally, Victor would summon me for war councils to help organize movements around the castle. I drew maps and compiled long lists about where our armory is located, where my men train, and the routes they usually follow. We even set up a plan to have food secretly delivered to the small folk at the citadel to help them survive the famine caused by Tricella's dark magic poisoning the soil.

Granted, no one really knows how much of what I know is still relevant. Maybe Kieran has infiltrated himself in the military ranks of Shadowvale too and fucked up everything I have built, but I am still willing to share.

"You can fool everyone else around here, but you can't fool me," Aries says, twisting his dagger in his hands.

I roll the soaked sheet on itself, trying to get as much of the water out before resting it into a wooden basket with the others. I can't help but remember I treated Sybil the same way Aries is treating me.

"For the sake of your people, I hope that the day you realize you and the council can actually trust me doesn't come too late," I murmur. According to the latest messages, the moles are getting closer to the access by the crypts. I pray to the Goddess the passage is still viable or the council will turn it against me and not grant me the help I need to go after Sybil. The mating bond tugs gently, and I feel excitement rushing from her side.

What are you up to, Sybil Vandeleur?

Drying my reddened hands on my breeches, I stand, lift the heavy basket and make my way back to the tents without so much as muttering a word to Aries who follows me instantly.

The whispers start rising as soon as I enter camp.

"Mama, look at him," a young boy says as we pass. Glaring intensely, the woman protectively gathers her son behind her flowing skirts and guides him away.

"Ironic having the Prince of Shadowvale wash our sheets," a teenage boy snickers with his friends.

"Why is he still here?" another asks.

Their eyes follow me with a mix of fear and suspicion and all I can do is lower my gaze, until an orange ball the size of an apple rolls to my feet. Angling the basket on my hip, I take the ball and search for its owner in the crowd, but no one claims it.

"Bella—" A woman comes running through the crowd in my direction, but something tugging at my black tunic catches my awareness. A little girl, no more than three years of age looks at me with determination. She has dirt on her cheeks, her knees are bruised, and her green dress has seen better days. But she does not seem to mind.

What really catches my attention, however, are her big blue eyes, void of the suspicion most people hide behind when it comes to me. She does not see the Crown Prince of Shadowvale and his unspeakable crimes, but a man holding her toy hostage, and it makes my heart melt.

The girl tilts her head and points to the ball I am still holding.

"Oh, I see." I smile and kneel to her level and give her toy back. If I had my magic, I could have made it roll on itself and fly but alas, I am still only an ordinary male. The girl, Bella ,smiles back and returns to her mother, who stands frozen in place.

As more and more eyes focus on me, I feel heat rushing to my cheeks.

What do I have to do to be seen as everyone else in this damn place?

Before I can take another step in the direction of the rods where I'm supposed to hang the laundry, a scream breaks the silence.

A man with blood dripping down his left arm hobbles past

us, his ripped sleeve fluttering in the wind as he yells in pain. I recognize him; it's one of the sentinels, tasked with protecting the perimeter of the camp.

"Shadow beasts!" He screams. I let the basket drop to the floor.

Shadow beasts.

Chaos ensues as more screams come from the west border, and I let my old instincts take over.

"Aries, inform the council, have every man and woman who can fight take arms. Everyone else must hide." My head snaps up to see smoke rising to the sky.

"If you think I am going to leave you, you're mistaken, Prince," the shifter spits at my feet. Pushing down the desire to punch Aries in the face, I take a deep breath.

"This is not about me and you, you stupid fuck. I have faced these abominations before. People are getting hurt and if you don't want your hands to be stained the same red as mine, go get that fucking backup!" I shout, indicating the way to the council building.

Aries blinks and narrows his eyes, studying me.

"I better not regret this. Go," he says suddenly. I don't hesitate before we both run in opposite directions.

A few tents down, I catch sight of a massive bull-like figure made of twisting shadows, with four menacing horns and a wicked spiked tail. It moves erratically side to side, taking everything out in its wake.

Great, they just keep getting bigger and uglier.

Feeling dangerously exposed without my magic nor sword, I look around and spot an axe leaning against a stack of wood. Without second thoughts, as the screams grow in the distance, I sprint in its direction.

"This'll have to do." I test its weight and take off toward the beast, who has a family of shifters cornered against a rocky wall.

Fuck.

Picking up a rock, I chuck it and the bull's massive head swings toward me. Its snort echoes through the air as it aggressively paws at the ground, smoke swirling from its flared nostrils. "Why don't you come pick on someone more your skill," I shout.

The bull charges, thundering toward me with unstoppable force.

Here we go.

Adrenaline surges through my veins as I brace myself, tightening my grip on the axe. With every step, the ground trembles beneath its hooves, shaking the very foundation of the street. I stand my ground, fearless, ready to face the monstrous creature head-on. As the bull closes in, I swing the axe with all my might, aiming for its colossal head. Metal clashes against shadow, sparks flying in a fierce clash of strength and darkness.

"Fuck." I muster all my strength, digging my heels into the ground at its brute force.

The bull retaliates, its tail whipping through the air like a jagged whip, aiming to strike me down. I dodge, narrowly avoiding the wicked spikes that could pierce through bone. Instead of finding its mark, the tail imbeds in the house behind me. The bull wrenches its tail from the wall above my head, sending plaster raining over me. I cough, trying to clear my vision as I scoot away from the beast and regain my footing.

My heart leaps in my chest as more screams from down the road tear through the air from either direction. If the shadow beast is here, it means Tricella is getting close.

Roaring with fury, the bull charges again, its eyes burning with malevolence. But I am relentless, dancing with death as I dodge and strike, a whirlwind of bravery and skill. With each swing, I chip away at the bull's twisted form, determination fueling my every strike. Blood pumps in my ears, drowning out the chaos around me as I fight for the innocent lives trapped in the alleyway.

Council be damned. If I had my magic, this fight would be over by now.

The clash of metal against shadow reverberates through the street, a symphony of defiance against the forces of darkness.

With one final, mighty swing, I cleave through the bull's shadowy form to its heart, shattering it into fragments of darkness.

Silence falls, broken only by the heavy breathing of the exhausted family and the victorious beat of my heart.

I lower the axe. The weight of the battle finally sinks in, as I take a moment to catch my breath. I kneel before the boy, who's shaking like a leaf, and place a hand on his shoulder as I meet his tear-streaked, dust-covered face. "You did well protecting your family, but I need you to continue to be brave. Go inside with your family and don't come out until we've cleared the others."

I rise to my feet and lock eyes with his father and mother, who are standing behind him, hand in hand. The father acknowledges me with a nod, silently expressing gratitude, and then guides his family indoors. I tear my eyes away as more screams fill the air.

Where the hell is Nero?

15
SYBIL

The chilly wind bites at my exposed skin, prompting me to pull my cloak tighter. The air feels thin and crisp, a stark contrast to the mild temperatures I'd become used to in the library. I turn in a circle, and my lips part in a mixture of awe and trepidation. With each step, my boots crunch through ankle-deep snow, immersing us in a winter wonderland. Towering pine trees surround us, their branches drooping under the weight of the glistening white powder. The bright white snow against the dark green of the evergreens creates a scene straight out of a fairytale, simultaneously breathtaking and eerie. It's as if nature has cast a spell on this place, isolating it from the rest of the world.

"How long does winter last in Shadowvale? In our village, we'd be preparing for spring plantings by now," I say, rubbing my arms for warmth.

"We're close to the Armaghdale forest border, according to the map," Marcelene says as she unscrolls the parchment. "But this close to the mountain range, I suspect the winter keeps her grip tight on the land." Pointing to smoke curling in the air, she continues, "It looks like the village is only a short distance away. We don't want to linger alone in the woods for too long. Even in the daylight, beasts hide in the shadows."

She starts in the direction of the smoke, bow in hand, and I quickly follow, my thumb caressing the hilt of my dagger.

"What will we do when we find the thief?" I ask, pushing a large branch out of my way. Above us, the songbirds fill the air with their chanting."I suppose question them to see if they–"

"Nero?" I cry out and run as fast as my legs can go as I see his giant frame lift an axe and bring it slamming down toward a shadow chimera, who dodges it with ease. The skin of his bare chest and arms glimmers with a sheen of sweat mingling with scattered scales as he stands to his full height and glances over his shoulder at me.

"Sybil?" Taking advantage of a momentary distraction, the beast pounces on Nero, knocking him to the ground. The snow turns red as its claws dig into his flesh. Meanwhile, three other males encircle another shadow chimera, swords in hand.

I swiftly throw my gear and Lemon to the ground, drawing both daggers. In the span of an instant, this place has turned from fairytale to nightmare. Next to me, Marcelene readies her arrow. Together, we run, eyes fixed on the creatures.

Nero struggles with the beast, flames dancing up his arms.

"I can't shoot from here. I need high ground," Marcelene says, looking around for a point of advantage.

"The trees," I say and make sure not to lose sight of Nero. "You have to climb on a tree. I'll distract the monsters. That should buy you enough time." I dart away. Leaping over a fallen log, I tap into my magic, feeling my body transform into my demi-form.

This has to work.

"Watch out!" Nero's warning cry reaches my ears, but it's

too late. A loud growl shakes the air before I am thrown into a tree and snow cascades onto my head, burying me under its thick cover. I start moving my arms and legs as the little air left in my lungs starts to burn. Cold seeps into my fingers and toes until I will myself to calm down.

I am not helpless.

Let the magic become you.

Reaching deep inside my magic well, I let the reins with which I have been limiting my powers my whole life fall. Warm and powerful light courses through me in a rush, and with a final exhale, I let it explode out of me. When I open my eyes, snowflakes are gently falling over me like in a dream.

The screeching sounds of the shadow beasts take me back to reality just in time to see a third one—its fangs bared and tail whipping—lunging toward me.

I roll to my right and dodge its attack, narrowly avoiding its razor-sharp teeth. Adrenaline surges through my veins as I slash at the creature with my daggers, aiming for its vulnerable spots. My dagger finds its home. Hot blood pours over my hand as the beast yanks away deeper into the forest, taking my blade with it. I turn, charging toward Nero, who still wrestles with the chimera.

"Over here, you ugly brute!" I yell, smacking a large stick against the trunk of the nearest tree. I hold fast to my remaining dagger, my knuckles blanching, chest heaving as the chimera pauses and glances up. It's all the time Marcelene needs as her arrow finds its mark in the shadow chimera's side. The beast howls in pain, momentarily distracted from its assault on Nero. Taking advantage of the distraction, Nero summons a blazing inferno, engulfing the beast.

The intense heat radiates through the clearing, causing the snow to melt beneath our feet. The scent of singed fur fills the air as the shadow beast thrashes in agony. Its resilience is astounding; it claws its way out of the flames, its eyes glowing with an otherworldly hunger.

I leap back into the fray, my daggers glinting in the fading light. Every strike is precise, every movement calculated just as I've practiced. The shadow beast retaliates, but I dodge out of the way and its claws slash through the air, leaving deep gashes in the tree trunks.

Marcelene's arrows rain down on the creature, finding their mark with deadly accuracy. The shadow beast howls in fury, its strength waning with each hit. We press on, refusing to relent, our teamwork seamlessly synchronizing. As the final blow lands, the shadow beast collapses to the ground, its form dissolving into shadowy wisps.

"Thanks, lass," Nero says as he pushes himself to his feet, the gouges in his flesh already knitting themselves together leaving dried blood in their wake. We all turn to face the remaining chimera who had taken down two of the shifters. Having transformed into their humanoid forms, they lay on the ground clutching their sides as blood seeped from their wounds.

"Thank me later," I say as the third chimera returns from the forest, heading straight for us.

With a roar, Nero grabs one of the fallen shifter's swords from the ground, flames licking up its blade, and charges toward the two remaining beasts. He jumps, using his wings to propel himself up into the air before landing on the creature's back and plunging it directly into the heart. The chimera lets out a furious howl.

My muscles lock up as the creature stalks toward me, chest constricted until I feel like I can't breathe.

A hero is a hero because even when hope is lost, even when everything you do amounts to nothing and shows no promise, you keep trying. You fight.

Filled with a renewed determination, I delve deep into the well of my magic. The chimera lunges toward me, but I am undeterred. A glow emanates from my hands as it arches above me. Ignoring the burning scrape of flesh tearing, I plunge my hands deep into its fur while its claws dig into my shoulders.

A scream tears from my lips as I channel everything I have into killing the beast. No, I am not channeling my magic, I am becoming light itself. My powers engulfs the creature, enveloping it until it dissolves into wisps of smoke and shadow.

Silence descends upon the clearing, broken only by our heavy breaths. Head pounding and vision tunneling, I focus on the feel of the snow against my heated skin, my beating heart echoing in my ears.

"Alpheaia, I never–" Nero drops into a bow, his wings sending a small gust of wind that knocks snow to the ground.

A wail of pain rents the air and I push past him. Not far away, three men lay on the snowy ground, their chests moving erratically. I fall to my knees beside them. There's blood every-where, and suddenly I'm back in the forest on my knees, as Kela bleeds out beneath me. Their pain is so intense I can feel it, feel their injuries without laying a hand on them. They are dying, like so many before them.

"I can't do this." My throat tightens and I freeze, my legs refusing to move. I failed Kela, and now I'd fail these people, shifters and elementals who were depending on me to take down a queen bent on using them for their powers.

"Ye can do this. I know ye can," Nero urges as he grips my shoulders, momentarily blocking the view.

"Wh-where is the healer? Don't they have a healer?" I can't keep the panic out of my voice and a cold sheen of sweat breaks out along my skin.

"We're too far from the village. They won't make it, lass. Tell me what ye need," he says, crouching beside me.

"Sybil," Marcelene's voice cuts in, and I turn to face her. She gives my hand a reassuring squeeze. "You can do this. Just like you practiced."

Closing my eyes, I inhale deeply. Lemon has found his way to our side and sits in the lap of the male propped up against the tree, licking his wounds.

"Help, please. It hurts." The wolf shifter, now in his humanoid form, writhes on the ground, clutching his leg where a large shaft of wood sticks out from where he fell. Blood oozes around the injury and has soaked his torn breeches. His partner, equally bruised and battered, sits wiping his brow. An earth elemental, I suspect, by the way the branches and shrubbery seem to lean toward him.

"It's okay, I'm not leaving you in this forest. You're coming back home with me," his partner whispers as he leans forward and presses a gentle kiss to the wolf shifter's forehead.

Breathe, Sybil. Breath.

"I need to focus on this one first. He's lost too much blood. The other two need their wounds cleaned, but they will survive with time." I nod and push my torn sleeves up to my elbows, letting instinct guide me.

"I've got your healing satchel," Marcelene says. "Dragon boy, we need hot water." She pulls a small metal pot from her bag and fills it with snow.

"As ye wish," he replies before grabbing the bowl and engulfing it in flames.

I kneel next to the young male shifter. My hands tremble slightly as I probe his flesh with my fingertips, examining the extent of the wound. Was it only a few months ago that I was in a similar position? Deep in the forest, my magic trapped just beneath my skin as I prayed to the Goddess that the extent of my healing knowledge could save Edmund.

"What is your name?"

"M-m-matthew," he says, sweat beading along his brow. I meet his green eyes, watching as the color drains from his face. Nero crouches across from me, Marcelene at his side with a stack of fresh linens and a bucket of steaming water.

"Okay, Matthew." I smile and reach deep into my magic, finding it ready to be molded at will. The young male's eyes are transfixed on my face and my horn. Using his distraction, I signal to Nero, who grasps the edge of the wood. The sound of tearing flesh is drowned out by Matthew's scream before he passes out and Marcelene gently lowers him to the ground.

I work quickly, cleaning the wound, probing with my magic to ensure no slivers of wood are left behind to fester before I will the muscles and tissue to knit back together. Lemon gingerly ascends to the wound, pressing his tiny paws against the man's skin, and I can sense the intertwining of our magic as the wound gradually heals. By the time I'm finished, my muscles quiver. I fall back, bracing my arms behind as I survey the neat pink scar running down his leg.

"Well, he'll likely be sore tomorrow," I say, exhaustion weighing heavily on me.

"But he will live to see another day, and use his leg. Not all are so lucky," his companion says, pulling him into his lap and gently stroking the hair away from his sweaty forehead.

Swaying on my feet from the excessive use of magic, I step closer to my friends.

"Nero, this is Marcelene. Marcelene, this is Nero. He's a half draken shifter, half elemental. I owe him my life."

"It's a pleasure to meet you," Marcelene says with a quick nod before turning the conversation back to more pressing matters. "You wouldn't happen to have seen a thief around here, would you?"

Nero pauses, eyebrows furrowed as he studies her.

"Hello," she says, snapping her fingers in front of his face. "I thought you said he was the smart one."

I roll my eyes, linking an arm with her. "Oh he is. He's just dumbfounded by your beauty. Nero, where is Aramis? I have so much to tell you."

"Lass, we've been worried sick about ye since the avalanche, but we couldn't dig ye out so we traveled south to the rebel camp to ask for help." He pauses.

"But?" I raise an eyebrow.

"So ye see, the rebels aren't exactly happy with the royal family right now or with what Tricella has been doing and all," he says.

The air suddenly fills with a blood-curdling scream from the village. My heart races as I instinctively look up, only to witness a monstrous bird of smoke and shadow hurtling toward the earth.

"Nero, where is Aramis?"

16
SYBIL

My heart pounds as I sling my healing satchel onto my back, tuck Lemon into my front pocket and run.

Where were all these shadow beasts coming from?

"Nero, how many warriors does the village have?" My legs scream as I push them to go faster, my breath coming in ragged pants. We must reach the village before that creature does.

"Sybil, this is the rebel camp. It's mostly refugee families."

I made it to the rebel camp.

The thought is fleeting but my heart goes out to Kela. She should have been here with me.

The roars of the shadow beasts grow louder, echoing in the air. My veins flood with adrenaline, heart pounding so loudly in my ears that it urges me to push even harder.

As we reach the west border of the camp, smoke billows from the burning tents, making us all cough and cover our eyes. A group of water elementals channel streams of water toward the flames, whilst wind elementals keep the flames from leaping onto other tents. The shock of seeing more elementals here slows my steps, but there's no time to linger.

"That way," Nero points to the left. We weave and dodge falling debris, sprinting through the chaos and leaping over burning wreckage. The camp is in chaos; hundreds are injured but I keep going. My magic–whatever is left of it–can help take the beasts down. I have done it once; I can do it again.

Our steps falter as the ground starts trembling beneath us. The movement is so sudden, people around us fall like leaves to their feet and tents crash down into heaps.

"What was that?" I yell as we round the corner on careful steps.

At the center of what was supposedly the heart of the campsite, a chasm has opened in the ground, and from it, a towering basilisk made of shadows emerges. Its bifurcate tongue slithers over sharp teeth the length of my forearm as it takes in the helpless people beneath it running like ants.

"Oh, Goddess me," Nero gasps, his eyes following the length of the basilisk.

"Nope," Marcelene says at my side as she notches an arrow into her bow. "I can do spiders, chimera and giant birds, but basilisks are where I draw the line."

When its entire serpentine length has emerged from the depths of the earth, its scales dark and sharp, the basilisk swings its tail, slamming into the nearest building. More warriors, swords in hand, approach but their determination soon falters as the creature's scales are too thick for mortal weapons. Earth elementals send debris flying in its direction whilst Nero uses fire to sear its face, but that only seems to anger the basilisk further as it tries to snap warriors from the crowd. Tiger shifters and earth elementals challenge the crea-ture but again, nothing seems to stop its rage nor cause harm. The snake emits a sinister hiss and swipes out its tail, knocking three men down into the chasm, their screams deafening.

"Sybil," Marcelene says, tugging my arm in the other direction where a dozen shadow wolves are attacking every tent, dragging out anyone hiding in it.

"Help them! I'll take care of the basilisk."

"Nero," I scream, trying to get his attention.

The echoes of arrows and the distant whimpers of canines serve as a comforting reminder that Marcelene is right behind me. I pull on my magic, hoping it will help Nero notice me, but I have exuded all my reserves.

"Nero! We have to get away from the buildings." The draken lands dangerously close to the creature with a thud and follows my gaze toward the main building who dangerously teeters, as if on the verge of collapse.

"We have to lead it away from here," I scream, pointing toward a path through the camp leading back to the woods.

He turns, flashing me a wide toothy grin before flaring out his wings and launching back into the sky. I take off running down the path, glancing over my shoulder.

Come on Nero, come on.

A fireball blasts from the sky above me, directly toward the serpentine beast. I instinctively cover my head and turn to watch. Nero shoots again, this time angling the basilisk in my direction. With a mighty swing, the beast falls and locks eyes with me, emitting an unholy screech before lunging toward me.

Oh.

My heart pounds in my chest as I take off running down the narrow road flanked by dilapidated houses. Cold sweat breaks out along my skin, mingling with the dirt and grime. Each gasp for air feels futile, as if my lungs have forgotten how to draw breath, but I shake my head to clear my vision and push on. After weeks spent in the library, my body is rebelling against the exertion.

Just a little bit further.

Nero keeps throwing fireballs from above, guiding the basilisk in my direction. His rough scales dig through the snow and ground. The sound of tents and huts breaking in its wake makes my heart clench. This is all these people have left of their homes, and it's all going up in flames.

As I reach a snow covered clearing outside the camp's border, I stop and turn toward the basilisk. The creature is only a handful of feet away and I pray to the Goddess this will work.

I roll my sleeves and drop my satchel before pulling on my magic reserve. This time, the light does not rush toward me as it did for the chimera. I have to scrape for it, find the last dregs. It feels like imploding. Everything hurts, I can feel my muscles straining, my throat closing. Tears stream down my cheeks, but I keep breathing, opening myself to the magic flowing in my veins.

One last push, Sybil.

Light explodes and I charge toward the basilisk, hands extended in its direction. I see warriors and shifters who have gathered at the edge of the clearing in aid covering their eyes, even Nero turns away from me. I channel everything toward the beast, screaming until I feel the ground beneath my feet shift. My body burns as if I am a star about to be born. The light seeps from my skin and my hair is so bright it blinds even me, until the basilisk is nothing more than wisps of shadows and heaps of ash.

My knees buckle, exhaustion taking over. Before I reach the ground, large hands grab me.

"Sybil."

A weak smile paints my lips. What a gift to hear Aramis' voice as I'm about to die.

"My love." A calloused hand cups my cheek, but I am so, so tired and my eyes refuse to open. *Magic isn't limitless*, I hear Cassara chide in my head, and she is right.

I hear murmurs and wings clapping so close to me I can feel their breeze on my cheeks.

"This makes no sense. The wards on the borders of the camp are supposed to hide us. I... I don't understand," someone says.

Strong arms lift me. They cradle me as my head perfectly nests in the nook between their shoulder and neck.

And I finally feel at home.

I have often come close to death, and it has always been a frightening experience.

There have been moments where I have felt only a step away from the veil and held onto life with my bare teeth wanting to survive. Yet, when I faced the basilisk, when my own magic had started to consume me, I was at peace. Content to sacrifice my life to save others. Now, as I stand on that edge, ready to cross into the next world and see my parents again, something tugs me back.

Come back to me, a gentle voice whispers in my ear, and I nod. I close my eyes and let myself fall backward into the silver lake to follow the golden strand calling to me.

I sit up, clutching my neck with both hands, coughing and panting. Confusion clouds my mind, golden light makes it hard for me to open my eyes and my heart beats erratically. Then, comes the pain. The stiffness in my body hits me and I struggle to breath, grieving the peace I had felt just a moment ago.

"Easy," someone says, sitting next to me. He takes my hand in his and squeezes gently. "Breathe, Sybil."

And I do as he says.

Slowly, he guides me down again until I'm lying on what feels like a hay mattress. His finger follows the edges of my face, and I linger in his touch.

Please, let it be him. I pray, not knowing what I'll do if I find out Aramis has not survived the attack.

My eyelashes flutter, eyes adjusting to the light and I weep. Tears stream down my face as I meet his piercing blue eyes. Silvery golden strands—longer than I remember—frame his hollow cheeks, graced with more stubble than I have ever seen on him. He holds a breath, his bottom lip quivering.

"You're alive," I whisper.

"You're alive," he echoes, and with the little strength I have left in me, I pull him closer with desperation. Our lips meet in a kiss that holds more words than either of us are able to proffer. I fist his tunic, one hand around his neck. Goddess, how can I ever live without this? Without him.

But is this the mating bond or my true feelings?

Aramis senses the change and unlocks the hold I have on him. He stands and I fight the urge to cover my mouth. His ripped pants are stained with blood and his tunic is slashed, revealing cuts and dried blood on his chest. There are cuffs on his wrists, ones I am familiar with. Aramis follows my gaze and shakes his head.

"The irony is not lost on me," he chuckles. I attempt to join but the pain in my side turns laughter into jolts of pain.

"Careful, Sybil. Your body is still recovering." In the little wooden hut we're in, there's only the bed I am lying on and the chair Aramis pulls closer to sit.

"Recovering?" I glance at my body then meet his gaze. "How long have I been out?" I strain my neck slightly to peek out the glassless window behind him, but the bed sits too low on the ground. Aramis leans forward, resting his elbows on his knees.

"What you did in the clearing the other day... you saved us but... you almost burned yourself up." He rakes a hand through his hair, a telltale signal for when anxiety is creeping up on him. I extend a hand and rest it on his knee. "You've been out nearly a full day."

"I only have vague memories," I admit.

"I was battling a shadow beast, on the west border." He shakes his head in disbelief. "It was chaos, Sybil. Men, women, even children have died before my eyes. And then I see this woman running through camp with a basilisk following her, and I think to myself, she must be utterly insane." I scoff, but Aramis' eyes look at me with so much apprehension it makes my heart burst. He catches a tear with the back of his hand and sits up straight.

"Imagine my surprise when that woman faced the basilisk, and I realize she was the most beautiful woman I have ever seen. The woman I love."

Tears stream down my face again but I can't move. Real or not real?

"I have never run so quickly in my entire life, Sybil. When I saw you heading to the clearing, I ignored everything else. I was not going to see you die right in front of my eyes. And then..." He rakes his hand through his hair again. "You lit up like a star in the night sky. You became the beacon of hope these people have been waiting for. But all I could see was your magic consuming you. I... I thought I'd lost you." He kneels at the bed and buries his face next to my stomach.

"I am alive," I whisper, caressing his hair. "I am here." Quiet sobs make his body jump.

We stay like that as the sun completes his descent, and

when the stars litter the sky, Aramis goes to get us some food and wood for a fire. I fight the urge to jump out of bed and look for the thief. Is he even still here after the attack? Is he alive?

There's so much I have to tell Aramis, Nero, and the rebels about my discoveries, so much we have to prepare. But even though my spirit is high, my body is a broken shell.

Time heals all wounds, my mother's voice lulls in my head, but time is a luxury I don't have.

"Everyone is safe," Aramis tells me upon his return. "Nero is taking care of your friend, the witch…"

"Marcelene, and I am not surprised. I had sensed a certain interest from Nero, but I don't think he'll have it easy with her." Aramis hands me a steaming cup of tea and helps me sit up in the bed. The fire casts shadows over his face, his eyebrows are furrowed, and I can sense there's something he is struggling to share.

"Tell me," I say, tilting my head.

He swallows and goes to adjust a log in the small hearth in the corner of the hut, turning his back to me.

"The Council wants to see you tomorrow. I have tried to give you some more time, but they've been waiting for you and the situation is bad." His large shoulders raise and fall with each breath, and I notice how much weight he has lost. What has transpired in the time we have been apart?

"The rebels had systems in place to help refugees, to bring food to those close to the castle, I even helped them plan a strategy to secretly enter the citadel and save the shifters in the dungeons. And now it's all gone."

"And you're carrying the guilt of it on your shoulders."

Aramis freezes and after a moment, he whispers, "I should have stopped her when I had the chance."

I rest my mug on the floor and slowly move my legs over the edge of the bed. They feel stiff and achy, but I welcome the cold floorboards underneath my feet. One wiggling step after the other, I reach Aramis and tug him up from where he crouches. When my eyes lay on his beautiful face as he towers over me, the bond in my core tugs me closer. Real or not real?

"I don't know what these people have put you through, but I see you, Aramis. We have all made mistakes in our pasts, but it's how we own up to them and try to do better that matters." I caress his cheek and wish he could see himself as I see him. "You are here, with me, with us, fighting. That *means* something. We will avenge those that have lost their lives and end Tricella's reign of terror. Trust me."

He takes my hand and kisses the back of it.

"I told you once, Sybil Vandeleur. I will follow you until the end of time itself, if you'll have me."

17
SYBIL

I drag myself by sheer will away from the injured.

After spending the night in the hut with Aramis–he on the floor as I lay on the hay mattress–I had woken up still aching but more energized, well enough to help the infirmary. Aramis had left to lend a hand with the reconstructions, needing to do something practical to help the people instead of sitting around the Council's table.

The morning had been somewhat awkward. Aramis had avoided my gaze and I felt like a fish out of water. After so many weeks of longing, I realize we have both changed, and the uncertain nature of my feelings keeps me stepping away from him rather than running into his arms.

An elemental with brown hair, Evolet, walks me to a newly erected tent at the center of the camp—the new home of the Council of Thorns.

"It's very kind of you to help with the injured. It is dangerous to stay here now that the Queen has found us, but we can't leave them behind," Evolet walks steadfast, and I struggle to keep up with her. Thankfully, Aramis had found some breeches and a tunic for me to wear after my dress had been ruined in battle, and it helps dodging all the rubble and broken tents.

"I may not be a healer in the traditional sense, but I do live by the healer codex. It's my duty to help," I say in between breaths.

All around us, there's silence at the camp, occasionally broken by the screams of those getting treatment. People are digging through the rubble, trying to save whatever remains of their belongings. So many tears are being shed, prayers are whispered at all hours, and rows of white linens cover the bravest of us all. But no one is alone. No matter where I look, shifters and elementals are supporting each other, strengthening that sense of community Tricella will never be able to break.

Evolet holds one of the tent's flaps open and nods for me to enter.

"We have to leave as soon as possible," a woman says. At the sight of her, I nearly fall to my knees. She is the exact copy of Kela.

The inside of the tent is a lot smaller than I expected, but then, there's about fifteen adults sitting around a makeshift table, including Nero and Marcelene. Half burnt maps are on display, everyone has exhausted expressions on their faces.

"According to the healers' reports, the injured need at least two more days before they can be moved. And even then, most will have to be carried on stretchers. It will be a slow and diffi-cult march," the man next to her explains, lovingly covering her hand with his.

"There's no more stalling. We have to plead for refuge in the Kallistar regi—"

"Sybil Vandaleur," the old man at the head of the table

interjects. With some difficulty, he uses the arms of his chair to lift himself, but I see his frail form shaking. Kela's mother on his right extends a helping hand, but the man signals her to stop. "My name is Victor Hawthorne, I am a tiger shifter and head of this council. Please, take a seat."

I sit at the other end of the table, back straight and Victor takes his seat again. Marcelene looks in my direction and smiles imperceptibly. Her usually pristine blond hair is darkened by ash, wrapped tightly into a bun. Even Nero, whose spirit rarely falters, has a lost look in his eyes.

"At present, the Queen's attack has depleted the rebellion to a point of crisis. We are not able to continue our missions until we can take the refugees here to safety. It is still unsure how the Queen found our location. We were assured the wards put in place would help hide us from the Queen's seer but alas, they failed—"

"Ten mole shifters, six Earth elementals and two owl shifters are currently digging their way to what is surely a death trap," a tall man with broad shoulders, chestnut hair, and a close cropped beard chimes in. "Let me tell you how the Queen found us. That scumbag of a prince has told her. I warned you all about this." He slams his hands on the table, and I jump at the sound and accusation.

"Aries, we have talked about this," a broad man sitting next to Kela's mum says as he shakes his head.

"Oh, so you're just going to let them die, like your daughter, Roger?"

Roger leans over the table, making his chair fall backward, and fists Aris' tunic, pulling him inches from his face.

Nero and three more of the rebels stand, ready to intervene.

"You better shut up," he shouts. Aris grinds his teeth but lifts his hands until Roger drops him and they all sit back around the table.

"Enough," Victor proclaims with his low guttural word. "The last couple of days have tested all of us but we cannot allow her to divide us. We are not going to abandon them, Aries."

A small female with pale skin, dark red hair, and brown eyes enters the tent. Victor gestures to her to come closer. "Phoebe, welcome. Thank you for joining us."

"Of course. I came to officially agree to infiltrate the castle," Phoebe says, squaring her shoulders. Two white ears twitch up from her hair as a white fluffy tail sweeps behind her.

People around the table start looking at each other in confusion.

"Absolutely not, it is too dangerous," Roger says and Aries agrees.

"What a great idea." Nero pinches his nose and I notice Marcelene biting her lip.

Phoebe balls her fists on the table as she stares the men down. "You can all say what you want. I am going. Between my shifter abilities and shadow magic, I'll go undetected. I can warn those in the tunnels and then attempt to go into the castle to gather information about how they found us."

"Shadow magic?" I ask, turning toward her.

Phoebe steps back and the shadows begin to waver until they swallow her completely from sight. My eyes light up and I'm at a loss for words. She shrugs sheepishly.

"My father was an arctic fox shifter, my mother was a shadow elemental. She was a chambermaid for the court of Queen Rose before she passed, Goddess bless her soul. I will use the crypts to access the castle. There'll be eighteen of us sneaking in, but they won't see me."

The room erupts into chaos, but all I can think of is that this could also be a chance for us to get some answers.

"Phoebe," I say. "Would you mind one more mission?"

Silence ensues and everyone focuses their attention back to me.

"Marcelene," Victor adds. "Has informed us about your discoveries at the library, Sybil. And of course, we have all witnessed your powers. But how can Phoebe be of assistance?"

"Well, we believe that Tricella is in possession of one, or potentially two, books about magic penned by the Goddess herself. We have a potential lead that could tell us more about them, but it would not hurt to double check." I turn to Phoebe, who's taking in every word I say with meticulous attention. "I don't know what the books look like, but they are some of the most powerful things ever created in Craeweth. I believe you'll know when you find them."

"I will try my best to find the information you seek, but now, if you don't mind, I will take my leave to prepare for my imminent mission."

She turns to Victor, who nods in agreement, and the young woman leaves the tent.

"What is this lead you're talking about?" Aris asks, arms crossed over his chest.

I meet Marcelene's eyes, trying to understand how much she has told them whilst a plan takes root in my head.

"Before I share the details, there's the matter of Aramis," I say, lifting my chin. "I understand your mistrust in his regards, but from what I have seen, he has proven loyal to the cause. Why continue treating him like the enemy? Would the enemy help you succeed? Kill the monsters he supposedly helped create and help rebuild your homes? Take those cuffs off him, for Goddess' sake."

Aris laughs, and I decide I'll happily slap him at the first occasion.

"You are not mistaken. Aramis has lent a helping hand to us all these last few weeks," Victor answers. "But the magic we have used on his cuffs is ancient, Sybil. We cannot temper with them even if we wished to. The cuffs will open only when Aramis proves his worth in the eyes of the Goddess."

"But he is free to go?" I ask, pointing my finger to the table.

Aries is about to jump out of his chair, and I wonder what the story between him and Aramis is, but before he can inter-ject, Victor exclaims a loud, "Yes."

I notice Nero's shoulders relaxing, eyes closing at this proclamation, and I revel in this little victory.

"Wonderful, in that case, I am looking for a thief."

"There is no way that scumbag down in the cells is the male you're looking for," Roger says as he leads us down the stairs. "We caught him rifling through the storage, pockets full of coins and stolen jewelry—not magical books."

"The magic doesn't lie," Marcelene says.

After the Council meeting ended, I had insisted for Nero to rush and get Aramis to join us on our way to the cells. Aramis' face glistened with sweat, his hair pushed back as he carried an axe he used to cut more firewood to keep everyone warm. He had only smiled at me, leaving some space between us, but inside, I burned.

Real or not real? I keep asking myself and feel like I am losing my mind.

"Didn't think I'd be back here so soon," Aramis jokes but I see his gaze getting lost in old memories.

"Ay, mate. I am sorry I could not get ye out sooner." The draken rests his arm on Aramis' shoulders. "But yer free now. Just windless." He snickers to which Aramis' grins.

I have missed this.

The cells are located outside the northern border,

concealed amidst towering trees. The aged building is adorned with lifeless grass that creeps its way up the walls of the simple, white-washed structure. Its exterior is unadorned, save for a substantial door and multiple diminutive barred windows leading to a lower level. Despite its plain exterior, familiar magic radiates off the walls reminiscent of... my eyes are drawn to the cuffs around Aramis' wrist and I shiver.

Roger inserts a big, rusted key in the main door, which creaks and objects.

"Axton," Roger calls as we follow him into the hallway one by one. He stops in front of the last cell and pounds on the iron bars. "Wake up, we have some questions for you."

A dark form in the corner moves, lazily stretching before he turns and centers his gaze on me. His hair is matted, clothes are stained, and the stench of human excrements coming from him is overwhelming, but I don't move.

"Oh, what a treat. Have you come to free me too, beauti-ful?" he says as he winks. "I told this here *prince* you'd nee–"

"Watch your tongue before you lose it," Aramis growls, hands clenching at his side as he glares at the male through the bars.

"Axton, I am Sybil," I say, crossing my arms over my chest at his leering stare. "We are told you are a brilliant thief, one of the best in Craeweth, the legends say? What an injustice having you locked up in here."

Roger and Aramis' heads shoot in my direction, confused at my flattering words to Axton.

"Oh what a lovely name for such a beautiful creature." He smiles, eyes twinkling. My stomach twists uneasily. "You are correct, darling. Axton Silverspark of Pruatho. And I can only agree, I should not be here. Can you help?" He winks, and I see Aramis' fists clenching with the corner of my eye.

"Well, I was actually hoping you would help me. I have

found this," I say and take the little piece of parchment with the dagger and heart out of my pocket. "At what is probably your masterpiece."

Axton's eyes shine in the light of the torches hanging from the walls, and I know I am pushing the right buttons.

"I don't know what you're talking about," Axton says, flicking at invisible dust on his shoulder.

"I think you do," Aramis growls. I flinch as he slams a fist against the iron bar, the sound reverberating through the room. "Answer them truthfully."

He turns back to me and runs his gaze down my body. "If you could sweet talk my way out of here like you did to blondie over here, I could be *persuaded* to remember."

"Ye will be respectful of the ladies, else we will have to persuade the information out of you in other ways," Nero says, standing to his full towering height and snapping his wings.

"The council has not passed judgment for his crimes of theft. They will not agree to free him just to give you answers," Roger says.

I turn and face the thief once again. "Come on, Axton. Are you trying to tell me another thief, much more brilliant than you, stole the most powerful magical artifacts ever created?"

"Sybil," Marcelene admonishes, eyebrows raised.

Axton raises up his hands in defense.

"Entering that mountain was a bitch of a job," he admits with a smirk. "Although stealing magical artifacts is behind me. She said she had told me everything she discovered during her studies, only coincidentally, she forgot to mention the gigantic spiders nesting underneath the bloody mountain." Axton shakes his head, but I don't say anything, hoping he'll just keep talking. "The queen tried to double cross me after delivering my end of the bargain. I barely escaped with my life.

So, I lied to her." His grin widens; this information will require leverage.

"What do you want, Axton? Apart from your freedom, that is."

"How about we start with better accommodation, although I am certain we won't be staying here for much longer. Awful noise those beasts make. I was almost relieved to be locked down here—"

"Deal," I say. Roger will not be happy.

"You see, when I reached that dusty chamber, I took both books as instructed by Tricella. Goddess, you should have seen her back then. The woman was nothing, small folk really. Had I known that bloody book would be the key to making her queen, I would have kept it!"

"Axton, focus," Aramis chides.

"Anyway, I get to our meeting point and the woman and her pet, tall, lanky guy, start screaming at me about why it took so long and then only deliver half of the payment. And as you said, sweetheart, I am not just any thief, I am a professional. So, I lied to her, and told her there was only one book."

"How did you prove it to her?" Marcelene asks.

"Secret of the trade, darl—" Nero grabs one of the bars and Axton rolls his eyes.

"Okay, okay. I use an invisibility amulet. Well, used, that's gone too, just like your precious book. I gave Tricella one of the books and decided to keep the other for myself, thinking I could sell it for a higher profit than what she offered." He gestures to me as if it's the most logical thing to do. "You don't hire a thief expecting him to be honest, darling. She was outraged, of course. You should have seen her! Until she saw the book and her eyes lit up and she set off into the sunshine with her pet."

This confirms Tricella's possession of the Book of Darkness.

"Where is the other book now?" I ask, barely containing the excitement in my voice. "Do you still have it?"

"Well," he laughs. "Am I free, Sybil?"

"Depends on your answer."

"There is one tiny problem." He crosses his arms over his chest and leans against the wall of the cell. "I don't have the book. It was stolen from me over fifty years ago by a great dragon, along with all my possessions–including my amulet–after I tried to take its golden egg."

"Ye tried to steal a dragon egg? Are ye dolt in the head?" Nero doubles over, laughing. "That's the most ridiculous story I've ever heard. Yer full of shit."

"Are you saying a *dragon* has the Book of Light?" My stomach plummets as I think of all the fairytales I've read of knights in shining armor fighting dragons who demolished whole villages. "I thought dragons were extinct decades ago."

"Aye, it's because they mostly keep to themselves as their numbers dwindle. Aramis and I used to–"

"Where is this dragon, then? And how did it come into possession of the book?" Marcelene interrupts Nero, and he looks at her like a scolded puppy.

"Well, after parting ways with Tricella, I set on the path Verdigris falls to find a boat to the island of Asthroth. I knew if I wanted a chance at selling something as powerful as the book, I had to go somewhere people don't ask questions but pay their dues. I was crossing through a mountain range when I heard this deafening screech. I looked up and a stream of fire exited this cave right above my head. Do you know how much dragon eggs are worth?"

When no one encourages Axton's dive into details, he rolls his eyes.

"Curiosity took the best of me, and I entered the dragon's den, who promptly tried to murder me but instead ended up taking everything I owned and I ran butt naked."

The thief looks down at his tattered boots and we're all in silence, trying to process the utter idiocy of this man.

"You're coming with us," Aramis breaks the silence and my head snaps to him. "You are going to take us to the dragon and help us get the book back."

Axton lowers himself to the ground, laughing maniacally.

"You all have a death wish. And I already worry about how the hell I am going to convince the Council to let him go."

18
ARAMIS

I have always known who I am, down deep to my core.

They don't leave you much freedom when you're born the son of the king. So, as prince, you're immediately forced to dress a certain way, walk, talk and think a certain way. I am not trying to hide behind the way I was brought up, I was still making choices even when I thought I did not have any. But now that everything that has ever defined me has been taken from me, I don't know how to rebuild.

The axe flies down with precision, and snow flies in the air when the log splits in two. It has been difficult finding dry enough wood for the fires, and after half of the refugees lost their homes, warmth is needed more than ever.

Another log splits in two.

A bloody dragon. How are we going to deal with that?

The cuffs on my wrist rattle against the axe's hilt. It has been so long since I have last felt magic cursing through my veins–the wind wrapping itself around my fingers–that I've become numb to the absence.

How do you prove your worth?

After meeting Axton, Sybil and Marcelene had returned to the infirmary to ready as many injured as possible for their upcoming travels. Two days, that's the time the Council has agreed on waiting before moving the camp, so we too have agreed to stay and help as much as we can before searching for the dragon.

Another log splits. I dry the sweat on my brow.

We find the dragon. We get the book. We kill Tricella.

I have been repeating the plan over and over in my mind, obsessively. The key to the plan is Sybil. Memories of her petite body bursting into light, with no control or direction, make me swing my axe harder and the log explodes and splinters. She could have killed herself.

I drop the axe and sit on the cold snow.

"Tired already?" Aries asks with a snicker.

"This is not the time," I wave him off, knowing that's exactly what's going to make him stay. Ever since Victor has assigned Aries as my guard, the shifter has been the bane of my existence. Although, fighting side by side during the shadow beast's attack has helped make him less of an asshole.

"I would have bet you'd be sneaking off at any chance to spend some time with your lady." He swings his dagger in his hands, leaning against a nearby pine.

"Are you here to give me love advice now, Aries?" I turn to him with furrowed brows and wipe the sweat off my forehead with the cuff of my sleeve.

"Fuck that. I'm just surprised you're here. And when you're not here, you're building tents or stretchers for the injured. Goddess, I've even seen you cook. Don't you think these poor souls have endured enough?"

I look away, suddenly feeling exposed by Aries' honesty. "I've been telling you since the day I first met you in the woods that I am here to help."

"And to get your girl back." The truth in his words makes my throat close.

Why wasn't I with Sybil?

I rake a hand through my knotted hair–Goddess knows, I need a haircut–and take some snow to rub between my aching hands. After a moment of silence, I take a deep breath and the words leave my lips on their own accord.

"I am not sure she still wants me. I am not the man I used to be, and I am still looking for the man I want to become."

After the first night spent in my hut, I have hardly had a moment to spare for conversations with her, except for the dinners shared with Nero and Marcelene around the firepit. She avoids my gaze, and every step I take toward her, she takes one step back. I saw her one night, resting on a pile of rubble, massaging her calves, and I could not take my eyes off her. I felt the pull of our bond, telling me to tend to her. To pick her up and run, take her to safety.

But she needs space. This is her destiny, I remind myself.

And I will hold her hand through it all, if she lets me.

"Aha, and I always thought princes had it easy with women!" He snickers. I wonder if I have willingly handed over more reasons for Aries to be unbearable to me.

I pick up the axe and raise it over my head, but pause as he clears his throat.

"I had a wife," he starts, so quiet I can hardly hear. I fight the urge to snap my head in his direction, but I pause, soaking in his story. "I lost her in one of the early attacks. We had no idea what the shadow beasts were at the time. They came out of nowhere and no one knew what to do." Pain laces every word and guilt rushes in like a punch in the gut.

"I'm sorry, Aries." I finally turn to him, setting down the tool. He is mindlessly rolling a golden band on his ring finger I have never noticed before.

"Her name was Emma. She had the spirit of a summer storm. She was headstrong and reckless, always getting herself into trouble to help others. I like to think the Goddess claimed her so early because she realized Emma had too much love to give and was going to become a Goddess herself if not stopped. She had always been one in my eyes." Aries scoffs and looks up at the sky.

The mating bond tugs in my core and I wonder if Aries and Emma were mates too. I shift my gaze back to my reddened hands, hoping the pain of the splinters will distract me from the ache in my heart.

"But I get you, Prince. Never, for a single moment have I ever thought I was worthy of Emma. The woman deserved every crown and jewel in existence, and I was a piece of shit with anger issues. But let me tell you this, now that she is not here, I regret wasting even a second not fighting for her, trying to find faults in something that was so... right."

I can hear the crunch of snow under his boots as Aries steps closer to me. He throws a little sachet with fresh bread next to me.

"For what it's worth, Aramis, you're not half as bad as you think you are. I just like taking the piss out of you. I don't know what the Goddess is expecting from you, but as far as I'm concerned, you're showing your worth. But don't you expect me to go soft on you." He crosses his arms over his chest and raises an eyebrow. "Now, get up and go show the unicorn some love."

Before I can respond, I hear her voice.

"Aramis! Come quickly," Sybil says breathlessly as she runs in my direction. She still has her healing apron ties around her slender waist, pockets full of vials and blood stains on its hem. Her cheeks flush deep crimson as they land on my bare chest, moving slowly to meet my gaze.

"Sybil." I straighten, stepping toward her as I feel the bond urging me to go to her, but I pause. "What is it?"

She shakes her head as if she's waking up from a stupor, hands twisting restlessly.

"Phoebe has returned."

Aries clucks his tongue and tosses me the tunic I had hung on a branch. "Let's go."

I quickly pull the fresh tunic over my head as we follow at her heels back to the council's tent. My eyes devour every movement she makes, hardly able to let her leave my vision. So close, yet so far.

"Sybil." I reach out and slide my hand down her arm until it encompasses her wrist. She inhales sharply and looks at my hand before meeting my eyes again. "No matter what happens, I will be by your side. We will take whatever news we can and plan accordingly to keep this village safe before we go after the book."

"I know." She nods, interlocking her hand with mine and giving me a reassuring squeeze. Marcelene turns the corner of the next tent and into our path.

"Where have you been?" Sybil whispers, and immediately drops my hand to turn to her friend. "You were supposed to be helping me yesterday with the healers. You didn't even come to dinner."

"I've been... around." Marcelene looks between Sybil, Aries and I before cocking her head to the side. Her feline slit pupils stare at us unblinking as her tail flicks back and forth behind her.

Why is she in her demi-form?

"What do you mean? What's going on?" Sybil looks over her shoulder.

"There is something strange going on in this village, but I can't quite put my finger on it," she replies with a shrug. "It's possibly nothing, just wound up from being cooped here, waiting for answers."

As we pass another group of tents, Nero turns onto the main path toward the Council tent and joins us.

"Evolet told me about Phoebe," he immediately says, but his gaze shoots to Marcelene, who bites her lip and looks in the opposite direction. I watch between the two and make a quick note to get some time alone with Nero to find out what is going on.

"Marcelene was telling us there's something going on here and I don't know how to explain it, but I think she's onto something," I say, the corners of my lips pulled down. I hadn't voiced the thought out loud yet, putting it off as just a manifestation of everything that had happened. But no one had yet managed to explain to me who the battered rat shifter who had attacked me in the cell was.

"Now, don't ye get that witch's feline cryptic senses affecting ye." He shrugs and gestures at this town. "These are yer people, Aramis."

I sigh as we arrive at the Council tent, I pull back the flap and gesture inside. "You're probably right. Let's see what the fox has to say."

The rising sunlight filters through the canvas, creating a muted tone as we are the last to take our seats. Nero, Sybil, Marcelene and I sit side by side amongst the council. Aries stands at the far end, the usual smug expression back on his face, but I have a newfound respect for the man.

"We are glad to have you returned to us, Phoebe," Victor says with a nod. "Tell us what you have learned."

Phoebe sits at the other end of the table. Her red hair is disheveled, dark shadows circle her wisp eyes. She probably traveled without stopping, aiming to get us the information she discovered as soon as possible.

"The shifters and elementals building the tunnels have been successfully warned of the threat. They're currently traveling back to the camp but agreed it would be safer to take different routes."

Everyone nods, relieved this first mission went as well as they could have hoped for.

"I successfully entered the castle through the water duct by the crypts," she continues, nodding at me in gratitude. "I eluded the guards and made my way down to the dungeons. The cells are still full of shifters, all alive, for now. But there's more. She's creating new monsters. Grotesque creatures the size of a minotaur, with menacing tusks protruding from their mouths, vacant eyes, and razor-sharp claws. They are made of flesh and bone rather than shadow, but that does not make them any easier to kill. I saw a guard cutting their limbs off, over and over, and they regenerated."

Gasps of horror fill the tent. There's no denying now that, if it comes to a full-fledged war, it will be one of the bloodiest Craeweth has ever seen.

"How many are there?" I ask, calculating the number of soldiers we'd need to have. The odds were stacked against us.

"I cannot say for sure. I stayed as long as I dared but did not explore the lower dungeons," she says with a flick of her tail.

"How many?" I ask again. Will I have to fight my own men? I need to get them out of there. Tricella cannot force them to fight for her.

"Aramis," Nero warns at my side.

"It will be a massacre, Nero. The shadow beasts. Now these monsters, look around you. If we die, the resistance dies. There must be something we can do to prepare for this eventuality. She has attacked once, what stops her from doing it again."

"We will leave this location by the morrow, but Aramis is right, we don't have the forces to launch an attack on the kingdom nor defend us from one," Victor replies.

"If we cannot find a way to break Tricella's hold on dark magic and on my father, war will be inevitable." I meet his glance over the table, heat flicking up my neck.

"We are hoping that by retrieving the Book of Light, there will be some inscription in it to help me use my magic to counteract her," Sybil says to break the tension. "But the book is kept captive by a dragon in the Rocheux mountains, we suspect. We will try our best, but we cannot rely solely on a single solution. Aramis is right. We need to prepare for the worst and hope for the best."

I clench my fists at the thought of Sybil confronting Tricella.

"Talking about the book," Phoebe continues. "I saw it. Only one, with a black leather-bound cover. I did not even dare get close; the evilness it was emanating... I have never felt anything like it."

"What about the soldiers?" Nero interjects. "How the fuck are they supporting her?"

"Well," Phoebe starts and quickly glances at me with apprehension. I rake my fingers through my hair and pinch the bridge of my nose, preparing for the news to come.

"They are shells. Eyes vacant. I believe they are under the same mind control as the King is. They will do whatever Tricella asks without batting an eyelid. This is how she's kept the elementals in check from rebelling against her. Her power is... extreme. It's like a virus and it's only growing stronger."

Sybil shifts in her seat next to me. She's sinking her nails in the palms of the hands, her breathing accelerating. I cover her hands with mine and when our eyes meet, I see my panic mirrored in hers.

The council members murmur between themselves. For a moment, it feels like it's only us and the burden we carry.

"Were you able to discern any of the queen's plans?" Aries drawls from the other end of the table, breaking our spell. A few members cast sharp looks at his tone.

"I found her advisor's chamber. The seer. I saw maps and battle plans not only across Shadowvale but beyond. The only area they're turning a blind eye toward is Caelo."

"That would mean crossing southeast through the mountain ranges." Nero frowns, looking around the room. "It would be an easier trip south to Kallistar."

"Kallistar is too risky with the queen's current motives. We'd be safer facing the mountain passage than we would facing her shadow beasts in the forest," Phoebe agrees.

"We will consider if moving camp there is a viable option," Kaitlin says and nods at Evolet, who promptly goes to circle in red the area on the map laying on the table.

"The seer also kept notes about you, Sybil," Phoebe continues and looks at her. Sybil squares her shoulders and forces a smile.

"They are still hunting you. Something about balance, and you being the key."

Sybil freezes and I squeeze her hand, sending her comfort down our bond, even if she probably does not feel it.

"What about the elementals she kills?" Kaitlin, Kela's mother, asks. The question takes me somewhat by surprise.

"What do you mean?" I ask. Nero matches my confused expression, but everyone looks at us as if we were stupid and Aries starts laughing.

"When the attacks first started," Victor explains. "Nero told us about villages known for the peaceful coexistence of elementals and shifters being attacked, and nine times out of ten, the only victims were elementals. The Queen of course, used this to weave the narrative that shifters were attacking elementals, and manipulated you, Prince, to start a crusade against us. But we never laid a finger on elementals."

My brows furrow, the cogs in my mind turning furiously trying to connect everything.

"We thought Tricella sent shadow beasts to target elementals, but did you ever wonder why there were never elemental bodies left behind? We thought she was experimenting on her own—"

"There's nothing about her messing with elementals. Her focus is on siphoning shifter magic alone," Phoebe explains.

"Something else is at play here," I whisper and worry about what is going to be the answer.

19
ARAMIS

Nero and I walk in companionable silence through the camp. Shifter and elemental children chase each other through the streets, their parents yelling after them to be careful, not knowing they'll be back on the snowy roads in less than a day. After the council meeting ended, sanctioning our next moves, Sybil and Marcelene headed to the infirmary, whilst the two of us volunteered to help load the few carriages available with the bare necessities.

Keeping up hope when everything seems to be doomed has been exhausting.

The late winter sun shines brightly above us, cutting down the chill in the air, but it does little to warm the absence of my magic flowing freely through my veins.

"What's on yer mind, Aramis? You're quieter than usual." Nero stares at me, shading his eyes.

There is too much on my mind these days.

"I have abandoned them, Nero. My men, the people at the castle, Edmun—" I sigh, exasperated. The thought of Edmund with the same far away eyes as my father makes me choke up, and I turn the other way, hiding the tears pricking at my eyes. This guilt has been gnawing at me since the moment I left Shadowvale, but now after hearing what Phoebe saw, it's consuming me. I should have gone back. I should have found a way to stab Tricella in the heart.

"Edmund is a smart lad." Nero interrupts my self-deprecating thoughts. "He probably ran from the castle after we left, sensing something wasn't right. And there's nothing ye could have done to change what happened to yer men." He rests a hand on my shoulder, but I can't find the strength to look at him.

"And what the fuck am I going to do if it comes to war? I am *powerless*, Nero. I will never get rid of these cuffs because I don't have any worth left in me." I look at my cuffs and feel as if I have one wrapped around my neck too, strangling me.

"Yer not *powerless*, let alone *worthless*, but clearly ye need a good arse whooping to remember that." I turn to him, surprised by his tone. "Now stop moping around, will ye, and find the captain of the guards ye've lost somewhere along the way. The old Aramis might have been a prejudiced and privileged arse, but he never stood down."

Nero points to the children playing whilst their parents are busy packing their few belongings, faces etched with worry. How many times have they done this? How many more times will they have to?

"Look around ye, Aramis. This is yer kingdom, yer people. We will find a way to protect and save them," he growls, his irises glowing molten gold in the dim light. "Who do ye think will sit on that bloody throne when Tricella is gone? I love ye, but we don't know the consequences the spell will have left on your father's mind. Ye will wear the crown, Aramis."

The truth of his words hits me and I nearly throw up.

"They don't want a murderer as their King," I say with conviction. "How can they look at me and see anything other than the man who has brought countless shifters to their death? What kind of king does that, Nero?"

Nero shakes his head. Scales glimmer underneath his skin as he loses his grip on his temper. "Ye have been so preoccupied with yer own worries and doubts, ye didn't even realize how much these people look up to ye now! They have seen ye rebuild their homes, chop the wood that kept them warm, share information that finally helped one of us infiltrate the castle. Yer a fool if you can't see their gratitude. And a prick if ye don't start appreciating it."

My best friend takes off to the woods and I stand frozen to the ground. A tree in the middle of the desert. Alone and desperate for water.

My eyes fall to the ground and I look at my hands. Despite being a prince, I've never had pristine hands. No matter the number of oils and butters my mother would massage through my fingers, the callouses from the hours spent sword fighting never left. But my hands have changed again. Cuts adorn every finger. They are an angry shade of red from the incessant cold, and the skin is dry and irritated. My nails are cracked, there's soil trapped underneath them and my callouses have gotten so coarse they feel like stones.

What kind of king has hands like these?

A king who's not afraid to work for its people.

The truth is a weak glimmer in front of my eyes. There for the taking, yet I stumble like a blind man. After a moment, I follow Nero to the woods where he's picked up my axe and is working on my stack of logs.

"I don't know what to do, Nero," I admit and it feels like lifting a weight off my chest.

The wood is cast in shadows as the sun is slowly making its descent. Shivers run down my spine and I pray spring will come soon. Alphaeia knows it will make travels for the refugees much easier. I take a deep breath, hoping it will slow my running mind.

"I thought... I thought having Sybil back would fix everything. Show me my place in all of this, but I keep feeling like the villain." I stumble on my words, but I am laying bare my truths now and there's no going back. "Fuck! I don't even think Sybil should forgive me for what I have done to her. I love that woman with every cell in my body, Nero. But there's no absolution for what I have done."

"Ye better shut up right now, Aramis, or I will have to punch the stupidity out of yer arse," Nero says, throwing the axe to my right as it finds its mark in the trunk of a tree behind me.

"Do it," I challenge Nero. I take off my leather jacket and throw it onto the snowy ground.

"Aramis—"

"Fucking do it, Nero. Or what? Do you think I can't take you anymore? Do you think I can't beat—"

"First blood?" He pulls off his shirt and crouches low into a defensive stance, holding another axe in front of him.

"And mar your beautiful scales?" I taunt as I yank the axe from where it's embedded in the trunk.

Nero lunges forward, his axe slicing through the air. I parry his attack with a swift flick of my wrist. Metal clashes against metal, sparks flying in the dim light.

"Is that all you've got, lizard boy?" I taunt, a wide grin on my face mirroring his own. I feint to the left, then quickly change direction, aiming for Nero's exposed flank. He anticipates my move, sidestepping with lightning speed. Our axes clash again, the force of the impact reverberating through our arms. I relish in the familiar feeling that vibrates along my skin.

"It's draken boy to ye, old man," he grunts as he swings his axe in an arch, forcing me toward the tree line.

"Old man?" I huff with laughter. I press forward, driving Nero back, relentless in my pursuit. Adrenaline pumps through my veins, fueling my every move. My axe becomes an extension of myself as I channel my pent-up emotions into each strike.

"Aye," he says as he launches into a series of rapid strikes. I parry each blow with unwavering resolve, his skill matching mine.

Melting snow and mud crunch beneath our boots as we circle each other, eyes locked in a fierce gaze. Sweat drips from my brow and my muscles burn, but I relish in it. The world around me fades into the background, leaving only the battle, the clash of steel, and the thundering of my heart.

"Remember that time we fought off those kids when we were younger–" I pant.

"Ye've got to be more specific, mate," he says, our axes clashing until he's up in my face. I push him off, and we both stumble a few paces back before crouching defensively.

"You remember Charlotte's daughter, Astrid Wren?" I pant, circling him and looking for an opening.

"Yer mother's lady-in-waiting's daughter?"

"Yes, the one you wouldn't stop talking about for weeks. Granted, what girl didn't you have a crush on in the castle?" I say. He rolls his eyes, but a grin tugs at the corner of his lips.

"Aye, didn't a group of the lord's sons steal her doll one time?"

"That's the one. It was four of them against the two of us." We continue our deadly dance, the clash of steel echoing through the silent forest. Time seems to slow as our movements become more precise, more calculated. Sweat-soaked and breathless, we fight with a fire that refuses to be extinguished.

"Even as boys, you always stood up for those in need," he says, his golden-brown eyes meeting my gaze.

My heart sinks, and the scar on my chest burns with phantom pain. I used to, until that night. However, I am different now; I have become the man my mother wanted me to be. A shiver runs down my spine, and I feel a ghostly caress against my cheek, but as I look around, I see nothing.

Silence fills the air between us as we circle one another. With a sudden burst of energy, I unleash a flurry of strikes, pushing Nero to his limit. His defenses waiver. A small opening appears. I seize the opportunity, driving my axe toward his chest. But Nero is not so easily defeated. With a swift sidestep, he evades my attack, retaliating with a powerful swing. His axe blade cuts through the air, aiming for my head. I duck just in time, feeling the wind of his strike brush against my hair.

"Getting tired there, Aramis? Should we stop so ye can join the villagers with less taxing chores?" He winks, and it fuels my next strike. I will not back down, not against Nero or anyone else. This fight is more than just a clash of swords; it's a test of strength, of will, of who I truly am. I will prove to my people I'm willing to do anything to protect them.

"You wish," I say as I feint to the left, then quickly change direction, aiming for Nero's exposed flank. He anticipates my move, sidestepping with lightning speed. Our axes meet again, the force of the impact reverberating through our arms. The cold air bites at my cheeks, but I ignore it, focused solely on him.

"I win," he says.

It's then I feel the sting on the side of my rips where his axe has left a thin slice in my side, blood mingling with the sweat plastering the linen to my skin.

"You bastard," I say with a grin, punching him in the arm.

"Ye smell worse than a pig rolling in shit, Aramis," Nero remarks, taking a swig from his canteen of water. The scent of sweat clings to him, his brown hair plastered to his head, and his chin covered in stubble.

"You should talk," I retort, accepting the canteen and quenching my thirst with a long gulp. "I didn't realize how much being locked in those cells for weeks affected me," I say, rubbing at the sore muscles of my arms. "I feel like I'm back in our first year of training again."

Nero laughs, and we both lay on the snow-covered ground. I feel the snow melting under my body heat and soaking my tunic, but it's a welcoming sensation. The setting sun casts a mesmerizing array of golden hues across the sky, painting a breathtaking scene as it dips below the horizon. Time is going by too quickly. There's still so much we have to prepare for our travels tomorrow.

"I don't like this plan with Axton. There is something about him that makes me uneasy," I say after a while.

"Aye, he doesn't seem like the best of people, but we dinna have any other choice, it seems. He's our only link in finding the book." Nero is right. My breathing finally starts to calm, but Nero is still panting next to me.

He better remember I still know how to beat his ass.

"I know," I say. "I just wish there was a different way—a better way. A way to avoid all this fighting and turmoil all together." My fists clench at my sides and I sit up. The smell of fresh baked loaves waft from camp as the cooks are getting ready to serve dinner. An idea strikes me but I tuck it away for now.

"How did you manage to stand by my side all those years?

You saw the pain I was causing under Tricella's orders but never left."

Nero follows my lead and sits up too, his black hair so disheveled it resembles a bird's nest. "For a hundred years, I've stood by yer side, Aramis. It wasn't easy, but I could see the real ye under all the pain. I know the male ye want to be." He stands and extends a hand in my direction. "Our past shapes us, but our actions help mold us."

I look up at him and thank the Goddess for gifting me Nero. Who knows what would have happened to me, had he not been in my life.

Taking his hand, he lifts me as if I weigh little more than a feather and I brush off the dirt and snow stuck on my clothes.

"When did you become so wise? Sure *you* don't want to be king? I'll let you try on the crown if you want?" I joke.

"Yer kidding me. When this is over, I want to sleep on the softest mattress in the whole of Shadowvale for a month straight. Find yerself another second in command. Although, I bet yer be busy anyways." Nero winks at me and my heart clenches. Will Sybil want to stay in Shadowvale, with me? "Aramis, trust yer heart. It's brought ye this far. Talk to her without pretending." I meet his golden eyes and know he is right.

The bond tugs me back to the camp, back to her. I nod and another weight is lifted.

As we make our way to the infirmary, with every elemental and shifter looking at us as if we're two children coming back home from a brawl. A thought comes rushing back to me.

"Are you going to tell me what's going on between you and the witch, or do I have to whoop your ass again to find out?"

Nero bursts into laughter, and I can't believe how good it makes me feel. Just because everything seems to be doomed doesn't mean I can't appreciate the little things. Like winding up my best friend.

"First of all, I whooped yer arse. Second, I don't know what to tell ya, mate. She's... she's something." He rubs his chin, eyes on the ground, and I know he'll tell me more when he is ready.

For now, I just need to find the courage to open my heart to the beautiful woman with the long, brown locks by the entrance of the infirmary tent.

The bands around my wrist heat up and I glance down, but nothing seems amiss.

20
SYBIL

S ybil." Aramis stands outside the infirmary tent with Nero and I have to take a double look because they look as if they've been rolling around in the dirt.

"What in all of Craeweth have you two been up to?" I ask in disbelief as I finish sorting out another medical bag for the journey. My back aches from spending the whole afternoon crushing herbs, seeping oils, and decanting balms to make sure the rebels are ready for any medical eventuality during their journey. Granted, it is not—by any means—a comprehensive selection, but it will help, should they need it. My eyes catch on the small patch of drying blood on Aramis' tunic and I raise my eyebrows. "What happened?"

"Nothing–" Aramis and Nero brush off their clothes and rake their hands through their hair, pouting like little children who know they've been caught. Aramis looks at me under his lashes and I can't help but laugh. The pure joy tastes sweet after so much worry and pain.

"What's so funny?" Marcelene peaks her head out of the

tent, and for the first time since knowing him, I see Nero blush. Marcelene shakes her head in disappointment and slips back inside, but I can hear her snickering.

"So?" I ask again and cross my arms.

"We... just... talked," Aramis says unconvincingly with a toothy smile and I almost gasp. He has not smiled at me, not like this at least, since we reunited. His blue eyes shine again, like clear water reflecting the summer sunshine. His shoulders are relaxed and his chin is lifted as if he's allowing himself to take up space again in the world. As if he's no longer afraid of his monsters.

My stomach turns upside down. How can these feelings not be mine when all I do is burn when he lays his eyes on me?

"Hungry?" He asks when words fail me. I nod. Aramis extends his elbow, and I interlock my arm with his as we make our way to the food tent.

"How are things at the infirmary?" Aramis asks. Even his tone has changed. He sounds secure in his words, not riddled by doubts.

"They're almost ready. There's only three people who are critically wounded and need to be carried either on stretchers or wagons. Ever since what happened in the clearing, I am worried to use my powers." The admission slips out of me, despite being something I had still not even admitted to myself.

"Unicorn power is raw light magic. The witches told you themselves. The Book of Light must have information on how you can weaponize it in a safe way, without hurting yourself," Aramis says and pushes a strand of my unruly hair behind my ear, leaving shivers behind where his skin touches mine.

The food tent is located at the center of camp, close to where the Council building used to stand, an easy location everyone could meet throughout the day and exchange a word or two. The cooks change regularly since they are all volunteers, and with different cooks come different recipes, making every meal different. But one thing never changes apparently, and that is the baker. Oscar, an earth elemental, has been the designated bread maker at camp since he joined. Thanks to his gift, he grows his own special crops. From them, he makes the most divine golden rolls, crunchy on the outside and soft on the inside.

Before we join the line, Aramis leans close to me and whispers, "I'll be back in just a moment."

I take a deep breath and will my legs to steady and stop shaking. Aramis sneaks into the food tent from the back entrance—usually reserved for volunteers—and I see as he greets one of the ladies at the counter with a hug. Her name is Heather. She's a panther shifter although she rarely shifts anymore after losing her husband during an attack. She joined the camp with her two boys soon after to escape capture from the crown. Heather smiles at Aramis and rests her hand on his cheek in a motherly gesture. Aramis keeps talking to Heather, but I struggle to read her lips until the two turn in my direction and I look at my boots, heat rushing to my cheeks.

A second later, I attempt another glance, and this time, he is speaking to Oscar. His mustache gives him a stern look, but soon he too is laughing wholeheartedly and looks in my direction.

Damn it.

I turn around, hoping it'll avoid more embarrassment.

They like him, I think, and the thought almost makes me tear up. The man blinded by prejudice is gone. My hand goes to rest on my chest where my heart beats so fast I wonder how my bones can keep it contained. Real or not real?

Aramis returns and wraps his arm around my waist. He's

carrying a cloth bag emanating the most delicious smell and I risk a peek.

"Ah—ah," Aramis chides. "I was wondering if you'd like to have a picnic, so we can talk."

Talk.

I swallow the knot in my throat. "That would be lovely."

We silently walk to the edge of camp and into the woods. The sun has set, and the sky is the most wondrous shade of blue, right before it darkens. Aramis takes me to a little clearing he's been using to chop wood for the fire. Most of the snow has melted, but the air is still cold, especially this time of day.

Aramis takes some of the logs and sets them together in a circle to light a fire. Memories of our days spent sleeping on the forest floor next to the fire, with Edmund and the others, come rushing back to me. How can so much have changed in so little time?

I sit on the trunk of a fallen tree not yet acquainted with the axe, and revel in the slowly growing fire. Rubbing my hands together, I close all the buttons of my wool jacket and watch Aramis almost awkwardly set up a makeshift buffet. Heather has wrapped some cheese in paper, there are some juniper berries and, of course, Oscar's rolls.

"How did you get all of this?" I ask, knowing there are strict rules about conviviality at camp and spending meals together to create a sense of community.

"Helping with the cooking has its advantages," he says with a wink and dives into the food.

In between bites, I ask, "How do you feel about tomorrow?"

"I came to this camp and immediately became a prisoner." His brows furrow and I worry I have asked the wrong question. "But now," he continues. "It almost feels like a home, strangely. I've never been very lucky with homes. The castle felt like home for a while, when my mother was still alive. Now I'm not so certain anymore. My permanence at this camp did not start splendidly, but now, it feels like somewhere I belong. Probably the only place in Craeweth I have made a difference. So, I am sad to leave, and scared about what's going to happen to these people. But most of all, I am scared about the uncertainty of it all."

He focuses on the piece of bread in his hands. The warm light of the fire makes his hair look like strands of white-gold and I'm mesmerized.

"I know what you mean. I am scared too. But I've come to realize that people are right when they say that home is more about the people you're with than the place itself."

Barely a whisper, still looking down at his hands, Aramis says, "I think you're my home, Sybil."

Unable to stop myself, I reach for his chin and gently lift his head. Our eyes meet and it's like opening a well. Anger, love, disappointment, longing, desire, all come crushing on me and I can't hold any of it in any longer.

"How long have you known?" I whisper and let my hand fall. I watch as his brows furrow. "When were you going to tell me?"

"I–" he falters before his head drops again and he sighs. "Since the night in the dungeon. I suspected long before then but lied to myself."

"Why?" I ask, my voice cracking and throat tightening. "Why didn't you tell me? If not there, then at the springs."

He runs a hand through his hair. "There are a million reasons, but none of them are good enough. You were the manifestation of everything I grew up hating and wanting revenge for, Sybil. I thought the Goddess was playing with me. I thought it was a cruel twist of fate but how can it be, when you are the reason for everything?"

He takes my hand in his, his hand is rough but warm to the touch,

"You made me question everything I believed in. You made me want to become a better person. You are the reason I have a purpose, a reason to exist, to keep fighting instead of letting my guilt drown me in my own despair. How can this be a trick? All I see is a blessing." Aramis shakes his head and looks up at the sky now littered with stars. "Do you really want to know why I didn't tell you?" He asks and I nod.

"I was scared you'd reject me. I am terrified of it, but that is not your burden to carry. Whatever you decide, Sybil Vandeleur, know that loving you has been the greatest honor of my life."

He slumps forward, elbows resting on his knees as he stares contemplatively at the fire.

My heart beats erratically and I can't decide whether I want to kiss him, slap him, or both. So, I run.

"Sybil!" Aramis calls after me, but I run deeper into the woods. I run until the tears rushing down my eyes dry up, until my calves burn and my breathing gets ragged. Until I miss an exposed root and go tumbling down on the ground.

"Balderdash!" I push to my feet, a sharp pain shoots up my left ankle with each step but I keep going. I need to clear my head. Every inch of me aches from the hours crouched over makeshift cots tending the wounded, not to mention the beating I took fighting the basilisk. I hadn't had time or magic to tend to my own injuries. What I wouldn't give for a bathtub full of hot water and some soap.

Aramis comes running soon after, sweat beading his skin.

"Sybil, wait. You're limping," he says, although I know, truly, he likes to chide me for my lack of balance, as he used to remind me. "Here, let me help you," he says, offering me a hand.

"Yes, yes. And no, I can manage on my own. I just—" A sharp pain shoots up my left ankle as I attempt to stand. How wonderful, exactly what I need the night before a long journey. I bury my face in my hands and force myself not to scream.

"You're not fine," he says brushing the pad of his thumb across my wet cheek. "I know you're brave and strong, but you're also injured and tired. You don't have to put on a mask for me."

He lifts me into his arms and my head settles perfectly against his chest at the movement, as if we were made for each other. Is this fate intervening once again? Aramis carries me in silence until we reach the edge of a frozen stream surrounded by large, smooth rocks faintly dusted with freshly fallen snow. He gently eases me onto a boulder next to the water and steps back.

"Why did you run?" he asks, crossing his arms over his chest.

"I—" The words catch in my throat and I sigh, meeting his gaze. "I don't know, Aramis. I am confused, I don't know what to feel. And when I feel, I don't know if it's me." I point a finger at my heart and Aramis' expression softens.

The stream gurgles quietly beside us, clusters of spring flowers pushing up through melting patches of snow still clinging to the earth. A lone bee buzzes to each tiny snowdrop blossom.

"You're worried our feelings aren't genuine?"

"How can I be certain of it, when there's this feeling inside of me, stronger than anything I have ever felt before? How can I separate my feelings from this fated bond tying us together?" I rest my hand on my chest, where the bond feels like a ray of sunshine slicing through me.

"It all happened so quickly. I always thought love needed time, that I would have to know a person—truly know someone—to feel this way. Everything we've been through *meant* something to me, Aramis. The night at the springs was the sole thing spurring me onwards whilst trapped under that mountain. I have to stop myself from touching you, from thinking about you every second because I don't know if that is me or this... this—"

He crouches in front of me and cups my face between his hands as I stare into his deep blue eyes. Sobs slowly rise through me, making my chest jump. Heat radiates off his strong, muscular thighs as they press firmly against the sides of my legs echoing the warmth blossoming in my core at his proximity.

"I love you, Sybil. Not because of the mating bond, not destiny, not even the fucking Goddess. I, Aramis Adrostos, love you so much it scares me sometimes. I don't care that we're mates. It does not change anything, you hear me?" He leans forward and presses his forehead against mine. He takes my hand and presses it over his beating heart. "You know this, Sybil. You've known it better than I ever have from the moment we've met. That's why my heart is yours."

My senses are flooded by his familiar scent of bergamot, cedarwood and leather. My hands find the front of his tunic and tighten in the fabric.

"But I do care, Aramis. I understand why you did not tell me sooner but I don't want fate to be what pushes us together. I want to choose you." Lifting my face, I press my lips against his. I can no longer deny wanting his touch.

"Then, let me prove myself to you. Let me prove that what is between us is more than just fate," he whispers, pressing a kiss to my brow before reclaiming my lips. His kiss is urgent and exploratory, one hand weaving through my hair, the other roving across my back. "Goddess, I missed you."

He leans back, eyes roving appraisingly down my body

before placing his hands possessively on my hips. My heart jumps in my chest, pulse pounding as heat pools in my core. He stands and pulls me flush to his body, our breath mingling in cloudy puffs in the cold winter air. My cheeks flush as I feel the thickness of him pressed between our bodies.

"A lifetime by your side would not be long enough for me," he whispers as he trails warm kisses down the length of my neck, the scruff of his beard scraping along the delicate flesh. "I want you. I want all of you. The bond be damned."

"Then, give me time," I whisper, taking his face between my hands and pulling back to look into his face. I rub my thumb along the stubble as I process my thoughts into words. "Let me spend time with you, let us get to know each other. Help me save our people, your kingdom."

"Sybil, I will wait until the end of time for you. I want nothing more than you by my side." He falls to the snow covered ground on his knees, pushing me gently, easing me back onto a large smooth boulder. "Not a moment has gone by that I haven't thought of you since that avalanche."

"I felt you," I whisper, lifting a hand to my chest.

"I didn't want to leave." His head drops, shoulders slumping. "I tried to reach you."

"I know, but it was meant to be. I had to do it alone, to prove to myself I could do it." My chest constricts as I remember the binding coils of the web around my body.

"And you did. You're a marvel, Sybil. But shall you ever need a sword, let me be—" His words cut off as emotions flicker across his face. "Reading."

"Parden?" I cock my head to the side, breath coming out in white puffs as I stare at the male at my feet.

"Reading. I like to read. Not many know. Nero teases me greatly for it. My mother, before she passed, was an avid reader and would read to the two of us late into the night when we were boys. My father thought it was a useless pastime and that we needed more time in the training yard, but she believed that stories helped us understand."

"I like to read too." I smile down at Aramis. "It was the one thing that kept me from feeling lonely. I could escape into a book."

"What else do you like, Sybil?" He asks.

"I like–" My breath catches as his warm hands slip under my skirts and slide along the back of my calves to my knees.

"Yes?" He grins, kneeling between my feet as fingers trace slow, lazy circles. Heat flushes across my body and up my neck, setting my magic singing through my veins. I glance down with hooded eyes, a lazy smile on my face.

"You're doing that on purpose," I say.

"Do you want me to stop?" His fingers pause and he stares up at me with stormy blue eyes.

Looking at me like that, I might lose my resolve. His touch feels so natural and comforting.

"No," I whisper, barely shaking my head. "I enjoy... planting. I know it's a menial task, but I love the feel of dirt between my fingers and reaping the rewards of harvest. If it wasn't for my knowledge of plants, Lemon and I would have starved those first few years before villagers started coming for simple remedies."

"I can't say I've enjoyed it. The only time I've had my hands buried in the dirt was when Nero kicked my ass in the training grounds. Don't tell him I said that; he will never let me live it down. Well—" His brows furrow and his fingers stop for a moment. "I suppose you can say I do have some experience with planting now. I have helped earth elementals cultivate some of the soil at the camp."

His gentle fingers continue tracing a path down my legs, skillfully unlacing my boots. As he slips them off, relief washes over me. With each stroke, the knots and tension in my muscles begin to unravel and a soothing sensation seeps into my weary body, a result of the battles fought against shadow beasts and long hours spent hunched over patients.

"We should not stay too long here in the dark," Aramis whispers, and reality comes crushing down on me. "We should also try to get some rest; tomorrow is going to be a long day."

I nod, sad to leave but feeling lighter. Aramis goes to take me into his arms, but I stop him.

"No need." I channel the smallest kernel of magic into my ankle and the pain disappears.

"I am all good again," I say, and jump off the boulder.

"You wicked little thing. You had me massaging your leg for nothing?" He shakes his head, a smirk on his face that makes me melt.

He takes my hand and we walk back to his tent, where I sleep for the first time with his arms wrapped around me, wondering what the morning will bring.

21
ARAMIS

I still don't think this is a good idea," Roger says, the sound of the lock turning and the creaking of the door accompanying his words. The musty scent of damp earth—the same one that had plagued me for the past few weeks—hits me with an almost physical force, causing me to pause with one hand on the door frame leading down the stairs. After the attack and worries surrounding the relocation of the camp further east to avoid Tricella's attacks, the Council of Thorns had agreed on leaving Axton to us. They understood the importance of finding the Book of Light, and in all honesty, I believe they were happy to get this headache of a man off their hands.

"Are ye okay there, Aramis?" Nero's voice reaches me from behind, concern evident in his tone.

"I'm fine," I reply, trying to suppress the nausea rising in me as I cautiously take the first few steps down the stairs.

I glare at the metal bands encircling my wrists, their cold touch a stark contrast to the icy absence of my magic. Each step I take down the stairs feels heavy, like trudging through a fog. We had risen at first light, when the sky was a blur of yellows and blues, and we looked at each other without saying a word. The uncertainty of change lingers heavily in the air for all of us, but we cannot let it stop us. Not now when we're so close to gaining something of value that can help us defeat Tricella. After rounding up my few belongings, I had left to meet with Nero and Roger whilst Sybil went to meet with Marcelene to ready our packs for travel.

Things between me and Sybil had also shifted, but it was a welcome change. The kind that is born out of growth—necessary change that will help us build stronger foundations for the future.

"Well, what fine company has come to visit me?" Axton's voice interrupts my contemplation, and I turn to face him through the bars. He performs an exaggerated bow, sweeping his arm, his voice dripping with sarcasm. "I'll have to apologize for the state of things; I wasn't exactly expecting guests."

"We're not here for teatime. We need your help," I quip and remind myself we have no other choice than to trust this asshole.

"You need my help?" He lifts a brow as he leans casually against the cell door, picking at his nails. "Well, isn't this quite a new song to sing, *Prince of Shadowvale*. Last time I saw you, you were threatening my life and slamming me against these very iron bars. Interesting, isn't it?"

"The council has granted us permission to release you on the condition that you hold your end of the bargain. You can count your lucky stars, Axton. You'd have rotted a couple more weeks in this cell for your crimes," Nero explains as he gestures for Roger to unlock the cell door. He hesitates, his eyes meeting mine in a shared glance of apprehension before he turns the key.

"Oh, what a show of mercy and gratitude! Shall I kiss all your feet now or can we do it after a bath? We've all been through a lot, I don't even want to imag—" Roger rolls his eyes and starts moving the key back in the opposite direction. "Okay, fine. Wrong crowd, I get it." He lifts his hands in the air and moves back from the door so Roger can open it. "So, just to make sure I understand the terms of this agreement. I take you to the dragon cave and I can walk free?" Axton watches us warily, his skepticism evident

"And you help us find the book, don't start twisting words now, thief," I say. The lock clicks and Roger swings the cell door wide. I extend my hand toward Axton. "Deal?"

The corners of his lips curl up into a grin, his eyes twinkling with mischief before he takes my hand, bending to place a kiss atop of it. "Deal."

I wrench back my hand in disgust and Axton starts laughing.

"Let's get going," Nero growls, his impatience evident. I grab Axton by the back of the neck and forcefully lead him toward the stairs.

Camp is a somber scene today as we make our way to the borders to meet with the others. The taste of dust lingers on my tongue as the ground—finally void of snow—is stirred up by frantic preparations. I meet the weary faces of shifters and elementals, etched with lines of fatigue and sorrow as they worked tirelessly through the night to dismantle the camp. Children with sleepy eyes clutch their worn-out toys in their little hands and look at their parents, wondering what made them all wake at this Goddess forsaken hour.

We pass a couple of carriages groaning under the weight of

the few tents and belongings they could afford to transport. Everything else is left behind in favor of traveling light and fast. Horse shifters agreed to carry the elderly to prevent slowing down the journey, whilst wind elementals focused their magic on making the stretchers gently float for as long as their powers allowed.

I see Heather with her two boys, backpacks on their backs, on their way to the meeting point for the journey through the mountains. The village would then separate into smaller groups to go through the mountain pass. The decision to separate was one Victor did not want to make but ultimately had to with how large the village had grown.

"Goddess speed, Aramis. May we all meet again," she says, her black hair hidden under a blue headscarf, her eyes glistening. She hugs me.

"Good luck to you all. We will meet again, I promise," I whisper in her arms and can't help but think that my mother's hugs felt just the same. I scruff the boys' hair. They are scared, but know they must be strong for their mama.

We continue through what's left of the camp in silence. Even Axton is at a loss for words at the powerful show of solidarity and resilience between the refugees. Supportive handshakes, reassuring pats on the back, and hugs are exchanged between family and friends who know the bond they share—forged in adversity—is their greatest strength to face the uncertain journey ahead.

You will wear the crown, Aramis.

Nero's words come back to me, and for the first time, they feel right. I want to be king for these people, for my people, because they deserve a ruler that recognizes the sacrifices they have made. I already owed a debt to these people, but now I owe them so much more.

We reach the northeast border and I see Sybil lovingly braiding a young girl's hair, and my heart stops.

"You're all set. The braids won't let those annoying strands fall into your eyes so you can see all the wonders you will encounter on your adventure!" She squeezed the girl's hand, who lights up with excitement. Sybil gives her a quick hug, and the girl rushes back to her mother, who's waiting for her with her hand stretched out.

What a gift, I think to myself, to turn someone's fear into exhilaration.

Sybil sees us approaching and joins our little party.

"Would ya look at that, the three of us back together on the road!" Nero says with a big grin on his face. "Well, the three of us and Axton here." He nods to the thief, who seems to be lost in thought.

"Actually—," Sybil begins.

"I am coming with you," Marcelene says as she walks toward us, backpack in hand.

Nero's eyes widen, and he shakes his head. "Absolutely not. Marcelene should head back to the library, where she will be safe."

"I will not go back to the library like some insolent child. Stop talking about me as if I am not here," she growls, glaring daggers at him. Sharp claws protrude from her fingers, digging into the marred wooden surface of the bowl in her hands, and I have to bite my lip trying not to laugh at how splendidly Marcelene is putting Nero back to his place.

"Down kitten, I did nae mean ye no harm," he says as he grins, eyes dancing mischievously at her. "I'm only looking out for yer well-being."

"Why don't you take your eyes and look after someone else," she scoffs, turning her shoulder against him, "Sybil Vandeleur, I vow blade and claws to stay at your side–"

Sybil places a reassuring hand on her shoulder. "Have no fear. I won't let the big lizard block you from accompanying me."

"And I volunteer to come as well," Phoebe's small voice calls out as she runs toward our little group.

What is happening?

"You've already done so much, risking your life infiltrating the kingdom to glean us answers of the queen's plans," Sybil starts, turning toward the petite shifter. "I can't possibly risk someone else's life for this mission."

"I have shown my worth," she begins defiantly, tossing her backpack to the ground. "Victor has blessed my decision and I can do more for the cause if I stay with you than with the camp. They are going to focus on safety, and I am not the type who likes to sit around. You might play a central role in this Sybil, but this is my war too." She starts putting her hair up in a bun, and then looks at me, challenging me to prove her point wrong.

"We could use her skills," I say at last, earning a sharp look from Sybil, to which I raise my shoulder. "She admirably made it into the castle and back unscathed and undetected."

"I won't put another *young shifter* at risk." Sybil's voice almost breaks and we all know she is thinking of Kela. "I don't want anyone to risk their life for me."

"You were not responsible for her death," I whisper, and tuck a stray hair behind her ear.

"That settles it, then." Nero sighs, glancing around the group. "Time to find a drag—"

"Wait!" My stomach plummets as a familiar voice calls out, and I turn to see Aries sprinting across the field toward us. "I'm coming with you."

Nope. Absolutely not. Axton is bad enough to deal with. I pinch my nose and wonder if this is a personal attack on my nerves. There is no way in all of Craeweth I am going to survive dealing with the two of them.

"No." I narrow my eyes, my muscles tensing. "Nero, tell him."

Aries tosses his head back and laughs, getting into my space but not touching me. "It'll be fun, *Prince of Laundry!*"

I look at Nero, begging for backup, but the son of a draken raises his shoulder and lifts his hands. "We're going against a dragon, mate. Aries is skilled in combat. You know better than me that strategically, he's an advantage."

"I am an advantage," Aries repeats and mockingly curtsies.

"For fuck's sake—" A muscle in my jaw ticks as I glare at the shifter that I'd only recently begun to tolerate.

"Aramis, Aries." Sybil pushes between us. "Now is not the time to fight and bicker like children. I know you two had a rough start."

"Ye could say it was a rough start," Nero chuckles, a twinkle in his eyes, but his grin quickly fades when Sybil shoots him a disapproving look.

"We don't know exactly what we're in for when we find this creature. As much as I hate putting another in danger, we could use a skilled fighter." Sybil reluctantly looks between the two of us. I sigh, conceding as I step back, but don't miss the smug look on Aries' face.

"I hope you did not think about leaving without saying goodbye." Victor's guttural voice makes us all turn. He is all dressed up in leathers, ready for the journey, but he is using a wooden cane. I silently vow to make Victor one of my counselors when I sit on the throne. Goddess knows the man has more at heart the wellbeing of himself.

Roger, Kaitlin and Evolet are also there.

"May the Goddess bless your journey and find the answers you seek," Evolet says and gifts us each with a water satchel. "I have bespelled them. They should replenish automatically for the next few weeks." We all nod in gratitude at her generosity.

"We may not be able to rid you of these cuffs, Aramis Adrostos, but we can return this to you as a sign of our gratefulness to you." Victor's gaze shifts toward me, his hand extending toward Roger, who swiftly moves to his side. The gleaming handle of a sword, tightly gripped in Roger's hand, emanates the familiar musk of leather. the sheath worn and weathered with time. Carved into the surface is the Adrastos house crest. Grateful, I acknowledge Victor with a nod, feeling the comforting weight of the weapon settle back into my grasp, familiar and reassuring.

"Be careful of the creatures that lurk at night. I don't know how deep into the mountains of Rocheux the shadow beasts may roam, but there are legends of other creatures with equally ferocious appetites." Victor rests both hands on the cane as he surveys our little party with a frown.

"Thank you," Sybil says. Lemon, sitting on her shoulder, nods at the council leader. He reaches up and gives him a scratch on the head. "We are indebted to you for supplying us on this journey. Especially with the needs of the villagers." A look of guilt crosses her face.

"There is no debt to be repaid. You have helped us so much over the past few weeks. All of you have." He glances at me, briefly meeting my gaze over Sybil's shoulder. "You have our support, should you ever need it," he says, but his brow furrows as he turns to stare northward toward the capital. "You may be the greatest key to our salvation and freedom, Sybil Vandeleur."

His words hang heavy on our group as we turn our backs on the village and step into the trees under the growing warmth of the morning sun.

22
ARAMIS

Three days go by with little change to our surroundings. The lull of conversation fades away as we venture deeper into the forest. The air grows thick with the earthy scent of damp moss and the sweet fragrance of wildflowers. Sunlight filters through the dense canopy, casting dappled patterns on the forest floor. The sound of rustling leaves and chirping birds accompanies our every step, creating a symphony of nature's melodies.

"So, how long have you been in Shadowvale?" Sybil asks Axton, breaking the silence.

"Oh, I come and go," he replies with a shrug. "I've traveled all over Craeweth, wherever odd and end jobs take me, but I always find myself coming back here."

"Were you born here?" She grabs onto the trunk of a tree for support as she steps up a small incline.

"Careful there," he says, placing a hand on her lower back to steady her.

Mine.

Jealousy burns deep inside as I glare at his hand, which lingers a moment longer than necessary on her. Ever since talking about the mating bond with Sybil, my feelings have become more erratic. The highs are incredibly high and the lows are more desolate than ever. I wish we knew more about how the bond works but alas, we have to find out one step at a time. Just as I promised her.

Sybil turns to Axton, a bright smile on her face. "Thank you."

As if sensing the growing tension, she turns her gaze back to me with a concerned expression. Lemon climbs up around her neck and peeks through her curtain of brown hair, his tiny head bobbing with each of her steps as his beady eyes stare at me expectantly.

Sybil turns back to Axton. "What would you say is the most beautiful place you've ever seen?"

"Hmm, now that is a tricky question. I've seen so many beautiful things in the world, but they all pale in comparison–"

"Why don't you elude more on this *creature* so that we know what we're up against," I say through clenched teeth.

"What can I say? It's a giant fire breathing beast of great proportions," Axton replies. "Thought they'd teach you basic mythical creature anatomy at Prince school. Do you want to know its color?" Axton asks mockingly, and I take a deep breath before I slam his face into the nearest tree trunk.

Marcelene speaks, her white striped feline tail whipping behind her. "Dragons do not give up their treasure lightly, and we cannot take a dragon down with just the six of us."

"Well, maybe your dragon shifter friend can sweet talk it into giving it up. You know, winged shifter to winged creature." Axton nods to Nero, who's been walking with his wings flared out the whole journey in case something attacks us.

"Draken shifters and dragons are very different," Nero says, crossing his arms. "While we possess similar qualities, we are about as similar as a unicorn is to a horse."

"Not to mention the average dragon is the size of a large mountain," Marcelene adds matter-of-factly but the dig at the draken does not go unnoticed.

"Oy, now if yer worried about size–" Nero starts, but Marcelene cuts him a sharp glance.

"We will figure out what to do with the dragon when we get there," Sybil says and continues walking in the direction Axton has been leading us. The woods' ground continues to be irregular; the melting snow has made the earth sodden and mud sucks at every step, threatening to pull our boots from our feet. Progress is slow and arduous.

"You're positive you know where you're going?" I ask Axton as I nearly trip on an exposed root.

"Who forgets their first time visiting a dragon's nest? I know where I'm going," he says, flicking invisible dust off his sleeves.

"It would be useful if you could give us more information than *I know where I'm going,*" Aries says as he hacks a branch from a tree in our path, sending pine needles scattering to the ground. "How many days will it take to travel? Are there any towns we can trade resources for?"

"It may have been half a century since I've been there, but the path is as fresh in my mind as though it was yesterday." Axton shrugs nonchalantly. "What would be the fun of telling you when I can show you? You'd have no need of me, then."

Marcelene tips her head up then stares around the forest. "Aries makes a valid argument. We might be far enough north to avoid the shadow beasts, but I'd rather linger as little as possible in the woods. We will need our rest soon. We've been traveling since sunrise, only taking a small break for lunch. We're going to burn ourselves out at this rate."

"This seems like as good of a place as any," I say as the trees thin out next to a small stream.

"Good enough if you want to sleep in the mud," Marcelene chides. Phoebe looks just as appalled at the idea of laying here.

"It's not a good idea to stay in this part of the forest," Axton says, looking warily around us. "There should be a small village, no more than a hundred settlements, about an hour from here if we keep moving on."

Could this be a trap?

Silence thick enough to cut with a dagger fills the air but we are short on options. Sybil glances up at the sky burdened with darkening clouds. The scent of petrichor lingers heavy in the air. "It would be nice to be under a thicker shelter than the trees should that storm hit us," she says.

"I agree," Marcelene says, sniffing the air. "It won't do us any good to get soaked to the bone this early in the spring."

"As the ladies wish." Nero bows with a wink before snatching back his pack from the ground.

We keep walking for what feels like an eternity and soon even the murmur of conversation ceases, replaced by heavy panting. Marcelene had shifted and flown in the direction Axton indicated to ensure the thief was not lying and to all our surprises, she did see an agglomeration of little wooden houses. Aris and Phoebe walked at the back of the group whilst Nero and I took the front line, following directions from Axton.

The gurgling of empty stomachs fills the silence when the tree line breaks open and down the hill is a small cluster of houses. But no smoke can be seen coming from the buildings, nor are there any other signs of life. The village is inhabited by ghosts alone.

"Do you think it's abandoned?" Sybil asks, twisting her fingers in the fabric of her skirt. Lemon stands on her shoulder and sniffs the air before glancing at me.

Nero shields his eyes from the glare of the setting sun peeking through the clouds and replies, "I can't tell from this distance. But I'd rather take my chances and find out either way."

"We have little to offer in exchange for a roof over our heads, unless they need healing." Sybil sighs, lugging her satchel higher on her shoulder. My fingers itch to carry the weight for her, but I know she's too strong headed to let me.

Axton holds up a jingling bag of what can only be coins and assures us, "Oh, don't worry. We will be able to afford a few rooms and a warm meal." He adds, "Don't ask questions you already know the answer to, unless you'd rather sleep out in the storm."

"Let's go," I say, biting my tongue. With Nero now in the lead, we all begin our descent down the steep and rugged decline into the valley.

Silence engulfs us as we cautiously approach the outskirts of the desolate town. The air is still, devoid of the usual rustle of clothes on lines and the murmur of people living their lives. Only a few of the houses still stand, and the ones that do have doors hanging askew, some torn from their frames entirely. Cracked windows, coated in a thick layer of dust, peer out like blind eyes, while wild vines snake through every crevice, reclaiming the structures with their relentless growth. The scene is one of eerie abandonment and a hasty departure.

"What do you think transpired here?" Sybil whispers.

"Tricella," Nero answers without batting an eyelid. We all turn to him and he gestures to a house with a collapsed roof. On its side run four deep gouges, the wood darker in the areas coated with dried blood. "These look exactly like the claw markings we've seen in the towns she's previously attacked, although it was rumored to have been shifters."

"I can see why someone would think that. The pattern

looks exactly like claws." Sybil walks over and touches the marks, hands glowing faintly with her magic. "But there is no trace of their essence. The attacks must have been at least a decade or two ago.

I leave the group to walk to the nearest house.

"Hello? Is anyone here?" I call out, stepping onto the porch of a modest single-story abode with a robust roof. The door, burdened by neglect, protests with a mournful creak, releasing a cloud of musty particles and stale air. The rotten floorboards creak under my boots. A solitary table with six chairs rests against the wall. Its surface is encrusted with grime and petrified remnants of half-consumed meals, as if the occupants had abruptly vanished mid-feast. A shiver dances down my spine as I venture deeper into the dwelling, my path interrupted by wispy cobwebs. The remaining three bedrooms, the bathroom, and the kitchen all bear the marks of hasty abandonment. Clothes still hang in the wardrobes, the beds have remained unmade, waiting to be filled again, and toys are scattered in the childrens' rooms. A whole life left behind, like so many other shifters had to do. Did these people make it to the camp? Do they sit in Tricella's dungeons or six feet under somewhere?

"You can come in!" I shout to my companions, who enter the main room one after the other. "It appears no one has set foot here in a long time. The house seems secure for the night, save for the thick layer of dust."

"I think it's safe to say we can stay here for the night. No matter what happened in the past, it doesn't look like anything is still haunting this place now, except for potential ghosts," Aries says uneasily as he takes off his pack and tosses it to the ground.

"There are only three bedrooms–" Sybil says, glancing at the hallway and back to our group. "Marcelene, Phoebe and I can take one, and the four of you can split between the other two."

"We should still rotate with someone on guard," I say, frowning. If there's anything we have learned in the last week at the rebel camp, it's that safety is an illusion. Especially when we know Tricella is still desperately looking for Sybil. My eyes meet hers and I can see she is thinking the same thing.

A boom of thunder rattles the walls of the house and we all glance outside the open door.

"The storm is coming quickly," Nero says, leaning out of the front door. "Aramis, Aries, Axton and I will see if we can find something to cook for dinner to fill our stomachs before the storm sets in, while the three of ye start up a fire to keep the wee beasties away." He clasps me tightly on the shoulder and gives me a look. I set my pack on the ground next to my sword and untie my bow and quiver.

"Do I look like a housewife to you?" Marcelene says tartly, pointing toward us. "I can bet you I'm a better shot than either of those two you're bringing with you."

"Oh, is that so?" Nero taunts. "Do ye want to make a bet on that?"

Marcelene snorts and tosses her head before grinning. "Don't you know cats love to play with mice? Why don't you and I see if we can catch some dinner before these two do?"

"Deal," Nero says. I frown at him over Marcelene's shoulder, but he only shrugs and grins before heading out the door toward the forest. Aries rolls his eyes and follows them, too.

"Sybil–"

"I know how to start a fire, Aramis. I was living on my own for years. Do you want my cloak? It's a lot warmer than the state yours is in, and I won't need it inside the house by the fire." She stares at the remains hanging around my neck before unpinning her heavy woolen cloak and holding it out to me.

"I cannot take this," I say, but the urge to pull it to my face and inhale her rich scent overwhelms me. I am to protect and care for her, but here she is caring for me.

"Go find us some dinner, otherwise we will never hear the end of it from Nero and Marcelene," she says as she and Phoebe walk outside and around the edge of the house in search of branches and logs for the fire.

"Alright, come on, Axton." I scoop up my bow and quiver from the ground before heading in the opposite direction.

I glance back as a low whistle cuts through the air.

"Well, isn't she a sight to behold," he remarks, his eyes gleaming as he watches Sybil walk toward some of the collapsed houses. "If you don't want her, I'll gladly take her, along with anything else she might offer."

I growl in response, yanking the cloak close to me and draping it over my shoulders, feeling the lingering warmth from her body. "She is not an object, nor is she offering anything," I snap.

Axton clicks his tongue, his voice filled with a mocking tone. "Hmm, I'm not so sure about that, mate. The way her ass moved as she—"

My fists clench as a crimson haze clouds my vision. "If I hear another breath from you about her, it'll be the last thing you'll say."

"And what are you going to do about it, Prince of Shadow-vale? They may have freed you from the cell but they've taken your powers," he says.

I grab his tunic and pull him toward me but when I see his wide grin; I realize I gave him exactly what he wanted from me: a reaction.

Sybil is my mate, but I cannot afford to lose control like this, just as she cannot lose control with her magic. I let him go and the cuffs feel heavy on my wrists. I can't even remember the feeling of the wind bending to my command anymore.

After a meek dinner of roasted hares and the two last rolls Oscar had gifted us before our departures, we settled into our rooms. Phoebe insisted on taking the first turn guarding outside and after much debate, I let her.

Nero and I take one of the children's rooms and since the beds are too small to accommodate two grown men, we look through the wardrobes and chests of drawers in search of any salvageable blankets that are not moth eaten. The floorboards creak as we lay down and exhale in relief as we finally take the pressure off our legs.

"We're a long way from home, my friend," Nero whispers in the dark, and I know he too is wondering how in Craeweth we ended up with a group like this and a suicide mission.

"I'm just glad you're here for the ride," I whisper back, and we chuckle.

Sleep comes quickly and without mercy. If the last night at camp spent with Sybil in my arms had been the best sleep I had ever had, this particular night is one of the worst. Nightmares of shadow monsters make me jitter, images of Shadowvale in flames, Edmund and all my men dead in a vicious and bloody battle, and Tricella on the throne, with my father's dead body at her feet.

Aramis!

Sybil's terrified voice cuts through the despairing images my brain is conjuring. I look for her in every scenario, horrified by what I'll see, but she's not there. *Aramis, please!*

My eyes snap open and I sit up, holding my hand to my chest as her voice reverberates through our bond.

23
SYBIL

Rain no longer pelts against the cracked window of the small bedroom I share with Marcelene and Phoebe.

We'd opted to sleep on the floor after the bed disintegrated from age when Marcelene tossed her bag on it. A slight breeze ruffles my hair, and it smells sweet like fermented honeysuckle.

The storm must have blown upon the window, but I remind myself that Aramis had checked the windows before retiring to his room. He paced around my chamber like an overbearing, protective beast, and I knew it was mostly because he did not want to leave me out of his sight. But as much as I craved his touch and warmth, I asked for space, and he granted me it.

"Stop it, Lemon. I'm trying to sleep," I mumble as I swipe a hand to push him away. His fur brushes against my face, making my nose tickle, but Lemon does not move away as usual.

I swipe another hand over my face and realize there's a hand, rough and hot to the touch, holding something under my nose. My eyes widen in shock as I stare into bright yellow pupils. I inhale to scream but my lungs fill with a powdery, sweet scent I have smelled before.

Corylorisis mushroom—used to paralyze someone as they maintain their conscious state. I had to learn that the hard way while harvesting in the woods next to my cottage.

My gut sinks, and I try not to breathe any more particles in, but the tips of my fingers are already tingling, refusing to move.

I try to move out of the constraints, wiggling my body left and right to see if Marcelene and Phoebe are safe before I completely lose control of my body, but it's a struggle.

His fangs glisten in the moonlight streaming through the open window as his massive form crouches over me. Holding my breath, I feel the spores rapidly working through my limbs. My tongue feels heavy as lead, and when I think I can't hold my breath any longer, darkness creeps into the corner of my vision. He removes the cloth and scoops my paralyzed body into his arms, stepping back toward the opening. My eyes move sluggishly over the room again, noting Marcelene curled around the small fire, fast asleep.

Is she alive? Have they drugged her too? Where is Phoebe?

I fight to keep my eyes on her, waiting for any sign of life, and when her chest rises and falls, relief floods through me. Hands lay on my body as someone passes me swiftly through the window to other shifters waiting outside. The smell of wet dog hits me as my face is shoved roughly against the waiting shifter's chest.

Aramis, Marcelene, Nero, anyone! Wake up!

I struggle to break free of my captor's arms, but my limbs are numb.

Both shifters pause, waiting to ensure no one hears them or is following, but silence ensues, and my heart sinks. I feel goosebumps crawling up my skin as the outside cold hits me. I am wearing a light blue traveling dress Phoebe found at camp, but the absence of my wool cloak is evident. How can no one have heard the commotion? Has everyone been drugged?

My body is jostled as my captors throw me over their shoulders and pick up an unrelenting speed, moving further away from the village. I look up at the night sky littered with stars. The canopies of trees above me scroll by as we move further away from the village, my friends. Aramis. A solitary tear runs along my temple. I scream internally as my thoughts begin to feel as sluggish and unresponsive as my body. My chest feels tight. My breathing comes out in short, shallow breaths, leaving me dizzy. Is this how it'll end?

No.

Think, Sybil, think. I take a deep breath, hoping the crisp night air will help me see things clearly. But as I do, something else comes alive within me.

I can feel the mating bond flaring to life like a lifeline.

This better work, I tell myself, and for the first time, I embrace the bond. The magic linking our souls brings warmth to my chest, it fills me and somehow makes me feel less alone. When I feel like I have the mating bond firm in my hands, I start screaming with everything I have left.

Aramis! Aramis, please!

I repeat those words over and over but there's no answer. Did they? No, I can't let my mind go there. Aramis is probably under the effects of the mushroom, just as I am.

"You've got her," a weasley voice says. I move my eyes as far to the right as possible but see only a wisp of hair. "Were you detected?"

"No, we vaporized some of the mushroom spores and

sprayed them into the rooms. See," the other man says while holding up a powder bag. "They're sleeping like babes." Yellow eyes peek into my field of vision and he snorts.

"Be careful where you swing that," the weasel voice snaps, grabbing it from their hand and shoving it into a leather pouch. "Do you want to knock us all out?"

"How long will she be incapacitated?" Yellow eyes calls out in a deep voice. "We don't have any more corylorisis powder. That shit is expensive."

"At least a few hours, but we will be far away from her companions and the prince by then. We can handle transporting one girl to the queen." He dumps me on the forest ground, my body aching from the impact as pine needles cut into my face and my skin through the fabric of my traveling gown. All I can see is their feet and the dirt below as they pace around.

Tricella.

Rage kindles deep in my gut and I scream internally, their conversation fading by the roaring in my ears. I have to get away. She can't have me.

Unicorn magic has the power to purify.

The corners of my lips curl up.

Power ripples in my veins as I call on my magic. The noxious hold of the corylorisis mushroom lessens, and the burning in my lungs subsides as I inhale a deep breath of the fresh night air. Nausea roils in my stomach at the use of so much magic at once. I had been more cautious with the amount of magic I pulled following the basilisk attack. The shifters' bickering and snapping come back into focus as my head clears.

"What's so important about one shifter? I mean, I know she's a unicorn, but what does the queen want with her?"

"We aren't here to ask questions. What does it matter,

anyway? Once she's delivered alive, we won't have to worry about the queen, the Council of Thorns, or anyone else. With all that gold, we can buy ourselves a ship and sail to start a new life somewhere else," yellow eyes growls, his long feline tail swishing impatiently behind him.

"Jessic will have the horses prepared for us but it'll take two days to travel to reach her. They should not be able to catch us on foot after that, especially with the prince's powers trapped. He's never going to break that spell." He spits on the ground and cackles. "Now pick her up; I want to get far away from here before they wake up."

I will my body to relax as rough hands grip me, and I'm hoisted over his shoulder. My nose collides painfully against his leather jerkin, and it takes everything in me not to cringe and cry out, giving away that the mushroom no longer holds me in paralysis.

I need to devise a way to escape without getting killed in the process. I have to bide my time and wait until they've settled to rest before we reach their other party to try to escape.

I lay on the ground, keeping my breath steady as they set up camp. The fire crackles, but I'm too far to feel its warmth. I shiver as the cold ground seeps into my bones and wish once again that I had my warm cloak with me.

"I'd kill for a warm bed and a cold beer," one of my captors grumbles. "We've been following them for days and have barely slept."

I hide my surprise and think back on our travels since leaving the camp. How did we not realize we were being followed? My chest tightens as I think back to the refugees and saying goodbye to the Council. I send a little prayer in their direction hoping they are all well on their way to the new safe point.

"Sunrise will be in a few hours. I'll take the first watch and then we will continue."

I wait as two of the shifters settle off to sleep, propped up against the trees. The wolf shifter who'd originally abducted me from the camp prods at the fire with a stick, sending sparks flying into the air. He yawns, stretching his arms into the sky. A loud hoot sounds from my left, and my heart jumps in my chest. My skin prickles as the shifter startles. He crouches defensively, muscles taunt as his bright eyes scan the night sky.

"Fucking owls," he grumbles as he picks up a rock and hurls it into the trees.

Marcelene!

I'm tempted to look, but I can't risk it. Is she here alone? How did she find me so quickly?

The sound of something crashing through the branches punctuates the stillness of the night. A great brown owl swoops down and disappears into the night sky. I sigh and close my eyes. It's as if hope had briefly fluttered within my grasp, only to be cruelly snatched away.

It was foolish to hope Marcelene had pushed past the effects of the mushroom's poison and alerted the others to find me. We were hours away from the camp, and by the time anyone arose and found me gone, our trail would be cold.

My heart pounds in my chest, its rhythm echoing in my ears, as the disappointment settles over me like a heavy fog. The weight of it constricts my chest, making it harder to draw in a steady breath. I can feel the tension in my muscles, the tightness gripping my shoulders and neck.

Be brave Sybil. A hero doesn't give up when it gets tough, they keep trying. Use your skills.

The wolf shifter pulls a flask from his bag, taking a long drought. I swallow, my tongue sticking to the roof of my parched mouth, likely a side effect of the corylorisis mushroom.

My body tenses as the shifter turns and walks to the other side of the camp. His two companions have fallen asleep, their breaths deep and even rhythms. The shifter on guard pokes the fire with a stick again, sending more sparks into the air along with the scent of ash that blows downwind toward me, stinging my eyes. I slowly blink, tears brimming my lashes.

He moves behind the treeline, and I hear the unmistakable sound of clothing being untied, followed by the sound of piss hitting the forest floor.

Now is my chance.

I shoot up as silently as I can, my eyes never leaving the two sleeping shifters on the ground as I back away. My palms sweat, and my heart races as I turn and run. Branches tear at my clothes and sting exposed skin. I don't care what direction I am heading in as long as I get away.

Raindrops cascade from the saturated branches above as I cautiously navigate the dense forest floor. Every step I take is measured; I focus on evading any treacherous exposed roots. Above, thunder reverberates, its booming presence accompanied by intermittent flashes of lightning that momentarily transform the obscurity into a fleeting spectacle of illuminated trees. Urgently, I tap into my reservoir of magic, propelling myself forward with increased speed, harnessing my demi-form's sharpened senses.

Pain lances along my skull as I'm yanked backward by my hair. I stare up into the snarling face of a shifter I haven't seen before. His sharp canines poke between his lips as his grip tightens on my scalp, his foul breath peppering my face.

"Let me go," I say through clenched teeth as I writhe against his grip.

"Well, what do we have here?" he snarls, his voice dripping with malice. I pull back my arm, ready to swing it into his face, but he's quick—too quick. He sidesteps, grabbing my arm and twisting it behind my back. I grimace, crying out as pain lances up my arm until it feels as though it's going to be pulled from its socket. He yanks me up against his chest, and I nearly gag as I feel his hot breath on the back of my neck. I summon every ounce of strength, every fiber of my being, and push back against him. With a burst of raw power, I kick my leg up into his groin, breaking free from his grasp as he doubles over. I spin around to face him once more, my body poised. Can I outrun him?

"Bitch," he growls and lunges, slamming me against the trunk of a tree before I have time to react. I twist, fighting for an inch of freedom, but he restrains my arms, rendering them useless, while the other tightens its grip around my throat, cutting off my air supply. The pressure is so intense that my vision becomes a blur of spinning stars.

Gasping for breath, I seethe through clenched teeth, "Let me go!" I struggle against his hold, desperately trying to break free, but he only tightens his grip, squeezing the life out of me.

As the edges of my vision slowly darken, determination surges through me. I lift my trembling hands, desperately scratching at his chest, but my limbs feel unnaturally heavy, as if burdened by invisible weights. A buzzing sound intensifies in my ears, growing louder with each passing moment, drowning out everything else. The sour stench of fear hangs in the air, mingling with the metallic tang of sweat. My arms give in to the overpowering weakness, gallingly falling limply to my sides.

"Oh, I don't think so. I'm not letting you go anywhere except to the queen. You've given us far more trouble than you're worth already," he taunts, his hold on my neck loosening slightly. Sensing an opportunity, I twist in his grasp, using his weight against him. In a moment of vulnerability, he loses his balance and trips, falling backward.

RUN!

I turn, palms scraping against bark as I propel myself forward but his sharp claws catch onto my skirt, causing me to tumble to the ground with him. The impact sends a jolt of pain through my body, but I refuse to let it hinder me. I scramble in the dirt, the earthy smell mixing with the scent of moss and pine needles that cover the ground.

I won't go down like this. This kingdom, the shifters, and the elementals need me. The Goddess chose me to be her undoing. Every movement is a battle against exhaustion, as I fight to regain my footing and stand tall once more. Dirt stains my clothes, but I ignore it. My eyes lock onto his, determination burning in my gaze.

"I will not go back to her," I yell. I pivot on the balls of my feet, my fingers instinctively reaching for the wellspring of my magic. The air carries the scent of desperation and fear. The beat of my heart quickens, urging me to escape. I'd be faster if I transformed into a nimble unicorn and fled. But before I can even contemplate the thought, I collide forcefully with the solid chest of the wolf shifter.

Pain courses through my body as his grip tightens around my wrists, his fingers digging into my skin. The sound of my gasp is drowned out by the pounding of blood in my ears. My vision blurs, stars dancing before my eyes as his clenched fist mercilessly meets my cheek. The metallic taste of blood floods my mouth as I inadvertently bite down on my tongue. Crimson droplets stain the ground beneath me. Defiance flickers within me, even through the pain, as I turn a burning gaze up at him. Brimming with tears, my eyes reflect a mixture of anguish and fury. He secures my wrists, binding them tightly with a coarse, fibrous rope. The motion knocks loose my family ring; it lands with a dull thud on the forest floor.

"You don't have a choice."

24
ARAMIS

I rush up from the floor, nearly slipping on the boots me and Nero have left by the door. My legs are unsteady, as if I've spent the night before drinking myself dumb. Even my head feels clouded. This is not normal. Her voice reverberates in my head and a sour taste fills my mouth. I slam the door open and break one of the rusty hinges.

"Can't ye hold yer piss until the morn?" Nero grumbles as he pulls the blanket over his head.

"Something isn't right," I hiss back as the hairs on my arm stand on end. My gut is filled with a sense of wrongness as I run to Sybil's room. A faint, unfamiliar scent like sweet honey lingers in the air.

"Sybil?" I call out at her door but am only met with silence. "Sybil, are you well?" I repeatedly slam my fist on the wooden door, nearly cracking the panel.

When no answer ensues, I push open the door to the girls' room, and my eyes are immediately drawn from the empty sleeping roll to the open window—no sign of Sybil.

I turn to the fireplace, where only coals and embers remain, and see Marcelene lying on her side, curled up in herself.

"Marcelene!" I call out but she does not move.

"Please don't—" I can't even finish the words and rush to her side, palms sweating and heart racing as I pull her on her back.

Marcelene's sharp feline eyes snap open, locking on mine and there's only terror in them. I exhale in relief as I see her chest barely moving up and down, but she lays on the floor like a puppet doll, her eyes begging for help.

"Nero!" I scream. The draken comes rushing in bouncing from wall to wall to help with his balance. When he reaches the door, he freezes as his eyes fall on Marcelene's figure. His hands hold the door frame with such strength, I hear the wood crack.

"I think she's paralyzed," I explain before he jumps to tragic conclusions. Nero is already at the witch's side, gently picking her up from the hard floor. Marcelene's body slumps in Nero's arms, but he's careful to support her head and make sure she can see what's going on around her. Her eyes fill with tears at the sight of Nero; the draken gently picks her up without saying a word, his nostrils flaring.

"What in Alpheaia's good name is going–" Aries rubs his eyes as he makes his way out of his room. His legs seem to be as uncooperative as mine, but his eyes are sharp. He inspects the girls' room and immediately understands what is going on.

"Where are Phoebe and Sybil?" He asks.

I rake both hands through my hair and look at the ceiling.

"Gone," I say, unable to add anything else when all I want to do is scream. Chaos ensues in my mind, wanting to do so many rushed things. I ultimately feel paralyzed in my indecision. I pace around the room, heart palpitating until Aries firmly rests a hand on my shoulder, and I stop. The shifter's eyes are set on mine. The resolution in them is a slap to my face, and I know I have to calm the fuck down. After I take a deep breath and nod to Aris in thanks, he straightens his back and crouches to the floor. He wrinkles his nose to sniff the air before letting out a feral growl.

"Corylorisis mushroom," he says, struggling to push himself back to his feet, as if his body was fighting his every command.

"Corylorisis mushroom?" I repeat, lifting a brow. "What does that–"

"It's a rare fungus whose powdery spores, if harvested correctly, can be used in small doses to induce sleep," he says, meeting my gaze, the air hanging heavy between us.

"And in larger doses?" I ask, body tensing as I already guess the answer.

"Temporary paralysis." He looks at Marcelene, his hands flex, claws peeking out as if shaking off the last of the effect of the poison. "An overdose would be lethal."

"How the fuck did Tricella find us so quickly and in the middle of Goddess damn nowhere," Nero shouts, still cradling Marcelene. Before I can answer, footsteps approach down the hall.

"What's going on?" Phoebe asks sleepily from the doorway. Her eyes widen when she notices the witch still unable to move. "Where is Sybil?"

"Where were you? I thought you were standing guard!" I whirl to face her, hands clenching at my sides.

"I-I was! I must have dozed off!" She stands up quickly, body trembling, and I notice she can barely stand—no better off than the rest of us.

A peal of thunder booms in the distance, shaking the small house. We all look out of the window, and the thought of her out there fills me with murderous fury.

"We've all been drugged. I don't think any of us would have been able to hear someone break in. Except for Marcelene, she might know something." The witch's petite body looks even smaller in Nero's arms, her colossal spirit having been blown out like a candle. Her eyes are barely open, lids fluttering from the exhaustion. Nero fixes her unbound blond hair out of her face with tenderness.

"How long does the paralysis last?" I ask Aries, who rubs his chin in thought.

"Difficult to say without knowing the dosage they used. Could be up to two days."

Marcelene's eyes widen in panic, and more tears fall down her cheeks. Thunder continues echoing outside, but it gets fainter at every outburst.

"We cannot wait. There must be something we can do now," Nero chides and mindlessly takes Marcelene's hand.

"If I remember correctly, red clover helps to eject the toxins from the blood system," Phoebe says, crossing her arms over her chest. "I can check Sybil's healing satchel to see if she has some, or anything else we can use to help Marcelene."

"That's a good idea, Phoebe. We also must perlustrate our surroundings; there must be something to give us a sense of direction, footprints in the mud maybe," I say, trying to think strategically instead of letting my emotions get the better of me, something Nero was clearly struggling to do.

"Where the fuck is Axton?" he growls, and we all turn to the hall.

I rush to the other bedroom, careful not to stumble on my own steps. There, half hanging off one of the kids' beds, lies the thief, eyes wide open but struggling to control any of his limbs.

"Arrimis" he slurs his words as his tongue almost hangs out like a dog. The toxins must have had a much stronger effect on him. I stand by the door frame and cross my arms over my chest as Axton tries to get on his feet. "A haaaand maaybee, maaite?"

I return to the girls' room, where Phoebe is crouched by Sybil's satchel, checking vile after vile. I see from the window that Aries is already outside, examining the area thoroughly.

"Axton's got the physical mobility of a worm at the moment, which is very fitting. I am sure he had nothing to do with this," I say, trying to keep my breathing in check before anxiety takes over.

"Got it!" Phoebe exclaims, holding up a glass tube with a reddish powder. "I just need to brew some tea." She runs out of the room, and I scoop Lemon off the floor where he's curled up and sleeping. He lets out a squeak of annoyance as he peeks open a sleepy eye, sniffing at my hands.

"You too, little fella?"

Lemon wiggles out of my hands on unsteady paws, climbs up my sleeve, and looks around the small room from his perch. I reach up to pat his head but pull away as he nips at my fingers.

"They can't have gotten too far." I try focusing on the mating bond, seeing if I can sense her but there's nothing. My magic still feels miles away from me. I clench my fists and stare at the metal wrapping around my wrists.

"Nero, if Tricella has her—"

"Stop, right now," he says. We stand there looking at each other while Marcelene slowly dozes off in his arms. "Focus, Aramis."

"Here." Phoebe comes storming back into the bedroom, holding a steaming metal cup. I take the few blankets and Sybil's wool cloak and prop them against a wall to help Marcelene lean against them. Nero gently lays her down, and with Phoebe's help, they move Marcelene's jaw and head to get some of the tea down her system. Nero and I look at the witch, then at Phoebe expectantly as she stands next to me.

"What?" the shifter asks, furrowing her ginger brows and then scoffs. "Are you expecting this to work like magic?" She shakes her head and says to herself, "Men really have to learn the art of patience. Leave the woman alone." Phoebe nods to the door. "She'll wake when she's ready. I'll stay with her."

Lemon crawls down my shoulder and settles in the pocket of my leather jacket. Nero and I take our swords from the main room to join Aries outside under the faint rain. The moon sits high in the sky but is barely visible through the thick gray clouds.

"The muddy ground held some of the kidnappers' footsteps," Aries says as he sees us approaching. "I even shifted and caught a scent but," Aries looks at us, confusion etching his wet face from the rain drops falling from his hairline. "They were shifters."

"Impossible," Nero says matter-of-factly and goes to inspect the footsteps himself as we follow. "Why would shifters want to take one of their own? Every shifter in Shadowvale knows about Tricella and the Council of Thorns by now."

"We're at war, Nero. People do desperate things for all sorts of reasons when they're frightened," Aries says and looks at me. It's a kindness that he thinks desperation drove my actions against the shifters. I crouch next to Nero to inspect the markings in the mud before the rain washes them away entirely.

Nero conjures his demi-form, scales glistening under the faint moonlight. He takes a deep breath as he closes his eyes.

"Fuck," he whispers. "Aries is right."

"How many?"

"Four, potentially five."

We stand again, worry clawing at me like a chimera.

"I can't wait longer," I say. "Nero, go back to the house and stay with Phoebe, Marcelene, and Axton. We don't know if they plan to return to finish the job. Aries—"

"I'll head west. Let's meet back here in three hours." Aries flashes me a grin, his sharp canines flashing. "Goddess speed, Prince." He crouches, his body molding into his wolven form before he extends his claws and launches himself into the woods.

I see Nero hesitating to let me go alone, his hand jostling with the hilt of his sword.

"She needs you," I say, looking through the window at Marcelene asleep in the golden light of the fire. Nero nods before returning inside.

I trudge out of the desolate village and off into the woods, heading east.

Where is she, my mate?

Sybil!

I call out her name over and over, reaching through the bond, hoping to catch even a glimmer of her to lead me in the right direction.

The woods are not kind at this time of night. I keep my senses alert as creatures lurk in the shadows watching me, waiting for me to trip and end up at their mercy. The familiar weight of my sword sheathed at my side gives me some comfort in the absence of my magic. But the wind carries screams and whispers, trying to play with my head. I shake them out before they can bewitch me and focus on the sounds of nature. The sound of water has me turning a sharp left and soon I come to a small stream. I kneel, cupping my hands in the freezing water and bringing it to my lips, but as I do, the mirrored image of the moon waivers in the rippling water.

Alpheaia.

I reach into my tunic and pull out the stone necklace,

letting it spin on its cord in the moonlight. No light pulses from within, and there is no sense of direction or purpose. I yank it off my neck, throwing it as hard as I can, but it bounces harmlessly off the trunk of a tree, landing in the dirt. It's useless.

Just how I feel.

"A prince now powerless and without a throne. Where has your little unicorn been stolen off to this time?" A musical male voice says behind me. I turn, unsheathing my sword, and see the silhouette of a shadow fae leaning against a tree trunk.

"What do you know?" I ask, eyes narrowing.

"Not everyone is to be trusted. You failed to listen to your instincts once. What is it telling you now?" My mind flicks back to the rebel village.

"Aries," I growl as my hands clench at my sides. But his attitude toward me had changed. Was it all just a ploy to lead me down the wrong path?

"Perhaps. The wolf does have a temper, but could he turn against his own?" he muses.

I rack my brain, trying to remember if anyone else stood out at the village, but I come up empty. My mind is only full of the kindness the refugees have shown me.

Aries seemed to be the least affected by the toxins. Could he have faked it? Did he agree to split so that he could have an excuse to run away?

"Tell me what you know, where is she?" I glower, grinding my teeth together. My patience is beginning to grow thin, and I am beginning to feel like he's the cat and I'm his mouse.

"Temper, temper, *princeling*. Anger does not become you without your wind to cool you down. Where are your manners? Did they lock those away along with your powers?" He gestures nonchalantly to my wrists.

I flinch at his words. "Would you *please* tell me who and where they've taken Sybil?"

"No."

I clench my teeth, feeling the pulse in my temples begin to pound. As I'm about to lunge forward with my sword, the shadow fae comes flying in my direction. Bony black hands grab my face as whisps made of shadow cloud my vision and wrap around my wrists and ankles, slowly lifting me in the moonlight shining through the clouds.

"Heed my words, Aramis Adrostos," the Fae's voice echoes in my head, making my every bone shake. "You are the tipping point. There will come a time when sacrifices must be made, when your soul will be a weight on the sacred steps of the Goddess's temple. She's been watching you. Your choices might look like they're your own, but like millions of water drops create an ocean, so do your choices. You will save or condemn your kingdom. Follow the bond, follow your heart."

I free-fall to the ground, nearly snapping my ankle. Shaking my head, I try to get the Fae out of my head, but when I turn to face him again, he's gone. I open my palm, and the gifted necklace I had thrown away begins to pulse with a faint glow as I turn northward.

"Fucking shadow fae." Lemon pokes his head out of my pocket and begins chittering.

"Yes, yes, hush. I know he was inadvertently trying to help without intervening, but did he have to be so cryptic?" I roll my eyes as I push northward through the foliage.

My chest constricts as I trudge deeper into the dense undergrowth. The eerie silence only adds to my anxiety, but I cling to the tenuous bond that ties us together.

Lightning streaks across the sky, followed by the booming sound that reverberates through the air. In that fleeting moment of light, I catch sight of a torn cloth fluttering in the wind, snagged on a bramble.

And Sybil's family ring.

25
ARAMIS

I sprint through the woods, the branches brushing against my arms and the ground crunching beneath my feet.

My heart pounds with every step as I try to keep my balance on the treacherous terrain. As the skyline lightens with the blush of morning, the rising sun battles with the clouds looming above, casting an eerie glow over the landscape. Breathing hurts, my muscles are strained and sweat drenches my brow but I keep running, Sybil's family ring safely tucked in my pocket with Lemon.

I scan the surroundings, hoping for any sign—any trace— that can lead me to her captors. With each passing hour, my hope wanes. My mind is drowning in thoughts of Aries' betrayal and Sybil's well-being, but I press forward, refusing to let despair consume me.

She has to be alive.

Almost in confirmation, the bond tugs in my chest, spurring me onwards. The branches viciously grasp at my clothes, etching deep scratches and tearing at the fabric. The rumble of thunder echoes from afar while the heavy gray storm clouds battle with the peachy glow painted on the horizon. The air carries the heavy anticipation of more rain, filling my nostrils with the earthy scent.

I can't afford to lose hope, not now. Not when she is so close to seeing me as a male and not a monster.

A distant rustling breaks the silence, making me slow down and become a quiet shadow. I follow the sound, heart racing, and I crouch low, unsheathing my sword. The morning breeze carries the unmistakable scents of sweat, damp fur, and smoke. Could it be Aries?

I move closer, careful not to be seen. A bellow of rage rents the air, followed by a loud smack and a small cry. Her cry. Rage floods my blood, hot as molten gold, and all thoughts of stealth leave my mind.

I step out of my hiding space, my steps confident, and sprint to the male. His back is to me and his hand is held high, ready to strike. One sleek motion of my sword and his hand drops to the ground as screeching screams echo in the woods. The shifter clutches his stump, and as he moves, I see Sybil bound to a tree with purple bruises forming on her cheek. Our eyes meet briefly, relief making her shoulders drop and her eyes glaze over. Before the shifter can move, I point my sword to his neck.

"I was going to say if you lay another finger on her, you'll lose your hand, but I got carried away." I raise my shoulders, but the man's face is the portrait of rage, his leathers getting soaked as his blood drips everywhere.

"You scum," the man screams. Three more shifters appear, one of them in their wolf form. I look at their faces, and a rush of relief washes over me as I realize they are not shifters from the camp. Maybe Aries is not such an asshole after all.

"Don't let him take her," the tallest of the four says, and

they all widen their stance, ready to defend what they think is theirs.

Too bad Sybil is *mine*.

With a surge of adrenaline, I twist my sword and charge at the wolf shifter closest to me. His eyes flash with a menacing yellow hue as his body contorts and reshapes. The air crackles with tension as my blade slices effortlessly through him, the metallic tang of blood filling the air as he crumples to the ground with a resounding thump.

I pivot swiftly, my senses on high alert, locking eyes with the remaining three shifters. In an instant, one of them morphs into a sleek, ebony panther, muscles rippling beneath its glossy fur. It lunges toward me, a blur of feral grace. I react instinctively, narrowly evading its razor-sharp claws. The impact sends a jolt of pain through my forearm, the searing sensation mingling with the adrenaline coursing through my veins.

"Aramis, watch out!" Sybil cries out.

As I turn, the panther springs toward me, its claws outstretched. I'm sent crashing to the ground, the impact leaving me gasping for air. One arm curls protectively over the pocket where Lemon has stayed hidden. Above me, the massive beast's eyes glaze over, and over its shoulder, my sword juts out of its back. With a grunt, I shove its weight off my body. Every inch of me aches, and the woods spins danger-ously as I push to my feet. The scent of damp earth mingles with the metallic tang of blood, filling my nostrils as I press on, fuelled by a potent mix of anger and determination. Before I can attack the man with the stump, he shifts into a battered rat —one I have seen before—and runs away.

"Aramis," Sybil gasps. When I look at her, the last shifter, a man my age, holds a dagger to her throat, but his hands are shaking.

"Let her go," I say as I narrow my eyes at him. I can't help but think that, with my magic, this confrontation would have been resolved by now.

"I-I can't!" The man says, his knuckles white from his tight grip on the dagger. Sybil's eyes are wide, but I can see she trusts me.

"The queen wants her," the man continues. Desperation laces his every word. "I appreciate the resolve," I say calmly as I wipe my bloody palms on my tunic before yanking my sword from the panther. The sight of the dead body makes my stomach turn—another shifter dead at my hand.

Don't be shy, let her see the true you, Aramis. You love to kill. Tricella's voice whispers in my head and catches me off guard. Was it real? Am I losing my mind? I nearly empty my stomach but hold my composure.

"But if you kill her," I continue, dragging my sword on the ground, "you won't have anything to bring to your Queen—"

"She is not my Queen!" the man screams, spitting his words at me. I furrow my brows in confusion, but Sybil uses the moment to her advantage.

Wielding her light magic, she burns the ropes holding her captive. She twists, jabbing her elbow into the stomach of her captor, who doubles over coughing and loses his grip on his dagger. I race forward, pick up the dagger, and slam the pommel of my sword into his temple. Holding his head, he slides down against the tree trunk Sybil was bound to and... he starts crying.

"Please—" he whimpers.

Sybil and I look at each other in confusion. I sheath my sword but keep his dagger in my hand.

"Tell us the truth or bear the consequences," I answer as Sybil stands behind me. Her eyes soften as the man keeps sobbing, and I think to myself that the woman truly is too good for her own good.

"Please don't hurt me. I have a family. I was just doing what I was told."

I lift his chin with the toe of my boot, forcing him to look at me. "Did you hurt her?"

"I-I-" he stammers, looking between me and Sybil behind me.

"I'll only repeat myself one time. Did you lay a hand on her?"

"N-no! Only just now to keep her from running." Tears stream down his face, leaving muddy tracks on his olive skin. "Only James touched her when she head-butted him."

The corners of my lips turn up in pride, but I make a mental note to teach her how to drop an opponent larger than her. She might have the right spirit, but the skills are necessary.

"Who gave the order? Do you act outside of the Council of Thorns?" I wipe the dagger against my pant leg before sliding it into its new home, the little sheath next to my sword, and cross my arms over my chest.

"Fuck the Council of Thorns," he spits at my feet. The clogs in my mind start turning, trying to put pieces together.

The shifter shakes his head and lets it fall forward hiding his eyes, "What have they done to help our people? Gathered them up in a little camp to play safe village while hundreds of shifters are still locked in her dungeons? How does that change things?"

I push down the need to defend the Council and Victor; I need him to keep talking.

"Peace," he continues with a sad laugh. "They want peace, but at what cost? The Queen does not give a shit about us shifters. Turns out, she does not give a shit about elementals either. Fuck, I don't think she has a heart because how can someone so cruel have one?"

Did you ever wonder why there were never elemental bodies left behind? Victor's voice booms in my head.

"You kidnapped the elementals living in the villages attacked by Tricella," I say, attempting to prove a theory.

After a moment of hesitation, he slumps his shoulders even further, defeated in his attempt to maintain control of the situation.

"What a fucking stupid plan, isn't it?" The man confirms my suspicions and looks at me. His blue eyes are bloodshot and surrounded by dark circles. I notice how run down his clothes are, how they hang on his body without shape. His cheeks are caved in and his fingers jitter. When was the last time this man ate something?

"We thought we could use the elementals to bargain with her. If she was going to threaten our people, we would threaten hers."

"Who is 'we?'" Sybil asks, stepping forward, head tilted.

"We don't have a name. All we want is justice. We're shifters, just like you, and we're tired of abandoning our homes out of fear. Tired of having to bow our heads. Do you want to know what Tricella said when we offered fifty elementals in exchange for fifty shifters?"

I hold my breath. What has become of this kingdom?

"Kill. Them. All," he enunciates every word as if he still can't believe them. "So we freed them all because we could not bear the thought of becoming as tyrannical as she is."

Sybil looks at me, and I can tell she is desperate to tell me something, but bites her tongue. Instead, she slowly approaches the man sitting against the tree trunk.

My hand flies to the hilt of my sword, ready to reach for her, but she holds up a hand to stop me and crouches in front of the man.

"You're all she wants," he says when they're on the same

level. His voice cracks. "We didn't want to sacrifice one of our own, but we were trying to save our families."

Guilt, hot and acrid, flows through me at the thought of the men I've killed. This deadly cycle needs to end.

Sybil takes the man's hands in hers, and her palms emit the faintest glow that makes his bloodshot eyes shine in wonder. Slowly, his bruises and cuts heal, his cheeks get fuller, and his complexion regains a healthy color.

"I forgive you," she whispers. "We are going to fix this, I promise."

The man nods at her in gratitude.

"Go. Go to your companions and tell them that the Council of Thorns showed you mercy," I say. "Then, go home to your family and take them far from here. Take the routes going east to the mountains. Who knows, you might find people willing to help you find some peace." Sybil smiles in my direction, and I continue, "There's honor in running away too, especially when it means safeguarding the most valuable thing you have: your life."

I glance down as I feel a barely discernible crack along the bands at my wrists, but they remain firmly attached, my powers inaccessible.

The man stands and brushes the dirt off his clothes. Sybil returns to my side and interlocks her fingers with mine.

"I will not forget your kindness, Sybil Vandaleur and Prince Aramis," the man says.he effects of Sybil's magic are unmistakable. He holds a hand to his chest and continues, "My name is Errik. I hope to meet you again one day, in a kingdom where we're all at peace."

He turns on his feet, walking westward as the sun finally peeks through the clouds.

I turn my back on him, and my eyes catch on her—a silent understanding passing through us.

I know she'd like to chide me for losing my temper, and she knows I'd like to tell her that she can't show mercy to every stranger she meets. But we both know we did the right thing—that we complement each other. Together, we will rebuild this kingdom and give justice to these people.

Not wanting to waste one more second, I rush forward to gather her in my arms, cherishing the weight of her against me. She wraps her arms around my neck, and I bury my face into her long brown hair, inhaling her familiar scent of lavender and black tea.

"I thought I lost you," the words a mere whisper. I push her back an arm's length away, and she slides her hands on my chest. Their warmth seeps through my wet clothes. I gingerly touch the blood blossoming on her cheek, and she flinches at my touch as I run my finger along the bone. "I don't think it's broken, just bruised. If I could kill him again for laying a hand on you, I would."

"You found me," she says, tears lining her eyes. She blinks, raising her hand to wipe at her face. The intensity of her gaze is about to make me lose my restraints.

"Sybil, I—" I go to kiss her, and our lips barely touch when Lemon squirms inside my tunic pocket squished between our bodies. He pokes his head out and chitters at me before climbing into Sybil's arms.

"Lemon!" she squeals and kisses the top of his head. He wiggles in her arms before climbing to curl around her neck and lick her injured cheek. The blossoming bruise fades under the creature's touch.

"This sassy rascal is nothing but trouble," I say as I rub his head. Lemon lets out a disgruntled squeak before climbing down her skirts to the forest floor. My hand brushes against her cheek. Her breath hitches at the contact, and her eyes meet mine. They are a sea of brown and green, a reflection of the wild forest.

"Thank you, for protecting him. For coming for me," she says, nibbling her bottom lip.

"Sybil," I say, cupping her face between my hands and tenderly stroking her cheeks with my thumbs. "I would move mountains to find you." I kiss her deeply.

26

SYBIL

Rain falls from the sky, peppering our clothes as our kiss deepens.

My body molds against his with a fervent embrace, the bond between us singing deep within me at the connection. His faint scent of cedar and bergamot radiates off his leather jerkin. My heart skips a beat, a soft gasp escaping my lips as I feel the firm pressure of his body against mine. The fabric of my chemise brushes against my skin, the sensation heightened by the intensity of his grasp.

His hands rove to my face, pulling a breath span from my lips as he stares into my eyes.

"I heard you call for me, Sybil. It drove me mad." He leans forward, gently cradling my face and resting his forehead on mine. "I thought I was dreaming but... I was terrified."

Reaching out to him was my first instinct.

Thunder forks across the sky, his words hanging heavy between us. Moments pass, and the soft rustle of the wind through the trees is the only sound. I look at his beautiful face in the light of the few defiant rays of sun brave enough to push through the rainy clouds.

I lift my hand and trace the sharp planes of his face and the golden scruff of his jawline. Watching him tremble under my touch, I press up on tiptoes to whisper in his ear. "I know, I called for you through the bond." His blue eyes widen as he reads the secret truth weaved between my words. "I don't know how I did it, but in that moment, all I wanted was for you to find me. I can no longer bear a single second away from you, Aramis."

There is so much I have yet to learn about the intricacies of the mating bond, but if there's one thing I know, it's that the bond never was in control of us or our feelings. We control it, it's an extension of our love; it binds us even when forces greater than us pull us away from each other.

His strong and firm fingers slide possessively into my hair and tangle in the strands. As he crushes his lips against mine, the force of our passion propels my back into the rough bark of the trunk. Raindrops, like tiny diamonds, scatter from the lush green branches above us, creating a symphony of pitter-patter.

He lifts me effortlessly into his embrace; my legs instinctively wind around his waist, causing my skirt to bunch up around my trembling limbs. "You're the most beautiful creature I've ever seen," he murmurs, eliciting a derisive snort from me. As he gently places me on a moss-covered boulder, his knees sink into the clean, damp earth, creating a stark contrast against the backdrop of my stained, torn, and blood-soaked clothing. The night's relentless storm has left me drenched to the bone, my hair a chaotic tangle adorned with the remnants of nature's debris.

"Aramis, I've been dragged around the forest through a rainstorm by greedy shifters bent on delivering me to Tricella. I am anything but beautiful right now." I motion toward my disheveled state, wincing in discomfort as the effects of the adrenaline fade. My palms bear the brunt of my desperate struggle, raw and bloody from my determined attempt to escape.

"You are a Goddess." He grabs my hands, turning them skyward as he presses the softest kiss against my wounds. I shiver in response as his kisses trail up the sensitive flesh on the underside of my wrist, the warmth spreading through my veins and desire building between my thighs.

I close my eyes, and the memory of their putrid breath and tight grip on my body comes rushing back. My body shakes at the fear of what would have happened had he not felt me through the bond and known where I was—had he not rescued me.

"Sybil," he whispers as he releases my hands, his hungry gaze sweeping over my body as he kneels before me. I feel a warm flush spread across my face as he locks his intense gaze on me.

"Aramis," I moan, bracing my hand behind me, the cold contrasting with the heat of him between my legs. "What about the others? They'll be looking for us. Someone could walk up on us at any moment."

"They won't." He smiles, meeting my gaze as his hands circle lazily on my inner thighs, each movement closer to my core.

"How–how do you know they won't?" I pant between strokes, reveling in the sensations coursing through my body.

"Because if anyone dares to interrupt us right now, Tricella will be the least of their worries," he says, running a finger through my exposed wetness and groaning in approval as I arch at his touch. "So beautiful, my pomme sucrée. There's so much I want to tell you."

"Maybe this isn't the best time to talk," I laugh, legs

squeezing against his shoulders. He places his hands on my thighs, tightening around them.

"Just a matter of perspective," he chuckles, then slides a finger across my center, his thumb gently circling my swollen bundle of nerves, raising a moan from my mouth. "You complete me in ways I never dreamed were possible."

"Oh, Goddess." My hips rise, seeking more friction, but he spreads a hand over my pelvis and presses me down. "I want you, Aramis. Right now," I whisper. I'm swept away by everything about him. His taste. His touch. His scent. All of it.

He slides another finger, then pushes inside me as he covers me with his mouth, flicking with his tongue. "Goddess, how long I've yearned for you to speak those words to me," he gasps, his breath ragged.

"Aramis." I can't focus through the blinding pleasure. I fist a hand through his hair, rocking my hips in rhythm to his thrusting, feeling the pressure build inside me, but he holds me in place. His responding growl vibrates against my sensitive flesh, sending me over the edge, and I cry out as I orgasm hard with his head buried between my thighs.

I feel as light as a cloud, held down to earth only by his grip on me. Waves of satisfaction hum along the bond tying us together. *Did all bonded mates feel this much from their connection?*

When my breathing slows, he gently pulls away and stands before me. I lift my hands, fingers trembling as I work at his leather belt.

"Are you sure? " He asks as he covers my hands with one of his, lifting my chin with the other to meet his gaze. "This isn't the bed of finest silk I promised you."

"Yes," I say, feeling confident. This is my decision.

Not the bond. Not fate. Mine.

He is mine.

I slip my hand under his tunic, feeling his warmth. "I want to know you, all of you."

He grabs the hem of his tunic and pulls it over his head, tossing it behind me. The rain has slowed to a drizzle, the sun's rising rays continuing to peek through the clouds and dancing with the shadows along his skin. He is still as my hands span across his abdomen, the ropes of muscle flex taunt under my touch. I skim over his chest, pausing at the healed, jagged scar.

"From the night they attacked when I was a boy," he says, placing his hand above mine. "The blade was poisoned, so it never healed properly. But that is the past, Sybil."

"I want you," I whisper as I push upward, pressing a soft kiss along the puckered scar. I let my hand drop, and I finish unbuckling his belt. He springs free from the confines of his breeches and I marvel at the length of him. I have seen many females and males in various states of undress in the little training I have had as a healer, but this is different. I watch the emotions dance across his face as I take my time exploring him. He inhales sharply as I tentatively run a finger along the smooth skin, then curl my fingers around his girth and begin stroking him. There is no denying the way he hardens even further under my grip.

"Sit back, Sybil," he orders, voice low and gravely. I drop my hands, bracing them on the velvety moss behind me as I lean back. His eyes glint dangerously, something animalistic rising to the surface as he bends toward me and grabs me around the waist.

"Did I do something wrong?" I ask, swallowing back my nerves. My chest rises and falls, straining against the soaked fabric of my chemise.

Have I crossed some sort of line?

"Did you do something wrong?" he chuckles darkly, positioning himself between my thighs. He places one hand on the front of my chest, pushing until I lean onto my elbows and stare into the rugged angles of his handsome face. "If you didn't stop, I was going to lose myself and bury myself inside you to the hilt until you screamed. I only have so much control when you have your hand wrapped around my cock, Sybil darling."

"Oh," I murmur softly as he slides an arm behind each thigh. He pushes them wide, tilting me back further until my back touches the cold stone beneath me. He leans forward, the heat from his hands a brand upon my skin. I writhe under his touch. "Oh gods," I whisper, back arching as he drags his tongue along my entrance. My body trembles from the wet heat of his mouth. I had never felt this way before, not even the few moments I had explored myself. My skin buzzes with a new energy and I feel like I'm going to explode again from his very touch.

"Aramis," I whimper as I thrust my hands through his hair, needing something.

"What happened to god?" he teases, nipping at the inside of my thigh.

"I want–" I squirm as he pauses, his stubble grazing the sensitive skin. I want more, I need more.

"What do you want, my pomme sucrée?" He asks.

"I want to feel you inside me," I writhe wantonly beneath him.

"This may be uncomfortable, but I'll go slow. Do you trust me?" he whispers against my temple as he positions himself over me, lining himself up with my entrance. His hands grip my hips as he slowly sinks inside me, stretching me inch by inch. I gasp at the discomfort when he seats himself fully inside me. He swallows the sound with a crushing kiss, holding his body still above mine as I adjust to the size of him.

"You are the most gorgeous, yet frustrating creature I've ever met. You're fucking perfect in every way."

When he came for me, I never imagined this is how it would end. Maybe it's the bond pulling us together, but everything we're doing now feels so natural.

The intensity of our kiss is heightened as he slips his tongue inside my mouth, tangling with mine. He begins to move in slow, shallow thrusts. The sharp bite of pain swiftly gives way to pleasure, and I let loose the breath I hadn't realized I was holding.

His moans reverberate through me, fueling the fire of desire that burns within. I arch against him, seeking more of his touch, my body craving the intoxicating pleasure he brings.

"I—" Stars form in my vision as my stomach tightens, forcing my body to arch off the rock as I come undone.

He presses a kiss along the base of my throat, smiling against my skin. "Good girl."

I moan in response, clinging to him as another wave of pleasure begins anew. My hips rock up, meeting him with each thrust.

"You will be my undoing and my salvation," he moans, lips hovering over mine. He buries a hand in my hair, tugging my head back as he withdraws from me. "We fit together like you were fucking made for me." With a fierce thrust, he enters me again, filling me completely. I inhale sharply, my nails digging into the moss beneath me. The rhythm intensifies, each powerful thrust pushing me closer to unraveling again.

His words, laced with desire, only serve to ignite the flames further. The way he tugs my hair, gently yet possessively, pulls me further into the realm of passion. It's as if he's unraveling the layers of my soul, exposing the raw vulnerability that lies beneath. As the wave of desire courses through my body, my senses heighten, every nerve ending coming alive. The kiss becomes more ravenous, our tongues dancing in a frenzied rhythm, exploring each other's mouths. With each slow, shallow stroke, I can feel my body adapting to him, the sensation intensifying, and the connection between us growing stronger.

"Yes," I murmur against his lips. Because it is. It felt so good, and at this moment, I wanted to know more about him. He promised to prove his worth—be a better male—and deep down his words ring true.

I realize he has the power to undo me, to break down the walls I've built around my heart against the actions of his past and the fear of fate controlling my future. Yet, he also has the potential to be my salvation, to offer a love that surpasses all boundaries. It's a risk I'm willing to take, for the spark between us is undeniable.

His grip tightens on my hips, his fingers leaving marks as he increases the rhythm. Heat builds within me, a wildfire ready to consume. As our bodies move as one, the intensity builds to a crescendo. With a final thrust, he holds himself still, allowing me to reach the pinnacle of bliss. I feel myself teetering on the edge, my body clenching around him, pulsating with ecstasy. The sensation is overwhelming, consuming me entirely as I surrender to the contentment that courses through my veins.

In this moment, I realize that our connection goes beyond mere physical reaction and a fated bond. It's a connection of souls, a profound understanding that speaks volumes in the silence between us. As I come down from the euphoric high, I can't help but believe that there is something more to discover, something worth exploring in the depths of this newfound connection. I may not be able to deny the mating bond any longer as it entwines with my true feelings.

27
ARAMIS

Fourteen days have passed since we left the rebel camp, and I don't feel like we are any closer to the dragon's lair.

I am beginning to wonder if Axton is all fable and no truth. After the events with the kidnappers, we returned to the road with our spirits slightly dimmed. Marcelene's experience with the corylorisis mushroom left her shaken up. The tea helped, but the terror of seeing her friend being taken and not being able to do anything to stop them had left an invisible wound on her. After hearing about the radical shifters, she recalled an incident at the village where she had noticed a man behaving oddly. He seemed to linger around the council tent, which caught her attention. Curiosity compelled her to confront him, but he swiftly fled. It was only in the aftermath, while she was recuperating that she realized the man with the yellow eyes was the same shifter who poisoned us.

Nero now carries her pack and always walks only a few

steps behind her. I see their stolen glances and wonder if something else happened after Marcelene's paralysis ended.

Aries and Phoebe were shocked to hear that another group of shifter rebels was attempting to overthrow Tricella using less conventional methods. The defeat that, even in a time of need, people could not come together under one banner was hard to accept, especially when the efforts of The Council of Thorns had made a significant difference to so many shifters.

My mind wandered back to Errik's story more times than I would have liked. The people of Shadowvale are desperate enough to be driven to murder to save their families— condemned to a life of hardship, to abandon their homes. There's nothing I can tell these people when I sit on the throne that will make up for their suffering. But I will try to make it right, should it be the last thing I do.

Sybil and I walk hand in hand. The group had settled into a routine, hiking as far as we can during the day, then camping at night under the trees with strict guard rotations to keep the beasts at bay. Food has become scarcer and the enchanted water satchels Evolet gifted us have started to waiver.

"How far away did ye say this dragon was?" Nero asks, shading his eyes as he looks upward through the canopy of trees. Murky gray clouds are beginning to roll in from the east, and we all wonder if it means there's more rain on the horizon.

"I'd say maybe another week east through the forest and then deep into the Rocheux mountains," Axton says as he rubs at his lower back. "This storm rolling in will hinder our progress and ache my joints. I bet that mushroom is still in my system. And I'm feeling a bit weary in my old age."

"You're lucky we didn't leave you to rot after forcing the coordinates out of you." I hoist the bag higher up on my shoulder.

"Now, where would the fun be in that? I'd miss out on such beautiful company," he says, turning to the three girls.

"Oh please," Marcelene says, rolling her eyes.

"What made you choose the life of a thief?" Sybil asks as he slows his pace to walk by her side. A muscle in my jaw ticks as I clench my teeth together, staring at his swaggering gait.

"Oh, I didn't choose the life of a thief. I set out to be an adventurer, but times are hard and food doesn't grow on trees," he says, winking at her.

"Food literally grows on trees. The saying is *gold* doesn't grow on trees," I say as I flick my gaze skyward.

"How did Tricella find ye, anyways?" Nero asks, crossing his arms over his chest.

"Well I was—"

The air crackles with electricity as a brilliant bolt of lightning slices through the darkness, casting an ethereal glow on the dark sky. A burst of crackling energy slams into a towering tree just twenty feet ahead and it explodes in a deafening boom. Flames erupt along the branches, their fierce glow devouring the wood before leaping hungrily to another nearby tree.

"Run! Stick together!" I yell, my voice drowned out by the raging wind. Pushing between Axton and Sybil, I grasp her wrist to pull her toward safety. Adrenaline surges through my veins, a tightness clawing my lungs as we scramble up the next ridge.

Sybil bends over, hands braced on her trembling legs, gasping for precious air. The wind whips her dark brown hair around her face, strands sticking to her sweat-drenched forehead. Lemon, her loyal companion, peeks out from her pocket, his curious eyes fixed on me.

"Are you okay?" I manage to ask, my breath ragged as I

attempt to regain control. Tenderly, I run my hands along Sybil's arms, searching for any signs of injury.

"I'm alright," she replies, strained but determined. She wraps her arms around my waist, seeking solace in our embrace, her head finding refuge against my pounding chest. I release a deep exhale but it's only for a moment.

"We need to find the others," I say with urgency. The flames keep growing, the searing heat makes me wince. If the rain does not start soon, this will become an inferno.

"Nero! Marcelene! Phoebe!" my voice echoes through the dense foliage as I try to keep track of the howling wind's direction to predict the flames movements. Charred branches are starting to fall from above; I take Sybil's hand in mind and look up at the sky. The green of the canopy is slowly turning into shades of yellows and reds. Fiery leaves start falling from the sky in a rain of embers. One lands on Sybil's shoulder and I immediately whoosh it off with one sweeping gesture before her clothes or hair catch fire. I pull Sybil toward me as a branch falls and impales itself on the ground before shattering into pieces. We keep running, trying to find a moment to cross over to where the rest of the group have run. The wind fuels the flames, which have created a deadly route through the forest, greedily consuming everything in its path.

I pull at the cuffs at my wrists.

"Get off," I shout, knowing my wind could contain this disaster instantly. "Fucking, come on!"

"Aramis," Sybil's soft voice breaks through the turmoil in my mind, her hand resting gently on one of the confining bands. "It's not forever. You will prove your worth. I know you will."

"Aramis!" I hear Nero's familiar brogue call out from our left. The flames start crawling up trees. The heat is so scorching I struggle to keep my eyes open. Sybil starts violently coughing as the smoke thickens around us. I pull out my water canteen and a bandage from her healing satchel and drench it in water. She looks at me with reddened eyes full of tears as I rest it over her nose and tie it behind the back of her head. Gesturing to her to breathe slowly, she nods. I pull the collar of my tunic over my nose, hoping it'll stop me from breathing in too much smoke, and scan what's left of the forest floor when Nero comes crashing next to us, wings spread open.

I push Sybil into his arms and gesture for him to fly her away from here. When she realizes my orders, she shakes her head, hands flailing in my direction. Nero wraps his hands around her waist and pushes himself skywards.

My eyes are stinging but before I can find a path out of this inferno, I see a fox. Hoping I am not hallucinating, I walk toward it, ducking and turning to avoid the fiery obstacles falling from the sky. Then, I see a wolf.

Aries and Phoebe.

My knees buckle and Aries comes rushing to me, urging me with his nose to get back up. Positioning himself to my right side, I sink my hand into his smoke blackened fur and use him to push myself up. We both run after Phoebe in her fox form as she finds the best way out of the fire.

When we reach a clearing, I let myself fall to the ground, exhausted and short on oxygen. Slowly, I turn my head to the right. Axton and Marcelene sit on the ground; their clothes are burned in places but otherwise, they look safe.

"Aramis!" Sybil runs to my side, pushing my tunic down and pouring water in my mouth, making me cough. My throat is sore and it feels like a clawed hand is squeezing my lungs.

"Breathe in, slowly," she commands, and I do as she says. When my eyes stop watering and my breathing regulates, Sybil gently punches me in the shoulder.

"Don't ever do that again, you hear me?" She says, pointing a finger at me.

I smile and feel a raindrop fall on my face.

Bloody brilliant.

The rain begins to pelt down upon us, and we all start laughing at the Goddess' questionable sense of humor. I turn to my right and meet Aries' eyes, still in his wolf form. He comes near, and before I can so much as thank him, he lowers his head and with a sudden, explosive energy, he shakes from head to tail, sending droplets of rain flying in all directions.

What have I done to deserve this?

"Now I'm soaked," Axton complains, shaking the water from his hair; I wonder if he took inspiration from Aries.

"Better wet than dead," Nero replies, his face streaked gray from the water mixed with ash falling from his hairline. "Phoebe was singed by some floating ash, but otherwise, we are safe. Are ye and Sybil unharmed?"

"Phoebe, let me see your burn," Sybil says, approaching the fox shifter, who stands to the side, cradling her arm. Pushing up the girl's sleeve, she lays a hand over the singed skin. A faint glow covers the burnt skin, and then she steps back.

"Wow, it doesn't even hurt anymore. Thank you so much," Phoebe says, examining the newly healed skin.

"The fire has pushed us away from the path. We have to find shelter before we catch our death of cold."

As if urged on by her words, the wind shifts and the rain-drops turn into hail and sleet,pelting at the bare skin of my face and hands.

Nero lays his pack down at my feet before launching into the air. Moments later, he drops to the ground, his boots crunching in the snow and slush.

"Well, I've got good news and bad news," he says, slinging his pack over one shoulder. "We've veered off the path by a lot, and the path ahead looks blocked by a rockslide. We'll have to climb instead of going through the valley."

"That all sounds like bad news," Axton whines, pulling his cloak tighter around himself.

"Well, the good news is that there seems to be a cave at the top of the next peak. We might be closer to the dragon's lair than we thought."

28
SYBIL

How are we supposed to get up there?" I shade my eyes from the sun finally appearing after days of incessant rain.

The six of us, with burned clothes and exhausted expressions from surviving a wildfire, stare up at the succession of snow-cloaked jagged peaks like the spiny back-bone of a monstrous being. The mountain's rocky face is steep and unforgiving, making me feel dizzy at the thought of having to climb all the way to the cave nestled on its side, hidden in the shadow of the other mountain close by.

"Please tell me there is a secret underground tunnel. A magical portal. Gosh, I'd even take one of those awful spiders dragging me up there. I hate heights," I groan as I turn toward Axton, who merely shrugs.

"I know as much as you know, love. If you think I consciously decided to *scale a mountain* the last time I was here, you are mistaken. You see that little path on that mountain?" he says, indicating a narrow wooden bridge hanging off the edge of the mountain. My knees almost buckle at the thought of stepping foot on it. "Hundreds of years ago, miners worked in these mountains, looking for Goddess knows what. But professionals like myself—"

"You mean thieves," Aries interrupts, and Axton rolls his eyes.

"It's still a profession, I'll have you know. Anyway, people built the bridge on the side of the mountains to access the caves and... have a look." He shrugs as he checks his filthy nails. "That's where I was going to take you, but to access that path, we'd have to walk all the way around this other mountain and up a very questionable ladder, if it's still there. If you want to keep walking that direction for, say, another seven days, I'd be happy to take you there."

"No, no more stalling. We have to retrieve the book." I steel my resolve, swallowing my apprehension as I scan the wild, rocky terrain, peppered with tufts of grass. The trees thin out dramatically over the last fifty feet, leaving only scattered scraggly seedlings dotting the mountain ahead with little chance of shelter. My eyes fall on my tattered brown boots, their soles consumed after weeks of travel. Alphaeia better keep me attached to this mountain because my shoes certainly will not. Aramis comes to stand next to me, his eyes still bloodshot and lips dry from the smoke he inhaled. I go to rest my hand on his cheek, magic tickling my fingertips, but he stops me.

"Save your magic. We don't know what will happen up there. I am well."

"I am the healer. I will tell you if you're well or not. Now, stop being such a hero all the time." I raise my other hand and rest it on his chest, light gently pulsating through his black tunic. Aramis closes his eyes, the relief apparent, and it makes me want to slap him for being so strong headed.

When he finally opens his eyes again, the blue of his irises are their usual shade. Aramis' breaths are more controlled, and the fatigue is gone from his shoulders. I raise my eyebrows at him and tug at the bond.

You're welcome.

I am still trying to understand how the bond works. The steady flow of Aramis's emotions always seem to be there when I focus on them, but ever since screaming his name during the kidnap, we haven't been able to talk mind to mind again. But that did not stop me from trying.

Like red lightning, Phoebe, in her fox form, comes bounding down the mountain after a quick run to scout the surrounding area. She jumps from behind a rock before her magic pulls her into her demi form—pointed ears peeking through her red hair.

"There seems to be a small path up the mountain, but it's narrow." She shakes her head, ears twitching. "It's not going to be an easy hike."

"No time to waste then," Nero booms, rubbing his hands together. "Ye better get climbing, worm," he says to Axton as he shoves him onward.

"Woah, I got you here," he protests, throwing his hands into the air as he stumbles.

"No, the deal was you get us to the book. I don't see a book laying around anywhere here," Aramis says, gesturing to the ground. A muscle in his jaw ticks as he stands above him. "Get up."

Axton scrambles to his feet, kicking dust into the air as he moves away from Aramis and brushes himself off.

"I, for one, don't want to be caught halfway up the mountain when it gets dark. Without the cover of trees, we'll be exposed to giant, bloodsucking bat creatures and goblins. I would take hiking over a chimera coming to look for a snack up here," Aries warns, counting deadly creatures on his fingers.

"Yes, yes, thank you wolf, I get the jist of it," Axton chides and we all try to suppress our snickers. "Not that it matters if we die on our way up the mountain when we're willingly entering a dragon's lair expecting to be welcomed for tea. Chances are, we'll die either way," the thief mumbles as he takes on the rocky ground.

"It would be smarter if we left the camping gear at the base of the mountain," Marcelene says wisely as she sets down her bag and begins unloading the items into a pile beside her.

"Less weight to offset our balance. Also, Nero, Phoebe, Aries and I would be faster if we fully shift. When we reach the top, we can assess the situation and think about a plan before entering the cave."

I nod, nibbling at my lip before casting my eyes over the small group. "I wouldn't blame any of you if you wanted to stay below—"

"I haven't traveled halfway across Shadowvale with you, Sybil Vandeleur, to be denied seeing a dragon's hoard first-hand," Marcelene says, putting her hands on her hips. Seeing her back to her old, commanding self fills me with joy.

Nero snorts behind us, and she glares at him over my shoulder. "If ye wanted to see a dragons hoa—"

"I wasn't talking to you—" she quips, narrowing her brows, but I don't miss how her lips press together to stop them from curling upwards, her cheeks glowing pink.

I unstrap my tent and sleeping roll from my healing satchel and tighten the strap along my chest. As much as it weighs, it's worth keeping. The lack of food and good sleep we had experienced in the last few days affected my magic's restoration cycle. I can feel it dormant within me, only a hand reach away, but the thought of using it for more than simple healing tricks makes my breath hitch and hands shake.

Noticing we're still, Axton grumbles as he pulls himself onto the ledge and edges along the steep incline.

"I'll take to the skies, but stay close," Marcelene says before her form wavers, shrinking in her feline shape. She stretches her wings, muscular legs bunching before launching into the air above us.

"See you at the top," Phoebe says before she and Aries follow Marcelene's lead and scamper up the mountain, leaving a cloud of dust in their wake

"I'll stay with me feet on the ground this time around." Nero takes the lead before me, his wings tightly tucked behind his back. Aramis' warm hand touches the small of my back before giving me a boost onto the ledge. The rough rock bites into my hands as I pull myself up.

"How long do you think it'll take us to reach the cave?" I say as I edge along the narrow path, staring at Nero's broad back and wings.

"I can nae say, lass." He shields his eyes and looks above us, where the mountains stretch endlessly. "But only a fool would climb this peak to steal from a dragon's nest." His lips purse into a thin line.

"It wouldn't be the first foolish thing we've done," Aramis says behind me.

"Remember that time ye decided to sneak out to see if basilisks laid golden eggs under the violet moon," Nero says as his wings tremble with laughter.

"What I remember was your oaf of an ass urging me on, knowing full well it was a fable," Aramis growls from behind me. "And my father made the two of us clean the stables for a week for our insolence."

"Aye, but for the look on yer face, I would have cleaned them for a month."

As we continue on, storm clouds roll in, swallowing the sun in their encroaching darkness and casting long shadows on the rugged terrain. The path up the mountain is a jagged ribbon of rock, twisting and turning unpredictably beneath my feet. My legs burn with exertion, calves stinging as the incline increases, and I must keep pushing myself upward. Every breath is a labored gasp in the thinning, cold air. Marcelene circles back around to check on us, signaling that the path above is clear before flying back ahead. Lightning flashes in the distance, followed by the boom of thunder.

A violent rush of wind suddenly rises beneath me, howling and whistling in my ears, and I waver, desperately clinging to the rough rock face as it mercilessly batters my bare face. My heart pounds like a thundering drum, the rhythm of fear echoing in my ears. I peer down, my vision blurred by the vertigo that threatens to overwhelm me, and the vastness of the valley below stretches out before me—splotches of vibrant green peek out between the jagged gray rocks, contrasting against the desolation.

"You've got to keep going," I tell myself, my voice barely audible over the roaring wind. I try to steady my trembling limbs with a deep inhale, but the rocky ledge crumbles. I slip on the loose rock and fall, landing hard on my hands and knees. Pain shoots through my palms as I scramble, trying to find leverage. My hands scrape against the rough stones, sharp edges cutting into my skin as I plummet downwards, the world spinning in a chaotic blur.

Searing pain rips along my shoulders as the unforgiving straps of my healing satchel dig into my skin but my descent seems to have stopped. I force my eyes open through the haze of pain, and I see Aramis, his face flushed red from exertion.

"I've got you," Aramis says. His grip on my bag is tight, his knuckles white with strain. Nero spreads his wings wide and flies behind me, helping to hoist me up as I scramble against the crumbling rock wall.

"Thank you," I whisper, turning my head. He presses a chaste kiss to my brow. My heart clenches in my chest at his words, heat flooding my veins at the simple gesture.

"I will always protect you," he says as he releases me and a chill runs along my skin as I break his gaze.

"Come on ye love birds, least Axton gets away," Nero says. "He'll likely get eaten by the dragon before we have a chance to search for the treasure due to his sticky fingers if he gets too far ahead."

Aramis scoffs behind me. "I doubt that. He's a spineless fool."

"There is more to him than he lets on," I say, looking up. Sweat beads on my brow as the sun rises higher in the sky, breaking through the gray clouds despite the chilly spring air.

Marcelene sweeps by, her broad white wings ruffling in the air. She lets out a long screech before pushing ahead of us. A rock falls from above, bouncing off the ground at my feet and tumbling over the edge. From our height, the valley below has begun to blur into a map of green and white. My stomach plummets as I realize how high we had already climbed.

"Don't look down," Aramis says, placing a gentle hand to the small of my back. I turn, brows furrowing, to face him. "Tell me about your childhood. A wise healer once told me talking helps calm the nerves."

I tilt my head forward against the steady surface of the cliff, letting the cold of the stone touch my face as I try to settle my breathing. I study the planes of his face. The corner of his lips curl up, a small dimple forming in his left cheek—one I have never noticed before.

"There isn't much to tell that you haven't already seen," I say as I take a tentative step, my hands gripping the rock before me. "My parents shared a small cottage with me in Bellevue. They mostly provided healing services to the village and surrounding towns, but occasionally they were called to the kingdom like for the birth of the Kallistar queen's infants."

"I remember," he says.

"That was before—" My throat tightens, tears pricking the corner of my eyes as their faces swim in my vision, the details blurring with time. I clear my throat, easing my way around a gnarled root sticking out in the path.

"You must miss them very much," he says. I nod silently, a gust of wind kissing away the tears clinging to my lashes.

"Does it ever get easier?" I turn and face him. "You lost your mother over a hundred years ago. It's been ten years since their passing, but it still feels fresh when I think about them."

"I spent so long letting my hatred for the people who killed my mother fester inside me that I didn't allow myself to grieve," he responds honestly. His warm fingers brush along mine as we inch along. "Tell me about the village, your pastimes, anything. Did your parents ever try to have another child?"

"They did, but unicorn shifters are rare. I don't even know my grandparents or if I have other family. My parents never spoke of them." I pause, watching as Nero awkwardly helps Axton scramble up to the next ledge before propelling himself afterwards with the help of his wings. He turns and extends a hand to me. My feet scramble against the stone wall as he helps me up. I roll onto my side on the small shelf, lungs burning from the effort of shoving my body up the steep incline of the mountain.

Aramis follows suit, dusting himself off.

"Come, my pomme sucrée. I've got you," Aramis says as he grabs my hand, our fingers intertwining. I give him a reassuring squeeze as he pulls me to my feet.

We follow closely behind Nero, nearly running into his back when he stops abruptly. "Can ye feel that?"

Axton pauses, crouching low as the path widens and the slope lessons.

"What is it?" I pant, resting my free hand on the wall next to me. The last rays of sunlight disappear as dark gray clouds fill the sky above us. Despite the chill in the air, sweat runs down my neck, soaking my chemise.

"I'm nae sure," he says, glancing up. Marcelene circles once, twice, before diving down and landing on the edge above us.

"Are we close?" I call up and she nods before ruffling her feathers and looking behind her as if urging us to hurry up.

We hastily scramble, hands grasping at the rough rock surface as we ascend the last twenty feet, until we emerge onto a vast, flat expanse of stone and the dark opening of a cave. Lightning splits the air, somehow casting the opening in more shadow The deafening crack of thunder follows. The mouth of the cave, once the same natural grayish brown of the mountain, is seared black from the dragon's fiery breath.

Beside me, Marcelene's eyes narrow into slits, her pupils fixating on the darkness ahead. A low whisper escapes her lips, "I have a bad feeling about this."

Rain pours relentlessly, drenching us within seconds, yet we're all waiting for someone to take the first step into what could become our final resting place.

"Looks to me like we have two options. Die burned to a crisp by dragon fire, or die by being hurled off this mountain and shattering our necks on the jagged rocks below," Aramis shouts over the howling wind, Without hesitation, we all break into a sprint, charging toward the cave entrance.

"Well, this certainly complicates things," Nero remarks, lifting a hand projecting a ball of flame. The jagged, soot-covered walls glisten with an oily sheen. Breathing is almost impossible as the air is thick with the acrid smell of smoke, charred rock and something else—something vile that makes my stomach turn. I lean forward to peer over Nero's shoulder and gasp. Bones of all shapes and sizes cover the entirety of the cavern's floor, and I realize with horror that death is the thing I could not put my finger on.

I can smell death.

"I think we're in the right cave," Marcelene says, toeing a pile of bones with her boot. "But we have a problem." She points to the back of the cavern, where two more tunnels go deep into the mountain and I feel deja vu.

"Which way should we go?" I inquire, my gaze shifting back and forth between the two openings. A growing aversion toward caves begins to take hold of me.

We all turn to Axton expectantly.

"Guys," he says, opening his arms. "You really think I remember?"

Aries unsheathes his dagger and starts swirling it between his fingers, eyes fixed on Axton, making the thief slowly step away from him until he backs up to one of the walls.

"Why don't you use your unicorn powers to feel which direction we should go?" He points at me, and my eyes fly to Aramis to ensure his sword is still at his side and that he is not severing Axton's hand. He rolls his eyes reading my thoughts and instead says, "Why don't we use you as bait?"

Aramis walks up to Axton and grabs him by the front of his tunic, hauling him up. "Which direction do we go, *thief?*"

"Let me go," Axton chokes, feet scraping against the stone wall. "I don't remember! I swear there was only one tunnel two hundred years ago!"

"Why would it need a second tunnel?" Aries scoffs, crossing his arms over his chest.

"Let him go," I sigh, softly touching Aramis' arm. He throws Axton to the ground where he sputters and coughs, rubbing his throat.

"We have to make a decision," Phoebe says, her gaze locked on the depth of one of the tunnels.

"Aye," Nero chimes in, picking up what appears to be a human femur and tossing it into the air. "Unless yer hoping to become a dragon toothpick. Let's pick a tunnel and stick together. If we come up empty handed, we can take turns watching guard and try the other path."

"What do you think, Marcelene?" I walk to her side where she's examining each entrance. "They both look and smell the same to me."

She sniffs the air before each opening. "They're nearly identical. But my instinct says we should go to the left."

"Let me shine some light," Nero says, scooping a thick branch from the floor between bones and lighting the tip. He hands the makeshift torch to me, then steps in front of Marcelene. "Axton, why don't ye lead the way?"

"I don't think–" he begins.

"Be a good lad now," Nero growls and Axton scrambles ahead of them, mumbling something about being unappreciated.

We travel together down the dark, damp tunnel, our footsteps resonating with a haunting echo. The air grows thicker, laden with the stench of sulfur, and I cover my nose with my sleeve.

"Look at this," I say, running my fingers over four thick, distinct claw marks carved deep into the rough stone, their width exceeding the span of my hand.

"I don't like this," Axton whimpers, his body trembling as he cautiously navigates the tunnel ahead of Nero and Marcelene. The floor is uneven, littered with the fractured remains of stalactites that have fallen from the ceiling.

Suddenly, a chilling gust of wind howls through the air, extinguishing the flickering flames and plunging us into impenetrable darkness.

"What was that?" I ask, reaching out blindly until my hands hit a warm chest and I find the familiar scent of cedar and bergamot.

"I don't know," Aramis whispers, pulling me close, his warm hand enveloping mine. "Nero? Light?"

"Working on it," he says as a small butterfly of living flame manifests in his hands. "Is everyone alright?"

The ground beneath me trembles and a deep rumble reverberates through the air, causing me to lose my balance and fall onto my hands and knees, the cuts from my plunge earlier on the side of the mountain reopening. Amid the deafening silence, a high-pitched scream pierces through, sending chills down my spine.

Nero's butterfly flutters above our heads, barely illuminating the space. I rub the dirt from my face, blinking to clear my vision as I count out our party members.

"We need to move," Aries growls, his wolfish eyes glinting in the soft flames.

The earth quakes once more and tiny pebbles rain from above, pelting my head and sending clouds of dust into the air. In that chaotic moment, Lemon, tucked away in my pocket, emits a small squeak.

"It's okay, boy," I cough, holding the edge of my cloak over my face as I try to peer around, but Nero's flame butterflies do little to cut through the darkness. I take a step forward when the ground beneath me crumbles away. Trembling and wide-eyed, I frantically claw at the unforgiving ground, my heart pounding in my chest as my feet dangle helplessly in the abyss.

29
SYBIL

I've got you," Aramis whispers, his warm hands enveloping my wrists. I can feel the rough texture of the crumbled stone beneath my fingertips as he helps me scramble up. Collapsing on my back, I feel the jagged edges of the ground pressing against me as I pant and shake with the adrenaline that surges through my body.

"Th-thank you," I whisper, pushing myself into a sitting position. The musty scent of ichor and stone fills my nostrils as darkness engulfs us once again. Nero's butterflies are nowhere to be seen. My magic responds effortlessly, my hands emitting an ethereal glow illuminating the cramped space around us. Before me, a gaping hole in the floor runs where I had just been standing, encompassing the entire width of the tunnel.

I turn my head and see Phoebe and Aries dusting themselves. There's blood running down Phoebe's face from a small cut on her forehead. Aries tears a strip of his tunic off and helps the shifter tie it around her head to block the blood from falling in her eyes. "Are you safe? Where is Nero, Marcelene and Axton?" I ask anxiously.

"We are safe," Aries confirms, although I see him limping. "What the fuck happened?"

"Nero!" Aramis calls out, his body tense as he scans the tunnel in my dim light. A chilling dread settles in my stomach as the silence resonates.

"How far down do you think it goes?" Aries asks, kicking a pebble toward the dark crevasse. I wait with bated breath, anxious to know the answer. The pebble bounces off the rocky surface, descending further and further until we can no longer hear it.

Terrible doubts start creeping in but no one dares to voice the possibility.

"Do you think it's safe? Why did the floor just collapse here?" I wonder, feeling out for anything amiss with my magic. "Do you think we could climb down?"

"There must have been a trap set to trigger the floor to collapse," Aramis says, feeling along the wall. He slams a fist into the stone. "Goddess damnit."

"I'm sure between the two of them, they'll be able to wrangle Axton and find us," I say.

"It's like they've disappeared into thin air," he says, with an exacerbated sigh. "You think they'd call up to us if—"

"I'm sure they're too far down for us to hear. Let's keep going. Perhaps we will find them further along," I whisper, squeezing his forearm. "I don't know much about dragons, but I know they protect their treasure hoard at all costs."

Silently, we backtrack to the other tunnel, making quick work of it. As we reach the broad landing of the cave opening, with its piles of bones, a shiver runs down my spine. I pull the dagger from the sheath at my side, relishing in its comforting weight in my hand.

"Sybil," Aramis says. I pause, turning to face him. He pulls me into the embrace of his strong arms, the warmth of his touch enveloping me. "I know this probably isn't the best time, but I- I don't know if we'll make it out of here alive." Our lips meet in a fevered, desperate kiss, igniting a rush of passion unlike his gentle teasing in the forest. As we part, our rapid breaths fill the air, mingling with the sound of our racing hearts. His hand tenderly cradles the side of my face, sending shivers down my spine. "I love you, Sybil Vandeleur."

"I–"

A growl reverberates through the air and the three of us shrink against the wall.

"Fuck, I think we've found our dragon," Aramis whispers, gesturing to follow him. "Let's go."

Phoebe and I cautiously follow Aramis as he leads us further into the widening tunnel, the scent of burning wood growing stronger with each step. Aries follows us, taking up the rear. I grip my dagger tightly, ready for whatever may come our way. As the tunnel takes a sharp turn, Aramis lifts a finger to his lips and my heart beats wildly in my chest as he disappears into the darkness ahead. Phoebe grabs my arm, claws digging into my flesh as another growl reverberates through the tunnel. Sweat beats my skin from the growing heat coming from the end of the tunnel. It mixes with the dust still clinging to every inch of me and my tattered clothes, making me feel itchy and uncomfortable. A moment later, Aramis appears again, gesturing us forward.

My breath catches as I round the corner into a vast chamber, illuminated by the flickering flow of the torches hanging off the rocky walls, its ceiling so high every sound echoes and I wonder how close it is to the mountain peak. The chamber is filled with so many riches that I wonder how it's possible that there's still gold left in Craeweth. Our eyes widen as we take in the dragon's treasure trove. Ancient tapestries adorn the chamber depicting kings and queens of old, the Goddess herself and creatures so ancient they no longer roam this earth. Despite their faded colors, the intricate patterns are still visible; some shine of their own accord as threads of gold are woven within the complex designs. The air is heavy with the scent of musty parchment and richness made of gold, silver and bronze. Heaps of golden coins of every shape imaginable form shimmering hills, reflecting the soft glow of the torches. Scrolls and books, aged and weathered, are haphazardly stacked against a wall next to piles of glistening gems of every cut and color, their beauty almost blinding.

"How will we ever find the book in this massive trove?" I whisper, apprehension twisting my gut. "We don't even know what it looks like."

I glance toward Aramis, who stands silently by my side, one hand holding his sword before him, the other clutching his chest.

"I hate to say it, but this is the first time I wish we had Axton with us," Phoebe whispers by my side and I give her a pursed lips nod. The thief had proven little worth saving getting us here, but he is the only one with intimate knowledge of what we're looking for.

"We don't have any other option but to find it," Aramis says, raking a hand through his dulled hair from all the dust he had collected. "Sybil and Phoebe, have a look around the chamber; me and Aries will stand guard by the entrance."

I nod and immediately make my way to the books at the far wall. Standing on the tips on my feet, I stretch my neck, trying to read the titles of some of the ancient books stacked on top of each other. The smell of old leather and paper pulls me back to the library of Harpalyke, and I can't help but think about

Cassara and Talia. What will they say if Marcelene... No. I push the intrusive thought out of my mind and keep looking.

My fingers itch, wanting to pick up every one of these books and scroll through the pages. Some of the books are so old, the golden foil of the title is gone, making them hard to read. Others are written in symbols I have never seen before. There's a book whose cover is made from the bark of a tree, whilst another is written on plates of silver so thin and shiny it's like looking into a mirror.

As I keep walking, however, my attention is pulled toward a lone painting resting against the wall of the chamber. Its thick wooden frame has seen better days. The colors have lost their saturation, but the more I look at the drawing itself, the more enthralled I become.

There's a unicorn on top of a mountain ledge. Storm clouds cover the sky, but the sun gloriously peaks out, bathing the rearing unicorn in golden light. It's difficult to interpret whether the unicorn is rearing out of celebration or distress. At the foot of the mountain lies a figure. A man, at first, then a woman. The man has golden hair and lies on his back, sword plunged in his chest. But then it's a woman. She too has golden hair with black ink running up her arms, her face sunken in as if life itself has been sucked out of her. Strange.

Come closer, let me show you! A melodic voice lulls in my head, and I step forward.

The painting changes. There's a wolf with dark fur hiding in a corner, lonely but loyal. A fox sits by the unicorn, its head tilted as if the fox too is trying to discern whether the figure at the bottom of the mountain is a man or a woman. Suddenly, it's a man again, and a river of crimson runs from his chest wound.

It's us! I turn to tell the others, but the words die in my throat. It's a painting of the four of us, but something is not right. Aramis should be by my side, like he promised. Until the end of time itself.

Pick me up, you'll see better! The voice begs, sweet like honey, and the man turns into the woman again. That's better.

I stretch out my arms, hands so close to the wooden frame I can practically feel its texture on my fingertips. Before I can touch it, a jolt of magic rushes through my right hand from my family crest ring.

"Ouch!" I cradle my aching hand and examine my ring, but nothing seems amiss. Until I lower my gaze to the painting again and the canvas is empty. I rub my eyes, trying to make sense of what happened and it dawns on me.

"Bespelled," I whisper as I step back from the painting. "Everything is bespelled!"

I turn and see Phoebe leaning down, hand outstretched toward a golden chalice with intricate carvings of the sun and moon embraced. The shine of the metal reflects in her green eyes, her fingertips almost shaking from the desire of owning this artifact. I run across the chamber, careful to avoid any of the riches laying precariously on the floor. I reach out, grabbing her by the wrist, and she snaps her head in my direction, her teeth almost baring at me. Slowly, I shake my head and see the haze of the enchantment vanishing from her eyes.

"What—" She retracts her hand, confusion etched on her face.

"We cannot touch anything. Everything seems to be bespelled to ward off thieves. Stay away from the objects. They like to talk," I explain and notice Aries and Aramis with their hands on their hilts, on the ready to take on a threat that is not there.

"Brilliant. As if the threat of being eaten alive by a dragon was not enough, now I need to worry about getting cursed by a cup," Aries rolls his eyes, looking suspiciously around the room.

"But what about the book?" Phoebe asks, rubbing her wrist. I wince apologetically, and she smiles in return.

"We will have to deal with that when we get there. Better not alert the dragon or trigger anything else before we do."

"You said in the library you could feel the power radiating off some of the books. Could you try to sense it?" Aramis suggests.

"If the Book of Light works the same way the Book of Darkness does, it'll emanate a power so strong it will be impossible to miss. I wasn't even near it and felt like a clawed hand wrapped around my neck urging me to come closer. It's as if it were alive," Phoebe explains. "Because you, Sybil, and the Book of Light share the same raw magic, it should be like looking for a part of yourself."

"That's a good point." I take a deep breath, close my eyes and focus on the room.

My magic hums to life under my skin and I feel the golden thread between Aramis and myself. I reach further, letting it flow freely through me, while keeping hold of my control. When I feel steady, I slowly exhale and let the power become me, just as Alexander had taught me. The light cursing through me feels exhilarating. It begs for more release and tastes sweet on my tongue, promising me invincibility. It would be so easy to let go; the power is right there for me to revel in. But images of the basilisk attack come rushing back. The feeling of my skin and insides burning as my power became uncontainable by my mortal enclosure. Getting so close to disintegrating both friend and foe.

Like blowing out a candle, I compress my magic and tuck it back into the deepest recesses of my soul. I cannot lose control again, not when my friends are in danger.

I stare at the stone ceiling, charred with smoke and ash. Hot tears line my eyes as I think of Rose's words. Alpheaia's words. They had chosen wrong. I wasn't strong enough for this. I cannot control this power. I am a liability. I can't even find a single book.

You have to choose someone else! I internally scream as my chest constricts.

I open my eyes to Aramis and Phoebe staring at me expectantly.

"Nothing." I sigh, head dropping. "I sense nothing. I don't think it's here."

# 30
ARAMIS

I t has to be here," I urge her, sheathing my sword to grab her arms. As her shoulders droop, the radiance of her magic dims, and a glimmer of silver forms along the edge of her eyes. "You can do this, Sybil. We didn't come all this way to be defeated."

"I can't do this." Her voice cracks and tears pour down her cheeks. I pull her against my chest.

"You can do this. I believe in you," I whisper into her chestnut hair, which has grown back to the length when I first met her. Before Tricella had shorn it off out of spite. My hands clench in its thickness as I pull her closer.

"What if Axton lied to us?" She looks up at me, hazel eyes bright. "What if Nero and Marcelene are dead, all because of this foolish mission to retrieve a book? We don't even know if it is here, let alone whether it still exists. The dragon could have burned it out of spite."

"Nero is alive. I just know it." I cradle her face between my hands, stroking her cheek with a thumb. "If the book is gone, we will find another way."

"She is too powerful."

The floor beneath us rocks violently and we're knocked to our knees, dust raining from the ceiling and the sound of cracking stones breaks the silence. I press my finger against her lips as I look around the cavern. Phoebe and Aries crouch behind us.

"Well, the thief wasn't lying about one thing. You better hope you're better with that sword, prince," Aries snarls, his body beginning to morph. His limbs elongate as fur rapidly covers his body. Dropping to the ground on all fours, he assumes the form of a massive brown wolf. His light blue eyes fixate on me, and he menacingly exposes his fangs. Gold coins tickle as they tumble down their piles as another rumble echoes off the stone walls.

Emerging from the chamber's entrance, a magnificent dragon stands, its sharp scales shimmering in shades of deep crimson and gold reflect the light from the torches. Powerful muscles ripple beneath its hide as it moves across the chamber, each limb ending in razor-sharp claws capable of cutting even stone to shreds. I notice the massive leathery wings folded against its back and bite my tongue, unsure whether I am stopping myself from gasping in awe or crying in fear. Two sweeping horns, gracefully curving backwards, sit on its head like a majestic crown. The dragon locks onto us where we crouch on the ground. Its eyes glow with a fiery intensity and it lets out a low, rumbling growl, unfurling its wings as it prepares to defend its territory.

"Run!" I yell, grabbing the two females by the arm and hauling them to their feet. We dodge around massive piles of treasure, heading in the opposite direction of the dragon, but Sybil's broken boots make her stumble. As she leans on an ancient ceramic vase, hundreds of golden coins fall in our way. One second of hesitation is all it takes, and the coins start melting under our feet, burning through our shoes.

Thieves, thieves, thieves. The coins sing.

I pull us out of the puddle of molten gold, frantically looking for a way out as we nearly run in circles.

"Over there!" Sybil yells, and we all run to the left toward a gilded carriage.

We change direction, charging toward the openings when we're battered to the ground by a gale of wind as the dragon flaps its mighty wings, launching itself into the air.

"We have to get out of here," Phoebe yells as we dodge under a golden arch to the right.

Sybil leans forward on her forearms, panting. "We can't leave until we find the book."

"We can't find the book if we're a charred pile of bones," I retort, wiping the sweat from my forehead. Aries crouches beside us, fur on end as he sniffs the air. "I'll distract it. Run to the tunnels."

I unsheathe my sword. "If the book is not in this chamber, it must be in another one. You are the only one who can find it."

"Stop trying to be so noble. You can't sacrifice yourself so we can escape," Sybil says as she glares at me. "I won't leave without you. We're in this together."

My chest constricts at her words, but I shake my head, gesturing around us. "We can't just stay here either."

"Aramis is right," Phoebe says as she grabs my wrist and pulls me toward the cave's entrance. "Let's go."

"No." Sybil freezes, her hazel eyes meeting mine. "There has to be another way."

Stubborn woman, I think to myself. Let me save you. I look around the room again, the dragon roving high by the ceiling.

The shining gold is starting to make my eyes water. There must be another way out of this hell hole. As I scan a corner of the chamber filled with statues of different creatures made of marble and gold, I notice a caving in the corner lowering into the ground. The shadows there look so dark, it must be the entrance to another, smaller tunnel.

"Look! There is another tunnel. We will meet there and look for Nero and Marcelene. On the count of three, you two go left and we will go right. One–"

A mighty roar echoes to our left, followed by a blast of fire. My arm jumps up to cover my face from the flames. Beads of perspiration form on my forehead, their salty sting making my eyes water.

"Too late, we stick together. You still don't have your magic. You don't stand a chance by yourself." Sybil grabs my wrist and tugs as she runs out from our temporary cover and back toward the entrance, dodging riches before we end up in a sea of molten gold.

My legs are burning by the time we reach the edge of the room. Dread plummets into my stomach as I realize it's not a tunnel, but an alcove filled with black diamonds.

"It's a dead end," Phoebe whispers, clinging to Sybil's arm.

"Where do we go?" Sybil yells, looking frantically around the room.

Aries suddenly turns to the right and takes off toward the opening of the room.

"Aries, no!" Sybil screams.

Time seems to slow as the dragon slides to a halt, eyes catching on the wolf as he darts between piles of treasure. The dragon sweeps out with its tail, slamming Aries' body into a pile of golden suits of armor. The shifter whines and I know he must have launched himself into the arms of death with only one thought in mind: reuniting with his Emma.

I cannot let that happen. Not today, not like this. Aries deserves to see the dawn of a kingdom where his people live in peace after everything he has sacrificed. Undeterred by the danger before me, I raise my sword and charge forward, trying to grab the dragon's attention. I jump, curling my body protectively over the wolf shifter just as the dragon's mighty claws slice through the air.

Pain like I've never felt before shreds through the fibers of my back. The sensation is so intense, I feel as if I am being rolled on shards of glass, cutting through every layer of me until my heart lays bare. I hold my resolve. Aries has to live.

"I'll say hi to Emma from you. Now run!" The rush of adrenaline silences through the agony. Grinding my teeth, I gather all my strength, rise, and push Aries as far away from me as I can. The wolf tries to get up again and comes close, but his hind legs are broken from the impact of the dragon's tail. Aries' eyes plead for me to run—to give him what he wants, but I shake my head. Blood pools in my mouth and I spit it out as the dragon's shadow looms above me.

All sound in the world has gone. Something tells me Sybil is screaming, but I am doing this for her too. I wish I could have kept my promise and stayed with her until the end of time itself. But it does not matter, she will be alive. And they will all be free, soon.

My hands are slick with blood, but I tighten my grip on my sword. One last round.

I open my eyes, widen my stance and bend my knees. Twisting my sword, I lift my gaze to welcome my demise as the dragon descends at speed, mouth wide open with the embers forming at the back of its throat.

I have proven my worth.

The bands around my wrist writhe before opening, falling to the ground. Power floods my veins, and I nearly fall to my knees. Three months of untapped magic courses through me like lightning. I call to it and feel it dance gleefully in response before I surround all of us with a ward. The dragon's claws slam into the barrier; it screeches and fights against it but it holds firm.

"Aramis!" Sybil yells and falls to her knees before me. Her sobs are uncontrollable, eyes puffy with tears. She holds my face in her hands with such intensity, I wonder if she'll ever let me go again. But she has to.

"We will be okay. I promise. Now go," I rasp out, pushing her away. "Take Phoebe, find the others, and escape. I will hold it off."

"No," she cries. I wince as she pulls me into her arms. "I will not leave you."

"You have to, my pomme sucre." A tear slips from my eyes as my throat tightens, the pain threatening to unravel me as blood pools from my back. "This is the only way."

I feel my magic waver against the dragon's continuous onslaught of attack against my barrier. With my last ounce of energy, I kiss her, pouring in all my love to her lips. "Save our people. Shine bright, my star."

3I
SYBIL

Without a beating heart, one cannot survive.

As healers, we are always told to guard the heart, ensure the blood keeps flowing. It becomes almost instinctual for all creatures to guard their hearts when danger ensues. Cut off a limb, and with good enough medication, you might still live. But tamper in any way with the most important organ in your body, and you will likely not live to see another morning.

The situation becomes dire, however, when your heart suddenly no longer lives hidden behind layers of skin and muscles, in the tight embrace of your rib cage, but outside of yourself. When it is suddenly no longer an organ but something someone else has power over—with the influence of life and death over you, over your heart.

Aramis is speaking but I cannot hear him. The fear of losing him makes my throat constrict, and air no longer reaches my lungs. I reach for him, fisting the once black tunic convincing myself that if I don't let go, he won't go through with this absurdity. Someone is trying to pull me away from him, but I keep him locked in my arms, his body shaking from the blood loss and the strain from using his magic against the dragon. He won't—he can't—hold for much longer.

"I cannot live without you," I finally say, the words barely audible as I force my body to continue to withstand the agony it's enduring. Aries lies not far from us, his broken legs still waiting to heal; his whimpers pierce the air as Phoebe, having given up on me, tries to move him out of the chamber.

"Run!" I shout to her, and the fox shifter looks at me. There is blood running from her nostrils. I can see the protest in her eyes.

"You have to come with us! We cannot lose both of you!"

"Find the others. Find the Council. Save us." Tears fill her green eyes, and she knows she has a duty to fulfill too. Her arms are wrapped around the wolf's middle, her face strained against the immense weight. My hands get progressively slicker with Aramis's blood, his body contorting as the dragon relentlessly slams against his shield, claws slicing through the invisible wind barrier, which seems to waver more and more with every attack.

"I am your mate, as you are mine. Until the end of time itself, you promised," I say as determination washes over me. Aramis's resolve wavers, and I take it as my time to strike.

I reach into my well of magic, and for the second time in my life, I let the power curse through me without restraint.

I channel some of my magic within him, willing his bloodstream to slow and his breathing to calm, pushing him to a point where his body will inevitably lose consciousness. Before his eyes fall shut, I kiss him as his eyelashes flutter, confused as to what is happening. The taste of blood and the salty tang of my tears mix in what is going to be our last kiss.

With a little nod, I urge Lemon to climb on Aramis' shoulder, and hope his ramidreju powers will be able to continue to heal him. Shifting into my demi-form, my horn appears, and it helps me prepare as the magic grows within me, an ethereal shine already peaking through my skin.

"Take care of him," I whisper to Lemon, who sneaks under Aramis's tunic before he closes those piercing blue eyes I fell for.

"I love you," I say as Aramis slumps into my arms, and the wall of air comes crashing down with him.

But the dragon does not seem to have realized yet. It flies to the top of the ceiling, gaining height for its last attack. Quickly, I channel more raw light magic into my hands, reveling in the familiar burn, and hope my gamble will prove fortuitous. I will it to lift Aramis out of my embrace. His body levitates, and I direct it to the mouth of the chamber—to Aries and Phoebe—before pushing myself to my feet.

"Hey!" I yell, drawing the dragon's attention. The light seeping through every cell in my body is so bright it almost blinds me, but before I let it consume me, I abandon myself to the familiar feeling of my body morphing into my full equine form.

The world around me is brighter, the smells sharper, and my magic seems to be... contained. The iron-rich scent of blood hits my nostrils, and I toss my head and whine. I paw at the ground, placing myself between the creature and the mouth of the chamber. The dragon comes flying down, claws outstretched in my direction. Before I direct my full power at it as I did to the basilisk, an ancient voice resounds in my head.

Unicorn. It says, low and rumbling, but I catch something akin to surprise in his tone. Flapping its leathery wings to arrest its descent, it hovers over me, and from this distance, I can see its razor-sharp fangs, yellowed with age.

Dragon? I pause, unsure what's happening. My magic reaches out to the ends of the cavern as I prance nervously over the coin-studded floor. It cocks its massive head to the side, studying me.

It has been three hundred and seventy-five years since the last time one of your kind crossed my lair. Why have you trespassed on my sanctuary, little one?

It sniffs the air before exhaling, blowing out hot steam that makes my mane billow.

I've come seeking knowledge. I carefully weigh my words, still unsure whether the dragon is a friend or foe.

After a moment, it blinks its massive eyes, tongue licking out, testing the air before it lands with a crush on a heap of golden coins, making them jump in all directions.

I have slumbered for decades. What use would my hoard have to one such as yourself?

Why does everything on this quest have to entail so many questions?

There is a great evil upon our land—

It moves restlessly, pawing at the coins as its massive tail whips back and forth.

There will always be evil in this world. Rulers are born and die. The brave protect and sacrifice. So is the way of the world. But you do not belong to their world. Why do you help them so?

I look up, meeting the creature's gaze.

I am Sybil Vandeleur, the last known unicorn. These are my people. I will protect them until my dying breath. I will lead them out of the dark tyranny and into the light of salvation.

The dragon raises its head, blowing a pillar of flame into the air. I flinch as ash falls around us.

Brave words for such a naive filly. Are you truly the last of your kind?

I stamp my hoof impatiently on the ground. Have the others escaped? Has Aramis recovered from his injuries?

I do not have time for this! I seek Alpheaia's Book of Light. Let us take it and we will leave you in peace.

The colossal dragon tosses its scaly head, causing the cavernous room to reverberate with deep, rumbling laughter.

Sybil Vandeleur, last of the unicorns. You do not just take from a dragon's hoard. We spend our whole lives collecting our treasures. To take from us would be to live a half-life, a cursed life, never able to find true happiness.

I hastily blink away the hot, angry tears welling in my eyes, determined not to let my emotions falter. I will not fault; I will not fail. With unwavering determination, I lock eyes with the beast, feeling the weight of its gaze pierce through me.

Without it, my people are in danger. My mate bleeds out his life force with every moment we wait. Please, I'm begging you.

The dragon shifts its weight onto its right leg, coins falling with every move. As it changes position, I notice the muscle of its left leg starting to spasm. My magic flows to assess the beast and confirms my growing suspicion.

You're injured.

I paw at the ground, and the beast cocks its head at me again, wisps of smoke escaping its nostrils.

It is an old, festering injury.

It sighs, glancing back at its hind legs.

Let me heal you.

I plead, dipping my head and horn to the ground in submission before the mighty dragon.

You would heal me while your mate dies only a few feet away from you?

I shiver as a cold sweat wraps around my coat, and I feel my heart breaking. I glance between the great beast and the male lying on the ground behind me.

Some wounds never heal, child.

Let me try, I insist.

I move slowly toward it. The dragon swings its giant head, its beady eye watching my every movement. Embedded in its hind leg is an iron band studded with spikes. The puncture wounds from the spikes are open and raw after centuries of torture. Their edges are dark, as if the flesh itself was dying. I sniff closer to it, careful not to touch it and immediately back away. Poison.

How?

The dragon rears its head as I gingerly prod the metal band.

Greed has creatures of all kinds do terrible things. Those who put that cuff on me no longer live, if that's of any consolation to you. But with their death, I also lost the key to get rid of this torment. I lower my horn to the leg, willing my magic to heal but the skin refuses to knit together.

It won't heal as long as the band is in place.

It turns to move away from me. Resignation echoes in the way it drags itself across the chamber.

Go. Take your prince and leave.

It collapses with a mighty sigh, lowers its head to the ground, and pulls its injured leg closer to its body.

No.

I stand back up and move to its hind leg, again lowering my horn to the band. Focusing on my magic, I will make it come forth, but don't focus on the act of healing—instead, a desire to free the dragon. The light pulsates in my horn, a beacon bright and pure. As if scrying away from the light magic, the black and oily poison seeps out from the dragon's wounds, dripping from its leg onto the ground littered with riches.

Begone.

The magic wavers under my touch, the band vibrating.

I am Sybil Vandeleur, and you will listen to me.

I rear onto my hind legs, and with a final push of my magic, I slam them into the metal band. It cracks under the force, falling with a dead thud to the ground, leaving eight deep holes in the dragon's leg.

You did it.

The voice inside my head is laced with disbelief as it sniffs at the spiked band on the floor, void of magic.

I waver, dizzy on my hooves but pull my resolve, ready to heal the wounds.

Stop, child. You've freed me.

The dragon turns its mighty head, and I meet it eye to eye.

But you're still hurt.

Its tongue snakes out before licking, where deep punctures have left their mark. I watch as scales begin to cover the holes.

I will heal now that the band no longer poisons the wounds.

I run my muzzle over the new golden scales, overlapping where festering puncture wounds had been only moments before.

What is your name?

I tilt my head to the side.

I have gone by many names, but you may call me Tarmyth.

It nudges me back toward Aramis.

Save your mate, horned one. His light fades, even now. Your little creature has used all its magic to sustain him.

I canter back to Aramis' side, falling to my knees. I rest my muzzle against his back, large silver tears flowing freely. Lemon weakly climbs onto my shoulder and collapses. I watch as the skin begins to knit back together on Aramis' back slowly, but he doesn't stir.

I will on my magic, pulling back to my demi form.

"Aramis," I sob. With aching muscles, I roll him onto his

back, the effort causing my breath to hitch in my chest. "Aramis, please hold on."

The silence stretches out; the faint drip of water echoing in the distance and the heavy breathing of the dragon behind us are the only sounds in the cavern. Tears stream down my face, their silver trails mingling with the crimson stains on the fabric of his torn shirt. Aries and Phoebe approach cautiously, paws padding softly on the rocky ground before they settle beside me.

"Sybil, we have to go," Phoebe urges, her voice trembling with fear and concern. Nervously, she tugs at the hem of her shirt, her fingers fidgeting with the fabric. I lift my gaze to meet her eyes, my brow furrowing in confusion.

"I'm not leaving him," I declare, my voice determined, though laced with desperation.

"I'm not sure how you tamed the dragon, but we can't stay here," she says as she grabs my sleeve, her gaze sweeping anxiously around the cavern. Her words hang in the air, and the tension is palpable.

"I'm not leaving him," I repeat, my voice steady, my resolve unyielding.

Pulling away from her grasp, I refuse to let doubt seep into my heart. "I can heal him," I declare, my fingers seeking the golden thread that binds us, pulsing with the magic between us. Gently, I cradle Aramis' head in my lap, my touch tender as I stroke his hair.

"Our story isn't over, my love," I whisper, my voice filled with longing. "Please don't leave me. I need you."

Reaching out with my magic, I search his body for further injury I may have missed but all his wounds are healed.

"Wake up, Aramis." My gut twists as I stare at his lax body in my lap, chest rising and falling in shallow breaths. "Your body is healed, Goddess damnit! Why won't you awaken?"

Aries' body morphs beside me, pain etched on his face as he leans against Phoebe, one of his ankles still not fully healed. "I think it's his magic reserve. He used everything he had," he growls.

"How long will that take to replenish?" I stare up at him with tear-filled, blurry eyes.

"I can't say." He shakes his head. "I don't know much about elemental magic."

I stroke the side of his face, his stubble rough against my palms, before reaching for the bond between us. I think of the day we traveled through the silver apple trees and the night under the stars in the luminescent hot springs, the picnic before leaving camp, and the subsequent burst of emotion that only brought us closer. I wrap all those slivers of happy memories and pour them down the bond.

Stay with me. I need you.

Closing my eyes, I let my head fall, feeling an ache deep in my soul. Lemon nuzzles at my cheek before curling around my neck.

And when I think I have lost the greatest gift the Goddess has ever granted me, Aramis draws in a shaky breath. Shakily, he lifts his hands to intertwine in my hair and opens his blue eyes. "I will always be by your side, pomme sucre, but don't ever do that again."

"Oh! Aramis," I lean forward, crushing my lips against his as chuckles and tears of happiness mix on my face. "Well, don't you ever do something dumb like that again either?" I say against his lips.

A scattering of rocks draws my attention, and I glance up. Footfalls echo in the tunnel as white and powerful magic permeates the space. I try to focus on it, and the magic calls to me as if it were alive. It feels as if someone is running away with a piece of my persona.

The book!

32
SYBIL

Thhhiiieeefff.

The dragon's voice reverberates again in my head before it lets out a mighty roar, causing the chamber to rock and vibrate.

Axton pauses at the cave entrance, a tome with a thick white leather cover and silver inscriptions held tightly to his chest as he edges along the wall. Where are Marcelene and Nero?

"Axton, you found it!" I push to my feet and head toward him.

"Sybil, thank the Goddess I found you," he stammers, his knuckles turning white. He grips the tome as his gaze flickers between me and the dragon behind me.

"Axton, where are the others?" Aries asks suspiciously, and my hand instinctively drifts to the hilt of the dagger strapped to my forearm.

"I-I don't know. We were separated in the tunnels after the

floor fell in." With every step I take to him, he slowly starts backing up, heading toward another tunnel.

My hair flutters as the dragon at my side exhales, then lowers her head, baring her teeth.

He lies.

"Axton, give me the book, and then we can go find the others." I hold out my hand as I reach out to him. His body tenses, sweat beading his brow.

He smells of my eggs.

"Are you certain?" Glancing up, I meet Tarmyth's gaze. Her large golden pupils dilate as she inhales. My brows furrow as she lets out another deep growl that makes the floor vibrate. In my peripheral vision, I catch Axton's sudden movement as he turns and bolts in the opposite direction. Before I can react, Tarmyth swiftly moves past me, slamming Axton against the wall with a sickening crunch. Her paw digs into the stone, claws sinking deep. The book drops to the ground with a thud, sending up a cloud of dust.

"Sybil," he calls out, his eyes wide with fear as he struggles in Tarmyth's merciless grasp. He coughs, blood splattering his lips. The dragon growls, her jaws snapping close to his neck. The reek of urine fills the air as a dark stain blossoms on his breeches.

This is the filthy mage who put that cursed trap around my leg. I've waited nearly five decades to repay him for stealing my egg, and now the time has come.

"Wait!" I cry out, running toward them.

Tarmyth growls again, her voice filled with rage, before knocking her tail into the tome. It skitters over the coin-strewn surface before stopping at my feet.

I believe this is the book you're looking for.

Bending over, I pick up the Book of Light, feeling its weight and running my fingers along the silver scrolling title on the front. I close my eyes and can't quite believe this moment is real. The book exists. The magic contained within it hums at my touch, sending warm waves of power coursing through my fingertips.

I shift my gaze to Axton, narrowing my eyebrows in suspicion. "Where are the others?"

"Dead." Axton glares down at me.

Lies. Tarmyth's voice fills my head as she sniffs his body, baring her long fangs.

"You lie," I say, hands clenching around the tome. He has to be lying.

"Tell it to let me go, and I'll show you their bodies," he says, fighting against the hold on him.

Axton screams in pain as Tarmyth's barbed tail lashes out, slamming his arm into the rock and severing his hand. The limp appendage falls, spluttering blood to the ground.

"You bitch!" He screams, writhing in her grip. "I should have killed you that night I stole your egg."

Are you done with his lies?

I nod. Exhaustion and my empty magic well make every gesture difficult.

As you have shown me kindness, I will show kindness to you, unicorn. Take the book and go, but the thief stays, or you will all die.

My head snaps to the dragon and then to Axton. He must read the surprise and worry on my face because the man starts frantically looking between me and the creature.

"What? What's going on? What does it want?"

I take Aramis' hand, the Book of Light held tight to my chest, and I nod to the dragon before leaving the cave. Phoebe and Aries follow as Axton's screams become louder, begging for help, until the sound of Tarmyth slamming Axton into the stone reverberates through the air, silencing him forever.

We attempt to retrace our steps, following the tunnel from which Axton had appeared, hoping it would take us to Nero and Marcelene. Our steps are slow and labored in the dark tunnel, all our magic reserves depleted to the point that I can only conjure a faint light. Aries has one arm wrapped around Phoebe's neck, still limping but finally able to stand again. Aramis looks as if he's died and come back to life which, in a way, he has. I squeeze his hand, knowing he, too, is picturing every worst scenario his mind can conjure about Nero and Marcelene's fate.

"Maybe one of us should try to go down the–" I begin, but before I can finish, we slam into another figure running through the tunnel.

"Sybil!" Marcelene's panicked voice cuts through the air like a knife. Her blond hair is covered in dust and cascading around her shoulders unbound. She has a deep scratch on her cheek and dried blood under one of her nostrils. But what makes me flinch is the look of fear and horror in her eyes and the way her hands shake as she grabs my shoulders.

"What is it?" I ask, unsure if I want to hear the answer. Nero is not right behind her as he usually is. "Sybil, it's Nero, he's hurt." My heart plummets in my chest, and I feel Aramis go rigid next to me. "We- We fell into the dragon's nest. There were eggs. Nero saved them from Axton. I–I don't know how to get back there; I just ran lo–looking for help." Her words come out in ragged breaths, her body shaking from the sobs she's pushing down.

"Go, please," Aramis says, looking at me, his hand on the hilt of his sword. "Let us meet outside, at the entrance of the cave."

"But you're still injured and I–" I kneel at his side, cold sweat breaking out along my skin as I begin to hyperventilate. I swallow over the lump forming in my throat. "My magic, it's empty."

"Sybil darling, you are more than the extent of your magic. I am not injured, thanks to you and Lemon. Go, save him." The corner of his lips pull up as he cradles the side of my face in his hand.

"I will stay here with the prince," Aries says, coming to stand next to us. I nod and take Marcelene's hand in mine.

"I have an idea," I whisper, and we run back to the dragon's trove chamber.

"Axton—he tricked us," Marcelene pants at my side as we push through the darkness. "He ran away with the book."

"Don't worry, we have the book. Axton is dead. Turns out dragons hold grudges." I reach out in the semi-dark and grip her forearm before urging her onward.

She smells of my eggs. Is the first thing Tarmyth says as we enter.

"She is my friend, Tarmyth. She would not harm your eggs," I yell to the majestic creature. "But there's a friend of mine in your nest who is injured because he saved your eggs from the thief's hands. I beg you for one last act of kindness. Take us there; help me save him."

You are too good for your own good, unicorn, the dragon chides. *It'll be their salvation, but will it be your demise?* Before I can ask the meaning of her words, she lowers her wing to allow us access to her back.

I sit by the curvature of her neck, thighs squeezing against the harsh scales that dig into my skin. Marcelene settles behind me, her hands wrapped around my waist as I hold onto two smaller protruding horns from the beast's neck.

When Tarmyth launches herself forward, Marcelene and I duck, not letting the wind push us back. With exceptional control, the dragon twists and turns through the labyrinthine tunnels, going up and down deeper into the mountain, where the heat is almost unbearable. The tunnel breaks into an extensive cave, but I don't have time to marvel as my eyes are drawn to the raised golden nest and the figure laying immobile atop it.

"Nero!" I cry, but the man lies still. A gust of wind blasts as the dragon spreads her wings, lifting us from the ground and reaching the top of the nest. Gently, Tarmyth helps us slide off her back, and Marcelene and I start running.

Crouching by Nero's side, I feel the adrenaline coursing through my veins as I lay my hands upon his neck and chest, searching for injuries. Despite the loss of consciousness, his face is a mask of pain, his pupils moving frantically under his closed eyelids. Probably lost in a nightmare that mirrors the gravity of his reality. As I press two fingers at the base of his neck, my palms quiver when I feel how weak his pulse is. A pool of blood is collecting under his scratched wings, staining the golden nest crimson drop after drop.

Marcelene crouches next to me, and I briefly meet her bloodshot eyes begging me to save him, before I return to Nero. With each shallow rise and fall of his chest, my breath catches in my throat, scared it will be his last. My hands clench tightly around his blood-soaked shirt, and I lift it, revealing a tapestry of wounds oozing blood. My knuckles blanch as I pull it back down, listing the minimal options we have in my head. I channel my magic, scrape for remnants, anything that will at least let me stop the bleeding, but nothing is there. Not a single drop of light curses through my veins while my mate's best friend readies to cross the silver veil.

"My magic is gone. I don't have enough to heal him, and he has lost too much blood," I confess, tears burning at the corner of my eyes. I hang my head, my hair falling forward, shielding my tear-stained face and hiding the guilt and shame I am feeling. I can't help but wonder if Alphaeia truly wants me to defeat Tricella. Is this the price of victory? Losing my friends one by one along the way?

"Tell me what you need," Marcelene says with desperation, resting a hand on my shoulder.

"I don't know. I have some yarrow ointment to stop the bleeding from the bigger wounds temporarily, but it won't last long. Not when his internal wounds are so severe." My hands shake as I pull open my healing satchel and rummage through it, searching for what I need to stop the bleeding. I can't just sit here and do nothing; I must try.

Lemon crawls out of my pocket and up to Nero's face, nuzzling and licking his cheek.

"He has a punctured lung, multiple chest wounds, and his wings are torn. Even with my magic at full strength, it would take weeks for him to heal at best. He won't be able to travel, and we can't stay here–"

"There has to be something we can do," Marcelene screams, pacing beside me as she holds her hands to her face. "If we were at the library, Cassara would know what to—"

"Help me turn him onto his side," I say, but Tarmyth turns and nudges my hands away.

He saved my brood from that filthy thief. I will fly you all to Harpalyke.

"Thank you." I throw my arms around her giant scaled neck before letting go and scooping Lemon into my arms. "But we have to meet the others on the ledge of the mountain first," I tell Tarmyth, who's already lowering her wings for me and Marcelene. After that, the dragon gently cradles Nero's body in her claws, and we are airborne again.

Aries, Phoebe, and Aramis stand outside the dragon's lair in the rising sun. I can't believe we have been trapped inside that mountain for almost half a day. They all seem to have recovered somewhat, although Aramis' gaze darkens as he sees Nero and a surge of grief courses through me.

When we're close enough to speak, Tarmyth rests Nero on the ground and gracefully settles on the landing. Her wings tuck in after she helps us dismount.

"Is he—"

"He's alive, but gravely wounded." Aramis rushes to crouch next to Nero, and I follow. He hands me the Book of Light and takes his best friend's hand into his, resting it over his own heart. I can see him methodically scanning his injuries, trying to assess just how severe the situation is before he allows himself to react emotionally. I rest a hand on his shoulder.

"He will live, Aramis," I say, and I know I have broken one of the cardinal rules of being a healer: never give false hope.

Aramis stands, his lips pressed in a firm line, and he pulls me into his embrace, the book crushed between us. Lemon lets out a squeak of protest before scampering up my shoulder.

"We have to go to Harpalyke. Now," Marcelene commands. "The dragon will take us, but even with me flying all the way there, I doubt Tarmyth will be able to carry the four of you on her back."

"No need to worry about that," Phoebe says as she brushes off her clothes and stands beside Marcelene. "Aries and I joined this mission to help Sybil find the Book of Light, which we somehow managed to do. Just as you somehow befriended the dragon that was intent on eating us." She scratches her head in confusion and looks at the book I hold tight to my chest, its magic humming secrets to me that I'm still struggling to understand.

"We will return to the Council of Thorns and report. Bring

them hope that not all is lost," Aries adds. "They should be on their way to the new safe place, west of here. If we keep up the pace, we can join them as they cross the river lands."

"But the shadow beasts?" I nibble at my bottom lip, glancing between the two of them.

"They don't travel this far north; even if they did, they can't catch me. Fox shifter and shadow elemental, remember?" Phoebe grins as she comes to hug me. "Plus, I've got this over-protective teddy bear to use as bait." She moves to hug Marce-lene, who's now crouched next to Nero.

Aries rolls his eyes and continues, "Save Nero, and then come save the rest of us. We'll be ready to fight next to you whenever you are ready. May the stars shine bright for you, Sybil Vandeleur." I bite the inside of my cheek and nod to the wolf shifter, grateful for all he's done, and I'm suddenly conscious that there's no guarantee I will ever see them again.

"And for the Prince of Laundry, of course," he adds with his usual wolfish grin as he mockingly curtsies to Aramis and goes to follow Phoebe, who's already shifting into her fox form.

"I have a name," Aramis says, hand tightening around mine.

"Oh, I know," Aries chuckles without turning. "Have faith, Prince of Shadowvale, change is coming."

We must make haste, horned one.

Tarmyth extends her wing as Marcelene starts shifting next to us.

"Follow me, and no stopping until we reach the library," she says, finger pointed at the dragon, and I can't help but admire the strength of spirit this woman has in commanding a dragon without batting an eyelid. Tarmyth must appreciate her attitude too, because her only response is a scoff.

I settle on the dragon's back and observe Aramis climbing over the membranous wing on unsteady feet. He sits behind me, strapping his sword sheath closer to his body while I tie knots in my dress around my ankles to ensure it stays put. His closeness conjures memories from another time we were sitting this close, but on horseback. Aramis wraps his hands around my waist, pulling me closer to him, his breath lingering on my neck.

"Have you ever flown on a dragon's back?" I ask as I feel his anxiety for Nero's safety grow.

"I cannot say it was an activity they offered frequently at the castle growing up." He moves from left to right, trying to get as much grip with his tights as possible. "You?"

"Well, this is my second time. I am practically a professional."

Hold on tight.

Tarmyth's voice rings through my head. A rush of adrenaline surges through my veins, and my stomach drops as Tarmyth's mighty wings beat. With the same tenderness as before, she scoops Nero and cradles him in her clawed embrace before launching us into the vast expanse of the sky. I lean forward, my face against her warm scales, holding the smaller horns at the base of her neck for dear life, and peer below. A breathtaking view unfolds beneath us, a patchwork of vibrant landscapes, rolling hills, and winding rivers. The sunrise casts its golden rays, painting the canvas of the sky with hues of orange and pink as we glide effortlessly through the clouds.

As the hours pass, I lean my head back on Aramis' shoulder. The cool breeze caresses my skin, blending with the warmth radiating from his embrace. My heart pounds in sync with the rhythmic flapping of Tarmyth's wings. She banks to the left deeper into the mountains, and Aramis tightens his hold, his touch reassuring and comforting.

"Look there," he says, his breath a warm caress against my ear as he points to a snow-white stag drinking from the stream far below. It lifts its head, watching our flight until it passes from view.

"They say the white stag symbolizes great change," I reply, turning my head.. Butterflies erupt in my stomach as he intertwines his fingers with mine.

"You have changed me. You are my salvation, and together we will bring justice to Shadowvale."

Marcelene lets out a piercing hoot before banking to the left toward an opening in the forest below, and Tarmyth follows. She releases Nero on the green bed of the clearing before landing next to him, her claws digging into the damp earth. As Aramis and I slip off the dragon's back, Nero lets out a moan.

"Nero!" I rush to his side, the pine needles biting into my knees. Aramis kneels across from me, his gaze fixed on his best friend. I touch his brow, burning hot with fever. His cheeks are flushed, and a fine sheen of sweat coats his skin. He mumbles incoherently as I pull the water flask from my healing satchel and turn to face Marcelene. "How much further?"

"The scouts ought to have seen our descent. They should be here any moment. But the entrance wasn't made for dragons." She glances up at Tarmyth, lips pulled into a frown.

Tell the winged cat she does not need to play host. I must make haste back to my eggs.

She hides her head under her wing and rubs her snout on her underbelly until shiny, dark crimson golden scales fall onto the ground.

A blessing for the war to come. Have an armorsmith craft you protection worthy of a queen.

She lowers her front legs and rests her head at my feet in a bow.

"I am no queen," I say, kneeling and pressing the palm of my hand to her snout. She lets out a puff of hot air.

Change is coming, horned one. Save your people, and should you have need of me, I will be there.

With a mighty roar and bellow of flames, she launches herself into the sky.

"Sybil!" Marcelene screams in horror. She's crouched next to Nero, holding his head between her hands. "Nero's stopped breathing."

33
SYBIL

I s he going to be alright?" Aramis hovers over his best friend, who lies writhing in one of the infirmary beds between us.

"I've done everything I can, and so have the healers here, but he took extensive damage. It's up to his body now to fight."

I lean against the side table, dipping the cloth into the basin of fresh water from the underground springs. My body aches, but I pay no mind to the discomfort as I focus on soothing Nero's fevered body. His breathing is labored, and his murmurs grow more coherent but still laced with delirium. The makeshift infirmary has rows of single white beds lining one stone wall, all with curtains wrapping around them. Despite being deep in the cool stone tunnels, the heat radiating off his body causes sweat to bead along my brow, plastering my hair to my face.

"He's burning up." I dab his forehead with the moist cloth. "Keep fighting, Nero," I whisper.

The high priestess and the Council of the white witches

had welcomed us despite their strict security measures. Granted, we did look as if we'd come back from the front lines of battle, all battered up with burned clothes, tattered shoes, a thick layer of dust on our skin and hair, and a barely alive draken. So whether their help was born out of pity or solidarity, we'll never know.

Thalia immediately took the situation into her hands, organized hot baths and nutritious meals for all of us, and instructed every healer in the library to help save Nero. After his lungs had stopped, they had to use a complicated emergency procedure I had only read of in my parents' medical books to restore them. The healers spent hours stitching his every wound, casting spells to close his internal bleedings, and brewing tonics to replenish the blood in his veins. When my magic had finally started to return, I joined them in the infirmary to lend my powers, but once the body starts to heal on its terms, there is nothing for my magic left to do.

I dry my hands, take the white healer's apron off, and hang it at the end of Nero's bed. Aramis sits on the mattress next to him, his gaze lost in thought, brows furrowed, while the book sits next to him. Since getting to the library this morning, we have not let it out of our sight.

I walk up to him and rake a hand through his golden hair. It is soft and smells like lilacs after the bath. With my index finger, I lift his freshly shaven chin until his eyes meet mine.

"We have to go. It's time to see if all of this was worth it," I say as I nod to the Book of Light and let my hand fall.

Aramis wraps his arms around my middle and rests his head on my stomach. "It was already worth it because it brought me to you."

I caress his hair, reveling in this moment where the world seems to have stopped, and we can finally breathe. "And it brought me to you," I echo his words. After a moment, I pick up the Book of Light. Its now familiar buzz fills my ears, and despite its heaviness, it feels like an extension of myself.

After rendering ourselves presentable again, I caved to curiosity and opened the Book of Light. Trembling fingers gently moved the ancient and yellowed pages as my heart raced, awaiting to be blessed with secret knowledge. Only to be met with symbols I had never seen, a language to me unknown, for which I was going to need the brightest minds Craeweth had to offer. Lucky for us, we are already at the library of Harpalyke.

"But now we must bring this to the witches and the scholars. You'll get to meet Cassara and Thalia, too. They know about you," I continue with a smirk and drag him off the bed and out of the infirmary.

"This isn't a language I am familiar with," the elder scribe, Zanthos, says as he sits down, rubbing the creases out of his brow. "Nor could we find it in any text on ancient languages."

"How is it possible to have an ancient text in a language no one has seen or heard of before?" Aramis says, slamming his fist impatiently on the table after hours of research.

"Could it be a cipher, or code?" I inquire and I rest my hand on Aramis' forearm. He glances up and nods apologetically before turning to the head of the table.

"It is unlikely," he says, flipping the pages. "There is no indication that it is written in code. It is a forgotten language, lost to time."

"Someone has to have the knowledge to read it," Aramis says, his muscles tensing under my hand. "Tricella has the Book of Darkness and is actively using it to teach herself dark magic. Is there a spell for translation? Or some other magical library who may have the knowledge?"

"Ow!" Aramis says as a quill lifts from the table and pricks his finger. He looks up, confused as to who or what made that happen, and I bite my lip.

"Be nice," I whisper as I cut him a glance. I grab his hand, running my thumb over the droplet of blood that wells on the pad of his offended digit, and let my magic heal the small wound. "Aramis is right. If Tricella has found a way to decipher its twin, there has to be someone with the knowledge."

"We have the most extensive collection of books in all of Craeweth," Marcelene says, crossing her fingers under her chin. Dark circles linger under her eyes and Cassara told me she has refused to eat—the worry for Nero too great to even look after herself. I make a mental note to talk to her in private.

"If Axton's accounts of his retrieval of the books were true, it means that Tricella has had the book for nearly two hundred years." I frown, staring into my teacup, watching the dregs float in the bottom.

"It's possible she had it translated all those years ago, and that person is no longer on this earth. While unlikely, it is possible," Zanthos says, rapping his knuckles on the counter. "You would have to look at someone or something ancient, difficult when it comes to living beings, of course, although there are creatures–"

"Zanthos!" Thalia snaps her fingers. "We all love a good history lesson, but the fate of our home is at stake here and time is running out."

"Of course," he says, nodding profusely and caressing his long white beard. "If not a living being then maybe an ancient institution might have records about a language as such. If the legend is true and this is one of the two books penned by the

Goddess herself, then you might be better off going to the temple to light a candle hoping she'll grant you the knowledge overnigh–"

"Nova Esther!" I say, pushing up from the table and knocking over my tea in my haste, everyone's eyes turning to me. The liquid instantly disappears, and in its place appears a fresh full teacup and saucer.

"Nova Esther?" Zanthos exclaims mid-stroke. "It's possible but a long shot. While not as ancient as the library of Harpalyke, the institution of Nova Esther does have some interesting tomes in their collection. After the war, however, we haven't had much communication. They too decided upon a more secure approach, and made venturing to their gates practically impossible for outsiders. They even disabled their portal that allowed us to directly travel to them," he scoffs. "But our portal is still able to take you to the last known entrance we have on record, on the edge of the Armaghdale forest. The rest of the way is up to you."

"But what would give them reason to help us?" I ask, remembering how much convincing Aramis had to do with the Council and I with the witches.

"The signs of looming war have grown exponentially since you left the library," Cassara interjects. "Thanks to your upheaval against the library's strict rules about neutrality, we've been sending scouts to different territories in Shadowvale." She points to six out of the twelve territories in the Kingdom. "Unrest is spreading as more of the soil continues to rot. She is becoming reckless in her attempts to find you. Shadow beasts have been spotted all the way to the Kallistar border. Mentions of her soulless guards marching through villages and causing upheaval are spreading," she continues, and I rub my brow at the weight becoming heavier and heavier on my shoulders.

"War is coming. Tricella won't be satisfied with just Shadowvale. We can already see that. From the plans Phoebe was able to see, she won't rest until she takes over all of Craeweth and that includes Kallistar," Aramis adds, crossing his arms. "We have to try. "And even if we don't manage to use the Book of Light to our own advantage, we will still need all the help we can get to face her. We must alert the King and Queen of Kallistar of what's on the horizon." The urgency in Aramis' voice is palpable.

"That would mean breaking the treaty between Shadowvale and Kallistar," Thalia notes.

"Tricella doesn't care about the treaty. Kallistar needs to know she plans to take them by force. They won't stand a chance against her, just as we won't without them," I explain, my voice filled with concern.

"We have to try," Aramis repeats, and looks at me.

Our eyes meet and I know he too is asking the Goddess when it will end. The traveling, the danger, the short hours of sleep and the constant worry of what is next. But we both know that the answer is, when our people are free. So we keep trying.

"The only question now is when do we leave?"I say as I stand. I turn and look at Marcelene.

"I'm afraid I won't be accompanying you on this journey, Sybil. The scholar council has asked that I step up and begin my transition into a leadership role."

My heart drops at her words.

"I understand, and I am very happy for you, Marcelene," I say, but the sad smile she gives me makes me wonder if she made this decision with her head but not with her heart.

"It looks like it's just the two of us." I turn to Aramis and stretch out my hand. "Nero will have to indulge in your hospitality for a little while longer, if you'll allow it?" I ask the witches, but I don't even have to finish the words.

"I will take care of him," Marcelene vows and looks at Aramis.

"That settles it then, we leave tomorrow," Aramis exclaims and reaches for my hand, ready for what is going to be another of our many final evenings before having to say goodbye to people we care about and venture into the unknown.

34
SYBIL

We climb down another flight of steps, only to end up on a quiet landing filled with more rows of shelves. My brow creases as I mentally retrace our steps from the infirmary.

"I'm sorry," I say as I face Aramis. "I thought this was the way to the–"

"It's okay," he says, grabbing my hand. His voice is a deep caress as I turn to face him. He presses a soft kiss to my knuckles. "You're tired, and it's been a long time since you've been here."

A warm fluttering sensation like a hundred of Nero's flame butterflies settles in my stomach as he pulls me into his arms.

"I can't believe it's the middle of spring," I say, heartbeat racing as I meet his eyes.

Silence stretches between us, broken only by the sound of our breathing.

"Sybil." His eyes are almost silver as they stare at me, and I feel a wave of power through the bond.

"Aramis?" The way he looks at me sets my skin on fire. I dart my tongue out to moisten my suddenly parched lips.

"Fuck, I love the sound of my name on your lips." He drops the towels and clothes to the ground and closes the distance between us, crushing his lips against mine in a kiss that's both demanding and hungry.

He pulls away, my body flushed and jolting with pent up energy. "We should–I mean," I nervously mumble. Heat creeps into my cheeks as I look around us. The mage lights flicker above. The rows are still quiet. No other being seems to be on this floor.

"Shh," he whispers, holding my face and pulling my attention back as his blue eyes rage like storm clouds. His hands glide down my body to my hips, pulling me flush against him before claiming my lips, slow and thorough. My heart begins to race in my chest, heat pooling in my core.

I moan, arching into his touch as our tongues dance together. I run my fingers through his hair, down the stubble of his cheek, and across the smooth planes of his chest. His muscles flex taut under my touch. My fingers grip the fabric of his tunic, and I know I'll never get tired of this male. My mate. I should have trusted my gut from the beginning and never let doubt push us apart.

His fingers comb through my braid until it hangs around me like a curtain. He breaks away, both of us panting, breathless as he pulls me tight against his chest.

"I'm sorry," he whispers against the shell of my ear, sending warmth flooding into my core. "I couldn't go one moment more without kissing you, without holding you. Knowing that you're real and this isn't just some sleepless delirium dream while I'm still stuck in that cell, powerless to save you."

I nuzzle against his cheek, the scruff alighting my senses. I deeply inhale his rich scent and melt into his embrace. I let my magic flow, my skin glowing as I reach for the thread between us pouring all my love and feelings through it. "I am real, this is real." I find his hand, entwining our fingers and bringing it between us where I can feel his heart pounding.

"The path ahead will not be easy, but I refuse to let Tricella or anyone else get between us. You're my mate." I feel the rush of power along the bond a moment before a gust of wind whips through the room, billowing my skirt and hair. He stares down at me, eyes hungry and heated.

"Truly?" His eyes search my face. "I thought–in the mountains–" He hesitates, and a muscle in his jaw ticks as he clenches his teeth together. "I thought I was going to lose you. I didn't want to spend the rest of my life without you by my side, not only as my mate but as my wife."

"Wife?" My heart beats wildly in my chest as he kneels before me and pulls a small carved silver wooden rose on a chain from his pocket. Every detail is intricate, from the blossoming petals down to the tiny thorns peaking around leaves. "It's not much. You deserve all the jewels and treasures in the world but–"

"It's beautiful." I run my finger along the edge of the rose. "Is it–"

"Yes, it's from the pomme d'argent woods from when we traveled together." He runs his hands through his unruly blond hair and stares up at me. "Be mine, Sybil Vandeleur. Will you stay by my side for the rest of time until the stars fall burning from the sky and the sea swallows the earth?"

"Yes." Tears prick the corner of my eyes as I smile down at him. "I want you. I want to be your mate, your wife." As soon as the words leave my mouth, he pushes to his feet and clasps the chain around my neck before pulling me into his arms burying his face into my neck.

"I want you more than anything, Sybil darling, and I vow I will spend my whole life showing you just how much I mean that."

My back hits the flat edge of a shelf, sending dust flying. I wrap my legs around his waist, my skirts pushing up as I arch against him. He trails a firefly line of kisses down my exposed neck and collarbone. His hand grips my exposed thigh, the other wrapping around my back. His touch sets my skin on fire, contrasting with the cool breeze of his magic stroking my skin, an inferno of heat and ice building inside me.

"Aramis," I gasp, writhing in his grasp. "Please."

"You don't have to beg for me, Sybil darling. I'm fucking yours." He nips at my neck, his hand roaming higher up my thigh in tantalizing circles. His touch is featherlight and followed by the breathy caress of his wind magic. My skin ignites into an inferno at his touch.

"As I am yours." My hands roam up the taunt muscles of his strong arms to encircle his neck and tangle in his short hair. I tighten my legs, seeking the friction I so desperately need. "I want you, only you, forever."

"You will be my undoing," he growls before taking my mouth in a kiss that melts away any coherent thought. I cry out against him as his hand roves higher, thumb circling my sensitive center.

"Please," I moan, my body arching of its own accord, seeking release. I lean my head back, cushioned by the soft moss. My eyes closing as delicious tension builds inside me.

"So demanding, my pomme sucre," he whispers as he increases his pace.

"Aramis—" I cling to him as my body explodes into a thousand pieces. I feel as though I will burn up from the inside out. Magic floods my veins pulsing in time with the throb in my core.

"Look at me," he commands, and I open my eyes, meeting his gaze. There is something like awe laced with feral hunger in his icy blue eyes.

A gust of wind blows against my wet core like a phantom hand and a hunger and lusty moan escapes me. Aramis lowers us both to the ground. He grabs the edge of my undergarments and rips them in two as he eyes me like a man starved. He leans forward, pressing a kiss to the side of my neck that sends a trail of tingles past my breast down to my core.

He slips a finger deep as he frees my breasts pulling a nipple into his mouth. I can't think—can't breathe—lost in the sensations his mouth, magic, and touch are causing.

"You are the most delightful, beautiful creature I have ever met," he growls against my flesh, slipping another finger inside me.

"And you are driving me crazy," I reply as every muscle in my body clenches, white hot heat searing me from the inside out. My release rips through me like a thunderstorm and he captures my lips against his as I cry out.

He gently withdraws his fingers, and I whimper at the sudden absence.

"Patience," he says with a smirk as he makes quick work undoing the fastenings on his pants and freeing himself. His hands grip my thighs, spreading them wide as he rubs the head of his cock against my wet, pulsing entrance. "You made me wait how long for an answer?"

"You're ruthless," I whisper feverishly. Something within me calls to him, craves him.

"I'm yours," he replies as he pushes into me.

My heart pounds in my chest, matching the rhythm of our

bodies moving as one. Every thrust sends a surge of heat coursing through my veins, igniting a fire within me that I never knew existed. The pressure of his grip on my face intensifies, his thumb caressing my cheek, leaving a trail of electrifying sensations in its wake.

"So beautiful," he murmurs, nipping at my neck.

I can't get enough of his touch. I hook my legs around his waist and he takes me deeper. The change in pressure and friction provokes a moan from my lips. I grip onto his shoulders, my nails digging into his skin, but it's not out of pain or desperation. It's a raw expression of desire, an instinctual need to hold onto him, to feel his strength and presence.

I lose myself in the depths of his gaze, my eyes locking with his as if they were the only lifelines in this sea of ecstasy. The molten adoration reflected in his eyes melts away any doubts or insecurities, leaving only an unyielding connection between our souls. It's a love so fierce and intense, it leaves me gasping for air.

The waves of pleasure ripple through my body, building and cresting with each deliberate movement. I am lost in a sea of sensations, each touch and thrust a symphony of pleasure that pushes me closer to the edge. Time loses meaning as we surrender to the intoxicating dance of our bodies.

"Aramis," I whimper, moving to match his pace. Every fiber of my body goes tight and tingly. He lets out a roar of pleasure, hand tightening in my hair as he throbs deep inside me. We fall panting beside one another and he kisses the corner of my mouth.

It's then I realize my skin is glowing as though I've rolled in luminescent lichen. He chuckles, kissing my surprised brow before lowering me to the ground. "You're glowing like a star, Sybil darling."

"I—" I stutter, staring at my hands gripping the front of his tunic. "This has never happened to me before."

"We will have to make sure we have curtains, lest everyone know what we're up to. You are shining brighter than any star shining in the sky."

I glance down at my glowing skin and chuckle before pressing my head against his chest, listening to the rhythmic beat of his heart.

"Let's go get you cleaned up," he says, kissing the top of my head and pulling me into his arms. I can't help but smile.

35
SYBIL

The morning came swiftly after a night of deep sleep. Aramis and I lingered in each other's embrace, reveling in the joy of having a comfortable bed, for once. But when Marcelene came knocking at our door to call us for breakfast, it had been difficult to even step foot out of bed. It felt as if the moment our toes touched the cold stone ground, this beautiful dream would be over.

But alas, our stomachs' increasing grumbling made the choice for us and, wearing the new clothes the witches had kindly gifted us, we walked to the common room. Aramis had just filled his spoon with the most delicious porridge when Cassara came running to us.

"The infirmary! Quick!"

Aramis and I drop everything and run up the twisting stairs and down the long corridor all the way to the room with the many beds. I storm through the door, heart in my throat, only to stop in my tracks.

"Nero!" I cry out, running to his bedside. "Oh, thank the Goddess you're awake."

"Fuck Nero. You're not allowed to die on me, brother." Aramis follows suit and grabs his best friend by the shoulders, peering into his face.

"Nae, only if ye stop yer persistent nagging and move yer ugly mug so I can see yer pretty mate." With a pained expression on his face, he tries to sit up, but his efforts are met with tears and clenched fists. "Oy, it feels like I wrestled with a thorny bush all the way down the dragon's mountain and lost."

"You've lost a good deal of blood and your body is still trying to heal after Axton–"

"Axton!" He growls, fists bunching into the sheets, eyes molten gold with fury. "I'll wring that–"

"Dead. He's dead, but we have the book. The dragon, Tarmyth–it's a long story but you needn't worry about him."

Nero breaks into a coughing fit and I rush to grab the flask from the table. Aramis gently lifts Nero's head, and I pour some of the cool water into his mouth to drink. His parched lips quiver as he takes small sips.

"And Marcelene?" he asks, face twisted in pain. Lemon uncurls his body from the foot of the bed and scampers over to Nero's left hand, licking his palm. "There you are, you little rascal."

"Here, take this. It will help with the pain." I grab a vial from my pocket and hold it up to his lips, pouring the draft down his throat. "She is safe. They are all safe, although Aries and Phoebe are back with the Council."

Nero's brows furrow as he takes us in. The traveling leathers we have on.

"What is going on?" he asks, confusion etching his face.

"I can't read it, no one here can," I admit, pangs of guilt settling heavy in the pit of my stomach.

"Now Sybil, yer a smart lass, I ken you can read," Nero says with a sigh, closing his eyes as he settles back down onto his pillow. His face is pale and drawn tight with pain.

"It's not that I can't read," I say, mopping his forehead with a damp cloth. "It's in a language neither I or Marcelene have ever seen before."

"That sassy feline. Are ye sure she isn't pulling your tail?" The corners of his lips pull up.

"She's not. That's why we came back to the library to find some answers." I smile as the tension begins to ease from his face.

"I'm sure ye will find an answer, Sybil. Yer the smartest unicorn I ken." He chuckles, peeking one rich brown eye open at me.

I can't help but laugh and shake my head. "Nero, I'm the *only* unicorn shifter you know."

"So, where are we going now?" he asks, and Aramis and I exchange a look.

"Nero, you're in no condition to travel, look at you," Aramis says, but the draken scoffs and lifts the sheets to get out of bed. A white billowing tunic almost reaching his knees is all he is wearing.

"Who says I am nae ready to travel?" Nero's drawls.

"I told them so." Marcelene's voice echoes from the door of the infirmary as she steps in. The two look at each other for a moment, a silence filled with unsaid words stretching between them. Aramis and I look at each other with curiosity. Nero remembers he is wearing the equivalent of a woman's nightgown and rushes back under the covers, red coloring his cheeks as he hides his gaze from the witch.

Marcelene comes closer to Nero's bed but leans on the wall

right in front of it, crossing her arms over her chest, but I see the relief in her eyes.

"I've been in worse shape than this, and I turned out just fine. Isn't that right, Aramis?" Nero's words hang in the air, his voice carrying a hint of defiance. Aramis throws his hands up into the air, the sound of his exasperation echoing in the room.

"I have already learned not to fight with a healer." Aramis turns, his movement causing the air to stir around him. He puts an arm behind my back, his touch sending a shiver down my spine. His thumb begins to caress in tantalizing, teasing circles.

I turn to Nero, ignoring Aramis' teasing. "If she says you need more time to heal, Nero—"

"I can make up my own mind of when I'm fit to travel. Plus, it's not like ye, Marcelene, and yer wee Lemon won't be there to look at my scratches."

Marcelene stiffens, her lips pursed tightly together. She lowers her head and starts fidgeting with the hem of her sleeve, something I have never seen her do.

"I won't be going," she declares firmly. Her words hang in the air, accompanied by a tense silence. The room feels heavy with anticipation.

"What do ye mean, ye won't be going?" He turns abruptly, his eyes narrowing. "Ye've traveled the last few months with us. Why quit now? Tired of my charming personality?" He winks, and Marcelene rolls her eyes.

"The library needs me." Marcelene's voice is filled with determination.

"Oh, well." He pauses, clears his throat and shrugs. "I supposed that makes sense. Can't have this place falling apart. Who knows what knowledge it contains that future genera-tions might need," Nero replies, but I notice a subtle shift in his posture.

"Or what help the three of you may still need," Marcelene replies, turning to me.

"You have a point. We may need help from the library, even with the power to defeat Tricella," I say.

"So," Nero begins talking to Aramis and me. "I am going to repeat this one more time: where are we going?"

Aramis sighs, pinching the bridge of his nose, defeated in the face of his best friend's resolve to join this new adventure. "We're going to Nova Esther. We're breaking the treaty and going to Kallistar."

36
ARAMIS

Sybil, Nero, and I step out of the portal into a small wooden hunting cabin.

The air inside the cabin is cool and filled with the scent of pine. Sunlight streams through the cracks in the wooden walls, casting warm golden rays on the rustic furniture. The sound of a crackling fireplace fills the room.

"How–" I start, staring at the fire.

"It's an extension of the library," Marcelene says as she glides gracefully into the cabin, her flowing robes brushing against the wooden floor. Two of the coven leaders, tall and imposing figures, enter behind her, their presence exuding power and authority. "We don't use it very often, but it used to be a safe house when we traveled more frequently. It looks like the library kept it up."

"Traveling through the forest on foot is going to take weeks," Sybil says, peeking out the side window at the forest.

"There used to be a small farm half a day's walk from here that breeds horses for travel," Marcelene says ,walking over to the large wooden table in the center of the room. "You should be able to buy a few to carry you to Kallistar."

"And how are we supposed to afford that?" Nero says, the bandages peeking from the collar of his traveling leathers. A thump hits the table and Lemon pokes his head out of my pocket to stare at the leather bag bulging with coins.

"If you don't overindulge," she says, picking up the bag and shoving it into Nero's chest. "This should be enough to cover the horses and any food or equipment."

Nero's wings snap out behind him, a flush rises up his neck as he holds the bag to his chest. The relationship between him and Marcelene had seemed tense after he woke up from his injuries, almost as if the draken struggled to forgive the witch for not coming along.

"Safe travels," Marcelene says to the three of us and the other two echo her words. "May Alphaeia show you the way."

Before Marcelene can leave and take a step toward the portal leading back to Harpalyke, Sybil drops my hand and runs to hug her. The witch freezes, but when she realizes it's Sybil, her expression relaxes and her arms wrapping tightly around Sybil's shoulders.

"I will miss you." Sybil's words are barely audible as her head is buried in Marcelene's blond hair.

"I will miss you too." The witch responds, and the two women unlock their embrace, tears streaking down their faces.

Sybil returns to my side and we go to exit the cabin as Marcelene returns to the library. Nero follows behind but I feel him waver. I look over my shoulder to make sure he is well and see that he too is looking over his shoulder. One last look before she goes. And as the portal swallows her in iridescent light, Marcelene glances back. We step out into the forest, and it's a sight to behold after the long winter. Birds chirp in the blue sky and the vegetation has a bright green sign that spring is finally here.

"Well, I always suspected, but the truth comes to light," a familiar voice calls out, its melodic tone resonating in the air.

I turn to see Kieran leaning against a tree, arms crossed over his chest, wearing his usual black, tailored robe, his towering figure casting a long shadow . A cocky grin dances upon his face and his eyes gleaming mischievously.

"Not a dog but a draken," he taunts, his voice laced with amusement as he stares at Nero's outstretched wings. I feel a surge of anger rising within me, causing my muscles to tense. My hand instinctively reaches for the sword strapped at my side. "You're looking worse for wear, *princeling*," Kieran remarks, his gaze shifting toward Sybil. His eyes linger on her and how the leathers hug her every curve. I clench my jaw, suppressing my desire to punch him in the face, at least not until we understand why he is here.

My grip on the sword tightens, my knuckles turning white.

"What do you want, Kieran?" I growl, my voice laced with defiance.

Kieran's lips curl into a sly smile.

"Oh here?" he says, pushing away from the tree. "It was simply a matter of finding what I was looking for. Or in this case, whom."

"You can't have her," I growl, placing myself in between the seer and Sybil.

"Oh, I'm not interested in the unicorn anymore. It's you, actually, whom I've been searching for. But she is a nice touch." He flicks a glance over my shoulder and I tense, meeting his gaze.

"What do you mean, you've been looking for me?" I pull on my magic, ready to protect Sybil and defend myself from this psychotic man.

"I thought the unicorn was what I needed. I've been looking for the tipping point, but I've realized it's not her, but you." His gray eyes meet mine.

A chill passes through my body, and I resist the urge to grab at the necklace pulsing under my tunic.

"The only thing you need me for, is to wring your neck." I move forward, fist clenched ready to punch him, but Sybil's warm hand grabs my wrist, holding me back.

"Kieran, you are not welcome here. We don't need you," she says, stepping to my side and entwining her hand in mine.

His eyes watch every movement like a hawk before a grin lights up his face. "Oh, but you see, this is the funny part. I think you do need me," he says.

"Why would we need the queen's whore to help us? You've done nothing but cause pain to my people and my mate." He flinches at my words, but then meets my gaze.

"You need me because I know where the one person who can read that book is," he reveals, his voice dripping with intrigue. My heart skips a beat, curiosity mingling with caution. His words hang in the air.

TRIGGER WARNINGS

Blood and gore

Death and violence

Sexually explicit

Arachnophobia

Abduction of an adult

Explicit language

Fire and destruction of a village

About the Author

Fleur DeVillainy is an American fantasy author. In the realm of imagintion, where love and enchantment intertwine, she crafts tales of extraordinary adventure interwoven with romance, internal growth and found family. By day, she brings healing to little hearts. By night, she lets her pen dance across pages, weaving magical worlds and captivating characters. When not weaving tales, she finds solace in baking, sewing, and gardening. Join her on the many whimsical journeys through words and discover the wonders that lie within. Check out her series The Vandeleur Trilogy, her comic series Wolf and I, and her co-written Calpa series today!

If you want to know when Fleur's next book will come out, please visit her social media and website.

ALSO BY FLEUR DEVILLAINY

The Vandeleur Trilogy

<u>Sky of Thorns</u>

Secrets of Thorns

Succession of Thorns (2025)

To Scorch a Quartz Thorns (novella)

Other/Standalone

Spellbound Scones

The Calpa Series

co-written with Johnna Dee

<u>The Clan of Mist</u>

The Clan of Luna (Fall 2024)

The Clan of Deception (novella)

www.ingramcontent.com/pod-product-compliance
Lightning Source LLC
Chambersburg PA
CBHW070427310726
48977CB00003B/867